WHEN
DARKNESS
FALLS

ALSO BY EMMA SALISBURY

When Darkness Falls

Emma Salisbury

Cover design by Author Design Studio

Interior design by Coinlea Services

For my family…

ACKNOWLEDGEMENTS

A lthough as a writer of fiction I tend to make things up as I go along, there are times when facts are required. The websites and reports referred to in my author notes at the end of the book were particularly helpful, and I found myself returning to the following books:

Forensics, The Anatomy of Crime, Val McDermid, Profile Books Ltd, Wellcome Collection

Forensic Psychology, Crime, justice, law, interventions. Graham M. Davies, Anthony R. Beech. Wiley.

I also found the BBC's 'My search for the boy in a child abuse video' by Lucy Proctor, shocking but thought provoking.

To Lin White for her patient guidance regarding structure which I fear she has repeated for each book – many thanks – one of these days I'll get it right! For Aimee Coveney for her brilliant cover design, I love that she captures the tone of each book with her images.

I am enormously indebted to Lynn Osborne, whose feedback and encouragement from day one has been invaluable. Thanks also to the sharp eyes of Sally Howorth and Sue Barnett – thank you for being generous with your time. For the little details that make a big difference to a plot – thank you Gill Oldbury and Steph Lothian.

I have a wonderful tribe of readers, some of whom have characters named after them in this book – I hope you like them when you meet them.

As ever, thank you to my family and friends for putting up with my overactive imagination, and bouts of absence, although I think something else was going on this year that was the main reason we were kept apart... And, thanks, of course, to Stephen.

PROLOGUE

She'd been standing on the pavement for no more than five minutes when his car pulled up at the kerb. Not long enough for her to consider the truth of what she'd been told, but long enough to understand the consequences if she called it wrong. She'd already flicked the finger at one guy who'd propositioned her. Offered her £30 for 'the works,' whatever that involved. The girls standing on the other side of the road kept looking over, not entirely unfriendly, certainly a lot more amenable than their pimp would be when he showed up. She wanted to explain that she wasn't on the game but they didn't speak English. Eastern European, most of them, Roma gypsies groomed by men who promised them a better life. What did it matter, she thought. In the end all promises get broken.

She hadn't expected him to reply to her text. Much less a request that they meet. But then life was a transaction, and he'd made it clear she had something he wanted. He stared in her direction until she made eye contact, beckoning her over with his hand. The passenger window lowered as she moved towards his car. Tentatively she crouched so that she was eye level with him. His gaze wandering over her like a butcher eyeing a side of meat. She waited, desperate for him to tell her that none of what she'd heard was true when her gaze settled on something lying on the back seat. Something that made the muscles in her stomach contract.

Without uttering a word, she opened the car door and climbed in.

SUNDAY/DAY 1

CHAPTER ONE

The eyes staring back at him didn't blink. Hadn't done for a while, by the look of it. Her face was bruised. There were traces of dirt around her mouth and nose, though that was likely down to the dog that had found her. An attempt had been made to bury the body but the freshly dug earth proved no challenge to Boris, nor the plastic she had been wrapped in.

Her body had been found fifty yards from a footpath in woodland frequented by joggers and dog walkers. The area had been secured and scene of crime officers had erected a tent to shield her from prying eyes. A cordon had been extended right back to the main road, but still, the lengths reporters would go to. Even so, thanks to social media, Salford would be rife with the gossip that a young girl's body had been found, long before it was reported on the news. At the entrance to the wood an officer stood with the three school age boys who discovered her when Boris refused to come when called. Parents contacted, the detective waited for their arrival before taking first account statements, telling them someone would be in touch.

The plastic had been wrapped loosely and fell open to reveal the victim was partially dressed. A loose-fitting jumper but no garments covering her lower half. After completing his initial survey, the pathologist made a small incision in her abdomen so a thermometer could be passed into her liver. It was usual practice when examining a corpse to take its rectal temperature when trying to determine time of death, but there was reason to suspect sexual assault. Initial examination completed, he clicked his instrument bag closed, said something to a colleague before getting to his feet. He turned to the heavyset detective staring at the victim. 'That's my golf tournament buggered.'

Detective Sergeant Kevin Coupland swallowed his response. He suspected Harry Benson was trying to keep things light but you could never be sure, the man was a prat at the best of times and today, well, today would hardly be classed as that. He watched the pathologist move away from the body and snap off his gloves. 'He hit her, then,' Coupland said, pointing to a scratch on her face, 'held her down too.' His finger moved to bruising just visible around her shoulders. Her fingernails were broken, which suggested she'd put up a fight.

'I really don't know why you lot bother calling me out,' sniffed Benson, 'when your *Ladybird Guide to Pathology* has clearly turned you into an expert.'

Coupland let his remark go; perhaps he had been stomping all over the medic's toes. 'Anything you care to add?' he asked, offering the closest he could muster to a smile.

'There are bruises either side of her larynx, and petechial haemorrhages in her face and eyes which indicates death by strangulation,' Benson informed him with just the tiniest hint of petulance. 'I can say no more than that, for the time being.'

'You can give me a time of death though.' It was a question, but the tone of it came out flat, like a demand.

Benson raised a bushy eyebrow. 'No more than twelve hours ago.'

Coupland nodded, swallowing down other questions he wanted to ask. The post mortem report would answer them soon enough, with far more accuracy and a damn sight less attitude than the man carrying it out. He could wait.

The black man standing beside Coupland thrust his hands deep into the pockets of his jogging bottoms and shivered. It wasn't the cold, Coupland guessed, registering the leather jacket over a hooded sweatshirt and the snug woollen hat pulled down over hair shaved close to the scalp. Like him, acting Sergeant Chris Ashcroft had been off duty when the call had come in. DCI Mallender had been at the other end of the city attending a fatal stabbing. It made sense that the day shift take this over from the beginning, even though neither detective was due on for another hour.

'Do you reckon it's Carly?' Ashcroft asked him, his gaze shifting from the teenager at their feet snuffed out before her time.

Coupland didn't for one minute doubt that it was Carly. Her face had been plastered all over the news over the last thirty-six hours. On the front pages of Saturday's edition of the local papers; even one of the nationals had featured her on its inside page. She'd been reported missing by her parents on Friday evening after going out to meet friends for a meal. A belated birthday celebration, arranged once restaurants had been given the green light to open their doors. Her father arrived at the agreed pick up point to give her a lift home, only she wasn't there. Her picture had been circulated by the MISPER team on social media but with no response other than sad face emojis and prayers for her safe return.

Carly had told her parents she was catching a bus into town. The investigation was escalated when the manager of the bus company informed officers there was no CCTV footage of her getting on any of the buses that picked up passengers at her stop from the time she left the family home, or the rest of the evening, for that matter. Her parents had taken part in a TV appeal. Her father, grim faced, had held up a photo of her while her mother stared into the camera and begged for anyone with information to come forward. It was the nature of her disappearance that had put everyone on high alert; it had all the hallmarks of abduction.

There'd been no ID found near the body, but the girl at Coupland's feet had the same style and colour hair as Carly. Wore clothes that matched the ones described in the last known sighting of her when she left home to catch the bus. It was bloody Carly alright. But there was a process to go through. A protocol of actions before her body could be taken to the mortuary for formal identification.

For Coupland, lockdown had barely existed. There'd still been murders, although not the opportunistic kind. With fewer people on the streets and pubs closed there'd been none of the pissed-up bickering that ended up with one of the parties getting a blue light ride to A&E. Long standing feuds had quietened too. It was domestic violence that had gone through the roof, couples cooped up together 24 hours a day.

There'd been some benefits to the change in his work pattern though. Giving evidence at trial via video link had meant less time wasted waiting around court to be called. While barristers conducted their cases remotely, dialling in from home, a section in the station canteen had been cordoned off with screens; a win-win as far as Coupland was concerned.

A SOCO used sticky tape to lift any suspect fibres or hairs from clothing and exposed areas of her body. Head, facial and pubic hair was sealed in a plastic bag to be labelled and collated in the chain of evidence log. This process took time. Coupland glanced at his watch. An hour yet before her parents' hopes would be shattered.

The morning air was cold, the sky littered with dirty clouds. What the hell had happened to summer? Coupland thought, pulling up his jacket collar to keep out the chill.

*

DCI Mallender's Office
'You OK, Kevin? You look tired.'

Coupland was sitting in the chair across from the DCI's desk, legs splayed as he rested his elbows on his knees, hands nursing a lukewarm coffee. 'Everyone looks tired at my age, boss.'

Using the thumb and little finger of one hand to massage the pulse points on his temple, he tried to remember the last night he'd had that had passed undisturbed. Not that it mattered much in the grand scheme of things. He was past the point where a good night's sleep would fix the lines around his eyes, or the bags beneath them that had set up camp on his last birthday and refused to leave. A change of career might slow down the crevice that was starting to form along the centre of his forehead. Short of joining a monastery nothing would hold it back. He'd long ago resigned himself to the fact his face looked 'lived in'.

'No sign of the Super? Not like him to miss a photo opportunity.'

'Local strategy meeting.'

Coupland cocked his head. 'And what's one of those, when they're at home?'

'He's on the steering group which directs the council regarding the regeneration going on in the city.'

'We're doomed, then,' muttered Coupland. 'Seriously though, who decides who gets these gigs? Are the names drawn out of a hat?'

'I'd be more interested in how those names got into the hat,' said Mallender, shrewdly. 'All the local bigwigs I suppose. People higher up the food chain than you or me.'

Talk of food chains made Coupland's stomach rumble. He'd intended to pick up something to eat at the 24 hour Tesco on his way into the station but one look at Carly and his appetite had disappeared.

Mallender perched his backside on the edge of his desk. 'Get dressed in the dark again, did you?' He pointed to the odd socks on Coupland's feet, one stripy, the other a washed out black now closer to grey.

When his mobile had rung he'd been pacing the floor with Tonto. An ear infection that hadn't impacted his grandson's lungs any, going by the decibel level he'd started to reach. Lynn had not been long back from a 12 hour shift. At least Coupland had managed a couple of hours' kip before the commotion had started. He'd told her to get some shut eye while she could. Her part time hours had gone through the roof of late; sickness absence was at an all-time high due to COVID and there were shifts to cover.

Amy had gone downstairs, was relegated to coffee making duty once her dad took charge. She scrolled contentedly through her phone while the kettle boiled, mugs containing decaffeinated granules beside it. Coupland had a knack of calming the boy. Of holding him close, his mouth to his ear, whispering his own daft version of nursery rhymes. *Humpty Dumpty was a big daft numpty. I know an old lady who did a big poo.* Tonto's eyelids had begun to close like a junkie mid-way through a fix, only to open them in alarm at the sound of the phone's shrill ringtone. Coupland barked his name into it, bouncing Tonto one handed while pulling funny faces to distract him from the cry that was threatening to return. He'd listened to what the caller told him. 'I'm on my way,' he'd grunted, taking Tonto down to Amy before the boy went nuclear.

He didn't think he'd done that bad, all things considered. The suit he wore most days had been folded over the back of a chair. He'd climbed into it on auto pilot, sniffing under the arms of yesterday's shirt before slipping it over his head. He hadn't bothered with a tie, decided he'd slip home later for a shower and change of clothes once the preliminaries had been taken care of.

Mallender on the other hand looked as sharp as ever. The only tell-tale that he'd been up all night had been the blond stubble which he'd shaved off in the gents half an hour before. The stabbing had been over in Tattersall, a neighbourhood feud that escalated once drink was involved. According to witnesses the victim had given almost as good as he'd got. His attacker had been taken into custody, was awaiting a check over by the duty doc. Unless there were premeditating factors a case of manslaughter would be filed. Mallender had handed the file to a DC in the Major Crimes team, to prepare for the CPS.

Shrugging on a padded jacket, Coupland got to his feet. He moved over to the window, stared down at the lines of vehicles in and out of the city. It never ceased to amaze him that the world kept on turning when awful things happened. It seemed disrespectful somehow.

He reminded himself that for most folk it was still early. There'd be sorrow soon enough when the news got out that Carly had been found. An outpouring of shock and anger. The cut-through where her body was found would be filled with shop-bought flowers and teddy bears. A vigil would be held with candles placed in jam jars. A procedure to follow that was just as rigorous as the one followed by any Crime Scene Manager.

'Ready, boss?' Coupland asked, turning to face Mallender who was sliding a comb through his hair.

Mallender let out a sigh. 'Don't think I ever feel ready for things like this,' he said, swinging his arm out wide indicating that Coupland walk ahead of him.

CHAPTER TWO

Carly's mother had collapsed into a chair the moment the DCI had uttered the words. Carly's father, silent at first, looked as though he would brave it till they'd gone. He stood facing both detectives, one hand gripping protectively onto his wife's shoulder. Mallender had accepted the armchair offered when Gary and Susan King had led them into the living room of the modest three bedroomed semi. Coupland had declined, the adrenaline coursing around his body making it impossible for him to be still. No more than an arm's span away from them he bounced on the balls of his feet, like a coiled spring ready for action. He'd thought about stepping back, adhering to the safe distancing guidelines that were still in operation when entering a member of the public's home, unless they were being apprehended. Decided the threat of a virus wouldn't touch the sides of what the couple were facing now.

'Are you sure?' Susan sobbed. 'Could it be someone else?'

Coupland cleared his throat. The DCI had been through all this; it was his role in this double act to repeat the information again in the hope it would sink in. 'There'll need to be a formal identification,' he said, looking from one to the other, his gaze resting on Gary, waiting until his head jerked a nod. 'But as DCI Mallender explained, the photograph you gave us of Carly, the description of her clothing…' He let his words trail off.

'We're just a normal family,' Gary began. 'How can something so abnormal happen to people like us?'

If Coupland had a pound for every time he'd been asked this.

'We live down to earth lives, nothing special. We work hard. We pay our bills, we live within our means. We're tough on the girls. We don't let them out unless they've somewhere to go to. Birthday parties, cinema with friends, sleepovers. I grew up on an estate where the kids hung around on street corners. Christ knows I was one of them. I wanted better for her.' He shook his head in confusion. 'What was the point of it all?'

'How are we going to tell her sister?' his wife asked, her brain navigating through the things that needed to be done.

The doorbell rang. Coupland stepped out of the room, returning with a young PC in plain clothes. It was the officer's first posting since he'd completed his family liaison training course; he tried not to look too eager. Coupland made the introductions, nodded when the officer offered to make tea.

'Has she been interfered with?' Gary asked. 'Has some bastard forced himself on her?'

His wife sobbed some more.

'We can't be certain yet,' Coupland said carefully, avoiding Mallender's eye. 'But it's a possibility.' A shiver ran through him, nothing to do with the cold.

'The sick fuck!' King yelled, his hand dropping from his wife's shoulder as he moved to go into the hall.

Coupland grabbed his upper arm. 'Where would you go?' he reasoned. 'Where would you start?' He'd found, over the years, this was more effective than telling victims' loved ones they couldn't, or shouldn't go after the bastard who'd caused them harm. Pointing out the practicalities was a much more effective way of putting a spoke in their wheels.

The man stopped as Coupland's words sank in. His face crumpled inwards, like a punctured football that had had the shape kicked out of it.

Coupland cleared his throat. 'We're going to do several things over the next thirty-six hours that may cause you alarm, but I promise you it's how this type of investigation needs to be handled, so nothing gets missed out at the beginning.'

'What do you mean?'

'Forensic officers will need to carry out a search of your home. It's routine, but it may uncover something that gives us a clue to where Carly might have been in the time she was missing. It might help us discover who did this. Your family liaison officer will help you pack some things, take you to a family member or friend. Just for the night. Officers will need to take some of Carly's possessions, to help us build up a picture of who she is and the sort of friends she has. Do you understand?'

'Do you mean like her laptop?' Gary demanded. 'We bought her a laptop to help her with her assignments. We installed parental controls, spyware, you name it. You're barking up the wrong tree if you think someone got to her that way.'

'Still worth a look. Our techies will be all over it in no time. They'll take good care of it. Do you have any questions?'

Two faces stared back at him, dead-eyed.

Outside, the world continued with its new 'normal.' Pedestrians giving each other a wide berth on the pavement. A woman wearing a face mask waited for her dog to finish squatting. Coupland shared a look with Mallender as he bleeped open his car. There was nothing to say that could make the situation better, so he turned his key in the ignition, released the handbrake, indicated and let several cars pass before pulling out into the road.

*

CID room, briefing
Coupland waited for the detectives to assemble around the desks at the front of the room. It was Sunday morning; a skeleton shift was in operation. Acting DS Ashcroft remained at the scene coordinating house to house inquiries at properties along the woodland's perimeter. DC Turnbull, Crime Scene Manager, would accompany the body to the mortuary once SOCOs had finished their work.

The photo of Carly at the top of the incident board was the one her parents had given to the MISPER team on Friday evening. It was a blown-up Polaroid taken on her actual birthday in the middle of lockdown. Grinning for the camera beside a stand of cupcakes in the family's kitchen. Who would have known that three months later she'd be dead?

Coupland leaned against a filing cabinet. Nodded his thanks to a young DC who'd handed round proper coffees made with a kettle before taking his seat. DC Timmins, known as Krispy because of his penchant for the famous chain's doughnuts, was the technical wizard of the team, but was also starting to engage in operational tasks. 'Fifteen-year-old Carly King left her family home at 5pm on Friday to catch the bus into town. She'd arranged to go for a pizza with friends. She'd agreed a pick-up time with her dad so when she wasn't waiting for him he knew something was wrong. It was only when he and his wife rang round her friends to see if she was still with them that they discovered she hadn't met up with them. She'd been sexually assaulted – probably raped, and strangled. Harry Benson has agreed to reschedule his list tomorrow to give Carly priority. With any luck he'll bump her up to first thing.'

'Why didn't her friends let her parents know she hadn't turned up?' asked a DC sitting at the front of the room.

'It had happened before. When she's grounded her dad takes her phone off her so it didn't seem that unusual.' DC Robinson had worked alongside the MISPER team when Carly had gone missing, making sure both teams shared information as it came in. He'd put together a victimology report ahead of the briefing. 'The DC I spoke to in the MISPER team described the Kings as a decent family. They're not known to police or to social services. Both parents are still married to each other. Mum works as a receptionist in a medical practice. Dad's a self-employed builder. Car, van, holiday abroad every year. They kept Carly on a tight leash. Dad's words not mine. Homework. Guides. Gymnastics. On Friday she left the family home to meet with friends. Her whereabouts after that are unknown.'

'Did she have a boyfriend?' asked Coupland.

'Her parents told the MISPER team she wasn't interested in boys—'

'—That doesn't answer my question,' Coupland cut in. 'This is a murder investigation now. Her friends might have more to say for themselves now the unthinkable has happened.' He made eye contact with Robinson, waited for him to nod as he made a note on the pad in front of him. 'Friends and family need to be traced, interviewed and eliminated as soon as possible. Teachers, anyone who came into contact with her. That way those closest to her can begin to process their loss.'

'If she had been meeting a boy,' asked Krispy, 'why would she let her friends think she was going to meet them?'

A shrug.

'Maybe she planned to meet them after,' said another DC.

Coupland turned to Robinson. 'Find out if she'd mentioned anything untoward happening. Had she noticed someone following her or hanging around the places she went to?'

'Was her mobile phone with her personal effects?'

'No. A bag containing a small purse with cash in had been dumped in a bin at the entrance to the park. There was a lip gloss and hairbrush inside it. Nothing else.'

Coupland turned his attention to Krispy: 'I want you to check out anyone with a history of sexual assault within a five-mile radius of where Carly was found. Let's not forget she was under-age, so include offenders with a history of sexually assaulting children too. I want them TIEd as a matter of urgency.' He waited for the DC to nod before moving on.

'The press are already circling due to the TV appeal on Saturday evening. The family is staying with relatives

26

overnight, but once they get back tomorrow the media circus will begin.'

Coupland's phone beeped indicating an incoming text from DCI Mallender. Coupland's shoulders dipped as he read it:

We're wanted in the Super's office NOW.

He got to his feet. 'Talking of circus,' he said, making his way to the door, 'I've been granted an audience with the ringmaster.'

*

Superintendent Curtis's office

DCI Mallender was already seated in Superintendent Curtis's office when Coupland knocked on the door, stepping in after being granted right of entry. He waited for permission to sit, angling his chair until he was semi facing the DCI beside him, so it didn't feel like they were two errant schoolboys summoned to see their headmaster.

'This case landed in our laps from the moment Carly went missing. Have you *any* discernible leads?' demanded Curtis.

Coupland regarded him. 'Not as yet, Sir. There's no obvious person of interest at this point but then the murder investigation is only just getting under way.'

It was as though he hadn't spoken. 'I mean,' Curtis persisted, 'less than 24 hours after Carly's parents go through the ordeal of appealing for information into their daughter's disappearance – in this very station – they're now going to have to come back and appeal for information about her murder.'

What he was objecting to was *his* ordeal; having to

stand in front of the press and admit their efforts to find Carly alive had amounted to diddly squat.

'We knew it was a long shot that if she'd been abducted by someone she'd still be alive, Sir,' Mallender reminded him, 'but however slim that chance was, we had to give the appeal a go.'

'And now we're facing the prospect of going back in front of the cameras to face a barrage of questions about how, given our claim that we were searching for Carly, it took three boys and their Jack Russell to find her.'

Coupland drummed his fingers against the sides of his chair. It was only a matter of time before Curtis put the blame at his door.

'I understand you coordinated the search for Carly, DS Coupland, alongside the MISPER team. So tell me this, how in God's name did you bloody miss her?'

It was as direct as questions got, Coupland conceded; he only hoped his direct answer was received in the spirit it was given. 'Not enough manpower, Sir,' he answered, pausing to make it look as though he'd considered his response when the answer really was that simple. Two teams had been tasked with searching multiple sites. They'd been focussed on three areas: the destination Carly had been heading to – a pizza restaurant in Eccles, the area adjacent to the bus stop, and her home. 'You want a faster response you deploy more officers, Sir, it's not rocket science.'

'I think what DS Coupland is trying to say is we prioritised our actions based on the information we had and the personnel available,' Mallender said, as though a translation was required. 'What we need to do now is focus our resources on finding Carly's killer.'

Curtis huffed out a sigh. 'The public needs reassurance that we are on top of this. That catching whoever is responsible for her murder is just a matter of time.' His gaze lingered on Coupland before returning to DCI Mallender. 'Manpower, overtime, whatever it takes. Just make sure we get the right result. And fast.'

Coupland bit back his response. Curtis wasn't a ringmaster, he was a stable boy. Shutting the proverbial door after the horse had bolted.

*

The play park in Tattersall was a no-go zone. For small children anyway. Several youths sat on swings, swearing and spitting, backs hunched against the cold. From a distance their demeanour was cocksure and intimidating; close up they were smaller, less able to handle themselves outside of their group. There might be shadow on their upper lips but it didn't need shaving.

A jogger ran past, keeping a safe distance. A couple on a bench were sharing a cigarette as they listened to music on their phones. A youth pedalled along the cycle path that circled the play park, saw the group huddled on the swings and made a beeline for them. He swung his bike to a stop, abandoning it on a clump of weeds as he made his way over. He wore a black anorak over a hoody that concealed jug ears and acne. His hands, which he'd thrust in the pockets of his low slung jeans as he made his way towards them, were already raised in greeting.

'Best brother,' said the oldest looking of the group, his fist raised in readiness to bump.

'Safe,' cycle boy replied, enveloping him in a hug like they were long lost siblings rather than part of a supply chain that traded drugs throughout the city. He reached into his jacket pocket and pulled out a bag. Waited while his companion pulled out two rolls of notes before making the swap.

'Police! Stop!' The jogger sprinted towards them while shouting into a radio as a police van screeched to a halt diagonally across the park's entrance.

The youth ran to his bike but the couple on the bench beat him to it; the male undercover officer wrestled him to the ground while the female officer cuffed him before reading his rights.

MONDAY/DAY 2

CHAPTER THREE

Not twelve months in and already Acting DI Alex Moreton wondered whether she'd made the right decision. Her transfer to Nexus House had been swift enough, the panel interview a formality that HR needed to rubber stamp. Her superior officers had made it clear that the promotion was hers bar the shouting. Her role, heading up the Children and Young People safeguarding team tasked with protecting and rehabilitating young people away from crime, was a new one. It wasn't as if she was putting anyone's nose out of joint, but still. The warm welcome extended by her superintendent on her arrival had expired by the end of her first week and since then she'd felt out on a limb.

Alex entered the room designated for her team and once more swallowed her disappointment. She'd seen bigger broom cupboards. It wasn't so much the size of the room that hacked her off, but what that size represented. How her team were regarded. She'd been given a screen to separate her desk from the detectives that reported in to her but it afforded no privacy. One to ones were conducted in a café down the road, unless there was a point to be made.

'The Superintendent's been on the phone for you Ma'am, said you were to ring him back.'

Alex acknowledged the DC who'd spoken with a nod, dropping her bag beneath her desk before pulling out her chair and perching on the end of it. Calls to the Super were usually followed by a summons to his office. No point in making herself comfy.

She took a moment to regard her team before reaching for her desk phone. When she'd first been introduced to them she'd had to bite back her frustration. Three women DCs and a male plain clothed community PC. The lack of male detectives in the group suggested this was viewed as a pen pushing exercise. Leaflet dropping, as Coupland had suggested when she'd first told him of the promotion.

This thought immediately made her feel guilty. She'd accepted the role because she wanted to make a difference; what right did she have to presume it was any different for them? From the start she'd tried to summon everything she'd learned from her online leadership course. Convey a confidence she didn't feel. On her first day she'd given them a potted career history and spent the next half hour listening and making notes when they talked about their own. One DC had been involved in Operation Steer, a project where youths met former prisoners to learn the realities of jail. Two other DCs had been school-based officers, working as part of Operation Gulf. The plainclothes PC had provided protection to crime families deemed to be at risk. She'd offered to take them all for drinks after work but they had family commitments that couldn't be changed at short notice. 'How about we put something in the diary…' she'd suggested. They had yet to organise a date.

Lockdown had put a hold on everything. Alex had wanted to be visible in the community – make herself known to the youth groups she'd be working with, but overnight everything stopped. Policing priorities shifted to one of containing the public, making sure those without good reason to be out stayed at home. She'd turned up to work each day but hadn't met any of the youngsters on her watch list until she'd been in the job four months. In the intervening time she'd set up a communication group with the youth leaders operating in her area. They'd offered limited online counselling to the kids on their caseloads. It had made sense to loan her team out to other syndicates when staff levels dropped due to officers self-isolating, but they'd lost their focus. Alex was determined this was not going to be a lip service provision. Since the ease down they'd been limping along, and Alex feared their motivation was starting to drift. If they wanted to stay in her squad they'd need to buckle up.

'Listen up, youth groups and after school clubs are operating once more. If we want this unit to stay open we need to focus on what we've been tasked to do, and that means telling your colleagues across the hall you're no longer available to bolster their numbers – we need to start prioritising community engagement.' She waited for them to digest what she said before adding, 'And to get a better understanding of the kids and support groups on our patch I intend to be hands on, accompanying you where necessary to get a better idea of your workload.' She kept her smile in check. Yes, she'd as good as accused them of being lazy. She didn't need to be liked. She just wanted to get things done. She called the Super's office, letting him know she was on her way.

Alex knocked twice on the closed office door, pausing just long enough for a mouthful of sandwich to be swallowed or a stray finger to be removed from a nostril before stepping inside.

Superintendent Urquhart regarded her for a full five seconds before rearranging his face into a welcoming smile. 'Acting DI Moreton,' he said, extending a hand to indicate she take the seat across the desk from him.

'Sir,' she said, lowering herself into the chair, noting the absence of tea and biscuits, which had been laid out in her honour when she'd moved to Nexus House at the beginning of the year.

'Duncan, please,' he said, in a way that brought her no reassurance.

'It's been a rocky time for everyone,' Duncan began, placing his elbows on his desk and forming a steeple with his hands. He regarded her over the top of his knuckles. 'I'm sure you've found it every bit as frustrating, watching resources being reallocated so we could keep the great unwashed indoors.'

Alex blinked. Was he letting her go? Was this his round-the-houses way of saying the team was being downsized?

'Let me get straight to the point. The mayor's office has been on the phone looking for good news stories.'

The division had come under a wave of bad press in recent months, two high profile ex-officers using the media to air their grievances alongside complaints from the public about arrests made during lockdown. No wonder the mayor wanted something he could put a positive spin on. Each unit was already tasked with posting key arrests made during each shift on social media, resulting in daily images of snap bags of skunk and confiscated machetes doing the rounds of Twitter and Facebook. Presumably the ones tasked with posting on Instagram had been sent on a training course – the images posted there were sharper, hard hitting: officers standing together in the wake of George Floyd. Happy Shavuot. Eid Mubarak. Manchester Pride. Alex was able to navigate her way through social media, though she wasn't sure she could do much to oblige in terms of content. 'We haven't had much of an opportunity to identify and engage with our client group, Duncan,' she began. 'I certainly can't magic any successful outcomes out of a hat.'

His smile faltered, momentarily, before resuming its politician's gleam. He was a carrot manager, much as Alex aspired to be. She'd read the psychology books, tried to work out how to meet him half way.

'The team is returning to normal duties now that they are no longer required to provide sick cover for other units.' She paused, daring him to over-rule her, insist that she was to do more with less. 'Which means that I can start to assess where and in what form our interventions can take to support these young people.'

He stared at her, his smile slipping. He needed something of substance he could take to the higher ups, and 'assessing possible interventions' made a crappy soundbite.

'I could produce a case study – anonymised of course – highlighting the impact our support is making to the young people who engage with us.'

Relief flashed across Duncan Urquhart's features. Already he was on his feet. 'Excellent!' he said, sweeping his arm towards the door signifying their meeting had ended. 'I'd like you to update me weekly on this, and prepare a report I can take to the monthly meeting chaired by the Assistant Chief Constable.'

'Sir,' Alex nodded, raising a brow as she headed towards the door. She'd committed her team to hitting the ground running and providing her with case study material that would demonstrate successful outcomes. How hard could it be?

*

Coupland looked on as the mortuary technician photographed Carly King. What remained of her clothing was removed and bagged. The plastic sheet she'd been wrapped in had already been folded and placed into an evidence bag to go to the lab for testing. Biological samples were taken – hair plucked, nails scraped, mouth, nose and sexual organs swabbed, ready for sending to the lab. He used a pair of tweezers to retrieve something from the inside of her thigh. 'This pubic hair doesn't match her own,' he said. Fingerprints taken, the body was washed. Every birthmark, scar, documented. Blood samples collected.

Coupland glanced up as Harry Benson entered the room, togged up in surgical gown and gloves. 'No show without Punch,' he muttered to Ashcroft.

They were standing in the viewing gallery, had a bird's eye view as the pathologist lifted his scalpel and began cutting a Y shape into Carly's torso from shoulders to groin. He'd known him professionally for several years, yet the pathologist looked no older than when he'd first taken up his post. He was younger than Coupland, though not by much, his dark skin giving him a healthy glow. He glanced up into the gallery, a smile flitting over his face as they locked eyes. 'You look like you've pulled an all-nighter,' he said. 'The job starting to get to you?'

Coupland tilted his head. 'Sleep's over rated,' he answered, 'it's all about power naps now.' Though it wasn't something he'd tried personally.

'You play any sport?' Benson asked.

'Are you having a laugh? When do I have time for that?'

'You could go running.'

'I run in my job.'

'Walking then.'

'I don't have a dog.'

'Do you need a dog to go for a walk?'

'Unless I want to look like someone's stalker.'

A pause, while Benson sliced and cut. 'Still smoking?'

'Just the one pack a day. Everyone has a vice.' He looked at the young girl lying on the mortuary slab and swallowed. At least his was palatable. 'Anyway, who appointed you my doctor?'

'Better your doctor than your pathologist,' Benson replied as he sawed open Carly's ribs and removed the breastplate. He began his inspection of her neck. 'The laryngeal cartilage is broken, as I suspected,' he told them, working his way along her body, weighing, measuring, more slicing. When he reached her genital area Coupland glanced away, dragging his phone from his pocket, began scrolling through messages he had no appetite to read, grinding his teeth as he did so. 'There's bruising to the labia, hymnal tears…'

Coupland filtered out the catalogue of injuries. There was only so much he could pack away into his Pandora's Box of horror. Only so much he could compartmentalise. He had no recollection of the post mortem ending. He couldn't recall whether he'd thanked Benson for pushing Carly up the queue or whether he'd walked out before the mortuary technician had got out his sewing kit. He told Ashcroft he wanted to get some fresh air, which the acting DS knew by now meant he needed a smoke.

Ashcroft had disappeared in the direction of the vending machine, emerging several minutes later carrying a froth-topped takeaway cup and a bottle of water. He had a knack of knowing just what Coupland needed, whether it was coffee, graft, space. Coupland nodded his thanks while drawing deep on his second cigarette. Let the smoke drift up from his nostrils.

'There's lots of posts on Carly's Facebook page now,' Ashcroft said, scrolling down his smartphone before passing it to Coupland.

Coupland squinted at one post. 'What's GBNF?'

'Gone but not forgotten.'

'Jesus.'

Ashcroft shrugged. 'It's only like RIP, but for the Peppa Pig generation.'

Coupland frowned. 'The Peppa Pig generation shouldn't need to be writing anything like this,' he said, handing Ashcroft's phone back. Carly's list of injuries kept circling in his head. He tried to blink the images away. He inclined his head towards the mortuary's entrance. 'Any idea why Harry big bollocks has taken an interest in my health?'

'I was wondering the same thing. Maybe the med school has run out of cadavers. He might be sizing up the next intake.'

'What? You think I'm going to leave my body to medical science? All those impressionable students thinking I was the norm?' Coupland blew out his cheeks. 'You can't improve on perfection. Some of us are just born with it.'

In truth his GP had been warning him to stop smoking for years. Had said at his last check-up he should reduce his caffeine intake too. The quack was a nice enough guy but when he started giving medical advice it was hard to play along. Coffee and fags to Coupland was like blood to a vampire. A necessary component of his life support system.

'So what's your vice then?' he asked, eyeing Ashcroft's bottled water suspiciously. 'You training for a marathon or something?'

Ashcroft shook his head. 'I like to look after myself, that's all.'

No reason to hold that against him, Coupland reasoned, dropping his cigarette onto the pavement to stub out with his shoe.

*

CID room, Salford Precinct station
Enlarged crime scene photos of Carly King appeared on the incident board beside the one from MISPER. Next to these a blown-up map showed the precise spot where her body had been found. A further map beside it covered a wider area: Carly's home, the bus stop she'd walked to and the pizza restaurant where she was due to meet her friends.

Coupland eyed the paperwork in his in-tray. Statements taken from houses and flats close to where Carly's body was discovered. He stood, allowing himself a stretch. His desk phone rang, which he answered on its second ring.

Harry Benson. 'I've emailed my PM report on Carly King through to you but thought you'd appreciate the edited highlights.'

Coupland wasn't sure that's how he'd describe Carly's injuries, but now wasn't the time for nit picking. He grunted in response.

'A couple of things I wanted to flag up, really. Firstly, the lab results are back on her bloodwork. We found traces of Fentanyl in her bloodstream. Which, for the uninitiated, is an opioid drug used primarily for pain relief but also as a sedative. It's one hundred times more powerful than morphine, and is fast becoming a best seller on the illegal Class A circuit. As well as the usual ingestion routes it can be administered in spray form – think of the type of gadget you squirt up your nose when it's blocked – which I would say is how it was administered here. I certainly didn't see any injection sites when I examined her body.'

Coupland digested this.

'It will have made her placid,' Benson continued. *'But not so placid she hadn't put up a fight.'*

Coupland swallowed. He'd picked up his pen whilst listening to Benson, had written down Fentanyl but bugger all else. He started circling the word. It was hard to keep up with the ever-changing drug scene. Especially the synthetic stuff that anyone with a garage and season one of Breaking Bad under their belt could throw together.

'The wounds around her vagina suggest her attackers had to force themselves on her.'

Coupland thought he'd misheard. He blinked. 'Attackers?' he said, catching Ashcroft's eye as he walked into the CID room.

Benson sighed. *'That was the second thing I wanted to tell you. There are two semen samples on the swabs we took from her.'*

Coupland slumped back in his chair, listening as he massaged his eye sockets with his forefinger and thumb.

By the time he'd finished the call, Ashcroft, who'd been watching him quizzically, was perched on his desk. He stared at Coupland's one-word note. 'As shopping lists go that's one hell of a party you're planning.'

'You've heard of it then?'

Ashcroft nodded. 'Its existence is certainly on the up. Whether it's a flash in the pan or becomes a classic drug of choice only time will tell.'

While Coupland updated Ashcroft on his conversation with the pathologist he scrolled through his emails until he found the PM report Benson had sent through and hit 'print,' gliding across the floor on his chair to collect it from the printer. He skimmed through it before passing it to Ashcroft. 'So the Fentanyl was used to stop her making a fuss,' he observed. 'Only she wasn't docile enough, by the sounds of it.' He summed up Benson's view entirely. He considered the implications. 'It can be administered via a nasal spray which suggests that this could have been an opportunist attack, it would certainly explain how her killer was able to overcome her without causing a scene.'

'What will you tell her parents?' Ashcroft asked.

'About her being raped by two men?' Coupland's jaw muscles worked overtime, as though he was chewing something hard to swallow. 'I'm not sure,' he admitted.

'But you won't volunteer it?'

Coupland levelled his gaze on Ashcroft. 'Yesterday they learned that their daughter had been murdered. Their world is still in freefall. I'll give them the information when I think they can cope with it.' His mouth stumbled over the word 'cope'. That wasn't what he meant at all. 'In a day or two they'll want to know more. The details. The how and the why. That's when I'll confirm that she was raped.'

Coupland slipped his hand in his pocket, felt the reassurance of his cigarette pack. He pulled it out, studying it as though words of wisdom had been written on the front of it rather than a government health warning. 'Will I tell them at that point, that it was two men that did it? Two pieces of the lowest form of scum? Those are the details that can keep, I think. They need time to digest the information we give them into bite size pieces.'

Each injury inflicted on their daughter would set off its own grieving process. To overwhelm them with so much information too soon would do more harm than good.

Ashcroft nodded. 'They'll need to hear it, though.'

Coupland doubted it. He'd found over the years, when dealing with parents of murdered children, one parent would emerge as the stronger of the two. Able to take sharp facts and remould them into something their partner could deal with. It wasn't always the husband who protected his wife. Many a woman would shield her man from news that could turn him into a killer. Damage limitation. 'I'll not hold anything back, if that's what you're meaning,' Coupland answered. 'Especially if this gets to court.'

Assuming they caught the bastards.

*

Afternoon briefing, CID room, Salford Precinct station.
Coupland was on his feet in front of the incident board. DCI Mallender sat nearby, writing notes in his Decision Log.

'Carly King was reported missing at 9.30pm on Friday evening. On Sunday morning at 7am her body was found in undergrowth in Oakwood Park.' Coupland pointed to a photograph of the locus placed on the board. 'During that time she'd been drugged and raped by two men.'

He let that sink in for a minute as he circled the room. Images he couldn't bear to see came into his head unbidden. The fear on her face. The struggle. The feeling of powerlessness as the drug seeped into her system. The hope that it would stop. The realisation it wasn't going to. He blinked them away.

'Her body had been partially wrapped in plastic. It's at the lab now for testing, I'm guessing it was used to minimise the transfer of particles during transit.'

'Any detail on the fibres?' Mallender asked.

'Not yet – Forensics should be able to tell us something by tomorrow.'

Coupland read out the key points of the post mortem report: The bruises, the tearing. That at least two men had caused these injuries. He explained how Harry Benson thought the Fentanyl had been administered. He circled the room as he spoke. Eyeballing each detective. 'I want you to do something for me. I want you to picture Carly's killers. Imagine them going about the place like nothing has happened. Think about what they're doing right now. Joking with colleagues. Chatting with customers. Buying groceries.' He looked at his watch. 'Picking their kids up from school.' He paused. 'Planning when they're going to do it again.'

He looked around the room. 'How does that make you feel?'

He didn't need an answer. The tension on the faces

staring back at him was enough.

Ashcroft spoke next. 'House to house inquiries have been carried out along the properties overlooking the park. I've read through the statements uniforms have taken so far,' he said. 'I've put them on your desk.'

'Concise version,' said Coupland.

'One household mentioned a car revving its engine about 11pm. Not unusual apparently. A young man lives along the lane, neighbours reckon he likes to let them know when he's home. He was out when officers called round so I thought I'd go and speak to him, along with a shift worker whose wife told them he was at work.' He hesitated. 'Unless you want me to leave it for uniform?'

Coupland rolled his eyes. 'No way. Subject to rest days and Christ knows what else it might be three weeks on Sunday before that lot get this action completed.'

DC Turnbull had arranged the removal of Carly's computer from the family home the day before. He provided an update. 'The tech team have been all over it this morning but there's nothing flagged up that's a cause for concern.'

'Any news on the missing phone?' Mallender asked.

Coupland shook his head. 'We've gone through the area with a fine tooth comb. Nada.'

'Find out from her parents what phone company she was with and get onto them. You'll be drawing your pension before they respond but might as well start the ball rolling.'

'I've already spoken to the family's FLO, boss,' Coupland answered, turning to Robinson. 'Can you follow that up?'

Robinson nodded, adding: 'I spoke to the friends she'd

arranged to meet, Sarge. Three girls in the same class as her at school. She was definitely supposed to be meeting them. There was no subterfuge going on, no secret boyfriend she was sneaking off to see. I asked if she'd had anyone show undue attention or follow her about but they said not. They were confident that if anything like that had been going on she'd have told them.'

'Any family members we need to look into in more depth?'

A shake of the head. 'It's not a big family Sarge, they're all accounted for. A brother on Gary King's side who lives in south Manchester close to their parents. There's an aunt on Susan King's side, several cousins.'

Coupland nodded. 'Talk to her teachers, see if there's anyone we need to be looking more closely at. Someone she spent time with or confided in. They'll need to account for their whereabouts like everyone else.'

Coupland spoke to the room: 'What's the significance of the location where she was found?'

A DC raised his hand. 'The park backs onto the East Lancs Road, giving access to several routes across Greater Manchester.'

'So, convenient for disposing her body then?'

'She was found approximately twelve hours after she was murdered. Someone had to find an appropriate spot to hide a body, dig a shallow grave, drag the body to it and cover it with earth.'

'A local then?'

'Or someone who did their homework.'

'Remember there's two of them. One to keep lookout while the other digs, it's a lot easier to transport a body if two people are sharing the load.'

Mallender spoke next: 'Let's get incident vans set up on both sides of the road where Carly waited for the bus. Put out an appeal for witnesses driving along that stretch of road in either direction during the time in question to contact us if they recall seeing a car stop close by. Remember Fentanyl was found in her system. It could have been used to subdue her, get her into the car without making a fuss. We're asking passers-by to recall something that may not have caused them alarm, may not have come across as untoward in any way. Under normal circumstances they wouldn't give it another thought. But we know now that they weren't normal circumstances, that a young girl's life was taken in a despicable way.'

The press were going to be all over this, and the Super too, because of it.

Coupland pushed the thought out of his head. He was trying to find a killer, not play to the crowd.

Krispy ran through the data he'd gathered regarding local sex offenders. 'According to ViSOR there are 252 registered sex offenders living in Salford. 643 if we widen it out to Greater Manchester.'

ViSOR, the violent and sex offender register, was a national multi-agency database of offenders classified as posing a risk to the public.

'I cross checked these figures with an Offender Manager listed on the local MAPPA team. Of the 252, 37 were returned to custody for breach of license, 65 were cautioned. 150 are being managed in the community.'

Registered sex offenders were monitored by police and probation officers through MAPPA, short for Multi-Agency Public Protection Arrangements. How long they were monitored depended on the severity of their crime and the terms of their release, or as a condition of a non-custodial sentence.

'Of those in the community, 30 are graded as high risk and 20 as very high risk. I explained I was pulling together an offender profile following Carly's murder and the DC I spoke to told me we need to speak to the sergeant based at the sex offender unit before we go near anyone.'

The words *pillar* and *post* came to Coupland's mind.

'They don't want us approaching them "gung ho",' added Krispy, 'though I'm not sure what that's supposed to mean.'

'It's what people hide behind when protecting their territory is more important than protecting the public,' Coupland explained.

'Kevin,' DCI Mallender cautioned.

Krispy continued, 'Apparently the way we approach them is through someone on the offender management team – specifically a MOSOVO trained officer.' This was an officer trained in the management of sexual or violent offenders.

Coupland looked up at the ceiling. 'Give me strength,' he seethed, 'Let me have their number and I'll call them myself. We're conducting a murder investigation and they're giving you the run around.'

'Sorry, Sarge.'

'Not your fault, kiddo, some folk get wind that they're dealing with someone still cutting their teeth and they make you jump through hoops for the hell of it. Nothing a bit of arm twisting from me won't speed along. Not literally of course,' he said, turning to grin at Mallender before he had time to object.

'Sarge, there's an outreach programme that sex

offenders get referred to when they're released. It's a condition of their license. I only got the number for the person who runs it this morning; I was going to pay them a visit this afternoon. Thought it might be a way of getting the information we need via the back door.'

Coupland nodded his approval. 'You've taken to the job like a duck to water since we've taken your 'L' plates off,' he said.

Krispy's cheeks shone with praise.

'Definitely worth following up and gives us something we can cross check against the information we get via the MOSOVO team,' Coupland agreed. He felt the familiar trickle of apprehension whenever Krispy went out in the field. 'You remember the ABC of being a detective, don't you, kiddo?'

'Assume nothing. Believe no-one. Check everything.'

Satisfied, Coupland nodded. 'Give the boy a doughnut. Remember we've got two ears and one mouth for a reason, listening is key. Just keep asking yourself, "Is this the action that will get us our evidence?" and you'll do just fine.' So much of the job was driven by technology these days, but good, old fashioned detective work still had currency.

Coupland called the Offender Management Unit, asked for the MOSOVO officer Krispy had been referred to.

'Your colleagues have been trying to put wheel clamps on my investigation before it's even got started,' he said after being put through.

'Ah, so you thought you'd get in touch and growl a bit. Am I expected to roll over at the sound of your name?'

'That's your call. But I'm staring at the photo of a schoolgirl who was raped and murdered over the weekend and if that doesn't compel you to assist us I don't know what will. We need to know who to exclude from our enquiries and who we need to look more closely at.'

'I know how it works, DS Coupland, but I also have a duty to maintain the safety of the offender, who for all intents and purposes has served his debt to society.'

Coupland stifled a yawn. 'You're based at Nexus House, right?' he asked, checking his watch.

A pause. *'Ye-es...'*

'Tell you what; I've got a meeting there this afternoon,' he lied. 'I could pop my head in the door, see if there aren't a couple of contenders you could point me in the direction of. Always helps to put a face to the name, don't you think? I could be with you in... shall we say an hour?'

'Okaay...' came the reply, though Coupland could tell she was anything but.

*

Ashcroft saw the downstairs curtain twitching as he stood on the pavement outside the red brick terraced house on Lancaster Road. He bleeped his car locked, nodding at the woman in the window before stepping up the short garden path to the front door.

The occupants of the house were Karen and Alan Hughes. Alan was a porter at the children's hospital, had been on shift when uniforms had taken his wife's statement. 'Saw a post on Facebook reckoning it was them travellers that did it, is that right?' said Mrs Hughes as she ushered Ashcroft into the front room.

He wondered where these rumours started. 'First I've heard of it,' he answered.

'I don't suppose they share important information

with those down the pecking order,' Karen reasoned. 'Strictly on a need to know basis, I shouldn't wonder.'

'Not if they want them bringing in,' Ashcroft replied, not for the first time wondering why people so fixed in their views bothered asking questions. Not like they were looking to be enlightened. He'd telephoned ahead, didn't want to waste his time going back and forth. Karen had assured him her husband would be in, and here he was, demolishing the best part of a bacon roll without a care in the world, certainly without the concern of someone whose home looked onto a young girl's burial site. Ashcroft introduced himself, his mouth tripping over 'Acting DS,' as though he was still trying it out for size. He paused, waiting for Alan to swill the remainder down with what was left in his mug. 'Wouldn't surprise me if it was those Asian groomers, can't keep their hands off our girls,' Karen chirped. There was an eagerness to her words, as though she wanted to be part of the drama unfolding beyond her front garden. Some folk got excited by other people's tragedies. Devoured them as their own. Tried them on for size until it was time to return to the safety of their own life. She buzzed around like an annoying wasp. Plenty to say but no offer of a drink or a seat. Ashcroft wouldn't have taken one anyway, besides, standing made him feel more in control. He preferred not to make any comment. He didn't have the luxury of being anonymous. *The black detective who came round to ours told me…* ' would whittle it down to him and no one else, so he was always on his guard not to give too much away.

'I understand you were on a late shift on Saturday evening?' he asked, turning his attention to Alan.

A nod. 'Shift finished at 11pm. I was back here about

half past. Karen has my dinner ready before she goes to bed, then I watch TV for a couple of hours, wind down a little. I went upstairs close to 1am, out like a log.'

'Access to the woodland is via the lane that runs in front of your house. Can you recall seeing any vehicle or person pass at a time that you would have considered late?'

'Where were her parents?' Karen piped up once more. 'That's what I want to know. You wouldn't catch me letting one of mine go out that time of night.'

Ashcroft turned his head, slow. 'She'd arranged to meet friends. It was hardly late.'

It was as though he hadn't spoken. 'You can't let them out of your sight these days. Turn your back for five minutes and there's no knowing what they'll get up to. No wonder they get themselves into trouble.'

Carly had gone from being a hapless victim to scheming minx in less time than it had taken to throttle the life out of her. 'Murdered, you mean?' he asked.

'I'm just saying. Sometimes they bring these things onto themselves.'

Ashcroft sighed inwardly; the designer beard that circled the edge of his mouth formed a thin line. He turned his attention back to her husband.

'Can't say as I heard anything out of the ordinary,' Alan told him. 'Mind you, with the TV on…'

Karen rounded on her husband. 'What about him up the road? He was making a right racket. I told the policeman when he came round. I said to him: *"I hope you have a word with him, tell him to be more considerate of others."* Do you know if he did say anything to him?' this question was aimed at Ashcroft.

'I'll be asking your neighbour the same questions I'm asking you,' was all he would commit to. 'Did you hear his vehicle though?' he pressed.

'Can't say as I did, but then like I said, I had the TV on.' He shrugged at his wife, as though sensing the row he'd get later.

'What make of vehicle is it?'

'Well, let me see, it's a van, I think,' said Karen.

'A Ford Transit,' Alan said, shrugging once more. 'I mean, I can't be certain…'

'Well you should be, the amount of time he drives it up and down,' his wife scolded.

Ashcroft shoved his notebook into his pocket and wrote them off as a waste of time. Still, he went through the motions, handed a card to them with a number they should call if they remembered anything.

*

Ashcroft rang the doorbell and stood back. Checked his notes that he had the right address when there was no answer. He rang the doorbell again, reaching into his pocket for his mobile to contact the person he'd arranged to speak to, Darren Yates.

A harassed looking woman flung open the front door, her eyes widening until she saw the ID held up in her direction. She tutted, jerked her thumb towards a path that led to the side of the house.

'I'm here to speak to—' The rest of Ashcroft's words drowned out by her decibel level.

'—Then you'll know one of your lot has already taken my statement,' she butted in, her face reddening. 'Coppers I mean,' she added, lowering her voice. 'It's him upstairs you want,' she explained, her thumb jerking once more. 'I'm his landlady. He lives in the extension, got its own main door round the back.'

'Your name is?" asked Ashcroft, consulting his notes once more.

'Janice Haig.' She hung back in the hallway, keeping her arm outstretched as though to keep him at bay.

Ashcroft understood her fear. The country was divided. The way some folk had carried on during the lockdown was shameful. As though they'd existed in a parallel universe. That the rules didn't apply to them because they were too rich, too educated, too thick to get infected, let alone pass it on. The social gatherings that uniformed officers had had to deal with were the tip of the iceberg. It wasn't just the lockdown that had spiked mental health admissions around the UK; the blatant disregard for it sparked a simmering fury that still hadn't been put out. Police units had patrolled the parks and large spaces, but they couldn't be everywhere and the fuckwits who'd carried on as normal knew that. The news agencies posted images of raves and protests on their front pages but it was the stuff that went on behind their neighbours' doors that got up most folk's noses.

Older officers compared it to the miners' strike. Folk remembering how people they thought were friends had behaved. Rifts forming that would run deep, grievances never forgiven.

'Comes and goes all hours,' Janice stated, in the same tone he imagined she'd have used for those who crossed the picket line.

Ashcroft nodded in sympathy, made a mental note to remind the uniform who'd taken her statement to take better notes. 'Sorry to trouble—'

The front door slammed shut in his face.

*

Darren Yates had unbrushed hair and a chin covered in fluff. Long limbs that hung awkwardly from coat hanger shoulders. The air in the flat was musty, as if the windows and doors were never opened. The place stank of stale food and farts.

'You were out when officers carried out house to house enquiries yesterday,' Ashcroft said after introducing himself. 'I take it you were working?'

He followed Darren into a cramped living room that consisted of a cheap foam sofa and slimline TV. A coffee table had the remnants of a kebab congealing on a Styrofoam tray. A pizza box beneath it. A tin of Golden Virginia sat beside them, though Ashcroft doubted that tobacco would be all he found in there.

'Yeah,' Darren said, flopping onto the sofa, oblivious to the cushions that threatened to swamp him. 'I work for myself. I'm a delivery driver. Order anything from any of the major online retailers and chances are I'll be the one dropping it off.'

'Keeps you busy then?'

'Yeah… Weekends are no different to weekdays now, s'pose it's been like that ever since lockdown. Can't complain though, money's good if you're willing to work all hours.'

Ashcroft balanced his backside on the arm of the sofa. 'What time did you work till on Saturday night?'

Darren frowned, as though remembering what he did two nights ago was a struggle. 'Let me see… Last delivery was dropped off about 7pm. Folk don't want you knocking on their door after that.'

In Ashcroft's line of work there was never a good time to come knocking. 'So, then what?'

'Back here, stared at whatever was on the box till it was time to call it a night.' He reached for the tin of tobacco, stopping as though he thought better of it. He leaned back into the sofa, eyeing Ashcroft. 'Good job is it?' he asked.

'Has its moments,' Ashcroft answered. 'Why, thinking of a career move?'

'Happy as I am. I work when I want, where I want. It pays the bills. That's the only reason we do any of it, isn't it?'

Ashcroft had a notion once, of making a difference. Not quite sure what difference he was making now. 'You didn't go out then?'

Darren screwed up his face. 'What?'

'After you came back, after dropping your last delivery at 7pm, you came straight home?'

Darren threw his arms wide. 'Where else would I go?'

'Girlfriend's? Family?'

'A big fat no on both counts. Maybe I should get a cat.'

Ashcroft turned his attention back to the coffee table. 'So who delivered your kebab? Or was the pizza on Saturday's menu?'

Darren's laugh was nervous. 'Forgot about that. I popped out to the chippy on the main road about 10pm.'

Ashcroft pulled out his notebook and wrote something in it. 'What did you do after that?'

'Came back here.'

'You sure?'

'Positive.'

'Did you see anyone else on this road?'

'No.'

'See any vehicles you don't normally see?'

'I didn't see anything.'

'Some of the neighbours commented you make a lot of noise, coming and going.'

'It's a noisy van. If I could afford a Tesla I wouldn't be living here.'

'Seems like a nice area.' House prices would certainly take a battering, body turning up like that across the road from them.

'Yeah. I mean I wouldn't rent someone's poxy studio flat. I'd buy one of those fancy apartments in the Northern Quarter. Rooftop views across the city.'

Ashcroft was with him on that. He got to his feet. 'Thanks,' he said, handing over his card. 'In case you remember something.'

*

Nexus House, a large modern office block in Tameside, was home to several Greater Manchester Police specialist units including Serious and Organised Crime, Sexual Exploitation, Major Investigation and the Public Protection Teams. It was also where Alex and her team were based.

'Kevin! It's so good to see you! I'd almost given up on you venturing into this neck of the woods, and now here you are.' Alex's voice when he'd called her during the drive over was enthusiastic, but he'd wondered if she was being polite. After all she'd gone up in the world. Could be forgiven for moving on in every sense of the word.

It became obvious her pleasure was genuine. After coming through to reception to meet him she'd given him a guided tour of the office she and her team operated from. 'I know it's a glorified stationery cupboard and I don't have any space to call my own but it's all we need really; I mean we're not doing our jobs properly if we're sat indoors all day.'

She'd taken him through to the canteen, had ordered a blueberry smoothie for herself and a double espresso cappuccino for him. 'Doc reckons I should be on the herbal stuff,' Coupland said, picking a table close to the centre of the room so he could see who was there.

'I'm guessing you put him straight,' she smiled.

A nod. 'Said I'd meet him halfway though. There's a jar of decaf in my drawer which I use when no one's around.'

They'd passed several officers as they'd made their way to the canteen, many of them had straightened themselves a little higher, tipped their head as they acknowledged Alex with a 'Ma'am.'

'S'pose I should be doffing my cap to you as well,' Coupland muttered, laughing when she looked at him, bewildered.

'Still feel a bit of an imposter, to tell you the truth.' A thought occurred to her. 'I must admit it's a relief being with someone I don't have to try and impress.'

'I think there's a compliment in there, somewhere,' he laughed, spilling some of his coffee before placing it on the table.

'To be honest I was starting to think maybe you were right,' she said flopping into the seat opposite him and taking a swig of her smoothie. 'I've only recently got the team back thanks to lockdown and now the Super's looking for some good news stories that I'm supposed to conjure out of thin air.'

Coupland lifted the cup to his mouth but didn't drink. 'Good news, eh? Did no one tell him he's in the wrong job?'

'It's what the public wants now. Helps them sleep better at night, apparently.'

'It's what the politicians want, you mean. Helps them secure votes from those not sleep deprived.'

Alex looked at Coupland and saw a tired man. 'Talking of sleep deprivation, I take it the little fella's still keeping you up?'

Coupland tried to find a bad word to say about the bandy legged grumpster but he just couldn't do it. 'He'll grow out of it,' he said instead.

Alex got the impression there were more pressing matters on his mind. 'I heard about Carly King, got any leads?'

Coupland shrugged. 'Nothing to write home about. Going to check on our friendly neighbourhood sex pests but need a heads up from the Offender Management Team on a couple of them first. I'm on my way to see one of the unit leaders now.'

Alex narrowed her eyes. 'You weren't here to see me after all, were you?'

'Maybe not entirely.' Coupland's smile was sheepish.

CHAPTER FOUR

DS Allison Round was nothing like her name suggested. Rather than a people pleaser who counted the calories, Coupland found himself face to face with a female Gladiator who lifted weights when she wasn't on shift. Hefty ones at that. Fake tan and dyed black hair that she wore in a ponytail, she matched Coupland in height – and attitude.

'Not sure there's anything I can tell you face to face that couldn't have been said over the phone,' she stated, shoving several coins into a vending machine before punching in the number for the drink she wanted. She gestured to the machine's window but Coupland shook his head.

'I had a coffee with Inspector Moreton before I came to find you,' he informed her, deciding it would do no harm to show he was pals with the higher ranks.

The look she gave him said she'd clocked the reference and had him marked down as a dick. Coupland sighed. You couldn't win them all.

The Sex Offender Management Unit consisted of a dozen officers trained to monitor Greater Manchester's most dangerous sex offenders. From what Coupland could see as his gaze wandered over the officers seated at individual workstations equipped with monitors and headsets, the majority of this was done remotely.

'We focus on those deemed to present a greater risk of

reoffending,' Round explained. 'We're not here just to do a head count. We're like their voice of reason at the end of a phone. There are occasions where we are the last line of resistance before they offend again.'

Coupland raised an eyebrow as he regarded his opposite number, nodded as though he was impressed. 'OK, that's the Disney version, what's really going on?'

Round blew out her cheeks – not easy, even her facial muscles were honed. She swept her hands in the direction of her desk, before widening it to take in those of her team. 'We've got a backlog of almost 100 overdue visits we're supposed to have carried out. I've been tasked with re-prioritising.'

'You mean downgrading their risk status.'

'That's not the only option.' Her tone was defensive. 'We can get them tagged.' She saw the look on his face. 'The number of people on the sex offenders register is growing by 7% a year.'

The force was having to manage a growing number of registered offenders with even tighter restraints on their time and resources.

'We're already asking them to self-report to their local station annually.'

'Whoopy-bloody-do,' said Coupland. 'I thought the whole purpose of visiting them at home was so that you could corroborate where they're living? Carry out assessments to check it's not too close to the local playground or school. How the hell does that happen if you don't go out and see them?'

'You're preaching to the choir but the cuts are made by those well above our pay grade.'

The problem started when sex offenders left prison.

Plans were not always made to manage their release, lack of suitable housing made it hard to limit their contact with children. Under the Sexual Offences Act homeless offenders were allowed to supply the address of *any* location where they could be found. A shelter. A friend's house. A caravan or park bench. Anything rather than be registered as 'No fixed abode.' The revolving door of the criminal justice system.

'So basically you're relying on your clientele to *tell* you they're behaving.'

'I wouldn't put it quite like that.'

'OK then, so how many have called you in the middle of the day, told you they've followed a woman into a car park or are standing outside a school? Go on, I reckon I can guess.'

'That's why we phone them, hoping that when they see our number flash up it pricks their conscience.'

'The smartphone equivalent of Jiminy Cricket. Got you.' Coupland could see he'd pushed more buttons than he'd intended. That any hope of cooperation was quickly evaporating. He tried a different tack. 'Look, we're on the same side. A girl on my patch was abducted, raped and murdered and I need you to fast track me a shortlist of contenders so I can eliminate them from the enquiry.'

Round considered this. 'Have you got the date she was taken and the time of her death?'

Coupland told her. Round sat down at her computer and logged into ViSOR. 'We record the calls and visits we make by date and time. I can search the system for the names of the offenders that officers from this team were engaging with during the time she was missing.'

Coupland waited. Watched the spreadsheet of names

reduce as the filters were added.

'OK,' she said after a couple of minutes, '10 names can be ruled out from our register of the highest risk offenders. I take it the perpetrator is male?'

Coupland nodded. 'Perpetrators.'

Round looked at him sharply.

'There were two of them.'

Another tap. 'If I discount the ones showing obvious lone operating traits, that leaves us with eight men.'

As roll calls went it made bleak reading. Beside each name a photograph and a precis of their criminal history appeared. Each one guilty of multiple rapes and several with a side order of murder. Out on licence because they'd served their time and the victims' families hadn't kicked up enough fuss at their impending release. Round studied each record. 'I have monitored these offenders for years,' she said pointing to several faces. 'Historically they've all checked out in terms of complying with the requirements of their licence – they haven't been charged with any offence for the last few years, have no civil orders against them and there's no intelligence that they may re-offend.'

Two names were left. 'These offenders haven't been registered as long so I can't give them the same clean sheet.'

Coupland felt a surge of adrenaline. Two names was more than manageable. 'We can have them rounded up in an afternoon. Check out their whereabouts for the dates in question.' He got to his feet. 'Thanks for your help. If you can email their details through to me I can leave you in pea—'

'—It doesn't work like that anymore. There's a protocol

to go through.'

Coupland remembered Krispy had mentioned something about it but he'd thought Round had been putting up a smokescreen because she'd been speaking to someone wet behind the ears. 'Protocol?' he said, his lips tripping over the word as though it was it the first time he'd heard it.

'These offenders are guilty of nothing other than we haven't been in contact with them for a long time. You can't just barge into their homes when the risk of harm from others who didn't know they were living there is high.'

'You mean vigilantes? Credit me with a bit more diplomacy than that.'

'No squad cars.'

'I heard you. I'm not a complete fuckwit.'

'No private vehicles either; if others do know about their offending history and are watching them there is a risk your vehicle might be traced, putting you and your family at risk.'

'Fine, we'll take unmarked cars.'

'Seriously, there can be no uniformed officers in sight.'

'Yep, I've got your drift.'

'In addition – the home visit must be carried out with a trained MOSOVO officer in attendance.'

Coupland's shoulder's sagged. 'You don't say. And where am I going to get one of those at short notice?' he asked, sensing the answer but hoping he was wrong.

'You're looking at her,' said Round.

Coupland sighed. 'I don't want these bastards to have reoffended any more than you do, but if I think that's what they've done then I'm not pussy footing around while you pull on your kid gloves.'

DS Round gave him a hard look. 'That's not what I'm doing.' She studied the two remaining offenders on her computer screen. 'It's been longer than it should have been since I last saw them but at least I've met them before which could prove useful. There may be small tells, changes in their appearance or behaviour that alert me to the fact something isn't right. Something that could pass you by.'

Coupland baulked at her arrogance, then remembered he was guilty of underestimating co-workers all the time. Even so, he could walk out of there and approach the Super for a warrant but that would take time and, Coupland accepted grudgingly, he didn't want to do anything that gave the pitchfork-waving nut jobs an excuse to bully someone trying to make a fresh start.

Round attempted a smile. 'I know I sound like I'm blowing smoke up my own backside but I do know what I'm talking about. Offenders like this are experts in manipulation, remember. The Yorkshire Ripper was interviewed twice and released by the detectives hunting him before being stopped by a PC for driving with false number plates.'

'Before my time,' said Coupland, even though she was around the same age. He threw his hands in the air in a show of surrender. 'I hear what you're saying. You. Me. A pool car. If you can head out now you've got yourself a deal.'

*

DS Round's face had taken on a pained expression since they'd pulled out of Nexus House car park in a two-year-old Audi A6, heading towards the first offender on their list. Coupland suspected he might be the cause. 'It's possible we got off on the wrong foot, earlier,' he admitted.

'Ya think?'

'I get accused of being pushy a lot of the time.'

'I can't imagine…'

'All I'm trying to do is work out which direction to take the investigation. Whether to look inwards at the family or out in the community.' Coupland paused as he stared through the passenger window. 'What's it like,' he said eventually, 'working with…' He didn't know her well enough to use the words that naturally tripped off his tongue when describing this kind of offender.

She looked across at him. 'What? Nonces? It does tend to kill the conversation when I tell people what I do.' Her throat made a rumbling sound which Coupland realised was a laugh. 'People are scared to seem too interested, in case that marks them out as having certain tendencies that make them look like a predator.'

Coupland turned to look at her. 'What got you into it?'

'I worked in the probation service; thought there was more I could do if I worked on this side of the fence.'

'And is there? I mean, back in your office you're swamped in paperwork with no sign of getting through it.'

'Doesn't the paperwork overwhelm *you* some days?'

She had a point.

'The cases can be overwhelming,' she conceded, 'but I've learned to switch off that part of my brain that responds emotionally, and focus on being the professional I trained to be.'

'How can you sit in a room with someone like that and

not want to punch them?'

She gave him a sidelong glance. 'There are days I've come close to it,' she said, 'reckon it's the same for you, too.'

Coupland shifted his gaze back to the window. Some cases affected him more than others. Some killers were contrite. Full of remorse. Others were bewildered or downright deluded.

Then there was the other kind. Like Carly's killers. The premeditated, hard-faced, cold hearted bastards that snuffed out a life like it was worthless. What he wouldn't give to be left in a room with them for five minutes.

He pushed the thought away.

Round spoke into the silence: 'Of course the job is hard. I'm a mum, I've got two children. If somebody harmed them I would want revenge...'

Coupland clenched his jaw.

'So instead I do all that I can to stop it happening again to someone else's child. Look at the reality. Prison sentences mostly have an end – there are probably only 30 or 40 people in the entire country who have a whole life sentence and will die in prison. The majority of sex offenders will be released one day. We have to manage them.'

Coupland suppressed a shudder. 'So, tell me about Craig Williams, then.'

Round paused to compose her words. 'He was 38 when he was convicted. Worked as a lorry driver, molested eight girls aged between 7 and 15 years old over a period of 20 years.'

'Sounds like a proper upstanding citizen.'

'He's 55 now. He got parole two years ago. The last

time I saw him he was applying to the council for an allotment. He'd started a subscription to Gardeners' World magazine while he was inside, told me he wanted to grow his own vegetables.'

It took all Coupland's strength not to roll his eyes.

Round pulled up outside a dingy looking building. 'It's a self-contained flat,' she told him. 'You've no idea how hard it is to pull something like this out of the bag for a single male. The last thing I wanted was for him to go into a hostel. He needs a routine. You can't get that when you're queuing to use the bathroom and your food shopping gets nicked.'

While they waited outside Williams's flat the door across the hall opened and a young woman backed out lugging a pram behind her. 'Looking for Craig?' she called over, her hand pulling the door to slowly so as not to startle the infant. They both nodded. 'He's over the road, picking something for his dinner.'

'Chippy?' Coupland asked.

The woman smiled. 'Don't let him hear you say that. It'll be soup tonight. He makes leek and potato on a Monday. Nice it is too.'

Coupland helped her down the steps. Wondering, if she didn't have a partner, who gave her a hand normally. One look at Round told him she was thinking the same thing.

She waited while the woman thanked him before heading towards a row of shops they'd passed earlier. 'I know. I'll have to move him. He shouldn't pose a risk until the child starts school, but still…' She shook her head in frustration. 'Just when you think you're making headway something else comes along.'

'You're not certain he won't reoffend, then.'

'How can any of us be certain? It's hard to manage every risk when they use cognitive distortions.'

'In English, if you don't mind,' said Coupland.

'It's when you convince yourself that a false notion is true. You know, "*She was asking for it*," "*She looked older*." Like the victim is responsible and the perpetrator is powerless.'

Excuses Coupland had heard countless times over the years.

'The skewed social views still held in our society don't help either.'

'What do you mean?'

'A man walks into an office and the female receptionist smiles at him. Should he ask her out on a date?'

Coupland could see where this was going. Men who assumed that every time a woman smiled or wore a short skirt she was coming on to them. The force wasn't immune. It still had its fair share of old fossils who tried to pass off their comments as banter. That had never been his way. He treated women the way he wanted Lynn and Amy to be treated. Double standards seemed plain hypocritical. He still got it wrong though. Coming to the defence of female colleagues when gobshites got too mouthy was demeaning, apparently, but at least he didn't try to get in their knickers. 'Look, I hear what you're saying, but it's a huge leap to this league,' he said.

'Agreed. I'm just making the point, that's all. That if women weren't seen as fair game in the first place, there might be less of this sense of entitlement amongst men like Williams.'

Coupland wasn't convinced, but knew better than

to get into a debate about it. There was no doubt that Round had read up on this, and the data she'd gathered, combined with her on-the-job experience would run rings round him if he tried to disagree. Sometimes it was better to know when to throw in your chips.

The allotments were separated from the maisonettes surrounding them by a six foot high wire fence with young trees designed to act as a screen when fully grown. A woman carrying an old Aldi bag stuffed with dirty potatoes held the gate open for them, clocking the lanyards round their necks.

'Probably thinks we're from the council,' Coupland said.

'Or preparing for retirement,' Round said, nodding at the grey showing through in his hair.

They followed the path that took them down the centre of the site. Past plots of earth marked out by wooden frames. A white-haired man with large glasses pushed a fork into the ground before standing on it to give it purchase. Medium build, wearing a green jacket and wellingtons, he looked like a retired geography teacher. Depth achieved, he tilted it backwards and forwards to loosen the soil. He was about to reach down and yank out whatever was down there when he glanced up, sensing their approach. His gaze settled on Round, as he arranged his features to give the impression of trying to place a face it was obvious he recognised.

'It's been a while,' said Round, 'thought it was about time I paid you a visit.'

A nod, his gaze sliding in Coupland's direction.

Round made the introductions, leaving Coupland to explain his presence. They'd agreed during the drive over that he wasn't to jump in with both feet. That although Williams was a serious offender there was nothing to tie him to Carly's rape and murder other than his victims were in a similar age range. Coupland agreed to keep his mouth clamped shut. For the time being, anyway. His attention returned to Williams. To the banter the ex-con seemed confident to adopt.

'You're looking well, Allison,' he said, a smile flickering on his lips. 'I'm surprised you've not been snapped up by now,' he added, his gaze sweeping over her left hand. She only ever wore her wedding ring on rest days, she'd explained to Coupland on the way over. Made a point of never giving anything about her personal life away.

'My work keeps me busy, Craig,' she answered, looking over the patch he was working on, nodding approvingly. 'You've been busy.'

Williams's nod was eager. 'Thought I'd get some onions while I was here,' he told her, 'I'm making soup.' He lifted the ones he'd loosened from the ground in case proof was required.

'Your neighbour told us it was leek and potato tonight,' Coupland said, 'same as every Monday.'

'Onions go in it too,' Williams said, defensive.

'Maybe they shouldn't,' Coupland said, ignoring the warning look Round sent in his direction. He decided to get to the purpose of his visit. 'Been watching the news much?'

Williams's gaze fell. 'Not if I can help it.' He dropped the onions into a bucket and pulled the fork free. Moved it from hand to hand as though trying to work out what it weighed.

'A girl by the name of Carly King went missing on

Friday.' Coupland studied Williams's face, looking for the twitch or blink or other tell that told him that after twenty years of abduction and rape he'd moved up another level. 'You might have seen her parents on the Saturday evening news appealing for information.'

Williams's hands settled on the handle of the fork, making Coupland think for a minute he was readying to strike him with it. He stared at Williams. Williams stared back. 'Her body was found on Sunday morning.'

'That's terrible,' he said, looking at Coupland as though reading out a line he'd rehearsed several times.

'That the best you can do? A girl is abducted, raped and murdered and it's all you can do to look mildly put out.'

'DS Coupland,' Round said. The look they shared was awkward, as though she was reluctant to pull him up in front of a third party but if she had to she would.

Coupland took a breath. 'Can you tell me where you were between the hours of 5pm on Friday evening and 2am on Sunday morning?'

'I'm a suspect all of a sudden?' He turned to DS Round, the accusation in his voice clear: 'I thought this was a routine check, not an appointment with the Gestapo.'

'We can carry this on down the station if you like?'

'That won't be necessary,' Williams interjected.

'It is if you don't have an alibi.'

Williams turned to DS Round. 'Do I really have to answer him?'

'Hey, I'm right here,' said Coupland. 'And yeah, that's pretty much how it works.' A sigh. 'You could clear this up right now if you just answer the question.' Coupland had waited long enough. 'You know what?' he couldn't bring himself to say the word 'mate'. 'This is the first time we've met but I reckon your best days are behind you, wouldn't you agree?'

'Depends what you mean.'

'Not as fast on your feet as you once were, I bet, more prone to slips and falls. Isn't that what happens when you get to a certain age?'

'I'm not there yet!'

Coupland looked him up and down. 'No, but in terms of prison fit you're over the hill. You survived it these last 20 years, but would you survive it again? The constant threat. The need to keep looking over your shoulder. To check your food…'

'DS Coupland I really think we should call it a day,' Round urged.

'Going back inside isn't an option for men like you. Too much damage has been done. Too many lost years. You couldn't hack it again, go through that whole humiliating process. Your victim pointing you out in a line up. Being labelled public enemy number one all over again. It'd make sense, when you've finished, to shut her up once and for all. Take your identity to the grave…'

'That's enough, DS Coupland. We're leaving now.'

Coupland turned to her. 'If I leave now I'm coming back with a convoy of police vans. For him,' he hissed.

'STOP IT!!!'

Startled, they both stared at Williams.

'I know what I did. I know, OK? I'm the one who has to live with it every single day. What I did to my victims… I left an emotional holocaust in my wake and nothing I do can repair that.' He looked at Coupland. 'I've turned a corner, I promise you. I'm not going back to being that person.'

For the first time Coupland began to doubt himself. It was easy to get carried away in the moment, to think someone was guilty because they fit the bill in so many ways. He was being sloppy. He shared a look with Round which basically asked, 'Is he playing me?' She was the expert in spotting manipulating behaviours, after all. A slight shake of the head told him all he needed to know.

'OK. I suppose it's possible I went off on a tangent. It happens sometimes.' His tone was grudging. 'But for Christ's sake tell me what you were doing so I can rule you out of this investigation once and for all.'

Another sigh. 'The thing is, DS Coupland.' Williams paused for breath, looked up at the sky for inspiration before ploughing on. 'The thing is, DS Coupland, I *was* in my flat. But I wasn't alone.'

CHAPTER FIVE

From the outside, Horizon House was non-descript. A red brick purpose-built office block just off the A580. Easily accessible from Worsley, Swinton, Boothstown. Manchester city centre was only fifteen minutes away. Anonymous. Krispy supposed that was the intention, for if passers-by knew what went on inside there'd be hell to pay.

The security officer manning the desk peered at Krispy before studying the ID he held up for inspection. 'You sure you're not on work experience, son?' he asked, laughing at his own joke whilst turning to eyeball his colleague who'd returned to his work station with a sandwich and a can of Diet Coke. The men were in their forties, fat heads framed by clippered hair. They leaned back in their seats, regarding Krispy as though he'd been sent to them for their amusement.

Ignoring their jibes Krispy straightened himself, explained that he was expected. The gobby one pushed the visitors' book in his direction, waited while he filled in his details. Krispy reached into his pocket and pulled out the keys to the pool car he'd driven over in so he could add the registration number.

'Drove here all by yourself?' gobby asked.

Krispy swallowed, wondered what DS Coupland would do in this situation. He laughed then, as though the men before him were stand-up comedians and between them had cracked the best joke ever. 'I did indeed,' he said, jangling the keys mid-air, 'and before you ask my feet *do* reach the pedals. Happy to demonstrate with a lift to the station so we can discuss wasting police time?'

The faces staring back at him didn't look so happy now. The gobby one's mate picked up the phone on the counter and tapped in an extension number. Told the person who answered there was a DC Timmins in reception, followed by a couple of uh huhs, before replacing the receiver. 'She's just finishing up with a group but I've to take you through to her office,' he said begrudgingly.

Krispy nodded, followed him along a corridor, beyond a bank of meeting rooms with large internal windows that ran the length of them. In one room a group of men sat in a circle facing a woman with spiky gelled hair. The men were pasty faced and weedy, not much of a threat to the jokers on reception if the situation arose, Krispy conceded. A ginger haired man with a widow's peak and gold rimmed aviator glasses was speaking. Beside him a middle aged man with a receding hairline and steel framed spectacles perched on the top of his head nodded in agreement. Many of the assembled group followed suit and Krispy noticed that most of them wore glasses, making him wonder if there really was a link between hours spent indulging in taboo sexual practices and poor eyesight.

If Dr Petra McGowan was surprised at how young the detective waiting in her office looked she didn't show it. Krispy rose to his feet, put out his hand before withdrawing it, remembering that wasn't how it was done anymore. Without the formal process of shaking hands his introduction felt hesitant, uneasy. His confidence ebbed away as his arms floundered, leaving the smile on his face stranded. He willed himself to remember what he wanted to say and do next.

'Please, don't stand on my account,' Petra said, moving towards her own chair behind a tidy desk. She unclipped a device as small as a pager from her belt and plugged it into a charger. 'There are panic strips in all the rooms but these alarms are an extra precaution,' she told him. 'Not that I've needed to use them often.'

Krispy looked through the window that looked onto an enclosed courtyard. It was similar to a prison exercise yard other than the men walking around moved in any direction they pleased.

'The men are enrolled on several classes, they need breaks like anyone else,' she explained.

'I didn't know this place existed,' Krispy admitted.

Petra regarded him. 'No reason why you would. I deal with your Sexual Offender Management colleagues, on a strictly need to know basis. Has to be that way, to ensure the men's safety. The public's memories run deep. As do their grudges.'

'I read up on your clinic before I came here. I didn't know half the crimes they committed were possible, if I'm honest.' Krispy faltered.

The doctor nodded gravely. 'I know. It can take quite a while to get your head around it, and trust me, it's right to be appalled at what they've done, but heinous as their crimes are, we can't lock them up forever.'

Krispy wasn't so sure. He had a DS and a team of murder squad colleagues who'd have pleasure debating that particular statement.

As though reading his thoughts Petra held up her

hands. 'OK, reality check: as awful as their crimes are, we don't have the resources to lock them up forever. So, if they're going to be released, we have to make sure they don't pose a threat to anyone.'

On that they were agreed. Even so, it was hard to believe that twice a week the city's worst sex offenders gathered here for classes, like Perverts Reunited.

Krispy mumbled something. He reached for his notebook and began leafing through it to give him time. It was hard not to be biased. To detest everything the centre represented because of the people it supported. Maybe DS Coupland had agreed to him carrying out this task because he reckoned he was the least likely of the squad to be jaded by it all. He hadn't seen what men like Carly's killers were capable of. Until now.

'Tell me about the centre,' Krispy prompted.

'I run a crime reduction programme for sex offenders. We've been running for ten years now. Most of the offenders referred to me pose a risk of serious harm if they are not managed correctly. Many of them have been given a SHPO.' Krispy began to write down the abbreviation, so he could look it up later. 'It's a Sexual Harm Prevention Order,' the doctor explained. 'It can include conditions preventing the offender loitering near schools or playgrounds, restrictions on undertaking certain types of employment, and limiting internet use. Failure to comply can result in jail.'

'So they're enjoying liberty by the skin of their teeth.'

Petra smiled like a teacher impressed with a dim pupil's progress. 'In a manner of speaking,' she said. 'Our focus here is on reducing their offending behaviour. I run a taster programme for those in custody prior to their release, a way of acclimatising them to what they can expect in terms of addressing the problem that got them sent there in the first place.'

'A taster course? So attendance isn't compulsory?'

'Coming here is a condition of their release but I can't help everyone. The sessions I run in prison are as much to help me identify those who can be helped as opposed to those who, for whatever reasons, are further down the line.'

'Shame you can't run the entire programme while they're inside.'

The doctor wafted his comment away with her hand. 'I understand why you would say that. But it isn't all about freeing up prison cells. If we want them to exhibit normal behaviours in the community then some of their training must take place in a community setting so they are able to put into practice the strategies I show them.'

That made sense, he supposed. 'So how does your programme work?'

'We have to re-programme their mindset, DC Timmins. Their urges.'

Krispy swallowed. 'And how do you do that, exactly?' He wasn't sure he wanted to know, but felt obliged to ask. It seemed to him that people in possession of a great deal of knowledge loved the opportunity to show it off.

'When offenders are registered with the programme we assess their arousal to certain stimuli, so, in the case of a paedophile that would be an extreme sexual attraction to children – and use this as a benchmark to monitor their progress. Over the following weeks we aim to reverse this arousal.'

'And how do you…' Krispy tried to form the right

words, '…achieve this?' There were many other ways he could phrase it, but this was the least likely to make it look as though he didn't approve.

'Many of our interventions take the form of cognitive restructuring sessions, designed to minimise old attitudes and beliefs.' She paused while Krispy wrote this down.

'I, er, I'm not sure I understand…' he admitted.

'Let me give you an example. We use olfactory aversion therapy—'

'I'm not sure what that means, either…' he interrupted, once again feeling this was the response the doctor was hoping for.

'We teach them to associate "negative" types of sexual arousal with a foul odour,' she explained, waiting for him to catch up. 'In contrast, we encourage "positive" arousal by getting them to masturbate whilst looking at images of adult women.'

Krispy looked at the floor; at least he'd have no difficulties explaining *this* part of the process to the rest of the team.

'Over time we can alter their sexual preferences and in the example I gave you even help them develop stable relationships with an adult partner.' She waited until Krispy put a full stop at the end of the paragraph he'd written. 'You told me on the telephone you are part of the team investigating that young girl's murder.'

'Carly King.'

'Yes, the whole thing is just despicable.' She turned her head back to the window, to the men who appeared to be forming a line to come back into the building. 'Is it that time already?' she asked, pushing the sleeve of her sweater to one side so she could check the time on her

Fitbit. She moved her head to face Krispy once more. 'How exactly do you think I can help?'

Krispy cleared his throat. 'We need to rule out known offenders before we widen the net.'

'A fishing exercise?'

Krispy shook his head. 'Offences of this type don't usually happen from out of nowhere. There's often a gradual build up to the point where murder feels like a natural progression.' Krispy reddened, as something occurred to him. 'But I think you already knew that.'

Petra's smile was kind. 'I understand the reason you are compiling your list, I'm not sure why you are speaking to me, rather than approach the Sex Offender Management Unit?'

A nod. 'We're just trying to be thorough. My DS is at the unit today but there's an awful lot of red tape to go through to get any sort of result.'

'So you thought you'd cut some corners?' Her smile had slipped, and her eyes were decidedly less good humoured than they were earlier.

'Hardly. I'm hoping any anecdotal information you give me can be cross checked against the shortlist we get from the SOMU.'

Petra nodded. 'OK,' she said eventually. 'I just don't want to be used as a point scoring tool. Procedures for approaching these offenders are put in place for a reason, that's all. A good day can turn badly very quickly in their world.'

As it does for their victims, Krispy thought, though he was learning very quickly to keep this type of thinking to himself. 'Carly was raped by two men before she was killed; it's unlikely the perpetrators are two random first time offenders.'

'Agreed. But I'm not an authorised profiler.'

'Anything you can tell me will be helpful.'

'Newspaper headlines have a way of tarring every offender with a single brushstroke yet in my experience one size doesn't fit all. Every individual has a set of circumstances that are unique to them, although some characteristics are shared: people who have sexual fantasies concerning children often fail to maintain relationships with adults closer to their age. They may have suffered humiliation in these encounters. An only child growing up in an isolated rural area, their development can be characterised by very limited social contacts. Others may display negative attitudes towards women. Offenders tend to have distorted views of children, who they view as submissive but also provocative. They tend to undervalue themselves.'

The murder squad didn't think very highly of them either, Krispy thought, though that was another opinion he chose to keep to himself.

It was as though she had read his mind: 'You can imagine how many people want to see programmes like these fail. We don't pretend to always get it right. Some people can't be helped.'

Krispy had been writing in his notepad but looked up as she said this. 'What happens to them?'

'Attending my programme is a condition of their parole. If they fail to adhere to the conditions of their licence, then they are recalled to prison to finish their sentence.'

'Is there anyone you're in the process of reporting who is in breach of their licence? Someone who's missed a session or two?'

She shook her head. 'As I told you when you called, attendance is mandatory.'

'Even during lockdown?'

'The sessions were run online. I'd email each participant with a secure link to an appointment. All they needed to do to join was download an app onto their phone.'

'And nobody missed a session?'

Dr McGowan hesitated. 'One client ran out of phone credit. He contacted me once he'd been able to top it up again so I gave him the benefit of the doubt.'

'How many sessions did he miss?'

'A couple.'

'Did you ask him to show you his phone, to verify his claim?'

'I operate a circle of trust with my clients. I didn't want to breach it.' She saw the look on Krispy's face. 'I made a judgement call. A failure to comply does not necessarily mean that he's committed an offence.'

'I know that. But it might mean he's thinking about it.'

*

Krispy reversed into the Pay and Display parking spot outside Alpaca House in Eccles, a converted Church of England 'Safe' house used as a bail hostel and temporary accommodation for asylum seekers. The double fronted property had been extended over time. The new extension was not as sympathetic to the original construction as it could have been. The original building featured period windows beneath a gabled roof with decorative wooden panels. In contrast the extension was little more than a breeze block lean-to with a single pitch roof. The ground floor windows and arched entrance were obscured from view by an unkempt privet. A bandy legged youth wearing a knock off designer tracksuit stood in the doorway smoking a roll up.

Krispy tried phoning DS Coupland, leaving a voicemail when he didn't answer. When Dr McGowan had given him Sam Duncan's contact details his original thought had been to pass them on to his DS for cross referencing. But then it occurred to him that if all they were going to do was pay this Duncan fella a visit anyway, he might as well do that now so they knew sooner rather than later if he was a person of interest.

He left another voicemail as he climbed out of the car, this time letting DS Coupland know his change of plan. He assessed the building as he made his way towards the entrance. The reception area consisted of a small wood panelled office with a toughened glass enquiry window. There was a buzzer on the counter top to call for assistance. A piece of A4 paper had been blu-tacked above it saying 'back in five minutes.'

Krispy headed toward the stairs at the end of the hall, passing a TV lounge with several foam backed chairs scattered around its perimeter. It had the appearance of a dentist's waiting room, except the coffee table was stacked with jigsaws, DVDs and an ancient Trivial Pursuit. A dartboard had been mounted on the wall above a faux leather chair, though Krispy doubted anyone sat beneath it by choice. A football table sat in the corner. The notice on the closed metal shutter across the entrance to the kitchen informed residents it was available between 8-10 am, and 6-7pm, all other times they were to use the microwaves in their rooms.

Krispy followed the signs when he reached the first floor, smelled the sweet aroma of cannabis that wafted from beneath a door at the far end of the landing. He knocked on the door to room 11, holding up his ID for inspection when the door opened a crack. 'Mr Duncan?' He waited for the man behind the door to nod before asking if he could come in.

'What's it about?' The man spoke in a whisper, forcing the young DC to lean forward.

'It's better if we talk inside,' Krispy answered.

The door opened wide enough for him to slip through the gap, clicking shut behind him once he'd crossed the threshold. The man looked unhealthy and pale and shrank against the wall as though avoiding any contact.

Krispy assessed the room. It was the middle of the day but the curtains were closed, plunging the single bed and sparse living quarters into a permanent gloom. A small TV was on but muted. A shopping channel ran an ad for nasal hair trimmers. There was a microwave and kettle on a small table. The en-suite bathroom consisted of a shower with no curtain, a sink with a tide mark round it beside an unflushed toilet. The room was cluttered with odds and ends. Mismatching ornaments and things you might find in a skip.

Duncan slid his gaze in Krispy's direction. Took in his narrow hips and gelled hair. The lack of confidence, making him appear childlike.

'Why did you come here?' Duncan demanded. 'I'm not supposed to have visitors.'

'I'm a detective,' Krispy answered. 'I've been speaking to your counsellor at Horizon House. I understand you missed a couple of sessions.'

Duncan looked put out. 'I explained it all at the time. She said it was OK.'

'I know. But you're not supposed to miss your appointments. It's a condition of your bail.'

'I didn't do anything wrong though. My phone ran out of credit, that's all.'

Krispy nodded as though the matter was done with. 'Can you confirm your whereabouts over the weekend to me? From Friday night through to Sunday.'

'Why? Has something happened? I haven't done anything wrong.'

'Can you answer the question?'

'I was here, where else would I be?' Duncan's face was pained.

'How come you ran out of phone credit?'

'There was a delay with my benefits. I couldn't top my phone up like I usually do.'

'Can I see?' Krispy felt out of his depth. He had no real grounds to look through Duncan's mobile but it would clear up whether his phone had been out of action when he'd said it was, or prove that he had lied. It was clear he had no firm alibi. But neither of those things made him a killer.

'I like to play Candy Crush,' Duncan confided.

Krispy loosened the knot of his tie. 'Any chance you can open the curtains? And a window too, to let in some fresh air.' He was starting to feel uncomfortable.

'I don't like people looking in.'

'You're on the first floor.'

'Someone might look up and recognise me,' Duncan admitted. He shifted his weight from foot to foot like a child needing the toilet.

Krispy tried to remember what Duncan's case file had said. Released a year ago after serving 6 years for abusing his neighbour's son. 'How long have you been here?' Krispy asked, deciding to distract him.

'A while.'

'Do you like it?'

Duncan's gaze roamed around the place as though seeing it through his visitor's eyes. 'It's OK. I know it's nothing special but the others leave me alone. I like being left alone.' His tone was brusque, as though he didn't like being asked questions either.

'I'm sorry I disturbed you,' Krispy said. 'But a girl was abducted and murdered over the weekend and we have to check that all offenders in the area can account for their movements. It's routine, nothing for you to worry about.'

A smile tugged at Duncan's mouth. 'I'm not worried,' he said, shuffling towards Krispy as he spoke. 'You're only doing your job. I get that.' He flashed an encouraging smile. 'Do *you* play Candy Crush?'

Krispy nodded, a feeling of unease settling on his shoulders like a cloak.

'We could play it on my phone if you like?' Duncan asked, his face brightening.

'OK,' said Krispy, thinking he'd be glad to be out of there and back at the station. A cuppa and a doughnut while he typed up his report.

'It's just over here,' Duncan said, beckoning Krispy to follow him to a set of drawers beside the bed.

*

Coupland's phone beeped as he climbed back into the

pool car. A voicemail from Krispy updating him on his visit to Horizon House. He gave the name of the offender flagged up following his meeting with the centre's counsellor. Sam Duncan.

He turned to Allison Round. 'What's the name of the guy we're going to see?'

She turned the ignition and indicated before pulling out into the road. 'Sam Duncan.'

Coupland hit the call back button; let the phone ring several times before cancelling it. He was about to try again when his voicemail beeped once more. Another message from Krispy: '*I'm outside the building Sarge, might as well go in since I'm here...If that's ok?*'

'Bollocks,' Coupland muttered, swallowing down alarm as he forced himself to think.

'What is it?'

'I've got an inexperienced DC about to knock on this fella's door.'

'How did he find out where he lived?' Round demanded.

Coupland looked away. 'I sent him to speak to a Dr McGowan who runs Hor—'

'—I know what she runs. I just can't believe she'd give out information like that.'

'For Christ's sake it's a murder investigation! That circumvents everything else!'

'Except now he'll be rushing in on his charger doing all the things I expressly asked—'

The look on Coupland's face told her something more was at stake. The smile she offered him was sympathetic. 'Handling rookies is like herding a box of frogs. Tell him to cool his heels.'

'I would if he'd answer his bloody phone,' Coupland muttered. 'Look, we're no more than fifteen minutes away.'

She applied more pressure on the accelerator. Long enough.

To cut. To maim. To kill.

'How long's your DC been with you?'

'Couple of years now.'

'He should know the ropes then.'

Coupland didn't answer.

'I mean, it's not like this is his first outing and he's got something to prove,' she reasoned.

Coupland responded with a grunt.

Round wondered what she was missing. 'What age is he?'

'Ten,' Coupland answered, explaining, when he saw the confusion on her face: 'Trust me. He's like a throwback to a bygone era. He's not even started shaving yet.'

Round wanted to laugh, but the tension in Coupland's voice cautioned against it. She pushed harder on the accelerator instead. Coupland's mouth worked as though he was trying to say something. She had to really concentrate to hear his words.

'He's from good stock, you know?' Coupland added. 'Imagine choosing to be a cop when crime is just a concept. When you've no real experience of threat or fear.' He realised too late that he was over sharing. That referencing his own childhood wasn't going to help anyone. He tried Krispy's number again. No answer. He glared at the traffic lights when they turned red.

'Nearly there,' Round said, like a parent might console a truculent toddler.

While they waited for the lights to change Coupland turned to face her. 'Anything about this wise guy I need to know?' His voice was loaded with anticipation.

'He drugged his victim before he raped him. An adolescent boy.'

One look at Coupland's face and Round had made up her mind. 'Blue lights all the way,' she said. 'Fuck the neighbours.'

Round had barely pulled up at the kerb when Coupland jumped out of the car. He barged through the smokers congregated in front of the building. Two steps and he was in front of the enquiry desk, banging on the glass partition with the heel of his palm. A guy in a shell suit pushed a sweeping brush half-heartedly, 'Can you not read?' he said, pointing to the sign above the buzzer. 'She's away on her break—'

Coupland held up his ID and glared. 'Tell me where Sam Duncan's room is. NOW.'

The man pointed to the stairs.

Coupland called out Krispy's name as he ran along the landing but there was no answer. 'No, no, no. Not a-fuckin-gain,' he gasped as he located the room. Fear wrapped itself round his heart like a cold compress.

He tried the door handle, which opened straight away. Looked down at the figure lying prone on the floor. Already his skin had the waxy pallor of the dead. Something cold and hard formed in his stomach. Coupland closed his eyes. Let his head drop and shook it. Tried to rid himself of the imagined horror before him.

'I couldn't get a signal to call it in, Sarge, had to go to the other side of the building.' Coupland's head had jerked up at the sound of Krispy's voice even though his eyes didn't register what they were seeing.

If it were possible to step forward *and* duck a possible cuff round the ear at the same time Krispy achieved it. Like a computer game character in the hands of a novice player he made his way towards Coupland. 'You OK, Sarge?'

Coupland looked back at the figure sprawled on the carpet. Wrists encased in handcuffs. A series of curses interspersed with a low moan. He waited for the thud in his chest to slow. 'I should be asking you that.'

'I'm fine. I'm sorry if I gave you a fright.' Krispy had heard about the rookie detective killed on duty, knew it was the reason Coupland had held him back. He could feel the adrenaline pouring off them both, for very different reasons.

'I did everything you taught me, Sarge. I remembered my ABC. He's missed two online consultations with Horizon House and despite claiming he had no phone credit there's evidence of call activity on the dates in question. Plus he doesn't have an alibi for when Carly was abducted. I was going to bring him in anyway but there was something odd about his manner…he was acting like he'd taken something. I wondered if it could be Fentanyl. I told him I wanted to bring him in for questioning and he tried doing a runner so I detained him.'

Coupland's breathing had yet to return to normal but he was damned if he'd show it. 'You've read him his rights?' he grunted.

'Yes, Sarge, and control are sending a unit over to pick him up.' Krispy's cheeks flushed. 'I was never at risk, Sarge. I checked out where the exits were when I entered the building and I didn't let him get between me and the door.'

Coupland nodded. It was hard to think properly. To clear sufficient space in his head to process what had just happened. Or rather what hadn't. The lad was bright, but he'd have to keep an eye on him. Working on a hunch and going off on a tangent was downright irresponsible. And a chip off the old block. He was flummoxed. Unsure whether to kick Krispy up the backside or take him for his first pint.

'Apparently Prince died from a Fentanyl overdose. Did you know that, Sarge?'

Coupland took a step back, wound one leg round the other in case the temptation to take aim was too much.

*

Carly King's family home

The house was busier now word had spread. Several reporters loitered in their cars; one killed time by scrolling down his phone, another picked his nose, inspecting the debris on the end of his finger. Someone had left a bunch of flowers on the doorstep. Coupland skim-read the emails on his phone, replying to some, forwarding others with instructions for the recipient. His shift had ended two hours ago but there was something he needed to do.

The FLO answered the door, saying under his breath, 'It's been like the Trafford Centre on Boxing Day since we got back.' Extended family members and friends congregated in the living room wringing their hands and passing plates of sandwiches which were placed on the coffee table untouched. 'The mother's upstairs having a lie down,' he added, leading the way to the cramped kitchen where two women unwrapped cakes and biscuits with all the fervour of someone whose future hadn't been obliterated.

The back door was open. Carly's father stood in the middle of the concrete-slabbed back yard chain smoking, his body obscured by a cloud of smoke.

Coupland stepped outside, greeting Gary King as he approached by holding up a cigarette packet. 'Thought you might need reinforcements,' he said.

King shook his head. 'Your man nipped out to the corner shop not long since and bought me some. He's been alright to tell you the truth,' he added, answering Coupland's unasked question. 'Everyone else can fuck off home for me.'

'I can get 'em to leave…'

A sigh or an exhale; Coupland couldn't be sure. 'What's the point? They'll only come back tomorrow. It's her family mainly. Mind you, my brother's on his way over, once he's picked up my mum and dad.' He turned to Coupland. 'Is it me or is this the worst family get together ever? I mean, I know they're all upset, but can't they be upset in their own homes? Why do me and Susie have to watch them fall apart? Not like all these tears will bring her back…'

Coupland lifted out a cigarette, pausing before putting it to his lips, waiting for King to nod his permission.

'Knock yourself out,' he said. 'It's a dying pastime these days,' he observed, without a hint of irony.

Coupland pulled out his lighter and lit up, letting the process give him time to couch his words. Robinson had called him after interviewing two of Carly's friends. There was no boyfriend, nor any interest in one for that matter.

'We've recovered Carly's bag, but we couldn't find her phone in it. The officers who were here yesterday didn't find it either.'

'I could have told you that you wouldn't find it. Don't you think we didn't turn the place upside down when we didn't hear from her? My wife kept phoning her number and I'd run round like a blue-arsed fly to see if I could hear it. We were convinced she must have left it at home. It was the only explanation we could come up with why she wouldn't use it. Apart from the obvious. But you keep that thought at the back of your mind, don't you? There's no point both of you being worried senseless. Searching for that phone gave us something to do.' Carly's father flicked cigarette ash into the ashtray balancing on the kitchen windowsill.

Coupland had taken a drag on his cigarette while King spoke. Had let the nicotine nestle in his lungs before exhaling long and slow. 'Carly's friends thought the reason she couldn't meet them was that she might have been grounded. They told my DC that whenever you stopped her from going out you would take her phone off her.'

King looked at him. 'It's hardly a bloody punishment if she can spend all evening messaging her friends.'

Coupland couldn't agree more, though Amy used to accuse him of being Draconian. 'How would you describe your relationship with Carly?'

A shrug. 'I'm her dad. She hates it when I wind her up in front of her pals and she takes the micky out of my clothes but if she's upset about anything I'd be the one she'd run to.'

'Could she have been keeping anything from you?'

He was already shaking his head. 'She wasn't at that

age yet. You know, boys were nowhere on the horizon, there was no reason for her to start keeping things from us or start confiding in her mum.'

Coupland wondered if his wife would be of the same opinion.

'I had no reason not to trust her, if that's what you're asking.'

Coupland wasn't sure that trust was the word. It was easy for their heads to swivel the wrong way once they got to high school. To compare their life to those around them and feel it came up short. He'd never *not* trusted Amy. He just hadn't trusted anyone around her. There were a couple of times, when she'd started getting a bit lippy, pushing boundaries he wasn't ready for, that he'd given her room the once over while she was out. She never knew that he'd done it, nor Lynn for that matter. As it was, he'd never come across anything to cause him alarm. No crack pipe in her underwear drawer, no shoebox full of condoms. It didn't cover him in glory, he knew that, but it helped him sleep better. He stubbed his cigarette in the ashtray before turning to head indoors. He'd ask Mrs King the same questions, if she felt up to it.

'DS Coupland,' Gary said, calling him back.

'Yes?'

'You asked us yesterday to let you know if we had any questions. Well I've got one for you now.'

'OK,' nodded Coupland.

'Since we got it so bloody wrong with Carly. Keeping her safe, I mean. How the hell do we get it right for her sister?'

*

Coupland's home was in darkness by the time he let himself in. Lynn wasn't due back for another hour and Amy had texted to say she'd nipped to the shops with Tonto. Coupland tried not to feel deflated. The house seemed soulless when they were out. Lacked warmth that had nothing to do with the central heating being off.

He took off his jacket, moved from room to room to close curtains and switch on lamps, re-fill the coffee machine, put on the TV. Even then it didn't feel the same. He couldn't fill the space the way they did. He found himself bumbling about, waiting until he could hear a key in the door.

He headed into the kitchen. Opened the cupboard under the sink. Pulled out a small black case by its carrying handle, laid its contents on the kitchen table. The blood pressure monitor his GP had advised him to get so he could 'keep on top of things.' He rolled up his shirt sleeve, fastened the monitor's cuff around his arm. With his other hand he reached for the TV remote control to search for a programme he could bear, before pressing the start button. He needed a distraction whenever he took his reading. Found that staring into space sent his mind hurtling to the latest investigation he was working on. Crime scene images vied for space in his head. He flicked channels, settling for a daft game show where even the host didn't seem to grasp the rules. Anything, to shut out the whir of the machine. He tried not to peep at the digits on the monitor's screen, his lip curling as the host read a question from the card he was holding that even Turnbull could answer.

Coupland rolled his eyes, his attention shifting to the numbers on the monitor before he realised what he was doing. He blinked. The machine beeped, signifying the reading had been taken. He peered closely, swallowing down disappointment. First attempts were always rubbish, he reminded himself, hitting the start button once more. The gameshow host announced an ad break. An advert for cut price funerals came on the screen using animated characters, making Coupland wonder what demographic they were aiming for. He sighed when the machine's second beep didn't indicate a better result.

Coupland switched off the TV, reached for his pack of Marlborough Lights and slid out a cigarette. He wouldn't light one in the house; even with the patio door open Lynn would smell it before her key had turned in the lock. Instead, he held it between his fingers, like a majorette holding a baton before the start of a parade. *Best of three*, he decided, already feeling the tension ease from his shoulders as he pressed the 'start' button once more.

The machine was packed away and the table was laid by the time Lynn popped her head around the kitchen door. A ready meal nearing its sell-by date was heating in the oven. Coupland saluted her with his wine glass, pouring one for her when she nodded in approval. Her eyes were shiny and her nose was free of make-up. He watched as she took a gulp from the glass, noticed that when she set it down on the counter top her hands shook. They'd lost one, then. He knew the signs by now, knew not to say anything unless she wanted to talk about it.

'It's ready,' he told her, re-filling his own drink before topping up the glass she held out to him. They could always have a wine-free dinner tomorrow, if their day didn't turn to shit.

'Can it wait?' she asked, the look on her face telling

him food was the last thing on her mind.

Coupland turned off the oven; he was in no hurry to eat vegetable lasagne either, truth be told. Lynn didn't ask him about his day. She'd been married to a cop on a murder syndicate long enough to know what happened in the days following the discovery of a body. She'd have worked out if it wasn't Carly's post mortem that was making him grim faced it was the difficult conversations he'd have had with her parents. She knew that if she looked into his face she would see too much and he'd hate himself for that.

He led her into the front room and sat beside her on the sofa. 'Tell me,' he said.

She looked down at her wine glass and nodded. 'We had a removal today.' A removal was when a newborn baby was taken into care. 'I was the one who took the baby away,' she said, lifting her gaze to meet his. 'His mother was in one of the side rooms on the maternity ward, the foster carers were in the room next door, waiting with the social worker. The interim care order stated the baby was at risk of future emotional harm, whatever that means. The mother had attended family court that morning, bleeding heavily and leaking breast milk but the decision stood.'

'Any idea why?'

A shrug. 'We don't get to hear about that. Don't want to know either, to tell the truth. She seemed alright to me.' Lynn pushed herself to her feet before leaving the room; returning with the opened wine bottle she filled both their glasses once more. 'I tried to make the day as nice as I could for her, you know? Helped her bath him and dress him in clothes she'd picked out. Took a video of them both on her phone. Then the time came and I had to literally lift him from out of her arms and hand him over. She smiled while I did it, but you could hear her sobs all the way down the corridor. I stayed late because she was being discharged the same day and she'd got to know me. He'd come to us because he'd shown signs of distress during labour. He's been given a clean bill of health. No reason for us to hang on to him. I walked with her to the taxi rank. This post-partum mother returning home with a bag full of baby clothes but no baby. All I could give her was a number for the Mental Health Assessment Team.'

Coupland leaned forward and slipped his hand into hers, the detective in him mentally working his way through the reasons a child could be taken from its mother. 'How about we open another bottle?' he asked, thinking the lasagne might seem more palatable if they were three sheets to the wind.

Lynn grinned, showing teeth already stained red from the wine.

TUESDAY/DAY 3

CHAPTER SIX

Krispy and Ashcroft were already at their desks when Coupland walked in. They looked up expectantly, Krispy already getting to his feet.

'Can you give me a minute?' Coupland said, opening the top drawer of his desk and reaching for a blister pack of paracetamol capsules which he dry swallowed. 'My head hurts like a bastard,' he groaned. Between them he and Lynn had polished off their week's wine allowance in one go, with an Irish coffee at the end of it, just for the hell of it. It wasn't often they went off the rails, couldn't think when they'd last had a blow out like that but sometimes it was needed. He'd slept well too. Hadn't heard Tonto once. Funny that.

Krispy gave Coupland's desk a swerve and headed to the corner of the room they used as a kitchen. 'Think everyone's in need of a strong coffee this morning.'

Coupland looked up sharply, wincing as two marbles dislodged and started bouncing around his head. 'You're OK?' he checked. 'That Duncan fella didn't hurt you or anything?'

'We should be asking how you are,' Ashcroft called across the expanse of desks, 'according to Krispy you looked like you'd seen a ghost when you found Duncan lying on the floor.'

Coupland forced the corners of his mouth into a smile he didn't feel. It was obvious they'd come in early to update him on their progress. It wasn't their fault his head felt like mince.

'Did you read my report, Sarge? I emailed a copy through to you,' Krispy asked.

'I did,' said Coupland, though in truth he'd only skim read it while sat outside Carly's family home the previous evening, before forwarding it to Ashcroft with a request that he interview this Sam Duncan and let Krispy ride shotgun.

The young DC was a bright lad. His measure of the team astute. His report on his visit to Horizon House had been concise and to the point. Written using words that people who only watched the celebrity version of quiz shows would understand. 'You might want to add a diagram for Turnbull,' Coupland commented, referring to the part detailing how the clinic reduced offender behaviour.

'You're happy with it then, Sarge?'

'What, happy with what appears to be a total waste of taxpayers' money? Castration would be cheaper,' Coupland answered, knowing that wasn't quite what Krispy meant. 'A clinic that stops molesters from re-offending and not a scalpel in sight. Who knew it was so simple? Shame this fella didn't get the memo.'

'That was the part of the programme he'd missed when he started going AWOL,' Krispy advised.

Coupland moved his head from side to side. The paracetamol seemed to be doing its job. Just as well, given he had a briefing with DCI Mallender in less than half an hour. 'OK, give,' he said, 'I'm guessing there's nothing to tie him to the murder, otherwise you'd have called me at home.'

'It *was* Fentanyl that he had in his room, Sarge,' Krispy told him.

'Cheap as chips apparently,' Ashcroft said, 'Due to the fact it's so potent. Anyway, as the saying goes, a little goes a long way.'

'Thought that was Fairy bloody Liquid.'

'He's been getting it for personal use.'

'He would say that.'

'That's not all. The caretaker at the hostel can corroborate he was present over the weekend Carly went missing, so he's not our man. The tech guys checked through his phone and although he used it on the dates he claimed he didn't have any phone credit, it was to call several estranged family members looking for a hand out.'

'You've corroborated this?'

A nod. 'More importantly, there is no untoward activity on it. We let him go last night but he was picked up by the offender management unit because of his breach of parole. Reckon he's just bought himself a one way ticket back to HMP Manchester.'

'We can eliminate Craig Williams too.' Coupland told them about his trip to the allotment. Another offender DS Round would need to read the riot act to, given his budding friendship with the young mother across the hall. 'He swears he's just being neighbourly. Claims he's started seeing a woman his own age and there's a chance it might grow into something. Says he was with her all last weekend.'

'I'm guessing his alibi checked out?' asked Ashcroft.

'Yup.'

'Did she know about his past?'

Coupland threw him a look. 'What do you think?'

Ashcroft nodded to the stack of papers on Coupland's

desk. 'I've left you copies of the statements I took from the two residents we'd been unable to speak to during the initial house to house on Sunday.' He started shaking his head as Coupland reached across his desk to pick them up. 'Both vague. Not worth proceeding with.'

Coupland dropped them back onto his desk.

DC Robinson walked in with a takeaway coffee.

'How's the appeal going?'

A sigh. 'About as well as you'd expect. One driver remembered seeing a blue Mazda parked just along from the stop. Another a black 6 series. Another saw a Skoda with a man sat on the back seat, but the witness couldn't describe him, reckoned it's hard to give a description because of the face coverings people wear these days. Everyone looks like they're holding up a post office, right? Anyway, by the time I'd driven out to speak to them they changed their mind and said it could have been a woman driving after all. Oh, and someone else thought they'd seen a teenager answering Carly's description walk alone in the direction of the town centre a few minutes earlier.'

'How did she get there, magic bloody carpet? Anything else?'

'No issues at school, Sarge. All her teachers check out and have alibis.'

A nod. 'What about this missing phone?'

'The phone company have tracked her phone signal to the bus stop but it was switched off at 5pm, the time she should have been catching her bus.'

Coupland's shoulders slumped. 'That's it? I've to go to the DCI and tell him we've got the best part of bugger all to go on?'

*

'We should have made more inroads than this, Kevin.' Mallender's lips were moving but it was the Super's words being spouted.

Coupland gazed at the space above the DCI's head. 'Nope, can't see any strings, which means the Super must be working you with his hand shoved up your—'

'—Remember the chain of command, detective sergeant.'

Oh, he remembered it alright. The higher ranks bawled him out and in turn he was supposed to bawl out his team, but he saw no sense in that. Winding them up would make them panic, see an increase in pointless arrests as they scrabbled around to get results, but it came at a price: an increase in claims of harassment and the press having a field day. Worse still, inexperienced officers treading where they shouldn't. He pushed thoughts of Krispy's close call out of his head.

'You've ruled out known offenders?'

'We've liaised with MAPPA and the SOMU. Both suspects that their system flagged up have been TIEd.'

'Even though one of them was found in possession of Fentanyl?' Mallender asked grim faced.

'Even though.' He knew it wasn't what Mallender wanted to hear but short of reading him a fairy tale there wasn't much more he could say. 'It was in a different format, boss, to the one administered to Carly. Besides, there was only enough for personal use,' he added lamely.

'Did you find out who his dealer is?'

Coupland closed his eyes. He hadn't had time yesterday

to prepare a list of interview questions, nor had he asked Ashcroft to let him see his interview plan. He intended to listen to Duncan's interview tapes after this meeting but given Ashcroft hadn't mentioned anything further about the Fentanyl he could take a wild guess that the answer was no. Getting him to cough up the name of his dealer in exchange for a get out of jail card should be easy enough. And a conversation with the dealer on the Fentanyl supply chain in the area could take them a step closer in identifying the person or persons who abducted Carly.

Irritated he hadn't made this leap while he was in the CID room Coupland got to his feet. 'Seems I've got to pay a couple of folk a visit,' he said, which was as much of an apology he could muster for being on the back foot.

Mallender inclined his head. 'Fine, but Kevin,' he said as Coupland reached the doorway, causing him to turn and cock his head. 'You might want to suck on a couple of mints before you speak to anyone.'

*

A quick call to Allison Round at the SOMU and a reluctant deal was made. She'd hummed and hawed at first, reminding Coupland that a breach of parole shouldn't be ignored. He reminded her that they wouldn't have been any the wiser if his junior DC hadn't contacted the clinic himself. She agreed not to recall Duncan to prison if he came up with the goods Coupland wanted. 'Assuming he's prepared to grass,' she added. Coupland was confident the nonce code of honour was right down there with sewer rats and sub-human forms of life that made amoebas look pretty shrewd.

Half an hour later DS Round called him back with a name.

CHAPTER SEVEN

When DC Robin Ward informed Alex he was meeting with a youth worker based in Pendleton she could sense his reticence.

'Sounds like the perfect place for me to meet the groups you've been working with,' she said in an attempt to reassure him, 'mind if I tag along?'

She caught the look that passed between him and the other members of the team. A mixture of apprehension and irritation, much the same that she'd felt when DCI Mallender used to accompany her anywhere. She enjoyed the feeling it evoked though, for it meant that bravado aside, it mattered to him what she thought. What she enjoyed much less, however, was the feeling of unease when she entered the community centre an hour later and came face to face with someone she'd certainly hoped had been relegated to her past.

Robin hadn't mentioned the youth leader's name when he'd talked about the centre. Said very little about her other than she was 'a decent sort,' and that she was more likely to engage with the police than 'the militant lefties who often run these types of groups.' When they entered the reception area a tall black woman was reminding a group of teenagers to use the hand sanitizer on the counter before they joined the session. She stood, hands on hips, watching as they did as they were told while groaning and swearing to make it clear they didn't take orders from anyone. She turned her attention to Robin and his companion, full painted lips forming a smile that only slipped when Alex came into view. The woman showed no sign of moving even though the teens in her charge filed into one of the rooms behind her. The two women regarded one another.

The black woman's corn rows were worn long now and loose, but there was no mistaking the almond shaped eyes and angular nose. The trademark scarf that hid the frenzy of keloid scars criss-crossing from her collarbone to her jaw. Shola Dube. Sacked from her job as community social worker following a case review of her conduct during a missing person's inquiry. A case review Alex had participated in. Witness statements confirmed Shola had been damned good at her job; if she'd been guilty of anything it was caring too much for the kids in her charge. Still, Alex had submitted her report knowing what repercussions would follow. She hadn't had any choice. You couldn't hold information back just to save someone's skin. Even so. It was a decision that still weighed heavily on her. Who could blame her if she asked Alex to leave?

Alex took a step closer, said, 'Shola...' waited for the other woman to respond. She hadn't changed in the couple of years since she'd seen her. Not in any meaningful way. Her style of dress was more casual, skinny jeans with a long sleeved t-shirt; the relaxed look suited her. Her demeanour was relaxed too. She'd been attacked by the father of a child on her casebook, a child whose life she saved through a selfless act of bravery. No one would have blamed her for retraining to become a librarian.

'DS Moreton...' Shola replied, her clipped, precise

accent rising at the end in enquiry.

'It's *Acting DI* Moreton,' Robin said, when Alex didn't correct her. 'I take it you've met before?'

'We know of each other,' Shola replied, her attention returning to his superior. 'Actually, I do recall hearing about your promotion…I'm sure it is well deserved.' Shola lived with a former colleague of Alex's, though she doubted, for obvious reasons, that her name came up too often in their household.

'Is there somewhere we can go and talk?' Alex asked, overwhelmed by the urge to clear the air between them.

Shola made a wafting motion with her hands. 'No need, DI Moreton. Let's leave the past in its place. We are both professionals. What's the point in bearing grudges? We deal with the aftermath of people trying to get even every day. Let's not make the same mistake.'

Alex bowed her head. There were things she wanted to say, to mitigate the actions she'd taken back then, but when she thought about it she realised the motive was a self-serving one. She simply wanted to make herself feel better.

'I take it there is a reason for your visit?' Shola asked, her head swivelling in the direction of the room the youths had gone into, the rising decibel level suggesting no one else was supervising them.

Oblivious to the tension, Robin explained the purpose of Alex's visit.

Shola raised a brow. 'Projects like yours come and go, it's grass roots organisations like this that give kids a fighting chance to make different choices. What do you propose to do for these children that we're not already doing?'

Alex sent an enquiring look in Robin's direction. He'd made no mention of Shola's resistance on his way over. But then he'd not mentioned Shola. Perhaps she needed to coach him regarding his communication skills, or manage her expectations. 'I'm not here to step on toes.' The last thing Alex wanted was for Shola to think she was about to oust her out of another job. 'I was hoping that by working alongside officers on my team you'd be able to refer youngsters to them who are at risk of turning offending into a career.'

Shola nodded as though she'd heard it all before. 'The children I work with have complex backgrounds.'

At least this was an objection Alex *had* anticipated. 'All my officers have been trained in Safeguarding. I promise you this isn't a tick box exercise.'

'As I've already told Robin, I have no problem with your officer working *alongside my team,*' she locked eyes with Alex as she said this, 'just so long as he doesn't get in the way.'

Just then a youth walked into the centre, hands thrust deep in pockets, hood up even though it wasn't that cold outside. He tried sauntering straight into the noisy room but one look from Shola and he pulled his hood down, a second look and he stomped to the sanitiser, muttering 'fucksake' before pressing the dispenser harder than he needed to.

'Why are you late?' Shola demanded.

'Got pulled in by dibble last night, you think that lot'd have something better to do…'

'Like what?' Alex asked.

The youth looked her up and down, a smile forming on his lips when he clocked the GMP logo on the lanyard she was wearing. 'On second thoughts, you can arrest me any time darlin'…' he said, smirking as he backed away from her, before heading in the direction of his mates.

'What's his story then?' Alex asked.

Shola winced as she shook her head, causing Alex to wonder if her scarf was chafing her damaged skin. 'Shaun Lowton. Dealing drugs since he was knee high. Before that a love hate relationship with school that saw him get expelled.'

'For the same thing?'

A nod. 'His teachers turned a blind eye when he started playing truant because they didn't want him in school.'

'But things have escalated?'

A nod. 'This boy has been on our radar for some time. I've tried on previous occasions to nudge him away from the family business but he keeps being drawn back into it.'

'What do the family do?'

Shola looked to Robin to explain.

'Class A dealing, mainly, Ma'am. They've been using him to recruit youngsters to sell nitrous oxide to school kids. His nickname's Laughing Boy.'

The silver canisters, not much bigger than bullets, were the latest legal high for the pocket money generation.

'He was referred to Shola last year through his social worker once he'd left school.'

Shola picked up the story. 'He seemed keen to engage at first, though I know that can be a front if they're trying to wriggle off the hook they've got themselves on. He completed a couple of literacy courses and I helped him get a job. On his second day with the employer he had to go into hiding due to a feud between his family and a rival gang. We're talking bullets fired into the bonnet of the family car.'

'Charming.'

'He was sacked from his job. Can hardly blame the employer, at the end of the day he failed to show up for work. He was reluctant to tell them the truth because they'd probably sack him anyway. Didn't want me speaking up on his behalf. Kids like this don't stand a chance, their family's lifestyle makes them unemployable.' Alex heard the woman's frustration. 'Despite what you just saw he's a nice kid, personable.'

Alex raised a brow, decided to take Shola's word for it.

Shola looked as though she was going to say something then changed her mind.

'What is it?'

A sigh. The first hint of a grimace on those full painted lips. 'Maybe we really are fighting a losing battle. You heard him just now. He's supposed to be keeping his nose clean while he engages with this group but his arrest puts him on sticky ground. He's already on a youth rehabilitation order – coming here was one of the stipulations – if he doesn't stick to the agreement then he risks going to young offenders. He's just been offered a mechanics course at the local college too.'

Alex shared a glance with Robin. 'Let me see what I can do,' she offered. 'I'm not promising anything but this is where our project could make a difference. Besides, I need to write up some case studies of what's happening in the area. Showcase best practice examples. You know the sort of thing.'

'Will it mean we get more money?'

'I can't promise you that, but wouldn't you like to show your old manager there's life after getting the sack?'

'When you put it like that,' she smiled. 'Now if you don't mind I need to go and sort this lot out….'

*

Plain clothed officers from the transport unit had been targeting drug dealers operating along cycle paths and walkways at several country parks over the last seven days. It had only taken a couple of calls to locate the officer who'd arrested Shaun Lowton, who was due in court at the end of the month. Alex explained her interest in the offender, stating her intention to get the case dropped if he could demonstrate a commitment to the Rehabilitation Order he'd already been given. Alex informed him that subject to Lowton's cooperation her safeguarding unit would be working with him and to update the PNC file accordingly, naming her as project contact.

She was trying to think of an 'angle' that would give Lowton his get out of jail card, without sending a message to his cohort that he was above the law. She needed something that would make him 'earn' the opportunity that she was giving him. She just hadn't figured out what it could be.

When her phone rang and she saw that it was Coupland, she was grateful for the distraction, unaware he was about to give her the opportunity she needed.

*

By the time Coupland walked into the cafeteria at Pendleton Community Centre Alex was already sat at a corner table, waiting, a pasty-faced youth beside her. Coupland studied him for a few seconds; the faux diamond studs in ears that stuck out at right angles from his head, the jaw muscles working overtime as though practising for the lies they'd spout.

He caught Alex's eye and raised a hand in greeting, causing the boy to look over at Coupland before slouching back in his chair.

'Twice in two days, and there was me thinking you'd forgotten who I was,' said Alex.

'Small world,' replied Coupland, 'one minute I'm conversing with a fine, upstanding member of the smack head community about how I go about getting my hands on Fentanyl, when Laughing Boy's name came up.' He swivelled his head until he and Lowton were eyeballing each other. 'He couldn't rate you highly enough. Brings a whole new meaning to Trip Advisor,' Coupland added, dropping down into the seat opposite before flashing a grin in Alex's direction. 'And when your name came up beside his on the PNC, I knew the day was going my way for once.'

Lowton sat upright in his chair in an attempt to gain stature. 'Nice to be in demand,' he smirked, performing an annoying little shoulder dance to show he didn't give a toss. Cocksure. Arrogant. In need of bringing down a peg or two as far as Coupland was concerned. A task he was only too happy to oblige.

'I wasn't after you specifically, son. Just someone like you. You know, the sort that sells misery dressed up as a good time.'

'I'm sensing some aggression.'

'Those days are gone,' Coupland said, leaning forward in his chair, 'unless you start pissing me off.'

'We talked about this,' Alex reminded Lowton. 'You told me that you wanted to start making a positive difference with your life. Now's your chance.'

Coupland regarded Alex. 'You really think this is a productive use of your time?'

'Stay in your lane, Kevin,' she warned, 'and tell us how we can help you.'

Shrugging, Coupland turned his attention back to Lowton. 'I've been looking at your CV. Quite a list of offences you've got there. Impressive, even for this postcode.'

'Kevin…' Alex prompted.

'Like I said, I heard you're the go-to kid if someone's looking to buy Fentanyl.'

Lowton screwed up his eyes. 'Fenta what?'

Coupland huffed out a sigh. 'Come on, son. Give your head a wobble, I haven't got all day.'

'Ah you mean Dance Fever?' A lazy smile spread over his mouth. 'It's my top earner at the moment.'

'You sell it as a nasal spray?'

A slower nod. 'Amongst other things. I can occasionally get the skin patches if you're willing to go on a waiting list.'

'I'm only interested in the spray form. Is there a way of telling one dealer's supplies from another?'

'I only sell the stuff,' Lowton replied, giving Alex a lame smile as he realised his error. 'I mean, I USED to sell the stuff. I've never made it.'

'But you know what goes into it?'

'I know it doesn't come from a plant, if that's what you mean. It's made in a lab.'

More likely some scrote's back bedroom in Tattersall, Coupland thought but he got the gist.

'The stuff I sell is Kosher, though. I know in powder

form it gets mixed with heroin and crack to make them go further. Let's face it, most spoon burners can't tell the difference, but I don't stock that.' He made it sound like he was an ice cream salesman discussing the merits of one block of vanilla against another. 'Fentanyl isn't laced with other products as it's so cheap to make. It's used to bulk up *other* products, though. If you buy heroin it might be laced with Fentanyl. You buy fentanyl, that's all you're getting.'

That was Coupland's theory of identifying the supply found in Carly by its chemical composition out of the window then. 'How many dealers sell it in the spray form?'

'Hardly any. It was a niche product I'd pretty much cornered the market in.'

'Your family must be so proud.'

Lowton puffed his chest out. 'It was my old man who set up the labs around Salford.'

Coupland smacked his lips in disappointment, 'Why do it? Why peddle poison for a living when you could get yourself a decent job?'

'Like yours, you mean?'

Coupland grunted. He wasn't sure he'd go near it with a bargepole if he had his time again, but it was all he'd ever known.

Lowton continued as though he'd given the matter serious thought. 'Hard times, innit? I mean, most employers don't want to take on more staff because of that virus, and I ain't working minimum wage for anyone,' he smirked.

'You'll end up in jail if you don't take the lifeline DI Moreton's offering. You know that, don't you?'

Lowton shrugged. In the world he moved in that

didn't register as a threat. You were more likely to get the kind of work he aspired to *because* you'd served time.

Coupland looked him up and down. 'You're not built for jail. Trust me, once you're banged up spooning takes on an entirely different meaning.'

That wiped the smirk off his face.

'How easy would it be to track down one of your buyers?'

'I don't keep a receipt book if that's what you're asking,' Lowton laughed, the smile dying on his face when he saw the look Coupland threw him. 'Sorry, but it just doesn't work that way. Have you any idea how many of these get sold a week? A lot of schoolkids buy 'em, sell 'em on to their friends. Teachers aren't wise to it yet, must think they've all got hay fever or something.'

'What about older clients?'

'Plenty of those too. Like I said, they can get high in public and no one's the wiser.'

'You'll have regulars though?'

A pause. He turned to Alex. 'Is he for real?'

Coupland banged his hand on the table. 'I'm right here, sunshine, and yep, you better believe I'm for real. Nickname, tag name, Sunday bloody name for all I care. And if you don't know their name tell me where you meet 'em.' Even as he said it Coupland knew he was on a hiding to nowhere. The chances of Carly's killer being among the names Lowton dredged up for Coupland's benefit were a hundred to one. He'd pushed him in the wrong direction, compelled him to provide information that was no more accurate than Mystic bloody Meg. He shared a look with Alex, could see she was thinking along the same lines. 'A girl's been murdered, Shaun. She had Fentanyl in her system. I'm sure you, and your family, wouldn't want to be associated with such a monstrous crime. I'm also sure you wouldn't want to waste DS Coupland's time providing names of people who don't exist.'

They both watched as Lowton wrestled with his criminal conscience. 'The best I can do is promise to let you know if someone dodgy comes along…'

'Much obliged,' Coupland drawled, thanking Alex in a tone that suggested she shouldn't have bothered at all.

*

Coupland rang Harry Benson from his car. 'How long would the Fentanyl have stayed in Carly's system?'

'It doesn't stay in the body for long. In a healthy adult, maybe eight hours. If we take into account her age and weight, maybe closer to twelve hours.'

'So if the drug was used to sedate her during her abduction, it must have been administered a second time for you to have been able to detect it.'

'Possibly more than that, depending what they'd intended to do with her.'

Coupland swallowed down a wave of revulsion. 'And there were no other drugs present?'

'I know how to read a blood test.' A pause. *'Maybe it'll be easier if you tell me what you're trying to work out and I'll try to fill in the dots.'*

Coupland knew that letting a pathologist know too much about a case before they examined the body could impact their objectivity. There was no fear of that now Carly's post mortem had been completed; besides, if he didn't share his concern they might overlook something crucial.

'I was trying to work out if there's a way of tracing her killers through the drug – if there was a way of identifying the supplier by the way that it's been cut. I know it can be used as a bulking agent, I just wondered if Carly had been given another drug laced with it.' It was unlikely, but he needed to double check what Laughing Boy had told him.

'Well, I can reassure you on that point. As far as the chemical construct goes the drug was pure. I'd say it was used because the killer wanted something that was fast acting and yes, I suppose they could have hoped that it would have been out of her system by the time they killed her as it's one less trace of evidence. You know, it's funny how times change. It wasn't something we routinely checked for but due to its rise in popularity we've started screening for it in most post mortem examinations. It's not a hard and fast rule, more a recommendation within the area health authority.'

'When did *you* start screening for it?'

'Oh, let me see now, about six months ago, round about the time Keri Swain was murdered. We weren't sure at first whether the cost justified it but a week in and bam, we got our first positive. I've tested for it ever since.'

Coupland's ears pricked up. 'Keri who?' he asked, sitting up straighter in his seat. For once Benson sounded a lot less confident. In fact, if Coupland wasn't mistaken, there was a definite tinge of being on the back foot.

'I was going to mention it,' Benson placated, *'but the investigation was conducted by a different murder syndicate and I know how prickly you fellas get about territory.'*

Coupland drummed his fingers on the dashboard. 'But now you *have* mentioned it …' he prompted, reaching automatically for his pen.

'Traces of Fentanyl were found in Keri's system too. Bear with me while I get her details up.'

Coupland heard the sound of keys tapping. *'OK let me read through her report, remind myself of the details.'* Another silence.

Coupland lit a cigarette while he waited. Was halfway down it by the time Benson came back on the line. *'Keri was the same age as Carly. She was raped too.'* Yet it was something the pathologist let slip next that set Coupland on alert. *'To be honest I didn't take to the SIO. His reaction to the fact multiple semen samples were present was that the poor girl was promiscuous.'*

Coupland's brow knotted. 'Hang on, are you saying she was raped by two men, like Carly?'

'I can't say that for definite. There were two semen samples present when I examined her. But there was no bruising around the genital area, unlike with your girl. We were able to get DNA samples from the skin beneath her fingernails, though to be honest the officers involved seemed to see this as an indication she liked to play rough, rather than she could have been fighting for her life.'

Coupland didn't recognise the name, let alone the case. He screwed up his eyes as he tried to remember whether there'd been a trial. 'Did they get any results when they ran the DNA?

'You're better taking this up with them.' Benson gave him the name of the SIO and the station he was based at.

The officer's name meant nothing to him, likely as not a face he'd recognise from attendance on training courses, no more than that. Made it trickier to go in asking questions, but he'd cope. He was more concerned with the feeling making itself known in the pit of his stomach, at the thought that the murders of Carly and Keri were connected in some way.

Coupland considered what the pathologist had told him. 'Any chance you can let me have a copy of Keri's

PM report?'

'Not without authorisation from the SIO she was assigned to.'

'I'll get it,' Coupland assured him. 'In the meantime can you run some tests to compare the semen and other trace samples taken from both girls?'

'No can do without the rubber stamp that says your boss is going to pick up the tab for it.'

Coupland sighed. 'Leave it with me.' There was nothing he liked more than going cap in hand for something that in his view was essential if the job was to be done properly.

'Look,' Benson placated, *'when you get your DCI's go ahead let me know and I'll make sure the tests are run as a priority, OK?'*

'Appreciate that, Harry,' Coupland said, his mouth tripping over the use of the pathologist's first name, but desperate times called for desperate measures. After all, Benson had given him the break he needed.

*

DCI Mallender's office

Coupland's conversation with DCI Mallender was short and to the point. It was the best lead they had and he wasn't about to let it get buried in a flurry of emails between two syndicates for the sake of following protocol.

Interest piqued, Mallender made the necessary call to the SIO in charge of Keri Swain's murder investigation at City Road station. When he ended the call Coupland was relieved he was still smiling, albeit his tone was cautious. 'He was defensive at first, until I told him we've landed a case here that may be similar and we wanted to compare the findings of the original PM report. He said he'd facilitate in any way he could.'

Coupland tried to hide his impatience. 'So we can get Benson to run those tests then?'

Mallender looked surprised. 'Don't you want to read through the report first, just to check it's worth taking further?'

Coupland stared at him. 'Suppose I could have a whip round in the canteen, see if we can't stump up the lab fees ourselves, or get Krispy to set up a GoFundMe page.'

Mallender sucked in a breath. 'Fine! Get the sodding tests done; just make sure you come back with some results, that's all.'

Ashcroft was at his desk when Coupland returned to the CID room, grinning. 'You got the green light then?' he asked, when he caught his eye.

'Yup,' Coupland answered, scrolling through his phone as he headed towards his own desk, a ping signifying he'd got new mail. 'Keri's PM report has just come through; I'll forward a copy to you, an extra pair of eyes and all that.'

Coupland logged onto his desktop PC, clicking on Benson's message before hitting 'send.' He fired back a reply letting the pathologist know it was all systems go for the lab work that needed to be done. Finally, he double clicked on Benson's attachment to open it, sat back in his chair and started to read.

'Bloody hell,' he said after a full five minutes of silence.

'It's Carly all over again,' muttered Ashcroft.

Less bruising, Coupland conceded, as Benson had already flagged up, but the marks on her neck, the defence wounds on her hands, were the same.

'We need to request Keri's case file. There are too

many similarities for us not to take this further.' He'd get no argument from Coupland on that.

'Do you know the officers mentioned in the PM report? DI Little and DS Clarke, based at City Road nick?'

Coupland shook his head. 'No, but I was present when the boss gave the DI a call.'

Ashcroft took a slurp of the coffee cooling on his desk and waited.

'He came across as a bit of a meathead by the sounds of it, took him a while to remember who Keri was. He was happy enough to play ball with the PM report but requesting access to the file will naturally put him on the defensive.'

Coupland knew how it worked. Collaborating with other stations caused a certain amount of friction. *My truncheon's bigger than your truncheon.* Emails back and forward between various superintendents until they were summoned to the chief constable's office.

'I'm happy enough cajoling Mallender into picking up the phone again, and if it's a blinking contest between me and the Super I know who my money's on, but playing politics with other syndicates requires a skill set I don't possess.'

'And what's that exactly?' Ashcroft asked, already knowing where this was leading.

'Diplomacy. Charm. The ability to see the other point of view.'

'That's a shame.'

'I wouldn't be so sure. You strike me as someone pretty much unflappable.'

'What's that got to do with being diplomatic?'

'When I'm backed into a corner I come out fighting.

It's all I know. I don't know how to make the other party listen without yelling for them to shut it first.'

Ashcroft suppressed a smile as he picked up his phone. 'Fine! I'll contact the city slickers in an attempt to pave the way for us, see if we can't all be grown-ups about it.'

*

Superintendent Curtis's office

There was a lot less banter in Superintendent Curtis's office. A lot more forelock tugging. And trying not to lose his patience was always a challenge. DCI Mallender had read Keri Swain's PM report when Coupland forwarded it to him, told him he had his full support in requesting the files from City Road station. He'd been on his way to a meeting with the Super, it made sense to raise it then.

'You think these cases are connected?' Superintendent Curtis said, removing his watch and lining it up within his pens beside the ink blotter on his desk. He regarded the watch face pointedly as though deciding how much longer he'd give the tetchy detective sergeant.

Mallender gave Coupland a meaningful look, waiting for him to get on with it.

Coupland leaned forward in his chair, shoulders hunched. 'I can't say for certain without looking at the file, Sir,' he said, 'which is why I'm here.' His look made it clear just how frustrated he was. 'The girls are similar in age. Both raped and strangled. The toxicology report on each of them shows traces of Fentanyl, but when DS Ashcroft spoke to the investigating officer just now he told him that Keri had come from a chaotic background. In his words: "Her mum was a junkie so it stood to reason she was too".'

'He actually said that?'

'More or less.' Coupland had given Curtis the edited version. Ashcroft had told him the detective's reply had been coarser than that.

There was a moment when Coupland finished that he and Mallender regarded Curtis, leaning back, behind his desk. Already distancing himself from the situation Coupland presented by checking the symmetry of his pen set.

Mallender jerked his head towards the Super's door.

Taking his cue, Coupland got to his feet and began a sideways shuffle. There was no point overstaying his welcome. Curtis's involvement in the investigation would be pretty low key unless a third body turned up. A thought Mallender was acutely aware of, given the look on the DCI's face.

Half an hour later, Mallender buzzed Coupland's internal phone. Told him the Super had given him the green light, and that the Super at City Road station had agreed to his request for access to Keri's case files. 'You're sure about this, aren't you?' he asked, once Coupland's whooping had died down.

Coupland's voice was laced with caution. 'Not really. But it makes sense. And that'll do for me now.'

Mallender muttered something under his breath. 'I would have appreciated your candour before we spoke to the Super, Kevin. You didn't mention any lack of confidence in your theory when you came barging into my office an hour ago.'

'You never asked,' Coupland replied.

'Do the words *skating* and *thin ice* mean anything to

you?'

'Ah, well you know what they say about that, boss. Never go round the same circle twice and always pack a towel.'

*

City Road police station was on the wrong side of the River Irwell for Coupland's liking but that aside, he knew precious little about it. An amalgamation of eight Greater Manchester stations, its gleaming multi story premises in Spinningfields looked little different from the banking and insurance office blocks either side of it, providing you ignored the yellow and blue squad cars parked out front.

Coupland hadn't exactly been expecting the red carpet when he and Ashcroft arrived at reception, but a bit of civility might have been nice. They were made to wait for half an hour, despite Ashcroft calling ahead and speaking to the DS on the case. When he enquired at the desk about the reason for the hold-up, he was told twice that the detective inspector knew they were waiting.

After thirty minutes the DS popped his head around the 'staff only' door and asked them to follow him to the DI's office. Like a baby delivered by Ventouse extraction, Detective Inspector John Little's forehead was narrow, sloping down to a wide jaw. Coupland expected him to be affable, given his mouth drew so much attention. Instead the opposite seemed to be true. The DI didn't get out of his seat to greet them, nor did his face flicker with the slightest bit of interest when Ashcroft made the introductions. Some inspectors went about like niceties were optional when dealing with the lower ranks, but most made the effort during the initial meeting.

Little's gaze lingered on Ashcroft. 'We've been trailing a gang in Cheetham Hill,' he said, 'You don't half share a passing resemblance to one of its main players.' He made a point of glancing down at the ID on Ashcroft's lanyard as though checking he really was who he claimed. 'Can't be too careful,' he smirked.

Ashcroft continued as though he hadn't spoken. 'I believe you were the SIO during Keri Swain's murder investigation,' he began.

'Gotta love this job sometimes, eh, fellas?' It was the first smile he'd cracked since they'd been ushered into his office. 'I could tell the investigation was a non-starter from the moment I clapped eyes on her.'

'How so?' Coupland asked.

Little pulled a face like he could smell something foul. 'The girl was a mess, and I don't mean the state she was found in.'

'What *do* you mean then?'

Little leaned back in his chair. 'You could tell a mile off she was chaotic. The facts bore that out: she'd been in care for ten years only to be returned to a mother who thought weaning herself off heroin was an achievement. Surprised you've not come across them, given she's from your neck of the woods. Tower block in Pendleton, can't remember the name of it.'

'What about Jamie Swain, Keri's father?'

A shrug. 'Nowhere to be seen. Problems started when her mum's boyfriend moved in. Another bloody junkie. It wasn't long before her mother was back on Class A. No wonder she'd run away twice the year before, the third time she never came back.'

'So she wasn't abducted then?'

Little screwed his face up. 'Her life had been one disaster after another. Wouldn't you run away?'

In all the years Coupland's father had raised a fist to him, he'd never thought of leaving. Didn't want to give the mad bastard the satisfaction. He shared another look with Ashcroft. This gobshite loved the sound of his own voice.

'Look, with no decent relatives to speak of she'd had no choice but to drag herself up. We see it all the time. Kids from tough neighbourhoods hardly move in the most salubrious of circles.'

Coupland's opinion of the DI had formed the moment he'd kept them waiting in reception. Nothing he'd seen or heard since made him feel that he'd been too hasty. 'So there wasn't a shortage of men that could have harmed her?'

The DI shrugged. 'It had to be her fella or a pimp. Let's face it, with girls like that they're usually one and the same.'

'Like what, Sir?' Coupland put on his confused face, though he knew damn well was the DI was suggesting.

'Sorry?'

'Girls like what?' Coupland tried not to sound arsey but it was second nature. Only three people had the ability to make him smile and none of them were in this room.

Little threw him a look that in no way hid the way *he* was feeling. 'I think we're done here. I'll have my DS show you through to the CID room where you can read through the file at your heart's content. If you've got any further questions, I suggest you direct them to him.' He raised his hand like a diner might in a restaurant, especially one that tipped well.

The detective who collected them from reception appeared as though he'd been waiting for the signal. 'This way,' he said, using his back to hold the door open.

Ashcroft stepped out behind Coupland, but not before pausing in the door way. 'Thanks for your time,' he said to the top of the DI's head, for Little's attention had already moved on to another task.

'How goes it in Bandit Country?' asked DS Clarke, laughing at his own joke.

'Same as ever,' Coupland replied, making a point of studying his surroundings.

'Look,' he said to Ashcroft, pointing to a door with a sign that said 'Gents'. 'They've got indoor plumbing too.'

Once the back biting was finished they found a seat in a quiet part of the office, began working their way through the box file Clarke brought to them. Every action log, every statement, every piece of evidence that would have been called on at trial if they'd charged anyone. Keri's body had been found on waste ground off Deansgate, the main road running through Manchester City Centre, which was why Little's team had picked it up. She'd been left behind a row of shops closed for refurbishment, her body wrapped in plastic, discarded like the cheap larger cans and condoms that littered the alleyway behind them.

Every so often Coupland glanced up, exchanging looks with Ashcroft, wondering if he was coming to the same conclusion. There were gaps in the evidence. Assumptions had been made based on her background. 'Multiple semen swabs' in Benson's report had been underlined three times. They might as well have scrawled 'slag' across the page in red ink. It was clear that they'd all but stopped putting in the effort within days.

'Coffee?' Ashcroft asked, nodding towards a Tassimo machine in a cupboard that looked like it had been converted into a mini kitchen. Microwave, kettle, a carton of milk beside it.

Coupland nodded a yes. He needed all the caffeine he could get to wade through glib comments and speculation dressed up as evidence. Besides, the DS who'd brought them through appeared to have gone to the same finishing school as his DI, if his hospitality skills were anything to go by. He stood chatting at a colleague's desk nursing a mug, his gaze every so often wandering in their direction.

In the kitchen Ashcroft located two cups, placed one under the machine's nozzle, added a pod, pressing several buttons until brown liquid began spluttering into it. He pulled out his phone, tapping and scrolling through messages, before turning his back to the door. Coupland's phone beeped, signalling an incoming text. He pulled it out of his pocket. He'd guessed right. Ashcroft's message was to the point. 'WTF?????? Seriously, are these guys for real?' he'd typed.

Coupland slipped it back into his pocket, shrugging as Ashcroft strolled back with their drinks.

'You've got him well trained,' the DS called over.

Coupland turned in his direction, though he'd already forgotten his name. 'Just happens to be his round, that's all.'

A nod. 'So, what do you reckon? You think it's the same punter then, who raped and killed your girl?'

Coupland glanced at Ashcroft before answering. '*Rapists*, you mean.'

The detective screwed up his eyes as though he didn't

132

understand what he was hearing. 'Plural? Christ…' he whistled. If he remembered the contents of Keri's PM report he showed no signs of it. 'So you reckon the same two punters did for your girl then?'

'It's a possibility we're looking into,' Coupland said. 'Though I'm intrigued why you would you use that term?'

The DS looked confused. 'I don't get you.'

'You said "Punters", as though the men were consorting with a sex worker rather than an underage girl.'

A shrug. 'She wasn't fussy about the blokes she went with, that's all.'

Coupland narrowed his eyes. 'Who told you that?' He shuffled through the pages of the file until he found the detective's first name. Derek.

DS Clarke looked flustered. 'It was just the impression we got, that's all.'

Coupland tried to keep his tone neutral. 'I'm still working through the file but I'm not seeing any reference to witness statements supporting that opinion.'

'Well, there won't be, will there? It's just a way of life for some girls. A form of currency to barter when they want something for nothing.'

Ashcroft frowned. 'Seems a bit out of order,' he muttered. 'They're just kids.'

Clarke glowered. 'Wind your neck in. No one asked for your opinion.'

Ashcroft regarded him. 'It's not my opinion. It's fact. She was only 14.'

Clarke sent a glare in his direction before turning his attention back to Coupland. 'Listen mate, it's bad enough we have to put up with the negative attitudes that exist in his community every time we step outside that door, can you not put a muzzle on him when you bring him indoors…'

Coupland blinked. He glanced sharply at Ashcroft who responded by shaking his head, as if urging him to let it go.

Coupland jutted his lower jaw forward. Pushed back his chair with more force than was necessary, his action causing several heads to turn in his direction. He could feel Ashcroft's gaze on him, willing him not to make a fuss.

Coupland flared his nostrils and took a breath. 'I think we've got a good measure of your investigation into this girl's murder,' he said. 'We'll need to take these files back to Salford, cross reference both cases, see if we can identify clear similarities.'

'According to the news your girl came from a good home. Unless she was leading a double life I can't see Keri's killer getting anywhere near her. Wasting your time if you ask me.'

'Good job I wasn't,' Coupland replied, slipping the paperwork back into the folder.

Ashcroft got to his feet, deliberately slow.

Coupland returned Clarke's stare. 'Do you seriously believe troubled kids don't deserve our time or are you just crap at your job?'

'Come on, it's common knowledge cases like this are a waste of everyone's time.'

Their raised voices had silenced the rest of the room. Sensing tension, two detectives on their phones paused their conversations to listen to what was going on.

'Not here,' Clarke said, indicating they step out into the corridor.

Coupland tucked Keri's file under his arm, keen, now he'd read its contents, not to let it out of his sight. He and Ashcroft followed the DS into the hallway. Stood quietly while he said his piece.

'Look, of course the daft girl didn't deserve to die but you know the saying, if you lie down with dogs you wake up with fleas. I mean, murders like this never come as a bloody surprise do they?'

'Jesus man, next you'll be saying they were asking for it and anything less than wearing a Burkha is provocative. Seriously, you need to stop talking.'

'You taken root?'

The throaty boom of DI Little startled Coupland, though it made sense one of Clarke's colleagues had sent for reinforcements.

'Derek here was helping to fill in a couple of blanks,' Coupland replied.

Clarke's response was more animated. 'I was just explaining that it's hard to put together an accurate victimology report when they don't sleep in the same bed two nights running.'

'My DS is right. The girl was a prozzie in all but title. Trying to trace the men who slept with her is like trying to find a ni…' he shared a smirk with Clarke before bowing to Ashcroft '…A *needle in a haystack*,' he concluded.

Coupland saw Ashcroft tense before arranging his features into neutral.

'We're done here,' Coupland said, any pretence at civility gone.

'You did well to keep your cool,' Coupland muttered as he pulled out of the station car park.

Ashcroft shrugged. 'Nobody likes an angry black man.'

'You can report them.'

Ashcroft studied Coupland's profile. 'What is this, the playground?'

'OK, I'll report them.'

A sigh. 'Really? What did you hear exactly? A bit of racial stereotyping? A bit of innuendo? A jibe? Water off a duck's back, trust me.'

Coupland was already shaking his head. 'You shouldn't let them get away with it-'

'LET?' Ashcroft spat. '*Let?*' He threw his arms wide. 'You're beginning to sound like those numbnuts back there. Next you'll be agreeing that girls like Keri have a say in how they're treated. Like there's some fucking *choice* in the matter. Trust me, there's no real choice, unless you want to go through every day bent out of shape.'

Shame rose up from the pit of Coupland's stomach. He stared at the road in front of them, stopping when the lights turned to red. He felt Ashcroft's gaze slide in his direction. Heard him exhale, anger spent. 'What you heard back there was nothing. In fact you being there probably made them mind their Ps and Qs. Anyway, I knew what I was signing up for.'

'So why did you join?'

'I'm a sadist.' He smiled. 'Ah, I don't know. I can barely remember the kid I was back then. I believed in time it would make a difference. That the public want to be served by people that look like them. The more diverse we are as a force the more chance we'll have of people trusting us.' He paused then, as though embarrassed talking about something so personal. Or maybe he was just tired of it. 'What I resent is people thinking I speak on behalf of a community. That I'm an expert on all things black.'

Hearing him speak, with his passion and his clipped vowels, Coupland could understand why the Met had wanted him as a poster boy. Curtis too, for that matter, though he knew better than to say that out loud. Even so. 'Those wankers,' he said tipping his head back to the station building. 'If they're like that with you, what are they like with some kid from Tattersall with his arse hanging out of the back of his jeans?'

It was a question that didn't need answering. They both knew how it would pan out. An accusation made and denied. Passed off as another kid with a chip on their shoulder.

Coupland hissed out a sigh. His Kryptonite was that he mistrusted everyone, yet it had been honed by years of experience. When someone showed a reprehensible flaw you didn't have to scratch the surface far to find another. Men who were racist were often misogynistic too. How could those officers serve without fear or favour? Could it be that Keri's murder hadn't been investigated with the diligence it deserved?

It was clear by the set of Ashcroft's jaw the conversation was over. Coupland nodded to himself. No point raking over old coals, he supposed. Especially ones that went so far back they were prehistoric. He accepted that. He really did. Didn't mean he fucking liked it though.

The cranes that dominated Manchester's skyline for decades had spread across the Irwell. Salford was on the up if you believed the hype. The landscape had become an architect's show and tell: glass buildings, multi-storey apartment blocks that wouldn't look out of place in London or New York. Bagging MediaCity had been a major coup. Developers continued to compete for the beautiful people they were sure would follow. Creative types happy to pay exorbitant rent to look out on roof top air-conditioning units and claim the view was stunning.

Along Bridgewater Wharf mills were being converted into upmarket apartment blocks. In Tattersall a new housing development was being built on the site of an infamous pub. Along Regent Road construction put on hold during lockdown was once more under way, each building a mass of scaffolding and hoists. In other parts of the city council properties built less than fifty years ago were earmarked for demolition.

'We've been talking about moving,' Coupland said. 'Not sure we could get much more for our money though, now.'

'Why bother?' asked Ashcroft.

'Be good to have a bit more space. For the little fella.' It sounded daft to his own ears. That someone less than two feet tall required so much room.

'What's the point?' Ashcroft said. 'Your daughter will be wanting a place of her own eventually.'

Coupland's brow furrowed. 'I can't see it myself. Too comfortable where she is.'

The truth was they'd all settled into this new set up like Tonto had always been around. He wasn't sure how he felt about that changing. Certainly not any time soon.

'What if she meets someone?' asked Ashcroft.

Coupland shot him a look that made him keep his head down for the rest of the journey.

CHAPTER EIGHT

Back in the CID room Coupland dragged one of the whiteboards idling at the back of the room over to his desk. A remnant from the previous year when the new police computer system was playing up, the bulk of them were now redundant, although Coupland still preferred to use them while brainstorming. He pulled out the crime scene photo of Keri and secured it at the top of the board.

As he tipped out the remaining contents of the folder onto his desk, he caught Ashcroft's eye.

'Not much to show for their effort, is there?' Ashcroft tutted. 'I've seen bigger investigations to find out who nicked the last of the milk.'

Coupland pulled out witness statements printed onto A4 sheets of paper, tapped them against the top of his desk to straighten them. 'Take a look through these, see if there's anyone we should be speaking to,' he said, handing them to Ashcroft.

'In relation to Keri's murder you mean? Or seeing if there are any links that lead to Carly?'

Coupland considered this. 'Both,' he answered eventually.

'So what's the official line? Are we sharing resources since our cases are similar or do you want to keep them in the dark for now?'

Coupland turned his head towards Ashcroft and

grinned. It was the first time the acting DS had seen so many of his teeth. 'You really think Fred Flintstone and Barney Rubble give a toss about this girl? You heard 'em. *"Girls like that"*. She was 14, for Christ's sake. They'll be in no hurry to invite us back.'

'They will if they smell glory.'

Ashcroft had a point.

'Update Clarke on progress at the end of the week. If he isn't interested, that's his look out.'

Ashcroft nodded. He poked around the files scattered on the desk top as though looking for something. He picked up a sheet of paper with a satisfied smile. He pointed to the opening paragraph. 'They've described Keri as a chaotic runaway, but what if she hadn't run away? What if she was taken, like Carly?'

Coupland sighed a yes. He'd thought much the same when he'd read through the file. The constant reference to her family background. She might have grown up on the other side of the tracks from Carly but it didn't make her disposable. DS Clarke had written off Benson's reference to the Fentanyl in her bloodstream as 'evidence of drug use' and the bruising around her genitals as 'liked to engage in rough play'.

While Ashcroft tried to make sense of the scant witness statements, Coupland searched online for news articles following Keri's murder. An hour later he decided to throw in the towel. The contrast in media coverage between both cases was startling. Images of Carly, a fresh-faced girl from a stable background, were splashed on the front pages of the national newspapers. Yet not one newspaper had picked up Keri's story.

'The problem is no one gives a toss if it isn't a perfect

family. If there are no doe eyed parents it doesn't make front page news, and if it doesn't make front page news it's as though it didn't happen.'

Ashcroft was just as frustrated. 'Names of her friends are recorded on file but there's no suggestion they've been contacted or interviewed. She'd been staying with her mother prior to her murder, but that's pretty much all there is.'

Coupland had heard enough. He hadn't realised he was on his feet until Ashcroft asked where he was heading off. 'To find out who Keri was. I think she's owed that much.'

*

Through the windscreen the rolling backdrop changed from bleak to bleaker. Shops boarded up during lockdown that couldn't afford to re-open. Those that did offered discounts to tempt customers over the threshold. The pavements were crowded but people weren't shopping, just glad to be out. The car in front of him stopped abruptly without indicating, swerving into a parking place. Coupland put his full weight on the horn. 'Arsehole,' he muttered, making a 'What the fuck?' gesture with his hands when he drew level with the vehicle in question.

He drove on, his thoughts returning to Carly King and Keri Swain. Two dead girls. Most people think life is some sort of equation. That what they get out of it correlates with the effort they put in, but the world doesn't work that way. It was easy to fall into the trap of it though, to think that kids could be kept safe if you did all the right things: Cooked healthy meals and read bedtime stories, sent them to the right schools and vetted their friends. A stable home.

All these things helped, of course, but weren't the Holy Grail. He'd wrapped his daughter in cotton wool yet he'd failed where it mattered. Not yet twenty, a single mother with a toddler who looked more like his serial killer father with each passing day. They'd ignored it at first. The way folk ignore other people's disfigurements. But recently Lynn had started to comment – out of earshot of Amy – that Tonto's smile, when he could be bothered, was crooked. She dug out the news clippings of Lee Dawson that she kept on a shelf in her wardrobe. Pointed to a photo the press had circulated of him following his death. 'Even their eyes are the same,' she'd said with a sadness that made Coupland's insides twist. He didn't need old photographs to remind him of the likeness. The eyes that blinked at him whenever he held his grandson close were the same as the ones scorched into his brain – the eyes of a maniac before he fell to his death.

For Coupland, pushing negative thoughts from his head was like rolling sand uphill. It wasn't that he was a pessimist, just a battle worn realist. He shook his head. He'd promised Amy he'd love that boy, and love him he bloody well did.

A pedestrian wearing a face mask stepped out in front of him, oblivious, causing him to slam his foot on the brake. The van driver behind him beeped on *his* horn. The pedestrian shook her head at Coupland as though he was in the wrong for not mowing her down. He lowered the driver's window. 'You're welcome!' he called after her.

Coupland knew Fitzpatrick Court like the back of his hand. Had spent a couple of years during his teens roaming the landings with mates when he'd gone through his rebellious phase. A phase some reckoned he'd yet to emerge from. Built in the 1970s, the distinctive blue tower block was scheduled to be demolished. With Grenfell style cladding and no sprinkler system it had been deemed by the residents not fit for purpose, another tragedy waiting to happen. Yet it had taken three years of petitions for the council to agree.

He was relieved that the lift worked, given Keri's mother lived on the 22nd floor. The interior didn't smell as bad as he remembered, though he made a point of not standing too close to the walls. The graffiti was uninspiring, sprayed-on tag names and marker pen hearts declaring undying love. A rainbow had been added between two giant penises, along with 'Thank you NHS' in red. Brought a whole new meaning to clap for carers, he supposed.

The doors along the balcony were painted blue to match the cladding. Coupland stopped in front of the number recorded in Keri's file. He rang the doorbell and, when there was no response, rapped his knuckles on the door as un-police-like as possible, so as not to cause unwanted attention from the neighbours. He cocked his ear at the sound of the TV volume being muted, standing back so he could be seen more easily through the spy hole when he held up his warrant card.

Through the distorted view of the circular lens Jackie Swain saw a solid framed man, serious faced. Two bolts were pulled back, a chain released, the latch slipped on the lock.

'Mrs Swain?' After he'd introduced himself, Coupland followed the woman into a living room that was cramped. A pair of jeans had been hung to dry over the living room door. Polyester knickers formed bunting along a radiator top. A pile of towels on the sofa meant he had to perch on its arm, forcing him to sit closer to her chair than she liked, he suspected, going by the way she drew into her own space, moving her feet away from his an inch at a time.

'I'm not here because there are any new developments,' he explained, sensing her anxiety.

She let out the sigh she'd been holding in. 'Oh,' she gasped, placing a hand on her chest, 'my heart was going ten to the dozen then. I thought you were going to say you'd caught him.' She narrowed her eyes, 'I haven't seen you before. How come you've not got them clowns with you?' She inclined her head in the direction of the world beyond her flat, which Coupland took to mean DI Little and DS Clarke.

'I'm investigating the murder of another young girl. Carly King. She and Keri were similar ages…'

'They'll never get any older,' Jackie observed, tugging her sweatshirt sleeves over her wrists before crossing one arm under the other and resting them on her stomach. 'Hang on,' she said, face clouding, 'Is this the girl that's been all over the news?'

Coupland nodded.

'I see,' she said. 'So, you're not really looking for the man who killed our Keri, unless you think he killed this other girl too.'

He tried to offer reassurance he didn't feel. 'The original investigating team is committed to finding your daughter's killer. If I discover something during my investigation that will help find the person who killed Keri I will share that information with them.' He looked her in the eye. It was a textbook police response. One that promised commitment, doggedness, endeavour. Words those tossers at City Road would need to look up in a dictionary.

Jackie made a noise that suggested she wasn't convinced either. The file he'd read earlier said she was 33 yet she looked much older. Haggard. Sallow skin and lines around a mouth that hadn't been near a dentist in a decade. She dressed like a protester. Camouflage trousers teamed with a top that said 'Fuck da System'. Strands of dyed orange hair snaked out from beneath a baseball cap. She lifted the fag packet perching on the arm of her chair and tapped out a cigarette. It was a brand Coupland had never heard of, though he doubted the folk who did their shopping from the back of a lorry or inside a pub toilet gave a toss about brand names.

Coupland pulled his lighter from his pocket and leaned forward to light it. She offered him one but he shook his head as graciously as he could. He allowed a silence to develop while he considered what direction his questions should take. 'Tell me about Keri,' he said eventually.

A shrug. 'Not much to tell. I suppose they told you she was in care for a few years?'

Coupland nodded.

'Long enough for us to be strangers by the time she came back to live with me.' She studied Coupland's face. 'If they told you that, then they'd have told you I was a junkie back when she was small.' She waited while he nodded once more. 'That was the reason I gave her up, you see. She wasn't taken from me. Not like people imagine. Me yelling as I run after the social worker's car.' She shook her head, 'No. I knew I couldn't look after her. Couldn't look after myself, to tell you the truth.' She waved the hand holding the cigarette over her head. 'Won't be long before this place gets demolished. Yet it's a palace compared to where we used to live. The word shithole didn't do it justice and I didn't see the point in looking after the place. I mean, you can't polish a turd. Anyway, stood to reason she was better off without me. I could see that every time I visited. Her foster families were decent people; I didn't blame them for being hacked off that she became foul-mouthed and narky after every visit. The thing is, blood's blood. I wanted her back with me and by some stroke of luck social services didn't put up a fight. Before I knew it she was standing on the doorstep clutching her little bag like Orphan bloody Annie. Truth is we'd have been alright on our own if I hadn't hooked up with Malky. Tosser of the highest order that one. Got me back on the gear, too. Keri was heartbroken, thought it meant she'd have to go away again.'

She looked away then, as though what she had to say was better said to no one in particular. 'The number of times I wish to God she had gone back into care. Maybe she'd still be alive if I hadn't kept begging her to stick it out. I kept promising I'd change, you see.'

'Where is Malky now?'

She clicked her tongue against her teeth. 'Long gone. Trouble was the damage had already been done. She'd started staying out late to keep out of his way, by the time he left she was going about with others as troubled as she was.'

It made a change to hear a parent admit their offspring wasn't perfect. The number of times Coupland heard someone's son or daughter had got in with a wrong crowd, he wondered how folk thought these crowds were populated.

'I heard she ran away twice,' Coupland said.

Jackie dipped her head. 'I overdosed a couple of times. It was her that found me. Freaked her out something rotten, it did. She went back into care for a short spell while I sorted myself out.'

'How are you now?'

Jackie looked at him in surprise. 'No one's ever asked me that before. To tell you the truth I have no idea.' She paused, as though trying to formulate an answer. 'Every morning I get up, have a wash, then sit here waiting for someone to tell me they've caught the bastard that took away the only good thing I ever had.' She glanced at Coupland but he said nothing, as though waiting for her to continue.

'I've had a couple of lapses,' she admitted. Her tone was hushed, like a sinner in the confessional. 'I couldn't accept she was dead at first. Started drinking myself into oblivion. Ended up in the odd fight at closing time, taking pot shots at anyone who claimed she'd brought it on herself.'

Without thinking, she yanked her sleeves up to her elbow like someone preparing to do a dirty job. A silver scar ran along the vein of her left wrist. Coupland's gaze settled on it, causing her to redden.

'I know I'm scum to people like you, but she was my kid and I loved her.' She flicked ash into a chipped saucer balancing on the arm of her chair, picked up her mobile phone and entered her pin code. She turned the phone round so Coupland could see the photograph of Keri on the screen. She looked older than 14. She had a stud in her nose and wore a top that showed her midriff. Jackie smiled for the first time. 'She was such a pretty girl,' she said.

She wasn't, Coupland thought. Not really. But that was hardly the point. This Keri, the living, breathing, smiling girl posing for the photo, was a damn sight more attractive than the image of the lifeless corpse on the whiteboard in the CID room. 'Can you tell me about the day she went missing?'

Jackie narrowed her eyes. 'Isn't there a file somewhere with all this stuff in it?'

'I'd like to hear it in your own words, if it isn't too much trouble?'

As it was, the notes in Keri's file were woefully inadequate. No one had drawn up a timeline of her actions that day. There was no certainty around the last time she'd been seen and who she'd been with. As far as Coupland was concerned the paperwork in Keri's file was only good for one thing.

He could tell by Jackie's reaction she wasn't convinced by what he said. But she told him anyway, her eyes pooling with tears that she refused to acknowledge. 'She'd been at the pupil referral unit in the afternoon. They were talking about her going back to school. Not sure how long that would've lasted, mind. The reality of it. But she was pleased they thought she'd made progress. We were going to have a takeaway to celebrate. Said she'd get her fella to pick one up while they were out. Only she never came back. You know the rest,' she said when she finished. She stared at him, daring him to come out with more trite words like the ones he'd trotted out earlier.

Coupland swiped a hand over his jaw, willing the anger rising inside him to subside.

A mother stunted by loss. Haunted by a perception her daughter mattered less somehow. That she hadn't earned the right to be engulfed by grief, the sorrow consuming her hadn't been earned. Coupland hadn't seen his own mother for over three decades but her loss when it came had knocked him off balance. It was too soon after lockdown to take the woman's hand in his. Some people weren't ready for that level of proximity. But he leaned forward in his chair. Showed her he was willing to breathe the same air as her.

'I can't promise that I'm going to find anything that'll bring Keri's killer to justice, but I *can* promise I'll lift every bloody stone to see what crawls out. Will that do for now?'

'For now,' she nodded, her fingers snaking along the silver scar on her wrist.

The tears in her eyes, still refusing to fall.

*

Coupland stomped into the CID room, the look on his face telling all but the foolhardy to stay clear.

'This can't wait,' Ashcroft told him as he approached his desk. 'Professor Benson's been on. He's had confirmation from the forensic lab – the skin samples beneath Keri's fingernails were not a conclusive match with that taken from Carly, simply because there hadn't been much of it; however, the analysis of semen and pubic hair from Carly and Keri yielded one positive comparison.'

Coupland considered this. 'You mean that although they were assaulted by two men, only one man assaulted them both?'

Ashcroft nodded.

This confirmation, though not entirely unexpected, rooted Coupland to the spot. The cases were definitely connected, but the number of perpetrators involved had grown. Coupland's lip curled. 'Dastardly and Muttley had the audacity to think Keri was killed by a "punter." How misguided can you get?'

Ashcroft nodded. 'Professor Benson reckons that the lack of defensive wounds on her body could just mean that she'd been given a bigger dose of Fentanyl because she had a higher tolerance threshold than Carly. The amount would be harder to detect if it had longer to work itself out of her system before she was killed.'

It was plausible. Coupland flopped into his chair while Ashcroft perched a buttock on the edge of his desk.

If Ashcroft had concerns about working with Little and Clarke he didn't show them. 'Did speaking to Keri's mother prove useful?'

'There's no doubt the family background is troubled but her home life had been settled in the lead up to her murder. Her mother feels Keri had pretty much been written off before the investigation got underway.'

'A fairly accurate assessment,' Ashcroft acknowledged. 'They never bothered interviewing her estranged stepdad, even though he and Keri had had a few run ins.'

Coupland's mouth turned down at the edges. 'Yeah but this was a sexually motivated murder.'

'That he should still have been eliminated from. Do you want me to take a statement from him?' he asked.

Coupland shook his head, distracted. 'Get Krispy onto it. The guy's not a person of interest by any means but it should have been done.' He was more interested in something else that he'd learned. 'According to her mother Keri had a boyfriend.'

Ashcroft's nod was impatient. 'I know. That was the other thing I wanted to talk to you about.'

Coupland regarded him. 'I'm all ears.'

'Well, I'm not sure how accurate the term boyfriend is for a start. He's a few years older than Keri and in my view should have known better.'

'Go on.'

'He was taken to City Road station for questioning a couple of times according to the file. Seems they were definitely interested in him.'

'And?'

'The interview notes are sparse. I called the station and spoke to Clarke, asked him for the first account interview tapes.'

The first account interview was the first interview with a suspect after they'd been taken into custody.

'He said he'd dig them out as a matter of priority, though something tells me he's not being entirely sincere.'

'If he gives you the run around let me know, we're going to have to work together on this whether we like it or not.'

Two syndicates working the same case was never a match made in heaven. And from what he'd seen so far of the set up at the other station, their enforced nuptials were destined for the rocks. There was no doubt in his mind which of the two teams would be doing the heavy lifting.

Ashcroft didn't look reassured by this.

'Spit it out, Chris, I'm no good at guessing games.'

'Thing is, I've met him. Keri's supposed boyfriend, I mean. During the house to house statements that I had to go back for the day after Carly's murder. I called round and took his statement! Nice as pie he was at the time. Bit strange though, don't you think, that despite me being there because Carly's body had been found close to where he lived, he never mentioned anything about his girlfriend being murdered.'

Coupland couldn't hold back the smile that tugged at his mouth. 'Yeah, very strange by my reckoning. I think you've just found us our first proper lead.'

WEDNESDAY/DAY 4

CHAPTER NINE

Hard-nosed. That's what they called you when you wanted to get on. Like it was an insult. A trait to be downplayed in polite circles, implying the part of you that cared and held and reassured didn't function anymore. You were a husk operating on auto pilot, oblivious to the pain of others. Alex had agreed to head up this unit because she couldn't stand that pain. Was sick of seeing the damage people inflicted upon each other. Safeguarding children meant she could throw them a lifeline. Put them on a path where they could flourish not spiral. What she hadn't anticipated was the sheer bloody volume. Since their meeting yesterday, Shola Dube had emailed her several reports on child protection. Each one made depressing reading, each case study as difficult to read as the last. No wonder social services were overstretched. It didn't help that the local mental health unit had stopped taking referrals for all but the most urgent children's cases, leaving the criminal justice system to pick up the slack. It seemed perverse that the only way the kids on Shola's caseload could access the help they needed was to commit an offence.

Alex's phone rang. A number she didn't recognise. She hit reply and gave her name. 'Shola!' she said when the caller returned her greeting. 'I'm just reading the information you sent through.' Despite their initial awkwardness yesterday she felt the youth worker was fast becoming an ally; they were both trying to achieve the same thing, after all.

'*This job isn't for the faint hearted,*' Shola said, as though needing to emphasise the point. '*The sooner you equip yourself with the scale of the situation, the sooner you can decide if it's for you.*'

'I'm going nowhere, Shola,' Alex replied. 'I know what I'm taking on.'

Shola let out a low chuckle. '*Please forgive me if I sound patronising, it is not my intention. It's just, we're the last chance saloon for these kids, and that really matters, don't you think?*'

Alex swallowed. Wondered what the opposite of hardnosed was. Sentimental? Shola had almost been decapitated in an attack; her actions were hardly based on sentiment.

'*There's a girl I want you to meet. I've been working with her for a while but I fear she's at risk of lapsing. I'm certain she's been the victim of grooming. Though it's not something she's willing to discuss. I hoped that you'd be able to speak to her, maybe she'll open up to you if you show her a side to the police she hasn't seen before.*' Be less hard-nosed.

'Of course,' Alex said, opening her notebook and reaching for a pen, 'give me the details.'

*

The girl flicked a cloth half-heartedly over a couple of tables and sighed.

'How many times! Use the spray Bethany!' the woman behind the Perspex screen moaned, pointing to an antibacterial surface spray she watered down every morning when she thought no one was looking.

'It's Bez!' the girl reminded her; taking longer than

necessary to move towards the 'cleaning station,' just to wind her up.

The woman tutted, her attention turning to a customer waiting to pay. Bez slipped in her ear buds, turned the music channel's volume on her phone up a couple of notches. Not so loud the old bag would hear, but loud enough to annoy the folk sitting around, eking out coffees that had gone cold long since.

'Can I get you another?' she asked a woman pointedly, knowing full well she ordered one mug of tea every afternoon and nothing more. Didn't even get a drink for the little girl beside her, who sat patiently, as though she understood the importance of this ritual. Large brown eyes peeped up behind a fringe that needed cutting, tensing when the woman spoke.

'If I wanted another I'd tell you,' the woman sniped without bothering to look up from her phone.

Bez was unruffled. She'd grown up in a house where voices were always raised, where sarcasm filled the toxic void in between.

Are you OK Mum?
What do you fuckin' think?

The little girl dipped her head, podgy hands pulling at the folds of a faded wool dress. Bez recognised her embarrassment, the shame, even at that age, that a mean-spirited parent could bring. She'd seen the duo a couple of times as they passed by the window. The mother yanking the girl by the hand to stop her dragging her feet, or grabbing her hood if she skipped too far ahead.

Slipping through the double doors into the kitchen, Bez searched through the lost property box until she found what she was looking for. A brown cloth doll with buttons for eyes. A stitched-on dress with a stain she was certain would come out in the wash. She took it over to where the child sat with her mother and offered it to the little girl.

The mother's head jerked up, all attentive. 'What's this!' she barked, causing the café owner to look over in their direction.

'Ah, don't mind this little one. She was sat in the window for months but no-one claimed her,' Bez said, waiting while her boss turned her attention back to the till. 'Would you like to look after her?' she asked.

Arms outstretched, the child looked to her mother for permission but the woman's attention had already returned to her phone. The girl looked up at Bez and grinned, her arms wrapping round the doll in an embrace.

Bez crouched down until they were eye level. 'What will you call her?' she asked.

The girl tilted her head, squinting as she gave it some thought. 'Brown Dolly!' she announced in a voice that made it clear the matter was settled. Bez had been serving another table when they left not long after, the woman yanking the girl's arm like she was keeping her from something. The girl yanking Brown Dolly's arm in return.

She'd been composing a text to a mate when a woman walked in and took a seat by the window, making her scowl. They didn't run a table service anymore, you were supposed to give your order at the counter where her boss lorded it over her all day. She never moved from that seat apart from going to the toilet. An opportunity Bez took advantage of now by scrolling through her phone for messages

On her return to her post her boss jerked her thumb

in the direction of the table's new occupant, her gaze dropping to the smartphone in Bethany's hand. *Better go*, Bethany's thumbs sped over the phone's keyboard, *Got a right one here*. Snatching up her pad and pencil she stomped over to the waiting customer.

'You're supposed to give your order at the counter,' she said by way of a greeting.

The woman didn't seem put out by her abrasive manner. 'I'll have a can of anything sugar-free,' she told her. 'Don't open it, I'll take it away.'

'Seriously?' Bez pointed to the pound shop across the road. 'You'll get a multipack of them over there a lot cheaper than we charge. Save you a fortune in the long run.'

'Thanks, but I'm feeling flush, plus I wanted to give you my business card.' Alex reached into her coat pocket, placed a card with the GMP logo above the Safeguarding Unit's number on top of the table.

Bez's face fell. 'What am I supposed to have done now? I'll get the sack if *she* thinks I'm in trouble again.' She stole a look at her boss who was busy giving a visitor directions.

Alex shook her head. 'I only wanted to introduce myself. Shola told me where I would find you. She did tell you I'd get in touch?'

Bez's face cleared. 'Yeah, but that was, like, only yesterday…'

Alex smiled. 'And here I am. What time do you finish?'

'I'm on all day today. But I'm due a break in, um, ten minutes.'

Alex's stomach rumbled. It was only then that she remembered she'd had no time for breakfast that morning.

'What sandwiches do you recommend?'

'I could make you a chicken wrap.'

'Make us both one,' Alex said, 'we can eat while I tell you why I'm here.'

Ten minutes later Bez arrived at the table carrying a tray with their lunch. The chicken wraps had been arranged on two plates, with a side of coleslaw and a handful of ready salted crisps. She placed a can of Diet Fanta in front of Alex and opened a Pepsi Max for herself. 'I've only got half an hour,' she warned. She wore a black t-shirt and jeans beneath an apron that bore the name of the café on the front. There were smudges of mayonnaise and ketchup around the middle. Her hair was long enough to scrape back into a ponytail, probably in an attempt to conceal the pink strands that had escaped from the hairband. She had several studs along the lobe of one ear, and a mouth piercing that was starting to look sore. 'I did it myself,' she said when Alex's gaze lingered on it. 'It'll be fine in a couple of days.' She had a slight lisp when she spoke, whether as a result of the lip ring Alex couldn't be sure.

Both obviously hungry, they tucked into their lunch without a word being said. Bez had placed her phone on the table top, glancing at it every so often before stabbing the screen with her index finger. Her nails were bitten down to the quick.

Alex swallowed the last mouthful of a sandwich that was much better than she'd expected, dabbed her mouth with a serviette she pulled from a dispenser in the middle of the table. 'Waiting for a call?'

Bethany screwed up her face, 'No…' as though using a mobile phone to make and receive calls was preposterous.

'I've read your file,' Alex began. 'You've been a busy girl.'

Following a conviction for mugging, the teenager was under an intense supervision order which meant she had to take part in supervised activities for 25 hours per week. Shola had arranged for her to do unpaid work at the cafe as well as attend two appointments per week with a drug worker. She was currently liaising with her school to see if Bez could return on a part time basis.

The girl shrugged. 'Drugs make you do stupid things.'

According to Shola, Bez had started smoking cannabis as a way of self-medicating. She suffered depression whilst at primary school but everyone around her thought it was something she'd grow out of. Now aged 15, she had a string of convictions against her and suffered from bouts of psychosis due to her addiction to skunk.

'Do you feel ready to go back to school?'

A shrug. 'You mean do I think I'll kick off again if I don't get my own way?'

Alex nodded.

'I don't mean to. Sometimes I can't help it, you know?'

'I saw in your file you were referred to a counsellor. Did you go?'

Bez pulled a face. 'I went to the first appointment. You know, where they suss you out. She kept asking about when I was little, which makes no sense to me. I wanted to talk about the day I'd had, not things I barely remember.'

'Are your meetings with the drug worker helping?'

'If you mean am I clean, then yeah, it's working.'

Alex didn't want it to look as though she was interrogating her but their time was limited. She formed her mouth into a smile. 'Are you seeing anyone at the moment?'

'What's it to you?' Guarded eyes looked back at her.

'Shola tells me you've been preoccupied recently.' She inclined her head towards the phone by Bez's plate. 'I wondered if there was a boyfriend.'

Bez dipped her head. 'Nothing like that,' she said.

Alex tried to remember the notes she'd taken during her phone conversation with Shola the previous evening. She didn't want to alarm Bez by referring to them. She recalled information she'd underlined several times. 'I understand you lost your mum a couple of years back.'

A shrug. 'It happens.'

'Had she been ill for long?'

'A while.' Bez sighed. 'If you're looking for something to blame for the way I am then don't bother. I got into trouble at school long before mum died.'

Alex nodded. There wasn't really anything she could do for this girl. There was no boyfriend to speak of, no obvious signs of coercion, no trouble at home. She seemed stable enough for now. The best she could do was tell Shola she'd keep her on her radar.

The sound of a throat clearing made Alex look over at the café owner who was tapping a finger on her watch indicating the lunch break was over. Alex gathered her things together while Bez cleared the table.

'Shola should stop worrying about me,' she said as Alex reached into her bag for her purse. She pulled out two crisp ten pound notes and placed them on the table. She'd drawn the money out for their meeting from the cash machine up the road. It was that long since she'd paid for anything with cash it felt like Monopoly money in her hand. 'Keep the change,' she said, hoping that since she wasn't paying her any wages her boss would at least let her keep the tips.

'Seriously, I'm OK,' Bez smiled, 'I know I get depressed sometimes but that doesn't mean I'm sad all the time.'

She waited while Alex stepped onto the pavement. Watched her pull up the collar of her coat before making her way across the road. A decent enough person, she thought. For a cop. A bit uptight maybe, but that was to be expected. If only she made a bit more effort with herself, dropped the newsreader look, she could look much younger if she tried. She pulled the corners of her mouth into a line, set about clearing their table.

And when I smile and laugh that doesn't mean I'm happy either.

*

CID room, Salford Precinct station

Coupland watched as Ashcroft returned the phone he'd been nestling in the crook of his neck into its cradle. He ran long ebony fingers over his shorn scalp, muttered something that if Coupland's lip reading was as good as he thought it was implied the person Ashcroft had been speaking to liked to pleasure himself on a regular basis. 'Problem?'

'I called DS Clarke back yesterday evening to see if he'd had any luck laying his hands on Darren Yates's interview tapes. He told me I had to submit the request in writing. I asked to speak to DI Little and was told he was in a meeting. I sent Clarke the written request he wanted by email, marking it urgent before I went home. I've been trying his direct dial number several times this morning and all I'm getting is his voicemail.' He huffed out a sigh.

You didn't become a cop for an easy life. He just hadn't anticipated quite so many problems on *this* side of the thin blue line. 'I don't want to interview Keri's boyfriend without hearing the tape first.'

'You won't,' said Coupland, 'Get your coat, let's pay them another visit. See if we can't put a rocket up their collective backside.'

A look of alarm flitted across Ashcroft's face.

'I'll get the boss to call ahead if that makes you feel better, smooth our passage a little. Though if that little toe rag doesn't start playing ball it'll be an entirely different sort of passage I'll be smoothing out for him.'

*

City Road station
DI Little and his hoppo were waiting in reception when Coupland and Ashcroft walked into the station building. 'Back so soon?' Little's smile looked plastered on.

'Can't keep away,' Coupland chimed.

'Suppose you'd better come through now you're here,' Clarke said, smile slipping.

They followed the DI and his lackey as he stomped to the 'staff only' door, waiting while he keyed in the entrance code before yanking it open. They took the stairs in silence, any pretence at civility long gone. DI Little led them through to his office but didn't bother shutting the door. He moved to the sanctity of the space behind his desk, regarding the interlopers like they were something he'd scraped from under his shoe. 'Your Super's been on the blower pecking my Super's head,' he began.

Coupland's eyes widened in mock surprise. 'Has he

now? Can't think why.' He noticed that DS Clarke had stayed in the doorway; either he wasn't allowed over the threshold without express permission or he enjoyed his vantage point from the back of the room. Coupland pictured him in school sitting on the back row flicking rubber bands at the girls in the front.

'Thing is, Coupland, I'm not sure why you couldn't have picked the phone up to me and told me there was a problem. I'm not sure why you had to be so cloak and bloody dagger about it.'

Coupland wondered if he had to go all the way round the houses, or whether a simple 'because you're a twat,' would suffice. He took a breath. 'DS Ashcroft tried to speak to you but you weren't available to take his call.'

'I was busy. Your boy should have called again.'

Coupland glanced at Ashcroft. He stared back, his face expressionless. 'He'd spoken to DS Clarke here by then and put his request in writing as he'd been instructed, but that was the last he heard from anyone.' Coupland shook his head, 'We're in the middle of an investigation and don't have time to bugger about.'

Clarke sniggered behind him.

Coupland turned, levelling his gaze on him. 'Shouldn't you be outside, snapping at passers-by?'

Clarke stiffened. 'You've got a lot to say for yourself.'

Coupland clenched his jaw but said nothing. He turned back to DI Little. 'Look, once we've got the tapes we'll be on our way.'

'I wouldn't mind but there's nothing to get excited about. Not really.' Clarke's voice came out as a whine. 'We'd questioned the lad because he hung about the same streets as Keri. They'd been out together a couple of times but it had fizzled out, only Keri's friends claimed that was more her doing than his. There'd been no forensics to place him with her, and his alibi stacked up.'

'Could you not have said this yesterday?' Ashcroft asked. His voice was low; even. Coupland could tell he was doing his best to keep it pleasant.

Coupland regarded Clarke once more. 'Who were her friends?' he asked.

'I can't remember!'

'Maybe they're mentioned on the tape.' The DS's laugh was a lot less cock-sure this time, a lot more uncertain.

His DI came to the rescue: 'You pick up a lot of information just poking your nose around and listening. You know, jungle drums and all that. No offence, like.' Little leered at Ashcroft.

Coupland clenched his jaw. He didn't look at Ashcroft for fear of what he might see. He knew how angry it made *him* feel. The effort it took not to drag the wanker out of his seat and drive his fist into his face. Better to bide their time, he consoled himself. Let the tosser opposite think he was getting away with it. For now.

'If your… colleague here had taken the trouble to phone again I'd have been able to save you both a journey. You see, we're having trouble locating the tape. Probably misfiled, you know how it goes. The point is we don't have it.' Clarke looked pleased with himself.

'Are you serious?' Coupland looked from one to the other to see if this was some sort of ill-timed practical joke.

The DI's eyes flashed like steel. 'Yes. But I can repeat what he said if you like.'

What Coupland would really like was to ram the smug

tosser's face into the top of his desk but he talked himself out of it. He threw his arms wide. 'Isn't it about time you started to co-operate, given we know both our cases are linked?'

'I can't give you what we don't have,' said Clarke. That annoying voice from the back of the room again. Like a wasp Coupland wanted to swat.

'I've done nothing but co-operate, DS Coupland. With you and your... minder.'

Ashcroft kept his face in neutral. 'You know my name and rank. I'd appreciate you using it.'

Both men looked at each other. 'Well, Acting DS Ashcroft, seeing as you asked so nicely...'

'How come there was never a TV appeal for Keri?' asked Coupland.

'You know how it goes. My Super refused point blank to run a television appeal on the grounds that it wasn't in the public interest. With a mum that looked vacant and a step dad off his tits there was nothing to evoke sympathy from the viewers.'

For once Coupland didn't doubt the truth in what he said. Keri just wasn't the right sort of missing girl to grab the public's attention. Her mother wasn't press conference material. The girl's background made it hard to build a 'campaign' around her. Murdered girls needed to be beaming photogenic angels to get air time whereas Keri had little going for her. Her teeth were too crooked and her hair too frizzy to ever make the front page of the evening news, other than for the wrong reasons.

'Besides, she was a runaway.'

There it was again. That tide of indifference, as though Keri deserved the harm that befell her. Coupland couldn't rein his temper in any longer. 'Jesus wept, man; did you not listen to a thing her mother said? Yeah, she'd taken off in the past, but at the point she went missing things were good between them. This assumption skewed your investigation from the start.'

DI Little stared Coupland down. 'I'd watch your tone, fella. I'm a higher rank than you. I think that deserves a little respect.'

Coupland sighed. 'Maybe it's the company I'm keeping but I'm all out of respect right now. I'm saving what's left of it for the dead girls I'm trying to get justice for, and their families.'

He turned to DS Clarke. 'Now, have you got that tape or not?'

'Like I said. It's been misplaced.'

Coupland nodded. 'Then there's no point in us being here,' he said, turning so abruptly the fuckwit beside him had to jump out of his way.

'So what do we do now?' asked Ashcroft as they headed back to Salford, City Road station nothing more than a receding image in his rear view mirror. This was why Coupland had a lot of time for Ashcroft. Most cops would have wanted to debate whether they'd just been fed a line. All he wanted was to get the job done. They could consider the reasons why an interview tape had gone missing later; right now they had a person of interest that needed to be interviewed.

'Bring Darren Yates in. See if we can't establish exactly what his relationship with Keri really was.'

*

Darren Yates had been standing on the end of a driveway

in Boothstown when he became aware of it. The silver estate that had turned into the cul-de-sac behind him had pulled into the parking bay beside his van, engine idling. He'd not given it another thought while he placed the parcel on the doorstep before ringing the doorbell. Stepping back when the occupant opened the door, so he could take a picture on his mobile of them carrying the delivery back inside. He pocketed his phone, his attention turning to the occupants of the silver estate as they stepped out of the car. He recognised the tall black man as the detective who'd taken his statement a couple of days before. He raised his hand in greeting, figured he and his colleague were calling at one of the detached houses on the cul-de-sac. He felt a trickle of unease when they moved round to his driver's door then stood there, waiting. He'd slowed his pace to give himself time to think. The smile on his face frozen.

'Darren Yates,' the black man said as he held up his ID.

'It's OK, I remember you,' he told Ashcroft, turning to the young man beside him. 'I suppose you're a detective too?'

Krispy nodded.

'I need you to come down to the station with us,' Ashcroft said. 'I've got a few more questions I'd like to ask you.'

Yates's mouth felt dry. 'Shall I meet you there?'

Ashcroft shook his head while the younger man opened one of the estate's rear passenger doors.

'How about you come with us?' replied Ashcroft. 'DC Timmins here will give you a lift back.'

*

Interview Room 3, Salford Precinct station

During their walk to interview room 3 Coupland agreed that Ashcroft should take the lead. Put into practice what he'd learnt studying for his sergeant's exams. Times were changing. Grilling suspects had shifted down a gear. Interviews were meant to be non-confrontational, information gathering exercises rather than interrogations. In Coupland's mind there was nothing wrong in presuming guilt if your suspect had been caught with their fingers in the till, but he kept his own counsel. Over the past year DCI Mallender had rebuked him several times off the record. More recently, he'd taken to recording these observations in his performance review: *DS Coupland's interviews are minimally planned and lack structure. He uses leading questions, interrupts suspects and can, on occasion, be confrontational.* Coupland had been happy enough to sign it off, what with it being bang on and all.

Coupland's role during this interview would be one of observer. Ashcroft's preparation was meticulous and he was good at building rapport. Coupland would focus on Yates's expressions, those little tells that separated the truth from the lie.

*

By the time Darren Yates left the station his t-shirt clung to his back. Sweat had formed dark patches beneath his arms and his crotch was damp. His left eye began to twitch. That black detective had been OK but the other one seemed to have it in for him. Didn't like the fact he hadn't told his colleague about Keri when he'd come round to his house to take his statement. 'Why would I?' he'd replied. 'He was here about that other girl.'

'Carly?'

'Yeah, that's the one.'

His questions had been relentless.

How did you meet Keri?

Where did you go when you went out with her?

Did you have sex?

The questions were different this time. The other cops, the ones that had picked him up when Keri's body had been found, they'd wanted to know if she had sex with other men. If she had a bit of a reputation. 'Was she a bit "Easy, like Sunday morning?" the cop with the funny shaped head had asked. It seemed to piss him off that he'd had to explain it was the line of a song. He'd told them back then that he'd never seen her with any men.

Not that it mattered. It's not like they were a couple or anything. That they couldn't see other people if that's what they wanted. He wasn't sure he'd been her boyfriend really, whatever any of them were saying now. Him and Keri, they used to talk about things, sure, though nothing those first cops had been interested in. She talked about school. How they'd put her in the thick class when she was in care, like she couldn't possibly be interested in History and English yet she loved reading. He'd buy her magazines when he got paid on a Friday. He'd take her for a drive out to Phillips Park in his van. They'd park up and share a bottle of coke and a joint while she read the problem page out to him and he'd have to guess the reply. They'd kissed a few times and every once in a while she'd let him touch her, but nothing more than that. He'd been a friend, he supposed. Though not much of one, since she'd ended up dead.

Coupland stood in the reception area watching as

Darren Yates climbed into the pool car beside Krispy. An oddball without doubt. Certainly a loner. A loner that according to the notes in Keri's file followed her round like a dog with two dicks. Was it about obsession? Had he fantasized enough about her to take things a step too far? To break her body then discard it when she'd turned him down. If so, how did Carly fit into the equation?

Back in the CID room he dragged a chair over to Ashcroft's desk, pulled on a pair of headphones while they replayed the interview tape.

Ashcroft: Tell me about the last time you saw Keri.

Darren: *Not much to tell. She seemed depressed about something.*

Ashcroft: Did she say what was troubling her?

Darren: *I didn't ask. People like Keri and me, there's always something to worry about, isn't there? Money, a place to stay, sometimes there's no point talking about it. Not like you can change it.*

Ashcroft: Did you try to comfort her?

Darren: *I might have put my arm around her a couple of times.*

Ashcroft: Did she like it when you did that?

Darren: *She didn't shove me away, if that's what you're getting at.*

Ashcroft: Tell me about Carly.

Darren: *I didn't know Carly. I know that she's dead. That that was the reason you came to my house, to take a statement. I don't know any more than that.*

Coupland: Have you ever had sex with underage girls?

Darren: *Not to my knowledge, no.*

Coupland: Do you have many mates?

172

Darren: *Not especially. Prefer being on my own.*

Coupland: Do you have any hobbies? Groups you belong to?

Darren: *Do I look like I go rambling in my spare time?*

Ashcroft: Doesn't have to be rambling… the gym perhaps, or a running group.

Darren: *You need specs if you think I look like I work out. When I'm not working I like to eat fast food and watch Netflix.*

Coupland: Talking of food, the night Keri went missing she told her mum you were going to get a takeaway. Where did you go?

Darren: *News to me. I wasn't with her that night. I was working.*

Ashcroft: I think you didn't do deliveries at night?

Darren: *I don't. I was at the warehouse loading my van up for the next day. Yuo can check with them if you like.*

Ashcroft wrote down the details Darren gave him in his notebook.

Coupland took up the remainder of the questions. 'We'd like to take a DNA sample.'

'Why?'

'So we can rule you out of the investigation.'

'Oh.'

'We'd also like to take samples of fibres from your van. Cross check them with the trace fibres found on Keri and Carly. Will that be OK?'

A pause. 'I don't see why not.'

'Is there anything else you'd like to tell us at this point?'

'No.'

'Anything you'd like to add to the statement you gave my colleague earlier in the week?'

'You mean like if I've changed my mind about something I've said or I remember something that I'd forgotten about earlier?'

'That's it, Darren, yes.'

'Well there isn't anything.'

'OK.'

'I know you're hoping that I'll confess now that you're going to take my DNA, but I've done nothing wrong. I said the same to the other detectives when they interviewed me at their station, only they believed me and chose to let me go.'

'So they didn't run any tests then?'

'No, I just said that, didn't I? Now can I get a lift back to my van? I've still got deliveries to make.'

Coupland removed his headphones and turned to Ashcroft. 'I hope for the sake of my police career the lab results don't match. If those gobshites chose not to take his DNA back when they were interested in him and he turns out to be Carly's killer I'll—'

'—You'll be second in line.' Ashcroft's voice was low, menacing. 'I'd love nothing more than to take those bastards down, but over something that doesn't make me look like I've got thin skin.'

Coupland thought that was an invitation to discuss their behaviour towards Ashcroft during their last encounter but while his brain tried to form the right words to kick start the conversation Ashcroft had moved on, berating the time it took to get DNA results back even when the boss was willing to pay to get them fast tracked, how in the absence of any other evidence relating to Yates it was a waiting game, pure and simple.

Coupland had spent more than half his life in the Job.

Had worked with great officers and downright wankers. The force wasn't immune to its fair share of bigots, like any industry. But the actions of individuals in a position of responsibility had far reaching consequences. The message it sent out about self-worth. Identity. He'd only been belittled by one man in his life. How must it feel to have to deal with that attitude on your street, in your city, in the institution that you worked for? He could see why Ashcroft preferred to keep his own counsel. Why he had chosen to man the phones when the Super had asked officers to stand on the station steps holding placards embossed with #BLM to post on the division's Instagram page. Coupland had given it a wide berth too. Had gone for a sly cigarette on the fire escape steps instead, making his own show of protest. So many headless chickens wanting to be seen to do the right thing, yet the only beneficiaries of this posturing were diversity consultants and their expertly written handbooks. HR had scheduled anti-bias training, but for what? So it could demonstrate commitment to an inclusive workplace should a lawsuit come across its door?

Coupland sighed. In his experience people didn't change. All you could do to modify their behaviour was threaten them with sanctions if they stepped out of line. But if the problem was bigger than anyone imagined, what then?

*

DCI Mallender's office
Mallender's expression suggested he was a lot less excited with the news they'd identified a common link between

both cases than Coupland had anticipated. 'If he's our man then where is his accomplice? Or is he working on someone else's say-so and he's the one who picks the girls up? But if he is then why hasn't anyone reported seeing his van near the bus stop Carly was waiting at?' His tone was sharp, like a rebuke.

Coupland furrowed his brow; he wasn't aware he'd done anything to hack him off so early in the investigation. 'We discovered the connection yesterday, boss, obviously we're putting our weight into finding known associates but we've not had the green light from the lab to say it's him yet.'

'Hasn't stopped you before.'

'Maybe I've learned from past mistakes. Look,' he added when Mallender frowned, 'we'll tread softly until his DNA test results come back. If they come back positive then we'll arrest him and put the pressure on to find his mate.'

'And in the meantime?'

Coupland's mouth turned down at the edges. 'In the meantime? I suppose we could put someone outside his home for the next couple of nights. Won't be short of volunteers.'

Mallender grunted approval. 'I've had a call from DI Little. Said he had a run-in with you when you went over there earlier. Anything you want to tell me about?'

'I'm more interested in what *he* had to say.'

'He didn't like the way you were questioning their handling of Keri Swain's murder.'

Coupland shrugged. 'Can't argue with that.'

'Anything you want to share with me?'

Coupland made a noise that sounded like a deep sigh. 'There's more dinosaurs than Jurassic Park. Little is a small-minded bigot who's done a stupendous job of forming Clarke in his own image. They make Neanderthal man look like Metrosexuals. There are huge gaps in Keri's file and we've just found out that that Darren Yates's interview tape has gone missing, only I'm not sure I believe them.'

'Little did mention that. He told me their EMU has undergone a refurbishment. New shelving, lockable cupboards, a lick of paint. No different to work we've had done here, one time or another. During that process some box files were destroyed in error.'

Sensing Coupland's cynicism Mallender ploughed on. 'To be honest, Kevin, it sounds plausible. At the end of the day they're not MI5.'

'Just as well, given their data protection's gone to shite.'

Mallender didn't contradict him. Coupland refused to be brow beaten: 'Add to that a lack lustre chain of evidence form where limited items were retained from the crime scene. No attempt at a timeline of Keri's final 24 hours, and the only statements written down are anecdotal. Now you and I both know paperwork isn't my cup of tea,' he ignored the look that flashed across Mallender's face, 'but you've got to question how they've stayed on the force this long.' All that was needed were a few bad seeds and before you knew it the culture of a place changed dramatically. Standards slipped. Co-workers turned a blind eye rather than complain. No one wants to get drawn into something that could end up biting them on the backside. Coupland shook his head. He'd never understood the ability of some folk to look the other way. To keep their head down. Make sure they don't rock the boat or muddy the water. Anything for a quiet life. As long as the kids that are murdered belong to someone else.

Mallender swore under his breath. 'Anything else?' he asked, eyeing Coupland.

Coupland considered Ashcroft's reaction if he shared his concerns regarding Little and Clarke's attitude towards him, decided he couldn't risk losing the detective's trust. He grunted a no.

'I'll speak to Superintendent Curtis, then,' Mallender sighed. 'Ask him to requisition every single piece of evidence collected from Keri's crime scene and get it sent here. You can put together a team to go through it with a fine tooth comb.'

'I'd rather someone from our Evidence Management Unit liaises direct with their EMU once the Super has given his approval. I'll send Turnbull too. He's not got an intuitive bone in his body, but he's a pedantic sod, that's why he's good at crime scene management.'

Turnbull only understood things he could 'see'. If something was recorded on the crime scene log but couldn't be cross referenced against the relevant evidence box he wouldn't leave until he found it.

'We need to get DI Little on side with this, Kevin. We're not investigating his team, we're just re-examining the evidence.'

'I don't get paid to smooth ruffled feathers, boss. That ball's firmly in your court, I believe.'

Another sigh. 'Look, I'm well aware of the different personality styles at play. Which is why I think we should start having weekly joint briefings here, just to make sure we're all working from the same page.'

Coupland couldn't be arsed summoning up a smile he

didn't feel. 'You're the boss,' he said, already thinking up ways to return Dumb and Dumber's hospitality. He was being petulant, he accepted that. But right now that's all he had.

FRIDAY/DAY 6

CHAPTER TEN

The key purpose of this morning's briefing was to officially 'merge' both investigating teams and spell out the rules of engagement. Coupland had swapped his rest day to the previous day, making sure he was on shift to roll out the welcome mat for the syndicate travelling through from City Road station. Although pissing in their coffee had been tempting, he'd accepted Ashcroft's point that if they didn't feel threatened at Salford Precinct, they were more likely to agree to the briefings being held there. Krispy had been despatched with money from the biscuit fund to buy pastries and an instant coffee blend that tasted as though it had gone through a machine.

Twenty minutes after the scheduled start of the briefing there was no sign of them. ''S'pose they could have had an accident,' Krispy said.

'Nothing trivial I hope,' Coupland replied, his look challenging Mallender to rebuke him.

The DCI glanced at his watch before stepping to the front of the room. 'I think we've waited long enough,' he conceded.

Turnbull, who'd been eyeing the doughnuts and cinnamon swirls laid out on a side table, raised his hand.

'Fill your boots,' Coupland sighed, sending a look to Ashcroft that said, told you.

Mallender tried to spin his introduction out as long as

possible, but it was hard to introduce a team that wasn't there. If he was hacked off he kept it hidden. Coupland spoke up next, running through the progress made on actions allocated earlier in the week. He'd positioned himself at the front of the room, his chair facing the murder squad, the investigation log book resting on his lap.

He nodded at Krispy to provide an update: 'Malky White, Keri's stepdad, checks out, Sarge. At the time of her disappearance he was dossing down with a pal on Langworthy Road. His mate had a win at the bookies and they pissed it all away in the beer garden at The Winston the night she went missing. There's CCTV showing them get kicked out after they started getting too close to regulars on the next table.'

'Right, said Coupland. 'Strike him off the list.'

Robinson reported there were still no discernible leads from the incident vans parked at the bus stop Carly was last seen at.

'Think we can safely knock them on the head too. Move Carly's poster to the bus shelter window.'

Coupland made a note in the log book.

Just then the door to the CID room opened. A red-faced civilian walked in ahead of the motley crew that made up Little's murder squad. Mallender had intended to greet them at reception but when they didn't arrive on time Coupland had phoned the desk sergeant, persuaded him to have them escorted through with minimum fuss; two cinnamon swirls sealed the deal.

Coupland waited while the detectives shuffled to the empty seats in the middle of the room before doling out the takeaway cups one of them carried in on a cardboard tray. Another opened a paper bag with the logo of the coffee shop round the corner across it, divvied up bacon and egg rolls between them, checking with his colleagues who had ordered brown sauce and who hadn't.

Coupland saw the confusion on the faces of his team, but said nothing. Little was flexing his muscles, that was all. Making a point. Besides, Krispy's reaction when he'd clocked the shape of the DI's head was priceless. Coupland introduced each member of his own team, invited Little to do the same.

'Right, let's get down to business,' he said once the formalities were over. The lab results concerning Darren Yates's fast-tracked DNA had come back. 'No match with the semen found on either victim,' he said, without missing a beat. 'Trace fibres found on Keri matched the fibres removed from the passenger seat of his van, which we'd expect given their relationship. His alibi checks out too.'

'No harm done about the missing interview tape then,' said Little, folding arms above a stomach that was no stranger to a fried breakfast.

Coupland bowed his head as though studying the paperwork on his lap.

'Surveillance came to nothing, unless you want to know how many people in Worsley shop on the QVC channel? Failing that I suggest we eliminate him from the investigation,' he stated, looking at Mallender for approval.

Mallender nodded. DI Little leaned back in his chair until the back two legs bore all his weight. Let the fucker break it, Coupland thought, their eyes locking. The glare Little sent back at him made Coupland wonder if he'd said it out loud.

'I reckon we need to be looking at this a different way,' said Little.

'What do you mean?'

'Well, at the moment you're scrabbling around looking for suspects that fit the bill.'

'Isn't that generally how it works?' Coupland replied, trying not to let the reference to scrabbling sting. 'We've eliminated those closest to the girls and checked the whereabouts of registered offenders. The purpose of this briefing is to see if we can now put together an offender profile.'

'I get that, but what are the chances two perverts met randomly and hit it off?'

Coupland shrugged, determined to keep his responses upbeat. 'Slim, I would say. But I don't think it's far-fetched to think that they made contact whilst inside, or while attending an outreach programme, it's how most offenders meet each other.'

Someone seemed to have hit Mallender's mute button, unless he was happy with the way Coupland was handling the interloper. Little rocked his chair forward until it was back on all four legs. 'Seems to me you've run into a blind alley.'

'Look,' Ashcroft spoke up. 'We're assuming that two men abducted Keri and Carly, and that both went on to murder them.'

'Keep up, sonny,' said Little, 'the DNA's—'

'All the DNA tells us is that two men raped them, but we now know only one man's DNA was found on *both* girls. We should open our minds to the possibility that one man abducted each victim for his own purpose, before taking them onto a third party – a different one each time. When they'd done what they wanted, the girls were disposed of.'

'What if these "third parties" are clients?' Coupland said slowly.

Mallender must have been thinking along a similar line. 'Remember Reedsy?' he asked. They'd smashed a human trafficking ring two years earlier. Albanian girls forced into prostitution by a Salford gangster who went by the name of Midas. Reedsy, AKA Austin Smith, worked for Midas, driving trafficked young girls round Salford to be sexually abused by men willing to pay shed loads of money to live out their darkest fantasies.

'How could I forget?' Coupland huffed out a sigh. He'd nearly lost his job over an accusation of brutality that Reedsy had made against him. He'd been murdered in prison on Midas's say-so to stop him identifying influential clients he'd taken the trafficked children to.

Mallender looked thoughtful. 'Remember the aftermath? The targeting of human trafficking gangs during Operation Naseby.' Operation Naseby had been set up to reduce the number of migrant children targeted for sexual exploitation. It had been deemed a success, but Coupland's face clouded as he considered a consequence that no one had anticipated. Every action caused a reaction, after all.

'The operation's success means that the supply chain of migrant children forced into sexual exploitation is dwindling,' he said, more to himself than the others in the room. 'To put it crudely, how are the perverts out there getting their fix now?'

'These abductions, and consequent killings, could

be orchestrated by a new gang, rather than individuals,' Mallender concluded.

Coupland nodded, his gut telling him they were on the right track. 'Keri had fallen through the cracks. To anyone in authority she was a problem kid. The kind who caused trouble and stayed out all night. The kind the public wouldn't miss, let alone give a toss about.' He looked at Mallender. 'What if there are others? Dead or missing girls whose absence hasn't caused shockwaves through a community.'

Mallender's solemn face told him it was worth pursuing. He turned to Krispy. 'I want to know how many reports there have been of girls that fit this MO throughout the city over the last twelve months.'

Krispy looked troubled. 'Carly hadn't been in care, she wasn't from a "chaotic" family either,' he said. Her father had made it clear to Coupland that he liked to know her whereabouts every minute of the day.

'She still ended up in harm's way,' a DC in Little's team said.

'How? By standing at a bus stop?' demanded Ashcroft. 'These girls didn't do anything wrong.'

'None of them did,' agreed Coupland. 'But Carly's set up is different to Keri's, there's no getting away from that.'

'Carly might have just been an opportunity that presented itself, one that seemed too good to miss at the time.'

Coupland considered this. 'Either they're already regretting taking Carly because of the attention her murder has brought, or they're happy to widen their net if it means keeping their clients happy.'

Coupland felt a lead weight form in his stomach as

something occurred to him. He looked at Ashcroft, saw he was thinking the same thing. 'What if they're already planning to take their next girl?'

'We need to put out a warning, starting with the schools,' Ashcroft suggested.

'Keri had been excluded from school,' Clarke reminded him.

'To social work departments as well then. Outreach departments, referral units, any organisation that comes into contact with teenagers for that matter,' said DI Little.

Coupland looked at Mallender. Little outranked him but Mallender had the final say.

'We could ask the council to circulate an urgent bulletin around the schools and their social work team on our behalf. Individual youth groups might be harder to reach speedily unless we put a message out via social media,' Mallender said.

'My team can do that,' offered Little, 'we can follow it up with visits in person to reinforce the message.'

'DS Coupland is responsible for handing out actions,' said Mallender. 'It's his decision.' It was obvious Mallender was throwing Coupland a bone. That he didn't really want him to get all arsey and allocate the task to his own team as a matter of principle. He was expecting him to respond like a grown up.

Even so. 'We don't want to give this gang a heads-up that we're onto them,' he said stubbornly, shifting his weight from left buttock to right. 'If the killers think we're on to them it may make them go to ground.'

'Better that than another victim, DS Coupland. I'm sure you wouldn't want that on your conscience.'

Coupland grunted something that resembled agreement. It was clear Mallender didn't intend to intervene any further. 'I'll update the log book. Any feedback to go through me though, yeah?'

'Wouldn't dream of going to anyone else.' The DI smiled, his gaze boring into Ashcroft as he said it.

Coupland regarded the detectives scattered around the room. 'Maybe I did go about this arse about face. Someone's dragging young girls off the street, not for their own gratification but for Perverts Anonymous.' He let that sink in. 'Who the hell are they?'

'We never found the guy that Zamia Gashi was being taken to,' said Krispy.

Coupland tried to blink away the image of the sports bag she'd been found in, the husk of her body stuffed inside.

'That's right,' said Ashcroft. 'The National Crime Agency weren't interested in him. They were going after the big hitters who were bringing the migrants in.'

The gang involved in bringing Zamia Gashi to Salford were now behind bars but it had gnawed away at Coupland that their 'clientele' had never been brought to justice. They were out there, roaming free, paying gofers to bring them other girls. Disposable girls.

'I think we're looking at an organised network here,' said Mallender. 'A network with manpower and resources to cover its tracks and access to people whose level of depravity knows no bounds.'

'I need to go back and speak to my contact at the Sex Offender Management Unit. All I was interested in last time I met with her was checking the whereabouts of known offenders on the register, but they don't operate in a vacuum. Many of them are part of a network too. A network of…' he struggled to think of a suitable word, '…scum. And if we wait long enough scum floats to the top.'

Coupland asked Ashcroft to allocate the remaining actions while he rang Allison Round. While he waited to be put through he noticed DI Little waft his hands at Ashcroft as though dismissing him. He kicked himself for leaving the inexperienced sergeant to handle him. He looked about for Mallender but he'd already retreated to his office.

DS Round recognised Coupland's voice before he'd had time to say her name; she picked up his anxiety too. He told her how the case had developed since they'd last met.

'Hell's Bells,' she said, like an old style games mistress to a pupil who'd turned up with missing kit.

Coupland stared at the receiver, frowning.

'Sorry,' she said, picking up his confusion. *'We're trying to clean up our act a bit over here. Some bright spark has introduced a swear jar. A fiver for every "F" word. It'll go towards the Christmas party. There's a hundred quid in it already and we only started the day before yesterday. Anyway,'* she said, clearing her throat, *'none of that matters. What do you need from us?'*

Coupland wished he knew. He described the offender profile outlined in the briefing. 'I need to find out more about the networks these guys operate in.'

There was silence on the other end of the line as she digested what he'd told her. *'Many offenders carry out what we categorise as opportunistic or premeditated abuse, Kevin. An offender might take a fancy to his neighbour's child, for example, another might be a sports coach who deliberately targets young boys between a certain age. In the most part these are practices they don't*

191

share or discuss with anyone else. Unless…'

'What?'

'If you're looking at someone who is taking girls to deliver to someone else, I'd be saying that you're treading on the verge of some really dark shit that—'

Coupland heard a raised voice in the background, something resembling laughter. Round's voice became muffled, but it was clear she was disputing something, *'NO, "shit" doesn't count as swearing!'* she hissed before apologising for the disturbance. *'My colleagues here are trying to make out that Shit isn't allowed. I mean, come on, we've got to have something left, otherwise I'll be bankrupt in a week.'*

She paused as though trying to remember what it was they'd been talking about. *'Let me give you the number of a public protection DS. She knows her stuff. She may be able to shine a light on what you're looking for.'* The line went quiet while she located the number. *'Good luck,'* she said after reading it out to him.

Coupland thought what his working day would feel like if he couldn't mutter the odd expletive. 'You too,' he said, meaning it.

*

Nexus House

Coupland had never been a big reader, He'd never had the time, or the inclination if the truth be told. But there was a quote gnawing away at him. Something along the lines of at 50, everyone had the face they deserved. He looked at the person opposite and shuddered. Hoped to Christ when the time came he didn't get the face *he* deserved.

Pauline Boydell was a Public Protection Officer,

attached to the Child Sexual Exploitation Unit for Greater Manchester. Thin like a reed, the start of a dowager hump could be seen beneath her polo neck jumper. The result of genetics, Coupland wondered, or a career spent hunched over keyboards as she trawled the internet following perverts. The lines around her eyes were heavy and dark, emphasised by black framed glasses which she took off and cleaned with a regularity that suggested habit, rather than need. Her face was devoid of colour save for a slash of red lipstick which had bled into the lines around her mouth. The Public Protection Unit was on the floor below the Child Sexual Exploitation Unit. It was situated at the end of a corridor that didn't have name plates on the doors, as though no one wanted to own up to what went on behind them.

They were seated around a small 'break out' table, three vending machine coffees at its centre.

'Alli called me straight after she'd spoken to you,' Pauline said after Coupland and Ashcroft had introduced themselves. 'She wanted to give me as much of a heads up as possible.' She took a sip of her coffee, pulling a face. 'So, you think the men you are looking for are part of an organised network?'

Coupland nodded. 'We worked on an investigation that the NCA ended up taking over a couple of years back, concerning a gang that had been bringing in Albanian girls to service wealthy paedophiles.' He told her about the investigation into Keri and Carly's rape and murder. 'We think whoever is responsible for those murders is trying to fill the gap left by that gang's removal.'

Pauline nodded. 'It's possible. I mean, one of the few sectors that haven't been hit by this bloody pandemic is the porn industry. In fact, COVID-19 was like manna from heaven. Child sexual exploitation across the country rose by 90 percent, up from last year. The pandemic motivated would-be predators to get a piece of the action. I do a lot of surveillance in my job, and I heard offenders openly discussing the fact that stay-at-home working was beneficial to them.'

Coupland considered this. 'More children were at home, schoolwork was moved online. Everyone's schedules were disrupted, it makes sense there were more potential targets for sexual enticement.'

Pauline looked at him as though he were simple. 'Not just that. More men staring at laptops all day. A potential new audience in the making. What do you think your predators are using your girls for?'

Now it was Coupland's turn to give her a strange look. 'Isn't it obvious?'

'Not necessarily. The young people I see in this unit are forced into sexual activity by multiple men. What you see as the end result is really just the start of a chain of events. A series of different enterprises, if you like. Were the girls drugged?'

Coupland nodded.

'Makes them compliant. Though sometimes these sickos want them to put up a fight. Either way, whatever form their abuse takes it ends up being uploaded onto the web.' She took another swig of her coffee, gulping down the remainder while encouraging the others to do the same. 'This stuff goes cold so quickly,' she told them. 'That's when it's really unpalatable, trust me.

'Have you got their photos? I can search our digital image database; see if they've appeared online yet.'

Coupland's blink was slow. 'Sorry?'

Pauline puffed out her cheeks. 'No, it's me who should be apologising. This job messes with your head. You end up thinking everyone is operating on the same level, but why would they? Why would anyone want to?'

'You think their abuse was filmed?' said Ashcroft.

Pauline nodded. 'It's a lucrative business. The person committing the act pays a hell of a lot of money for the privilege of performing whatever perversion takes their fancy. If the abuse goes online straight away there's additional revenue when it's live streamed, not to mention pay per view income from the sad sacks that watch it at home.' She paused, 'There's a market for watching their murders too…'

'This can't be happening here though,' Coupland said, 'not in this city. We'd have heard about it before now.'

'How?' said Ashcroft, 'Not like the victims can tell us.'

'I don't have to work in vice or drugs to know where the knock off shops and shoot em up dens are,' said Coupland, 'but I haven't seen anywhere peddling this…' He couldn't think of a word that did it justice. Filth? Depravity? For once he was at a loss.

Pauline's smile was sympathetic. 'Digital camera, tripod, laptop, and a room large enough to swing a cat. That's all they need. A back bedroom or lock up would do it. It's happening in Airbnbs too. Remember, their audience isn't the dirty old man brigade who used to queue up outside dodgy cinemas back in the day. This clientele is logging on in their lunch break. Or at playtime.'

'Jesus,' Coupland muttered. He pulled his phone from his jacket pocket. Tapped on the screen until he found the photos of Keri and Carly, then slid the phone across the desk to her. She moved over to a bank of computers against a back wall, used what looked like a supermarket scanner to scan the images onto her PC.

'If there is a match,' Ashcroft asked, 'will your search throw anything up that could help our investigation?'

A shrug. 'It's a bit like going on YouTube and searching for your favourite band. Sometimes your search will throw up the original track recorded in the studio and it's like you're in the same room with them in terms of sound quality and visuals. Other times you'll end up with a low quality recording of someone playing the CD in their bedroom, the music track jumps all over the place and the lighting is rubbish. I can't say at this point what the search will throw up, if anything. It's probably better not to speculate.'

Ashcroft nodded. 'We're talking about the Dark Web, though, right?' The dark web was an internet area beyond the reach of mainstream search engines.

Pauline nodded.

'So it's not something you can accidentally fall into while googling cycling shorts or whatever else it is that men with too much time on their hands look for?'

'The days of husbands claiming they didn't know where the link they'd clicked onto was going to take them are long gone. The people that go onto the dark web know what they are stepping into. Whoever sent them there will have warned them about covering their tracks. There are "gateway sites", that show would-be punters how to disguise themselves by setting up anonymous IDs with untraceable payment methods. A lot of thought and planning is required to do this.'

'So, you're saying you need a PhD if you want to join

Perverts Anonymous?'

'Not at all. You've got a TV subscription package?'

Coupland looked uncertain for a moment then smiled. 'You mean like Netflix?' he said, nodding.

'Registering on the dark web is like joining one of those service providers. Once you've set up your account you're in. You can peruse to your heart's content.'

'So, you don't become a member on the back of a whim,' Coupland said, satisfied.

'You don't need fancy devices either. The global expansion of personal computer and smartphone ownership has made it much easier for people to indulge their perverted fantasies. Remember, the dark web is vast. It sells over 350,000 different illegal items from drugs and guns to pornography. It even operates a rating system for speed of dispatch and delivery.'

Coupland wondered how that might work:

Need to get your rocks off in a hurry? This is the site for you.

The skunk starter packs are sensational value. Order before midnight and you'll be off your face by lunchtime tomorrow.

During his time in CID Coupland had witnessed up close the effect the internet has had on crime. It was like the invention of the motor car – enabling criminals to escape and reinvent themselves in the blink of an eye. Now someone was doing this on his patch though if he had anything to do with it, they wouldn't stay invisible for long.

'It'll take several hours to run this programme,' Pauline told them, keen to crack on with her own burgeoning work load while the software ran its course, 'but I'll let you know straight away if we find anything.'

*

Nexus House

Alex valued her body mass index too much to venture into the staff canteen under normal circumstances but she'd an hour to kill until her next meeting and her sugar levels were starting to drop. She ordered a cheese toastie and a coffee and had just hovered her debit card against the contactless payment machine when she noticed the little girl sat at the far side of the room. She picked up her tray and moved towards the officer looking after the child, her brow furrowing.

'Social work is trying to find emergency foster care for her, Ma'am,' he explained. The child looked happy enough, eating a sandwich and drinking a fizzy drink the PC had dipped into his own pocket to buy. He turned away from the child and lowered his voice. 'Her parents were arrested in a money laundering raid. No friends or family that could have taken her short term, apparently. Think the mother was hoping to tug on the arresting officer's heart strings but it's not the first time she's been hauled in so he wasn't falling for it. How many lives do these parents get?' It was tough; there was no getting away from it.

Alex took a seat at the next table and shared her toastie with the PC. 'Got kids of your own?' she asked, becoming wary when he dropped his gaze.

'Wife's had two miscarriages,' he said.

Alex mumbled that she was sorry, decided to move the conversation on to safer ground. 'I've got a meeting with a cluster of head teachers,' she told him, 'trying to persuade them to let excluded kids return to school but under the supervision of our youth offending team.'

'Makes sense, Ma'am, children need structure.'

A catering assistant wandered over to Alex's table and began clearing it. Alex looked at her watch; saw that it wasn't long until her meeting started. She got to feet, her gaze shifting to the little girl, one arm clasped around a brown doll in a grubby dress. 'Has she asked after her parents at all?' she asked, watching as the girl reached with her other arm for the fizzy can, swigging from it like an expert before offering some to the doll.

The PC pursed his lips and shook his head before blowing out a sigh. No Ma'am, going by her demeanour she hasn't missed them one little bit.'

By the time Alex's meeting with the cluster heads had finished, three out of the four high schools in the area had agreed to reinstate excluded pupils under a trial scheme which stated that if they stepped out of line during school hours it would be Alex's team who dealt with them. A lot of the problem behaviour was low level 'indiscipline'. Nothing significant in its own right – answering their teacher back, larking around repeatedly so the lesson was disrupted, winding up the other kids. All things which in normal circumstances – smaller class sizes, more teaching staff, a punishment system that returned some control back to the staff – would have been dealt with in-house. Add to that a catchment area that included several crime families, little wonder the teachers refused point blank to chastise certain kids.

Alex was relieved one school had resisted her pitch; her officers would be stretched as it was, but if she was to deliver results she had to be prepared to take risks. One of the schools that had agreed to her proposal was the one attended by Bethany Davies. 'I'm sure Bethany will be thrilled when I tell her the news,' she'd said, cutting in front of Olive Blair, the head teacher of Bez's school, before she could leave. It had been Olive's reluctance to take Bez back when Shola approached her that made Alex come up with the idea of relieving schools of the burden of managing problem pupils themselves. 'She knows how important the last couple of years at school are. I'm confident with our support she won't let you down.'

'It's not me she'd be letting down,' Olive warned. 'Seems to me she's got a real champ in her corner, now. Just be careful, though, that weight of expectation can sit heavily on their shoulders.' Alex had bristled at that, though she'd tried hard not to show it. Her team was offering kids like Bethany Davies and Shaun Lowton, AKA Laughing Boy, a way out, not adding to their burden.

Coupland was bleeping a car open a few bays down from hers in the staff car park. A pool car, which meant he wouldn't be able to smoke in it. She grinned at Ashcroft as she made her way towards them. Fair play, it had taken her ages to work that one out. 'You stalking me?' she asked, realising that she missed this. The craic. The relaxed way of speaking with people you'd worked with a long time.

Coupland barely glanced in her direction. He seemed pre-occupied.

'Everything OK?' she asked.

'Ignore me,' he said, brightening at the prospect of lighting up while they talked. 'Just spent the afternoon in the Public Protection Unit.'

Alex shuddered. 'Rather them than me. Safeguarding's hard enough. It skews the way you look at things. Every child that crosses my path becomes a potential candidate.' She told them about the little girl in the canteen. 'I found myself checking up on her after my meeting. Just in case, you know. Turns out her parents were released on bail so she got to go home with them after all. Even then I find myself wondering if this was good or bad news.'

Coupland blew smoke out of the corner of his mouth, careful to keep Alex and Ashcroft out of harm's way. 'To give some kids the protection they need you'd have to sit outside the delivery room,' he said, thinking of the baby Lynn had removed from its mother earlier that week.

'How's the investigation going?'

Ashcroft sent her a warning glance. *Don't ask,* it seemed to convey, *if you need to be somewhere else anytime soon.* 'Two victims now, thanks to a mishandling of an investigation by the Ant Hill Mob over at City Road. Apart from that, everything's tickety-bloody-boo.'

Coupland stubbed out his cigarette. 'There's a chance both girls are victims of a dark web network operating on our doorstep.'

'Christ. Look, if I can help in any way you know where I am,' she offered.

'Yeah,' said Coupland, sounding more like his old self now his nicotine levels were replenished, 'feet up in front of the TV watching Bake Off, now you're working regular hours,' he commented, making a point of looking at his watch. 'In fact scratch that, you'll be home in time for Pointless.'

'To think I was having second thoughts,' Alex muttered to herself as she returned to her car. 'Must be bloody mad.'

*

Coupland saw the number from SOMU flash up on his smartphone screen when his mobile started to ring. He hit the 'reply' button before telling Allison Round she was on loud speaker so Ashcroft could hear at the same time.

'Look, this might not be anything,' she began. 'But an offender by the name of Patrick Jameson was released yesterday. Turned up at Swinton nick with his wife to register. I got the notification through as usual. Only this time I paid him a welcome visit. Just to verify his address.'

Coupland heard the smile in her voice. 'What was he sent down for?'

'Distributing indecent images of children.'

Coupland waited.

'He lives over at Worsley Woods.'

'Very how do you do.'

'Adamant he's done nothing wrong of course.'

'Would expect nothing less.'

'But then he told me something I thought you'd want to hear straight away.'

CHAPTER ELEVEN

Patrick Jameson lived in a substantial detached property in a secluded development of three houses in Worsley. Located 6 miles to the west of Manchester and 5 miles to the north west of Salford Quays, it was reached via a private, access-only road. Ashcroft parked in front of the middle house. They could have brought a fleet of squad cars and there'd still have been room on the ample driveway. Established bay trees in matching pots stood either side of a double front door. 'Nice.' Coupland climbed out of the car and gave an appreciative nod.

'Did you hear that?' he asked as they waited for their knock to be answered.

'What?'

'Exactly,' he said, referring to the silence. Built on the edge of Worsley Woods, the houses were muffled from the sounds and rhythm of the city. You could live here and not be aware of night shelters and food banks, of drug addicts sleeping off their fix on park benches. If you didn't see them, Coupland wondered, did they cease to exist?

Appearances were deceptive. If Coupland hadn't read the file DS Round had sent through to him an hour before, he could be forgiven for thinking he and Ashcroft were sitting in the elegant front room to discuss the merits of setting up a neighbourhood watch scheme. Instead he had to remind himself that the retired civil servant seated opposite had been found guilty of sharing images of children so vile the judge had refused point blank to let the jury see them. The brief course he'd attended on child protection warned against jumping to conclusions based on appearance when it came to sexual exploitation. Most culprits looked like middle management commuters rather than dirty old men.

Jameson wore an open neck shirt tucked into beige slacks. When he crossed the room to examine their warrant cards there was an air of entitlement about him, even after his stint inside. His hair was shorter than Coupland suspected he normally wore it, what with prison barbers offering a limited range of style options.

His wife wore a shirt dress belted at the waist. Her hair was long but she wore it up, Princess Anne style. They both wore slippers, and had looked put out when the detectives hadn't offered to remove their shoes when they'd turned up twenty minutes earlier.

They'd gone through the preliminaries of introductions and turning down offers of tea and coffee. Coupland wanted to spew at the thought of them drinking tea together, wondered what in God's name his wife was thinking of staying married to him.

'Your colleague was very keen that I tell you exactly what I told her,' Jameson said, lifting a china cup and saucer from the tray his wife brought in and placed on the coffee table. 'She said it might help you in relation to your current investigation. Obviously I'm keen to help in any way that I can.' He seemed pleased with himself, happy to play the role of upstanding pillar of the community once more.

Coupland nodded, sent Ashcroft a look that said *Let*

him have his moment.

'It's been such a terrible time, one we're all keen to move on from,' said his wife, Sally, taking her place beside him on the sofa, placing a reassuring hand on his knee. 'Yet it's so very typical of Patrick to put the needs of others first if it means he can be of service.'

'Very commendable,' Coupland said, the look he sent Ashcroft signalling that he play along.

Ashcroft bobbed his head up and down, humming in agreement.

'It's the least I can do,' Jameson said, turning to face his wife before covering her hand with his own. 'Then we can put this whole sorry business behind us.'

'He's only on this damn register because it's procedure,' Sally chimed.

Coupland nodded once more, albeit slower this time.

'It was the same with his sentence. We'd expected a community order but the judge had no choice.'

'It must have been a shock,' Ashcroft said, relaxing into his role.

Coupland gestured to furniture dotted about the room that looked as though it had been handed down several generations. Certainly not something you'd get in your local DFS anyway. 'Must have been very hard to go from all this,' he said, sweeping his arms wide, 'to shitting in a bucket.'

Patrick blinked. 'It's been very difficult for me to talk about,' he said. His thoughts didn't seem to stretch to how difficult it was for his family to deal with. Or his victims to endure.

'Our son hasn't spoken to us since… it all came out,' added Sally. 'If I want to see our grandchildren I must visit them alone.'

Coupland saw it then, the first chink in her armour, but in the blink of an eye it was gone. They'd both read the file that DS Round had sent over, but Coupland asked the question anyway, wanted to make the bastard squirm. 'Tell us why you were sent to prison, Patrick.'

A sigh. 'I find it hard to say out loud what I've done.'

'Take as long as you need.' Coupland mustered a smile. 'We're not going anywhere.' He didn't care if it came out as a threat; the man was living in his own little bubble, and not the kind that Boris Johnson kept banging on about. The psychological contortions men like Jameson employed to play down the severity of their crimes was beyond belief.

Sally took his cup and saucer from him and returned it to the tray with her own. She excused herself before carrying the tea things from the room.

'I take it that's your cue to speak freely,' Coupland said.

'None of this has been easy on her,' Jameson admitted.

It was the first thing he'd said that Coupland could accept. 'We're waiting,' he prompted, showing his teeth.

'I used the internet,' Jameson said. 'To look at pictures of children.'

Coupland baulked at his use of 'pictures', as though he'd been perusing holiday snaps or family photos taken around the Christmas tree. Layer on layer of minimisation, distancing himself from the abusive acts he'd undertaken. 'At first I was taken in by the imagery of it.'

'Imagery?' Coupland repeated.

The man smiled awkwardly, looked at his hands before answering. 'Many of them were smiling in the photographs. I thought they were enjoying it.'

Coupland leaned in close. 'Are you for real? Did it not occur to you that they were being threatened in some way, or had been drugged?' Did he really think they were models who at the end of the session would get to keep the clothes they were wearing and be given a lift home?

'And when you finished looking?' Ashcroft prompted.

'I downloaded some of the images onto my PC.' There'd been a video of a toddler stored on his hard drive. 'I shared some images with people I'd met in chat rooms, that's all.'

'Nice,' Coupland said.

Jameson seemed to take umbrage. 'Hardly distributing explicit material in the real sense of the word!'

His lack of victim empathy alarmed Coupland but someone on the MAPPA panel had seen fit to sanction his release. 'If you say so.'

'My lawyer told me that all kinds of upstanding members of society commit these crimes, accountants, solicitors, high court judges. It's not as if I'm like those paedophiles you read about in the tabloids. It's not like I'm the one doing the touching.'

Coupland turned to Ashcroft. 'Jesus, it comes to something when perverts start to distinguish themselves from their cloth cap comrades.'

Jameson's responses might have come from behind a glaze of arrogance but he had a point. His middle class neighbours might shun him but he wouldn't arrive home one day to find 'Paedo' sprayed across his front door.

'Tell me about the chat rooms then,' prompted Coupland.

'It's where you can go to let off a bit of steam. Talk to people with similar interests, you know the sort of thing.'

Coupland doubted he meant gardening and car maintenance, but hey ho.

'I used to go on to find out about new sites, or new…'

'Go on, say it,' Coupland prompted, his tone a damn sight less amenable than it had been before.

A sigh. 'Young girls. Someone in the chat room started talking about "passmen", saying that they'd log into the chat room and see what people were looking for.'

'Like market research?' Coupland asked. 'Only instead of asking whether you preferred Labour or Lib Dems it was schoolgirl or babysitter?'

Jameson dropped his gaze. Studied his hands once more. Probably knew every vein and wrinkle, Coupland didn't wonder. A slow nod. 'Something like that…' he whispered. 'I didn't take it seriously at first. I mean, it's all make believe on these sites. No one's who they say they are. Why should anything they say they can do be true either?'

Coupland's mouth turned down at the edges as he shrugged. 'Did these *passmen* ever join in the conversation?'

'No. But every once in a while something would happen. Someone might say, for example, there were too many Asian girls, then next time you logged in there'd be a banner advertising a Brighton Babe or a Manchester Minx. It was a bit like when you're looking for a lawnmower online then for days afterwards you're bombarded with loads of adverts because the advertisers track your cookies? Well, it was a bit like that.'

'And you've no idea who these passmen are or where they're from?'

'Of course not! What the hell do you think I am?'

Rather than answer and risk another complaint being

lodged against him Coupland excused himself, blaming a dodgy prostrate. He left the room but instead of following Jameson's directions to the downstairs toilet he headed towards the kitchen.

Sally was stood by the back door, her hands encased in a pair of marigolds as she smoked a cigarette. She jumped at the sound of Coupland approaching. 'He doesn't like me smoking,' she said, ignoring the look that flashed across Coupland's face.

'Everyone has a vice,' he said, accepting the cigarette she offered. He lit it, drawing up the smoke before exhaling through his nose. 'Though for most of us it's low level. A sneaky takeaway when you're supposed to be on a diet. No real cause for concern. Your old fella though, he's taken guilty pleasures to a whole new level.'

'He couldn't help himself.' Her words were hesitant. A woman unused to making herself heard. 'After a while they become addicted.'

'Kept telling you that, did he?' Coupland asked. 'I can't help wondering when they trot out that line… I mean, how many times does it take to "become" addicted? Two goes, three? Do they have to log on twenty times before they realise they've got a problem? Or is it thirty before they've worked out they're a sick f—' Coupland stopped. It wasn't her fault she'd vowed to love a nonce in sickness and in health. Even so. 'Didn't it worry you? About how much time he spent on his computer, I mean.'

Her neck flushed pink. 'Not really. I suppose there were moments, when I look back over that time now, but there was no reason for me to question what he was doing.'

'Weren't you ever curious? About what he must have

been looking it?'

'If you think I had any idea—'

'That's not what I'm saying. Just thinking aloud. You know, idle curiosity.'

She let out a lungful of smoke. Coupland took the opportunity to do the same. 'I suppose there were times when he left the room and I'd wander over…'

'And?'

A pause, while she put her thoughts in order. The result of being married to a man with an answer for everything, Coupland supposed. 'He'd locked the screen and I don't know any of his passwords.'

'Did he ever leave his computer on when he went out?' She shook her head. 'Didn't he trust you?'

'He said it was a habit from work he couldn't shake off.'

Coupland barked out a laugh. 'I bet he did.'

She crushed the cigarette, waited for Coupland to do the same, placed the stubs beneath a potted rose. Snapping off the rubber gloves, she returned them to the cupboard under the sink. 'You think I'm a fool, don't you?'

Coupland scarcely missed a beat. 'Yes, love, I do. He might be the one fresh out of jail but you're the one living a sentence. You might see your grandkids every now and again but while you live here they'll never get to stay over. Never play hide and seek in the upstairs bedrooms or go on a treasure hunt in the garden. Seems to me you're willing to give up a lot of things for a man whose convinced himself he's done nothing wrong.'

Ashcroft appeared in the doorway. 'Reckon we've outstayed our welcome.'

'The feeling's mutual,' said Coupland. 'You take care

now, Mrs Jameson,' he said, meaning it. He followed Ashcroft into the hallway. 'And think on.'

*

CID room

Coupland was at his desk when the call came in. He'd been working his way through his emails: lab reports he'd chased up confirmed the same plastic had been used to wrap both girls in. There were no distinguishing characteristics. It was the type that came off a roll – the kind found in any common or garden DIY store. The fibre comparisons from both bodies drew a blank, suggesting the girls weren't killed in the same location. Shoulders hunched, he added this information to the report he was typing up for DCI Mallender, which included his meeting with Pauline Boydell at the Public Protection Unit and his subsequent visit to the Jamesons.

Ashcroft was on his computer checking through the limited house to house enquiries conducted following Keri Swain's murder. His reading punctuated every once in a while by a sigh or a four letter word. The rest of the team were away from their desks following up actions on both investigations, knocking on more doors, asking more questions. Most days felt grim once an investigation got under way. Either frustration set in because you weren't progressing fast enough, or the more you delved into someone's murder the darker the world around you became.

Neither was aware how dark their world was to become.

Call it a sixth sense but Coupland knew instinctively

when his mobile rang what the call would be about. He pulled it from his pocket, already signalling to Ashcroft to get ready to leave. He barked his name into the receiver.

It was Pauline Boydell. *'I'm sorry,'* she said, *'but there are images of both your girls on the site.'*

'We're on our way,' said Coupland, getting to his feet as Ashcroft followed suit. They were already in the corridor, Ashcroft holding up his car keys signalling he wanted to drive.

Coupland nodded, distracted. It had gone quiet on the other end of the line, other than a sharp intake of breath. DS Boydell's tone was low, but firm. *'Our equipment is state of the art, DS Coupland. The digital recognition software has rated the likeness of Keri and Carly at 100 per cent. I've already verified it. You don't need to come in.'*

Coupland didn't break his pace until he was out in the car park, waiting while Ashcroft located his car. He put the phone onto loud speaker.

A sound of static, as though Boydell was also on the move. *'I mean it. The site's seriously fucked up. Don't expose yourself to it if you don't have to.'*

Ashcroft unlocked the car with a bleep. Both men climbed into it, secured the seatbelts across their laps.

In the silence Coupland looked across at Ashcroft. 'You sure you want to do this?' he asked. Ashcroft nodded. Coupland remembered something Patrick Jameson had said. About going online to meet others with similar interests. Men who logged in and watched what happened to Keri and Carly as a form of *entertainment*. 'We're coming in,' he said to Pauline, gritting his teeth in readiness.

CHAPTER TWELVE

It stood to reason a shit day was going to get much worse.

The darkness Coupland had been expecting, had finally hunted down, was far murkier than even he had anticipated. The job was unpredictable, he knew that much. Took him to places he didn't want to go to, exposing him to situations that were impossible to forget. He'd had the audacity to think that after all his years on the force that he'd seen it all. That there was nothing left to shock him, to render him utterly bloody speechless. He realised now he'd been having a laugh.

When they'd arrived at the PPU, DS Boydell showed them into a small office with nothing in it other than a computer and several sets of headphones on a table in the centre of the room. After closing the door, she joined them at the table. 'We found Keri and Carly on a site called Utopia,' she said, dropping into a chair. 'It specialises in adolescent and preadolescent girls. It's been running for a couple of years.'

She raised a hand to quell the questions she sensed were coming. 'Every time our officers manage to close it down it rises like a phoenix, even more impenetrable than before, and we have to go on the hunt for it all over again. It's like virtual cat and bloody mouse.'

While Coupland, then Ashcroft, took a seat either side of her, she logged into the site using a fake ID. 'Maybe it's easier if I print out screen shots?' she'd offered. 'There's no need for you to see all of it.'

'Just play them,' Coupland had grunted. 'Sooner we crack on the better.'

Without uttering another word Boydell pressed play on two sickening videos in a library of depravity. Within minutes Coupland's certainty that he was right to be there wavered. A sideways glance at Ashcroft told him he was thinking the same thing. Only seconds in and Coupland's mouth filled with something sour tasting.

Swallowing it down, he sank back in his seat, forcing himself to watch. What he saw on that screen drove into his stomach like a fist. The sounds jarred him too. Crying. Grunting. The cameraman's heavy breathing. When the videos had ended DS Boydell had stood back, keen to put a distance between her and the computer screen. At least she had the grace not to say I told you so.

There'd been other names on the home screen. A list of names with video clip icons beside them: Stacey. Jackie. Sam. Chris. Jenna. Coupland stopped reading. Whether there were ten names or a hundred, he couldn't bear to see them. What they represented, *meant*, to loved ones. He massaged his eye sockets with his finger and thumb.

He hesitated before looking at Ashcroft in case the look he gave him was an accusing one, blaming him for making him endure it. Coupland was after all, the more experienced of the two.

Ashcroft pushed back from the desk and got to his feet. There were creases round his eyes that hadn't been there earlier. 'I'll go and wait in the car,' he said, before leaving the room.

'I'm sorry your victims ended up here,' said Boydell. 'I

can't think of a worse ending to a life. To know someone doing this to you cared so little.'

Coupland cleared his throat. He tried to stand but he felt off balance; his legs seemed unwilling to play ball. He held onto the desk for support.

'It's the shock that does that,' Boydell commented. 'Let me give you a minute,' she said, making her way towards the door. 'I'm down the hall if you need me.'

Coupland waited for the door to close. He waited until he couldn't hear any footsteps in the corridor beyond. He placed his hands on the top of his head. They felt cold. He screwed his eyes shut, breathing in and out slowly until his heart rate returned to normal. Eyes open, he dropped his hands to his sides. Clenched his fists. He wanted to punch something. To reach into that computer and drag out the men that inhabited that world. Make them experience the pain and suffering inflicted for their entertainment. He no longer felt sick, unless feeling sick to your stomach with rage counted. He moved across the room. The unsteadiness in his legs had gone. He wanted to run, kick and stamp, put the adrenaline coursing round his body to good use. He wanted to go back to Patrick Jameson's house, drag him and his deluded wife here, see if the sick fuck still thought he wasn't doing any harm.

'It's not as if I'm like those paedophiles you read about in the tabloids.'

'He couldn't help himself.'

'It's not like I'm the one doing the touching.'

Coupland's breath snagged in his throat. He rubbed the heel of his palms into his eyes, tried to erase images that would stay with him always.

It was quiet in Ashcroft's car. Both men aware of the

other's breathing. As though on automatic pilot, Ashcroft turned the key in the ignition, flicked on the indicator before pulling out into the road. Coupland's car was back at the station but he wasn't ready to go home. He needed to let off steam, decompress before anyone he cared about asked him how his day had been. He turned to Ashcroft. 'Fancy getting shitfaced?'

Ashcroft pretended to consider it. 'I know just the place.'

*

'Nice,' Coupland said, nodding his approval. He followed Ashcroft along a stripped wooden floored hallway lined with photos of European cities, into a modern kitchen. 'How long have you been here?' he asked, his gaze sweeping over the open plan kitchen with shiny worktops. Probably never used the cooker, Coupland consoled himself. Microwave meals for one, he shouldn't wonder, though not takeaways, given Ashcroft's athletic build.

''Bout a year,' Ashcroft answered. 'Thought it was about time I put down some roots.' He moved to the fridge, pulled out two beers which he opened before handing one to Coupland.

Coupland took a grateful swig, his gaze sweeping the room. A blackboard beside the fridge with a shopping list written in chalk: coconut milk and Kaffir lime leaves. A shelving unit contained jars of multi coloured pasta and spices stored alphabetically. Above it a collection of cookbooks from Hairy Bikers to Joe Wicks. 'Didn't have you down as a cook.'

'You make it sound like I'm in the Masons.'

It struck Coupland when Ashcroft laughed, that it was

a sight he didn't see often.

'I try to keep it healthy during the week but come weekend I'll make a big pot of curry and work my way through it.'

Coupland had to stop himself from drooling. 'My idea of heaven that, though Lynn's not so keen. She was a Korma girl when I met her, she'll just about tolerate a Bhuna if there's a shedload of raita within arm's reach.'

'It doesn't have to be hot to be flavoursome. I'm trying Indonesian at the moment. I could give you some recipes…'

Coupland narrowed his eyes. 'Are you taping this conversation?'

Ashcroft laughed once more. 'If you change your mind…'

The last time Coupland had worked closely with Ashcroft was during Alex Moreton's maternity leave. He hadn't been sure what to make of him back then. Wasn't sure he had the staying power for what must have seemed like a parochial station compared to what he'd been used to at the Met. He'd stepped into Alex Moreton's shoes with ease, though Coupland would never dare tell her as much. He realised now that he'd made no effort to get to know him beyond casual enquiries about his weekend. He'd got a lot on his own plate back then, but even so. Ashcroft's ex still worked for the Met, if he remembered it right. It occurred to him then that other than a liking for the gym he knew little about him.

His flat was smarter than Coupland expected, going by his own limited experience of living on his own. Then again, the hours they put in, not like they were inundated with free time to turn anywhere into a pigsty.

They moved into the living area, two grey leather sofas facing a chrome coffee table. A book the size of a doorstop in the centre.

'So you're a boxing fan?' Coupland said, sliding the book towards him, locking eyes with a close up head shot of Muhammed Ali.

'Not especially. My dad is though. Thought if I started reading up on his hero we might have a bit more to talk about.'

'Let me know how that goes,' said Coupland, acutely aware that if his old man had any interests beyond smoking and putting a bet on he didn't know about them. He wondered what Amy would say about *him*, if pushed. *He moans all the time and is crap at DIY.* He resolved to make more of an effort with Tonto. Kick a ball about. Buy them a season ticket to the football. Drink Bovril at half time. He wondered whether that was still a thing, or whether the stands at the ground only sold lattes and frappuchinos these days.

An iPhone docking station sat on a console table by the window. Compact speakers either side of it. Coupland nodded in its direction, furrowing his brow. 'How do you play your CDs?'

Ashcroft tried to suppress a grin. 'I don't have any. All my playlists are on Spotify.'

He might as well have said grandad at the end of the sentence. Coupland's mouth turned down. Amy had made them go digital a few years back. Lynn had packed up his music collection into a plastic box, the opening times of the local charity shops written on a post-it note stuck onto the lid. The box was still in the boot of his car, lurching from one side to the other whenever he took a sharp corner. Every so often he would swap the contents of his CD changer with The Stone Roses and Oasis, taking the longer route home so he could enjoy his guilty secret in peace.

'Suppose you save everything onto the Cloud as well,' Coupland observed, sounding mystified, having never fathomed out the point of it.

'Only family photos,' Ashcroft answered. 'I mean, I love my sister but I don't want photos of her kids cluttering up the place.'

Coupland hummed his agreement but reckoned that's where the age difference between them really showed itself. That or his years in the job. The appreciation of life. The kids they came into contact with in their line of work were rarely smiling or happy or even alive. To capture them on camera doing what they do best – being children – was a blessing.

Coupland took another swig of his beer. Moved over to the window. The shit summer they'd had was long gone. Grey days followed by 4pm black skies were already the norm. He wondered if they'd get a holiday next year. One that didn't involve packing face masks and hand sanitizer. He wondered what Tonto would make of the sea.

'I couldn't do what Boydell does,' he said, staring at the bleak sky. He wondered what Ashcroft's view was like in the daytime. Other than road works and crawling traffic. He swallowed. Sensed Ashcroft was waiting for him to bring up what was on both their minds. He hadn't been sure, on the way over, if they were going to discuss it. Not sure he'd wanted to, if he was being honest. But now, with a drink inside him, there was something he needed to say, to lessen the weight that was starting to press down on him. 'Watching that stuff day in, day out.'

'Makes me sick just thinking about it.' Ashcroft lifted the bottle to his lips. Took a swig. 'I wanted to rip my eyes out. Thought I was going to throw up right there and then.'

'That why you left?'

'Had to. Couldn't trust myself to speak.'

'Back there,' Coupland said, not looking at Ashcroft, not looking at anything anymore, if the truth be told.

'Watching that footage?'

Coupland grunted a yes. 'It didn't seem right.'

'A bit too voyeuristic you mean?'

Ashcroft had hit the nail on the head. 'Yeah, that's it.' Coupland paused as he tried it out for size. Nothing but a fag paper's width to separate *them* from the twisted fucks who tuned in regularly. 'Wasn't that the point of it though? To see what they see?'

'I don't know. I feel like I'm no better that the sickos that tune in and pay a fee.'

'Grubby you mean?'

'Yeah. Like I've been contaminated, only no amount of handwashing's going to get rid of the stink of it.'

Coupland remembered something DS Boydell told him when she stepped back into the viewing room. 'It's all about the Dopamine apparently,' he said.

Ashcroft looked at him.

'Your brain releases it when it associates a certain activity with pleasure. I looked it up. Some people get a dopamine "rush" when they go shopping, others when eating their favourite food or snorting their drug of choice. Some people enjoy that rush so much they want to do it again and again to the point where the periods in-between lower their mood.'

'You see that with addicts all the time,' said Ashcroft.

'This is exactly the same. When junkies develop a tolerance to a substance they crave more of it, or in the case of these perverts the images they seek need to be more and more debased.'

It was clear Ashcroft had had enough. 'What do you reckon about the "Passmen" Jameson talked about?'

Coupland turned to see Ashcroft returning from the fridge carrying two more bottles. He'd already texted Lynn to tell her he was going to be late. She'd offered to pick him up, hadn't put up any resistance when he said he'd get a taxi. '*And I already know you love me,*' she'd added, '*You don't need to announce it at two in the morning when you fall into bed.*'

Coupland suppressed a smile, swapping his empty bottle with a new one, taking a slug from it before wiping his mouth with the back of his hand. 'Not sure I believed him at first, but then he's got no reason to lie.' In jail passmen were the inmates who earned special privileges. They bagged the cushy pantry jobs but could also be responsible for cleaning. Either way they got paid the best rates. Had the ear of the prison warders too. They were the eyes and ears of the jail and if you got on the wrong side of them they could make your life a misery. It was possible that on a sex offenders' wing, or the VPU – Vulnerable Prisoners' Unit, to give it its proper name – passmen could find themselves in an advantageous position, mixing with the big players, establishing networks of their own.

'What's in it for them?' Ashcroft asked.

'Apart from the obvious? Securing work on the

outside. Getting paid to feed their perversions would be pretty high on that job description, I would imagine,' replied Coupland.

Ashcroft didn't look convinced.

'Someone must be making it worth their while to do all the fetching and carrying.'

'You make it sound like they're picking up dry cleaning rather than snatching kids off the street.'

'A job's a job.'

Coupland shoved his hands into his pockets. Try as he might he couldn't rid himself of the on-screen images of Keri and Carly in their final moments. The older he got the harder he found it to believe that the law had all the answers. Especially when those answers were a lot less satisfying than taking matters into his own hands. Doling out punishments he felt each crime deserved. He blew out his cheeks. 'Contact the local prisons, find out the names of passmen that have been released in the last 12 months.'

Ashcroft moved over to the blackboard in the kitchen. Wrote down the task. He caught Coupland's eye as he turned, 'What?' he asked defensively. 'You sure *you're* going to remember everything come tomorrow?'

Coupland hoped to Christ he didn't. He swilled his mouth with the dregs, wondering if Ashcroft had a decent takeaway on speed dial.

MONDAY/DAY 9

CHAPTER THIRTEEN

Coupland had been at his desk since the crack of dawn. A weekend off had refreshed him, reminded him of the reason he got up every morning. A rare family meal out at a restaurant they trusted, followed by a walk along the canal. Tonto straining to be let out of his buggy. 'Not like he can get far,' Coupland had argued when he'd undone the pushchair's clasp. He was crawling now and into everything. Coupland had fixed gates to the top and bottom of the stairs and locks on all the kitchen base units apart from the one with the pans in because letting toddlers make noise was good for them, apparently. Tonto chunnered his thanks as his grandad plonked him on the grass beside the war memorial.

'Did you check for dog poo Dad?'

'No Ames, the sooner he learns life's full of shit the better…'

'Don't swear in front of him, Kev!' chided Lynn.

Coupland looked at his grandson and rolled his eyes. 'Ah, you'll get used to it,' he said, stepping away from Tonto backwards, clapping his hands to keep his attention. 'They worry too much, though they mean well, but if it's fun you're after then I'm your go-to guy.' He spread his arms wide and squatted down, rolling his tongue around his mouth like a New Zealand All Black chanting the Haka.

'OMG Dad, LOOK!' Amy had squealed. Tonto

pushing himself to his feet, spreading his arms out for balance, moving bandy leg style towards Coupland. He couldn't explain the fluttering in his chest. Hoped it was a good sign. That he wasn't about to drop down dead and rob them of this happy moment. Three more steps and the boy was in his arms. He lifted him up and instead of doing aeroplane noises as he swung him round he held onto him tightly, just for the sake of it.

The rest of the weekend involved a further trip to B&Q, for corner protectors this time once a full blown risk assessment of the downstairs rooms had been carried out.

'Sarge?' Krispy had passed by Coupland's desk three times in as many minutes. He now hovered beside his chair looking miserable.

'What's up?' Coupland asked, distracted by a commotion at the door as DI Little and his cohort swaggered in laughing and joking and worse still a full hour before the briefing was due to begin. As far as Coupland was concerned, arriving too early was as unforgiveable as arriving late. They proceeded to set up camp at the front of the office even though the chairs hadn't been moved yet.

'Go and show 'em where the canteen is while I nip and tell the boss they're here,' he said getting to his feet, 'buggered if I'm going to babysit them for an hour till the briefing starts.'

'But Sarge—'

'I'll be back in a minute.' Fifteen if he could stretch it out to include a medicinal smoke. 'When Ashcroft gets in tell him he's holding the fort.'

'Yes Sarge.'

Mallender wasn't best pleased that the City Road station crew were already in situ but he tried not to show it. He'd clocked Coupland's glum face when he appeared in his office doorway and had made the mistake of asking if there was a problem. 'Can you make more of an effort to get along? It's easy to fall into a comfort silo when you work with the same faces day in day out.'

'You've been watching those staff development programmes HR keep sending round again haven't you, boss?' he said, slumping into the chair opposite, his face brightening now he had Mallender's ear. 'I know it can be good to collaborate with others but I don't like them. They're either lazy or inept, I haven't decided which.'

Mallender turned his attention from the emails on his screen to the detective in front of him. Coupland wasn't the Super's cup of tea, or many people in authority's preferred choice of blend, for that matter, but there wasn't a single front line officer, uniformed or plain clothes, who didn't respect him. He had a tendency to be suspicious of career cops, and an open dislike for the overly ambitious, which had been known to cloud his judgement. 'Are you satisfied with the effort they've put in on the actions you gave them?'

Coupland's cheeks coloured. 'I haven't passed on much to them. I'm not convinced it'll get done properly.'

'Maybe they'll raise their game to prove you wrong.'

The boss had a point. Some folk were like chameleons. Imitating the behaviour of the people they worked with. Next to an arsehole they'd be an arsehole. Next to someone who gave a damn they'd try and raise their game. Coupland doubted it as far as DS Clarke was concerned but he'd run out of steam. Besides, the investigation had grown from one murder victim to two. He had no choice but divvy the tasks up more evenly before each member of his own team became just the teensiest bit hacked off that they were doing the work of two people. 'You've got a point there, boss,' Coupland agreed, rising from his chair. His compliant manner causing Mallender to stare at the seat he'd vacated long after he'd left the room.

*

Joint briefing, Salford Precinct station
In the end Mallender agreed to start the briefing early. He let DI Little speak first as a courtesy, using his phone to catch up on the emails and messages he normally attended to in his office first thing. Coupland gave the DI his full attention. Convinced he was slipshod he was determined not to let corners be cut on his watch.

'The education department has agreed to circulate a bulletin around all schools warning female pupils to be on their guard. It recommends not travelling alone and not to take lifts from anyone unless previously arranged. A letter is going out to parents of all high school pupils this afternoon. The duty social work team and community healthcare trust are going to contact relevant youth groups. We've drafted a series of social media posts that have been approved by the press office, and have asked the youth agencies to re-post them to their followers as a matter of urgency.'

Try as he might Coupland couldn't find fault with it so he nodded grudgingly.

Ashcroft's report was grim. He spoke about their visit to the PPU and the Utopia site where videos of Keri and Carly had been found. He kept his voice neutral, his attention focussed on the note pad in front of him. He described what they'd seen, how the video images had been pixelated to obscure the identity of the men in each clip. 'DS Boydell explained that the men in each video have paid big bucks for the "privilege" of being the one on screen. It's likely that the person who abducted the girls is the gofer – bringing the girls in and disposing of them afterwards. Their "reward" is the opportunity to abuse them too – but not to kill.'

'So who's doing the killing?' asked DI Little.

Ashcroft's shoulders sank. 'It's definitely the guy on screen, he's paying big money for this, remember.' He exchanged a look with Coupland. 'I guess we need to tell you how both videos end…' he said, trying but failing, to hide the catch in his voice.

Krispy's report was next. Savannah Glover went missing from a local authority children's home 12 months ago. There had been no sightings of her since her disappearance. 'The case was treated as MISPER because she'd run away once before, although she'd returned voluntarily on that occasion.'

Krispy had circulated a social work report on her. Coupland skim read through it: Savannah's case worker referenced her propensity to 'grant sexual favours.' She was 15. Care home staff complained about a 'boyfriend' and 'pimp' in his mid-20s visiting her and supplying drugs. The relationship was condoned by social services. Krispy attached interview notes with a social worker, but read out a summary stating that at no point had anyone attempted to find out the man's identity. In the meantime Savannah had been assigned a drugs worker and advised to smoke heroin rather than inject it.

'Jesus wept, was this the best we could do for her?' Coupland said, looking around the room, incredulous. 'Who was the MISPER team handling this?' he demanded.

Krispy's cheeks flooded. 'The case was handled by Central Manchester Division, Sarge.'

'Yeah but which station,' Coupland persisted.

Krispy looked as if he'd been struck dumb.

'Spare the lad his blushes,' drawled DI Little. 'What he's trying to say is it was dealt with by our MISPER team. It was referred to me to see if I thought there was any merit in treating the disappearances as suspicious, only I didn't.'

Coupland's brow knotted. 'Why didn't *we* pick up this shout?' he asked, turning to DCI Mallender when he saw that the children's home was close to Buile Hill Park.

'Control diverted calls out to other stations during the incident last year when that teacher ploughed a minibus into a group of schoolkids.' At the time it had initially been classified as a terrorist attack. 'We had our hands full, Kevin,' Mallender reminded him, matter of fact.

It was clear DI Little viewed someone of a lower rank questioning his decisions as insubordination. That he expected his word to be the final one. But this was Coupland's case, albeit DCI Mallender was the overall SIO, and if something didn't feel right he wasn't going to sit on his hands because some tosser didn't like getting his feathers ruffled.

As it was Mallender stepped up to the plate. 'What were the reasons that made you come to this conclusion?' His question was more considered, non-threatening, a lot more palatable than anything Coupland would have come up with.

In return, Little addressed his reply to Mallender, the only person in the room he didn't outrank. 'You know what it's like,' he sighed. 'The girl was troubled; everything about her was messed up. It's about priorities.'

'You mean who deserves our time more?' Coupland asked.

Little replied, his answer still directed at Mallender. 'At the end of the day, yeah, isn't that what it all boils down to?'

Mallender made a point of nodding, as though the DI spoke with the wisdom of King Solomon instead of a lazy chauvinist. Like his opinion had been given due consideration. Coupland admired how the boss did that whilst making it look sincere. Then, that only mattered if you gave a toss what others thought.

'On balance we need to look at this case again,' Mallender concluded, looking at Little as he said this. 'I want you and Clarke to work with Kevin and Chris on this. Given what they have learned about Utopia we need to find out if this girl has suffered the same fate as Keri and Carly. If that is the case,' he said this slowly as though emphasising the point, 'then we'll need to work back to when she was reported missing and establish a timeline.'

Little arced his body towards his cronies, muttered something out of earshot which Mallender chose to ignore, likely putting his truculence down to embarrassment, but Coupland wasn't so sure.

He stared at him until the man stared back. 'Any issues with what the DCI has just said?' he asked, continuing to hold his gaze.

'Absolutely none,' Little responded, when he realised Coupland wasn't going to let it go.

'Then that's dandy,' replied Coupland, stretching the corners of his mouth into a smile. He turned to Krispy. 'Have you managed to get a recent photo of this girl?'

'Yes, Sarge.'

'Let me have it and I'll send it on to DS Boydell.' He told them about the facial recognition software her unit used to identify victims whose images had been uploaded to the web. He studied the photo Krispy handed him. Too many hair extensions had left Savannah's hair wispy. She wore it scraped back into a bun on the top of her head. Large gold hoops hung from her ears. She looked like a typical teenager. Defensive. Vulnerable. And now very possibly dead.

Ashcroft had been on shift over the weekend. He'd compiled a list of passmen released from the Vulnerable Prisoners' Units at HMP Manchester and Wakefield over the last 12 months. He explained the significance to the rest of the team, describing his visit with Coupland to Patrick Jameson's home. How he'd told them about passmen who hung around the chat room he frequented before he went to jail. His claim that they were keeping Utopia stocked with victims. 'The job of passman tends to go to those serving longer sentences, so there weren't that many who matched our profile. Four came closest. Two have been contacted by officers from the Sex Offender's Management Unit, and their whereabouts for the dates our girls went missing have been confirmed. The other two moved away not long after their release but we're talking Lancaster and the West Midlands, both commutable distances, so I contacted the local force in each area. Both offenders registered with the relevant stations when they relocated. The offender in Lancaster's alibi checks out, but I've just taken a call from a DC in Sutton Coldfield. The other offender – a Maurice Kennedy – can't account for his whereabouts.' Something was troubling Ashcroft. 'Thing is, his DNA doesn't match, otherwise his name would have been flagged up when the semen taken from both victims was sent for testing.'

'It tells us he didn't rape them, though he could still be the guy doing the fetching and carrying,' reasoned Coupland.

'And murder?' asked a DC from the back of the room.

Coupland shook his head. 'Remember, they've been killed by someone prepared to pay a hefty premium for the privilege of doing it on camera.'

'Why risk going back to jail when you've only just got out? Whoever has done this is going to get serious time,' Ashcroft persisted.

'Unless they get away with it,' Coupland said. 'Prisons are full of people who think they're cleverer than they are.' Coupland understood Ashcroft's reluctance to get too excited about Kennedy until he'd been interviewed but his reticence that he would risk his parole was misplaced. It was more than just about money too; they'd already borne witness to that. Perversion. Addiction. Compulsion. A deadly combination. 'You heard what Pauline Boydell said. This is a lucrative business. Punters pay a premium to be the one carrying out the abuse. And remember, their identities are never shown on camera.'

'We're talking significant money, you reckon?'

'We're talking murder. It'd have to be. If that's someone's fetish, abusing their victim before snuffing them out on tape, then that's something they'd be willing to pay through the nose for, I'd have thought.'

Coupland looked over at Turnbull and Robinson. 'Fancy a road trip?'

Both detectives nodded eagerly as though two hours on the M6 was a treat. Turnbull made a note on his pad to download an expenses form before they set off.

'If this fella can't give a decent account of himself to you don't pussyfoot around,' warned Coupland. 'I want him brought back here so we can remind him of that Northern hospitality he's so obviously missing.'

Coupland updated the whiteboard while he waited for the stragglers to leave, biding his time by working out in his head the best way to broach what needed saying. When Little and Clarke had got to their feet at the end of the briefing Coupland had asked if they wouldn't mind waiting. He'd made a real effort not to make it sound menacing; even so, Little hadn't looked quite so cocksure.

Ashcroft, having updated the day's action log, pulled his chair across to sit with them. Coupland dragged a plastic chair from a stack at the back of the room and moved beside him. He turned it so the back of the chair was between his legs as he sat astride it, his arms leaning on the back rest.

'There's always that moment,' he began, his voice low enough and steady enough to show he was being reasonable, that he could be reasonable when push came to shove. 'That point following an abduction, where the "golden hour" has tick-tocked itself away and you know that what you are looking for now isn't a person but a body. I've always wondered if it's like that too, for the victim. You know… now humour me here… imagine for a minute you're in a locked car boot. You're bound to think "Well, so and so'll miss me, they'll raise the alarm,

234

keep looking for me till I'm found." But what if it isn't like that at all? That girls like this…' He held up the social work reports on Savannah and Keri. 'They already know that no one gives a toss. That it's pointless putting up a fight because there's no one to come riding in on a white charger and save them. Imagine that being your last thought?'

DS Clarke looked uncomfortable, like he was trying to pass wind without making a sound. His DI stared at Coupland. 'Getting a bit ahead of yourself, mate. We don't know there's any connection as yet between Savannah and the existing investigation.'

Coupland jerked his head in a nod. 'Yeah, you're right. I mean, there's no reason to be concerned about a missing fifteen-year-old that no one has heard from in the best part of a year, is there, *mate*? Got kids yourself?' A grunt. 'Right, next time one of 'em is late home, just tell your missus, "If they're not home in the next 12 months they're grounded." See how that works.'

'I'm divorced.'

'Why doesn't that surprise me?' Coupland muttered, turning to Ashcroft as though saying 'over to you.'

'We need to pay the children's home a visit. Speak to the staff originally interviewed.'

Little's face was a picture. 'You want four detectives to rock up at their door, mob handed?'

Ashcroft refused to be browbeaten. 'If it makes up for the inactivity over the last year, then yes.'

'That's sorted then,' Coupland said, rubbing his hands together triumphantly. Despite his bravado, he felt as though the investigation was slipping away from him. More victims coming out of the woodwork yet still no real person of interest. He and the rest of the enquiry team needed something positive, a lead towards someone they could begin to lean *on*.

*

Sandilands Children's Home was midway along a leafy residential street of private homes overlooking Salford Royal Hospital. Built in the 1930s, there was little to set it apart from the houses that flanked it other than the number and age of cars on its driveway. Five-year-old hatchbacks with a nearly new saloon. Staff, Coupland assumed, given the children sent there were moved on once they turned 16. The neighbouring house had a four wheel drive Mercedes parked in front of it, a new one at that. A low wall divided both properties. The owners weren't too snippy about the residents next door then, Coupland observed.

'Seems to me we're going about this heavy handed,' Little griped as they approached the home's entrance. 'Or are you just trying to make a point? I can see that we should have acted differently. I'm not sure how rubbing our noses in it will help.'

Coupland rounded on him. 'Keri's mother told me she'd claimed all along that she hadn't run away.'

'She's bound to say that, though isn't she? Especially in hindsight. Can't give too much credence to it though, I mean, she probably didn't even know what day of the week it was, at the time.'

'Do you need to know what day of the week it is to know someone hasn't come home?'

Their voices trailed away once Ashcroft rang the buzzer. Coupland forced his features into a smile. The public needed to think they worked in unison. The force, after all, liked to portray itself as a family. But didn't most families bicker?

*

The plaque on the door said: Stephen Bryant, followed by a stream of letters after his name that denoted he was an expert in something. Along one wall shelves stood thick with books on child psychology. On another, an array of photos: youngsters who had passed through the home's front doors, Coupland assumed. On another wall, a photo of Stephen himself in cap and gown, holding an academic scroll.

Coupland had called ahead to explain the purpose of their visit: that Savannah Glover was no longer considered missing, but a potential victim in an ongoing murder investigation. He'd arranged for Ashcroft and DS Clarke to interview the staff who'd been on duty when Savannah had been reported missing. Coupland and Little were to question Bryant, Sandiland's Manager.

'That *poor* girl.' Bryant shook his head as he eased himself into the chair behind his desk, indicating that both detectives take the seats opposite. '*Such potential.*'

'Yes,' agreed Coupland.

'*So much to live for.*'

He sounded, Coupland thought, as though he was rehearsing what he'd say to the press, once they came knocking. 'An unconscionable act.' A pause. 'Heart-breaking.' Coupland waited for the inevitable word. '*Tragic.*' If they were playing platitude bingo, Bryant had just scored a full house.

'You weren't on the premises when Savannah went

missing?' he asked.

Bryant blinked. Coupland hadn't intended it to sound like an accusation, but he could see from the manager's expression that it had. 'I can't be here all the time, detective sergeant.'

Coupland bowed his head as though accepting the rebuke. 'We understand that.' This time his tone was placating, reasonable. 'But there doesn't appear to have been any urgency to get in touch with the police at the time.'

'I reported it the moment I became aware.'

'So it's usual practice for staff not to report any cause for concern to you straight away?' Coupland pushed on, his mouth widening in a manner that only those who'd never crossed him would find comfort in. 'I get that in your job runaways are more commonplace but from what I understand Savannah was starting to settle in here. Surely when you heard she hadn't come home that should have rung alarm bells?' His voice, like a sub machine gun fired at full pelt, 'Given all that *potential* she had.'

'I resent your suggestion that I was lax in some way. Besides, the officers who took down Savannah's details didn't seem unduly worried.'

Coupland threw a look at Little before replying. 'Perhaps they were influenced by the way she'd been described.' Coupland referred to the report he'd read during that morning's briefing. The comments he'd consigned to memory: 'Her "propensity to grant sexual favours". The fact she had a pimp. A dealer.' Coupland sniffed. His dislike of the man was primitive, as though he gave off a scent that truly got up Coupland's nose.

'This isn't a young offenders' institution, they're not

kept under lock and key. They're allowed to go out when they choose and we can't vet their friends.'

Coupland stared back, wide-eyed. 'Should girls that age be friends with *men*?'

'How do we know who they consort with when they leave here?'

'Oh, I think you'd have had a damn good idea, unless you don't bother reading the reports from her social worker. And why would you use the word consort? Does that mean you disapproved, but still did nothing?'

DI Little, beside him, seemed to have been struck deaf and dumb.

'Anything you want to ask?' Coupland asked, clocking the startled look that flashed across his face.

'I think you've covered it all,' he drawled.

'Have we met before?' Bryant asked him, peering at his misshapen head. 'Your face seems familiar, although I'm certain the officers who responded when Savannah went missing were in uniform.'

Little cleared his throat. He slipped an index finger beneath his shirt collar and gave it a tug.

'DI Little is part of a murder squad like me,' Coupland explained. 'We usually get involved once a body has been found but evidence that has come to light leaves us in no doubt Savannah suffered a similar fate to the victims of a current case we're investigating.'

'What evidence?'

Coupland took a breath. Relayed the information Pauline Boydell, the DS from the PPU sent him by text not half an hour since. 'Savannah and two other girls have been found on a child abuse site that goes by the name of Utopia. Their abuse and murder were filmed and put online.'

Bryant slumped back in his chair. 'Dear God!' he exclaimed, his mouth opening and closing but nothing more came out.

Coupland's phone rang. When he slipped it from his pocket to glance at the screen Ashcroft's name flashed up. 'Excuse me,' Coupland said, before hitting reply.

'They won't speak to us.'

'What do you mean?' Coupland growled, already understanding the gist of it.

'They kept us waiting for fifteen minutes, then both came through at once to say they'd been advised not to speak to us without someone from the union being present.'

Coupland ended the call, exchanging a look with Little before deciding he'd gone toe to toe long enough. Sometimes you needed to take a swing. He levelled his beady eye at Bryant before continuing. 'What I don't understand is why, given how keen you are to help in any way, you've blocked my officers from interviewing your staff.'

Bryant reddened. 'Not blocked, exactly, I need to obtain guidance.'

'Do you?' Coupland asked, leaning in close. 'Really? You knew we were coming,' Coupland reminded him, 'it's why we didn't just drop in, which we'd have been entitled to do.'

'I also have the right not to speak to you without a union rep or the local authority solicitor present, but I wanted to be cooperative.'

Coupland coughed up a laugh. 'What's cooperative about making us come back?'

'I'm sorry,' Bryant said sounding anything but. 'I've

made my decision. I'd feel happier not saying anything further without consultation with the management team.'

'Suit yourself,' Coupland said, rising out of his chair.

Little got to his feet quickly, eager to be on his way.

Now they were leaving Bryant seemed keen to say his piece. 'I've already spoken to the head of Social Services.'

'No surprise there,' Coupland shrugged. In his experience arse covering began the moment condolences were trotted out.

'They're satisfied that every procedure was followed.'

Coupland stopped, swivelling on the spot like a champion ice skater, until they were face to face once more. 'Then those procedures need looking at, because one way or another, a girl in your care ended up dead.' Coupland held the man's gaze for longer than was necessary. Satisfied he'd made his point; he turned and left the room.

CHAPTER FOURTEEN

It was his smile that gave him away. There were no other clues to be found in his medium build or mousey hair that skimmed the neck of his sweatshirt and curled above his ears. His clothes were too young for a man approaching forty, his trainers a bit too 'street.' None of it enough to earn a second look, until you clocked his prison smile. Broken teeth poked out of inflamed gums, their enamel a dull grey. No amount of brushing would cure his halitosis, thought Turnbull, as he tried to reduce his in-breaths. Beside him, Robinson turned his head towards the kitchen window, willing someone to open it.

Oblivious, Maurice Kennedy sat across from them around his sister's cramped table, hands circling a can of Red Bull. He'd nodded while Turnbull had made the introductions, waiting until he'd finished before offering to make them tea, coffee, a cold drink perhaps? Pleasant enough, though some might consider it stalling, since he didn't join the detectives seated at the kitchen table until his sister let herself out of the flat, remonstrating with two small children to stop bickering as she did so.

'I see you served your time at Monster Mansion,' Robinson said, using the name by which HMP Wakefield was known due to the number of sex offenders detained there.

'Could've been worse,' Kennedy shrugged, though at the end of the day it was hard to be grateful. Prison was prison when all's said and done.

'You were a passman.'

Another shrug. 'What of it?'

'Can you tell us what that entails?'

'You drove down from Manchester to ask me that? Turn up to any jail in the country and some lag'll put you right.'

'Yeah, but that won't be *your* take on things, will it? And that's what we've come to find out.'

'There's nothing much to tell really. You're a glorified cleaner in many ways. You're expected to keep the landings and common areas clean. Yeah, it pays well – but we're not talking picking up manky socks and replacing the soap. You have a lot of time to kill when you're inside. Too much time and not enough imagination. Sometimes the other cons leave little presents lying around, and I don't mean the kind you find under your tree at Christmas. Other times they'll piss under their cell door just for the sake of it. When someone moves out of their pad we have to clean that too – unless they've topped themselves or someone's given them a seeing to. If that happens the screws bring in a special agency. For the blood and guts, you know. Infection risk apparently. For everything else,' he jerked his thumb towards his chest, 'it was down to me.'

'What's in it for you, though?'

Kennedy regarded Turnbull. 'Only someone who's never served time would ask that,' he chided. 'You get to spend longer out of your cell. 23 hours a day inhaling your padmate's farts is enough to send anyone doolally. Plus, the screws trust you more. They let you know in advance if something's going down, like if the cells are getting turned over or the sniffer dogs are being brought in. It means you can tip off the cons you want to keep on the right side of. Or pass the information on for a fee.'

'What do the other prisoners think of that?'

A shrug. 'When you're inside your world becomes small. Things you wouldn't normally give a toss about start to matter. Someone walking round a landing when all you've got to look forward to is three strides to the cell door and back if you're lucky. It gets up their nose that you're doing something that they're not, but like I said, the grass isn't always greener. Yeah, I had the screws' ears and money in my pocket. But if someone left a turd on the landing it was me who had to clean it up.'

So, passmen were glorified cleaners. Turnbull shared a look with Robinson. They'd worked together for so long they could second guess each other's thoughts and once more their opinion aligned. The DNA held on file for Kennedy since his previous conviction hadn't flagged up as positive when the lab ran tests on the DNA found on both victims, meaning he couldn't have raped them. However, as a passman on a sex offenders' wing, he was certainly equipped – in terms of skill set and lack of moral fibre, to 'clean up' after the girls' abusers and dispose of their bodies.

'How come you moved down here?' Robinson asked him.

'I needed a fresh start. I can't return to my mum's, it's a condition of my license. Besides, she keeps having her windows put through since my release. Feelings are still running high.'

'Bet she still lets you visit though?' Only a mother could look at a human stain like Kennedy and see a scuffed knee in short trousers. It was unlikely he'd want to lose that.

'Once or twice,' he said, studying the can in his hand.

'When was your last visit?'

'Not sure I can remember, to tell you the truth.'

'We could wait for your sister to come back, ask her when she last let you borrow her car.'

Kennedy placed his can on the table and sighed. 'Why do I feel like I need to speak to my brief before I say anything else?'

'I don't know, Maurice, why is that, I wonder?'

'Could you have paid your old dear a visit the first weekend in June?' Turnbull asked, referring to when Keri Swain was murdered. 'Or the back end of November last year,' when Savannah Glover went missing. 'Carly King was abducted and killed the weekend before last,' he added.

'Right. I'm not saying anything more without my lawyer being present.'

*

Nexus House

Inside the partitioned corner that Alex called her office her desk phone began to ring. Traversing the narrow room took no time at all; she picked up the receiver and spoke into it. She recognised the caller's name but it took a few seconds to put a face to it. Or the school she was associated with for that matter. Grove Academy. The high school that had been reluctant to take Bez back before Alex's intervention. The ambitious promise she'd made, making her unit take responsibility for every returning pupil's misdemeanour. She sighed. For her unit, read her. To give Olive Blair her due, she wasn't trying to score points. She sounded too tired for that. Like this was one of a long list of calls she'd have to make that morning causing nothing but disappointment so the sooner she could get on the better. The sooner Alex told her she was as good as her word, that Bez was her responsibility and hers alone, she'd leave her be.

Alex should have sensed things weren't going to go the way she'd hoped by Bez's response when she'd called into the café where she worked after her meeting with the cluster heads. She was a bright enough girl. Smart enough to get a set of decent grades if she applied herself, a set of average ones if she didn't. One thing was certain. She wouldn't get any if she failed to turn up. 'Not sure I see the point,' she'd said to Alex, matter of fact.

Alex recalled how affronted she'd been. 'Education is like a ladder, it can help you move out of the situation you're in.'

Bez hadn't looked certain. 'To what though? Another room with a trap door in it?'

For some reason Alex had taken her response personally, found it hard to bite back her irritation. She was passionate about this project – why weren't the recipients of it passionate too? 'I don't understand why you're being so negative,' she sighed, her response eliciting a look from Bez that bordered on pity. It was hard, when your life had always been a certain way, to see a different perspective.

'Maybe that's all I've got?' Bez replied.

Alex had felt the first trickle of impatience. Like when her sons played up when all she wanted to do was put her feet up and binge watch a box set on TV. Luckily they were at the age where she could pack them off to bed. 'Just give it a try,' she'd coaxed. 'One week. Look, I'll have a word with the owner here; see if she'll keep your placement open while you make up your mind.' She stole a glance at the sour faced woman behind the Perspex screen. Her work would be cut out for her but she was willing to give it a go.

Bez threw her a look. 'Like I want to wipe manky tables for nothing? That is so *not* an incentive.'

'So what is?'

In the end they'd agreed she'd go back to school part time. Three days per week starting Monday. Only Monday was here and the head teacher was using convoluted words to tell her how pissed off she was. Bez hadn't turned up. No phone call. No explanation. A teacher drafted in from the pupil referral unit kicking their heels outside the head's office. Alex heard Olive Blair's frustration. She felt it too.

PC Ward looked up while she shrugged into her jacket. She'd taken to calling him Gunner, which he didn't seem to mind. He'd moved up from the Midlands; his Black country accent made him drag out his words. 'I'm going to do this' sounded like 'I'm gunner do this,' and so the name had stuck. He flashed her a confident smile. He had good news. 'The DS from Pendleton station has confirmed they're dropping the charges against Laughing Boy. I'll ring him and put him out of his misery.'

Alex nodded her approval. 'Remind him that's all of his nine lives used up in one fell swoop. I don't want to find out he's set up a drug outlet via the garage repair network.'

'Bring a whole new meaning to the term pick up service if he did, Ma'am.'

Alex regarded him. I do believe Gunner's cracked his first joke, she thought. Perhaps the team was starting to gel after all.

Alex's optimism was short lived when she pulled up outside the address Shola had given her for Bez. The Birchwood estate was earmarked for redevelopment. Most of the tenants had been rehoused with only a handful of stragglers remaining, those who'd bought their properties under the council's right to buy scheme and were now in a stand-off following the paltry amount offered in the compulsory purchase order, stuck with dead-weights no one in their right mind would want to buy. According to Shola, Bez didn't have any brothers and her father was in his forties, so the driver of the car she was climbing out of didn't fall into any of those categories. White, mid-thirties, she reckoned, though through the car's windscreen it was hard to get a good look. A neatly trimmed beard made him look respectable but that didn't stop Alex from wondering who he was.

Using her phone to take a photo of the car's registration number as he drove off, she waited while Bez let herself into the pebble-dashed maisonette before calling her mobile. After a couple of rings a guarded voice answered. *'Hiya?'*

'Just thought I'd see how your first day back's going.' Alex chirped.

A pause. *'Yeah, fine. Not supposed to use our phones during the day though.'*

Alex frowned at the effortless lie. 'That rather depends where you are, doesn't it? I'm standing outside, Bez. Let me in,' Alex barked.

A curtain moved in a bedroom window overshadowed

by a huge satellite dish. Two minutes later, the front door opened. Bez looked different. Alex had only ever seen her in the black jeans and t-shirt of her café uniform. The colours had washed out of the top she had on. The fabric her leggings were made out of was way too thin. Worn loose, her hair hung about her like rats' tails.

'Have you taken anything?' Alex asked, peering at her pupils.

'Feel sorry for your kids when they're older,' Bez sneered.

'Stop it,' Alex snapped, regretting sharing personal information in an attempt to gain some common ground. During their last conversation she'd managed to coax out of her that she wanted to work in a nursery. Alex had told her she'd need to go back to school, but had promised to find a more suitable placement. All she had to do was keep to her side of the bargain. The words *lost* and *cause* came into her mind but she was determined not to throw the towel in yet. 'You were supposed to be going into school today. What happened?'

'I overslept.'

'Who else lives here?'

'My dad.'

'Where is he now?'

'Asleep. Don't wake him.'

Alex detected the alarm in her voice, a quick glance at the stairs behind her. 'Can I come in?'

Bez dropped her voice. 'Better if you don't.' She pulled the door to behind her and stepped onto the pavement in bare feet. 'I'm sorry, OK? I didn't realise what time it is. I'll go in now and grovel if you like.'

Alex's mind was elsewhere. 'Who was that I just saw

dropping you home?'

'A friend.'

'Bit old, isn't he?'

'Is there an age restriction on who you can be friends with? What is this? I'm late for school. I didn't break any laws, so I don't know why you're pecking my head.'

Alex waited in her car while Bez changed into her uniform, then drove her into school. Not just because she didn't trust her to go in by herself but so she could quiz her some more about the nameless man who'd dropped an underage girl home early enough for it to look like they'd spent the night together. Each question was met with silence no matter how casual she'd made it sound. 'Does this man give you a lot of lifts?', 'Does he offer you anything else?' OK, maybe the questions weren't so casual, Alex conceded, but she had to start somewhere. 'Look, I just want to know that you are OK,' she said, when even to her own ears it sounded like she was subjecting Bez to the Spanish Inquisition.

'For God's sake!' Bez snapped irritably. 'Why does it matter?'

'Because I can help you.'

Bez's laugh was the saddest thing Alex had heard in a long time. 'You're so interested in some random guy you see giving me a lift. If you must know, I asked him for some dope and he offered me a freebie if I hooked up with him. It's no big deal.'

'Is your dad aware of what's going on?'

'He wasn't there. I lied. He stayed over at some woman's he's seeing.'

Alex shook her head. She knew it made her look like some prissy headmistress but then wasn't that the role she'd taken on? 'What's going on, Bez? You seem to be breaking all your agreements in one go.'

'What do you care?'

'Because it's my job.'

'Maybe that's the problem,' Bez moaned. 'I only ever come into contact with people paid to care about me. Besides, you might come over all nice but most of your lot don't give a toss.'

'What do you mean?'

'You people have no idea what it's like.'

'Then tell me!'

Tell her what? Bez wondered as she regarded the detective. That she'd been in cars with older men that were stopped and searched by police and none of them questioned who she was or why she was in there. That a celebrity caught snorting coke is 'wild' but a local kid caught getting off their face is a junkie. Rich folk go to rehab and poor folk go to prison. Life wasn't fair. End of.

'Doesn't matter,' Bez sighed, pushing open the car door and stepping out.

*

Nexus House

Back in the office Alex ran the number plate of the car Bez had got a lift home in. Aiden Nichol. No previous convictions, yet she'd seen him dropping off an underage girl who was unwilling to divulge the reason. Perhaps Nichol would be more forthcoming, Alex reckoned, deciding to pay him a visit.

The woman who answered the door was more soft around the edges than plump. Long brown hair she took time styling framed a face that put her around the same age as Alex. She looked tired, but that was explained by the bundle of energy running headlong down the hallway towards his mother, wrapping chubby arms around her leg as he waited for the stranger to go. Mrs Nichol smiled at Alex pleasantly, the smile remaining in place even after being shown Alex's police ID. 'I'm afraid Aiden isn't here,' she said when Alex asked if her husband was in. 'I'm surprised you didn't go to his work first. He practically lives there as it is. Is this about the break-ins? I keep telling him he needs to bring in better security, why have a dog and bark yourself? He can't keep staying over just because the guards are useless.'

'I'm afraid I didn't take his work address down,' Alex told her, 'Perhaps you can…'

'Give me a minute,' the woman said, moving to a small table in the hallway, cajoling the boy to move in step with her. 'Here,' she said, holding a card out to Alex. 'Try him on the mobile first, save yourself a wasted journey.'

Alex thanked her before returning to her car. What was a grown man, a married one at that, doing driving round with a young girl when he'd a wife and son waiting at home? It was a question Alex could have asked Mrs Nichol if she'd wanted to set the cat amongst the pigeons, but there was no point ruining the woman's day just yet. Besides, there were connotations to this that she needed to be clear about.

Leaving the business card on the passenger seat beside her she turned on the ignition and headed back to Nexus House.

TUESDAY/DAY 10

CHAPTER FIFTEEN

Turnbull and Robinson were at their desks bright and early. Their interview notes typed up and emailed to Coupland, a paper copy waiting for him on his desk. They'd called him before putting Maurice Kennedy in the car, didn't want to be accused of being overzealous. Turnbull not quite understanding why Coupland had sniggered when he'd said that.

'What did you make of him?' Ashcroft asked. He'd been copied into the email, had read through Kennedy's responses to their questions, had already started making notes in preparation of drawing up an interview strategy.

'A shifty saddo. He couldn't account for his whereabouts on the dates our victims went missing. There's a good chance he was visiting his mother but we felt the hatches needed battening down a bit, especially since his sister drives a car similar to the one spotted close to where Carly was last seen.'

'Let's not get too carried away,' said Coupland. 'Witnesses said they saw a blue car, that's all.'

'Kennedy's sister's car is blue.'

Coupland said nothing. It needed checking out but he wasn't going to work himself up into a lather. They were a long way from finding any evidential material. Still, he didn't want to piss on their chips. 'Write him up on the board,' he instructed. 'He doesn't come off until we've filled in all the gaps.'

Coupland retrieved his mobile from his jacket pocket when it started to ring. The call wasn't expected and at first he wondered why he'd been contacted at all. He'd meant to programme Pauline Boydell's direct number into his mobile but hadn't got round to it. Not that it took him any time to place the name, and certainly no time at all to place the team she worked for.

'We've arrested a man who's been accessing Utopia. He's downloaded footage of your girls. Others too. My DI is interviewing him now. Thought you'd want to know.'

'Thanks.'

'I'm not saying he's any use to your investigation. Just wanted you to know we keep going after these bastards. Every one of your victims matter to us just as much as they matter to you.'

Coupland tried to unsee the images that Pauline saw every day. No wonder she permanently looked as though she'd seen a ghost.

'This job, you know, it makes me laugh.'

Coupland knew when people said that they meant the opposite. That in Pauline's job there'd be precious little to laugh about. Except the sentences handed out once each case made it to court.

'These men are adamant they're not abusing kids. This one's no different. "I'm not the one touching them. I'm merely looking at pictures, and not even actual pictures – just using the internet really; using the internet to look at pictures." Fucking pictures. Does he not see that it's men like him, that create the market for child abuse. Is it so difficult to understand?'

Coupland sensed she needed to vent.

'Three years. That's likely what he'll get. Many will claim that's reasonable for a cheap thrill online but it's so much more than that.'

'You're preaching to the converted, there,' said

Coupland.

'You know, the men you're after might be the ones that physically drugged those girls and abused them before throttling them to death. But that bastard in the interview room and every other pervert that logs onto that site had a hand in their deaths. If I had my way I'd throw away the key on the lot of them.'

There were a few more keys he wouldn't mind throwing away once the inhabitant of the cell had been locked up, Coupland thought. He wrote down Stephen Bryant's name, circling it over and over with his pen until it cut through the page. Dereliction of duty or neglect? He wasn't sure that it mattered.

'Ready?' Ashcroft asked, looking up from his desk when Coupland's call ended. He held up a clipboard containing typed up interview questions.

'Let the dog see the rabbit,' said Coupland.

*

Interview room 3, Salford Precinct station
They'd gone through the preliminaries. The tape was running and already Kennedy's solicitor looked on, bored. He'd caught Coupland's eye a couple of times and looked away, as though the shame of representing a paedophile was more than even he could bear.

'It's good of your sister to let you borrow her car whenever the mood takes you,' Ashcroft said.

'She lends it to me in exchange for keeping an eye on her kids when she's working.'

Coupland studied Kennedy's face but there was no humour in it. He was serious. 'Come back to see your mum often, do you?'

A shrug. 'I know I'm not supposed to, but you know how it is.'

Coupland didn't. He could only imagine, and even then he couldn't be sure how much of that image was wishful thinking. 'Weekly? Every fortnight?' he prompted.

'I'm not sure…'

'Monthly, then…'

'Not as often as that. Petrol doesn't grow on trees. Besides, the neighbours still watch her house. They're quick to post pictures of me on Facebook if they see me within a mile of the place.'

'And yet still you come.' Coupland looked down at the printout in front of him. 'Your sister's number plates showed up on ANPR cameras placing it at Lancaster Road and Bank Lane on six separate weekends over the last twelve months. I'd like to know more about three of those weekends starting with the weekend before last, especially since your mother claims she didn't see you.'

A nervous laugh. 'Of course I was there! She's covering for me. It's what mothers do.'

Coupland didn't need to take his word on that. The number of mothers who'd stared him down over the years, swearing Billy or Jonny or whatever their numpty was called wasn't at home, that they were home alone and shouldn't be harassed like that, while Billy or Jonny hot footed it through the back door and over the fence and straight into the arms of the uniform officers waiting for them.

'Let me speak to her, explain why she needs to tell you the truth,' Kennedy offered.

'Not sure it matters, to be honest,' Coupland said eventually. 'You could have turned up with a takeaway on the Friday night and stayed right through to Sunday lunch and you'd still have had time to abduct a young girl then dispose of her body.'

'Excuse me?' Kennedy's lawyer spoke next. 'I'm sure my client's car wasn't the only one recorded by ANPR cameras for the weekends in question. Will you be interviewing drivers of those cars or is this just a fishing trip?'

Coupland turned to him. A duty solicitor from a firm of 24 hour defence lawyers in Swinton, bad posture emphasised a lockdown belly. 'I bet that looked good on you once,' he said, inclining his head towards his straining suit.

The lawyer clicked his tongue. 'I'm guessing his DNA isn't a match otherwise you'd have charged him by now.'

Coupland's smile faded. Ashcroft had already flagged this stumbling block up but at the time it seemed worthwhile checking him out. Plus, he'd got form for abduction, Coupland reminded himself, settling back in his chair. He felt at home in an interview room. Removed from the social niceties expected by ordinary members of the public on the outside, in here he could cut to the chase, even if being confrontational was resigned to the past. 'What is it with that get up?' he asked, smiling to himself when Kennedy's lawyer regarded him in alarm until he realised Coupland was addressing his client.

'I like keeping myself up to date, nothing wrong with that. I can't help it if I look young for my age.'

'You don't look young. You look like a middle-aged man who got here by skateboard, and that's creepy.'

Ashcroft looked confused that they weren't sticking to his interview strategy but he had the sense to watch and learn.

Kennedy leaned back in his chair and folded his arms. You had to have thick skin to be a paedophile. He was sure he'd had worse insults lobbed at him than being creepy.

'What is it you want to know, DS Coupland?'

'Remind me what you did time for?' The information was contained in Turnbull's report but he slipped the pages back into the folder before closing it. Placed his hands either side of it, the tips of his fingers making contact with the table top, like a pianist readying himself to play.

'It was all a misunderstanding,' said Kennedy.

'That's not how the jury saw it.'

'She used to walk through the park on her way home from school. She'd wave at me for Christ's sake.'

'You? Or the boys in her class you'd started talking to. The ones who gave evidence in court, who said you'd started turning up where they always went for a kick about before they went home?'

'I thought they were my friends.'

'They were half your age. Correction, a *third* of your age.'

'Didn't bother them.'

'You were plying them with cigarettes so you could hang out with them.'

'They were happy to take them.' He caught the look on Coupland's face. 'I'm just saying,' he shrugged. 'The blame goes both ways.'

'Is that right?' Coupland muttered.

Ashcroft, cottoning on quick, turned his mouth down at the corners as though Kennedy had a point.

'And what about the victim herself?' Coupland's voice had lowered several octaves. His vowels were flatter. His tone bordering on aggressive. 'Looked older than her age did she? The way they dress these days. Was she egging you on? No wonder you couldn't help yourself. You followed her home. When she told you to get lost you dragged her into nearby bushes and assaulted her so badly she needed reconstructive surgery. If her neighbour hadn't heard her crying Christ knows what else you'd have done.' A shudder ran through him and he struck his fist hard against the table.

Coupland turned his attention back to the lawyer. '*That* is why I think he's capable of abducting young girls, so if it's alright with you I'll crack on.' He received a curt nod in response. 'Now, unlike my colleagues who travelled down to collect you, I know damn well what a passman does and doesn't do.'

'Glad to hear it.'

'I'm more interested in the work that's goes on off the books, shall we say.'

'I don't know what you mean.'

The most unlikely friendships were formed in jail. The person you met on the bus coming away from court was a face to latch onto once inside. It was harder for the sex offenders, once their conviction came out, but if the other person was of a similar *inclination*, it could be the start of a beautiful kinship. 'I've heard passmen get a lot of perks. Running drugs or tobacco on the landing. Turning a cheek where necessary, especially for a slice of the pie.'

'On occasions, I guess.'

'Every prison has a food chain. Even on the sex offenders landing. Someone will have been pulling your strings.'

'It wasn't like that! I kept my head down, I did my time. Now I'm out, living off state handouts, bunking up in my sister's spare room. No little side-lines.'

'So if someone offered you the chance to make money you'd jump at it?'

'No! Not if it involved what you're saying! How many times have I got to say it!' He looked at his lawyer. 'I need the toilet.'

Coupland formed his hands into a 'T' shape. 'I think we could all do with some time out,' he agreed, getting to his feet.

DCI Mallender thundered towards the interview room as Coupland stepped into the corridor. His heart sank for a moment, wondering if the DCI had been watching through the observation mirror, was coming to bollock him for banging the table with his fist or anything else he'd seen that he'd taken exception to. 'Reckon I'm for it now,' he said to Ashcroft, only half joking. 'I can assure you it was all in context, boss—' he began, as Mallender locked eyes with him.

'Ashcroft can finish up here,' instructed Mallender, brooking no argument. 'You need to come with me.'

'I was going to get his mum to come down and give a statement, confirming his visits,' Ashcroft said quickly, seeking approval.

Coupland shook his head. 'She'll not give a statement, it'll incriminate him regarding his breach of licence. Have a quiet word with her. Tell her it's important but it *will* be off the record.'

Ashcroft nodded.

Coupland could feel the DCI's agitation. He kept pace with him as they headed towards Mallender's office.

Something big was on the DCI's mind. Coupland waited while Mallender closed his door behind them.

'This entire investigation has come under scrutiny.'

'Oh yeah, who by?'

'Well for a start, the ACC's been onto the Super wanting to know why we haven't initiated a joint investigation with Child Sexual Exploitation and Serious and Organised. The Super's over at Nexus House now, agreeing a "collaborative" strategy.'

'Why aren't you there?'

'I wasn't invited. Nobody operational will be. We're talking Gold Command level.'

Coupland considered the implications of this. 'Are they going to take the case away from us?'

The look Mallender gave him said it was a possibility.

'Christ, I've been run ragged trying to extricate back histories on these girls and you're telling me I might have to hand it over to a specialised unit.'

'Isn't it about the result?'

Coupland narrowed his eyes. Of course the result mattered. But so many assumptions had been made by other cops, decisions taken that he didn't agree with, what confidence did he have in anyone reaching the *right* result?

Coupland thrust his hands in his pockets. 'Carry on,' he said, explaining, when Mallender's brow knotted, 'You said "For a start…" so I'm guessing there's more.'

'The head of Children and Families Services rang me personally to complain about an abrasive detective who'd berated the manager of Sandiland's care home. Ring any bells?'

Coupland shrugged.

Mallender reeled off words he'd consigned to

memory: 'Threatening, belligerent… Accusing him of being slipshod.'

Coupland baulked, 'Come on, does slipshod sound like a word I'd use?'

'You know the point I'm making, Kevin. Was there a need to alienate the manager or was it purely recreational?'

'I can assure you I got no pleasure from it. And if he felt threatened then that's because my questions must have hit a nerve. I just need to find out why.'

'Then maybe this'll help. We've been invited to a multi-agency meeting determining how this investigation will proceed in relation to Savannah. We'll be joined by the head of the service and Stephen Bryant himself. Don't look so put out,' Mallender said, clocking the expression on Coupland's face. 'The fact this has been arranged at such short notice shows how much they want to engage with us.'

'Or control the access we're given. Anyway, what's the point if the big boys are going to sweep in. They'll want to put their own stamp on things.'

'This investigation has thrown up a discrepancy in the way young people in the care system are being treated. It needs to be looked into, and documented. The council can't turn their backs on this. Yes, it's a different enquiry altogether, but if that's kick-started in some way by pursuing your line of enquiry then so be it.' Mallender's smile told Coupland he was throwing him a bone; that he'd managed to turn a complaint against him into an opportunity. The DCI was some salesman. Coupland's face brightened. Even desk jockeys got things done.

*

It was agreed that the enquiry into the disappearance and murder of Savannah Glover was to be held at social work headquarters in Swinton, a short enough drive from the station once the school run was over. Coupland's role was to take notes, make sure they stayed on track as these things had a tendency to grow arms and legs, and most importantly keep his mouth shut.

Mallender had made this demarcation line abundantly clear during the drive over. 'I'll do the talking, Kevin. Thanks to your little spat we've still got some bridge building to do.'

Coupland let Mallender's words wash over him. He turned on the radio. A talk-show presenter welcomed listeners to a phone-in with the mayor. He was keen to talk about the regeneration going on across the city; something the council were at pains to emphasise would benefit everyone. Coupland raised a brow. How an explosion of high-end tower blocks and skyscrapers helped those on the arse end of a council waiting list during a housing crisis was beyond him. Apartments a-plenty for executives and football players, yet little in the way of affordable homes.

'Our next caller works for a charity,' said the presenter. 'She claims that she and the other volunteers who worked at a homeless mission were evicted from their premises because the land next door was being developed.'

A forty-a-day voice boomed over the air. 'I don't claim anything, thank you very much; I know it for a fact. The area across the road from us was developed into apartments. It was obvious folk moving in there wouldn't want vagrants on their doorstep. When it closed 12 months ago we were told it was being done up but the work hasn't even started. It was just an excuse to get us out. Pure and simple. It'd be nice if someone would come out and admit it.'

'Is there anything you'd like to say to that, Mr Mayor?' the presenter prompted when a reply wasn't forthcoming.

There followed a series of coughs which Coupland assumed was a tactic to buy time. 'Um.' The articulate elected official of ten minutes ago appeared to have left the room, replaced by someone unable to string two words together. 'I'm going to have to look into this before I comment. However, I can assure you that I'll put this at the top of my agenda.'

The presenter thanked him for coming in before announcing the next track. Happy Mondays' *Step On*.

'I missed a trick there,' Coupland grumbled.

Mallender turned in his seat, regarded his gobby sergeant who every so often managed to surprise him. 'Fancied going into local politics you mean?'

'No boss, listen.' He turned the music up, his eyes taking on a slightly wild look as he jabbed a finger towards the radio. 'I don't have a musical bone in my body but even I could o' played the maracas.'

When they arrived at the council buildings they showed their IDs to reception before making their way to the conference room on the first floor. A long table had been set out; the chairs around it evenly spaced to allow for social distancing. Individual note pads and biros, water glasses, and a copy of the agenda were placed at each setting. Felicity Thompson, the head of service chairing the enquiry, greeted them and made introductions. Several senior social workers were joining by video conference; the manager whom Coupland had got on so well with yesterday was attending in person, Coupland noted, together with the local authority solicitor. DI Little and his hoppo were also present. Only right since they'd made such a ham-fisted job of the original investigation or lack thereof, if they were really going to boil down to the truth of it.

Coupland noted the absence of coffee and biscuits. The chairperson, clocking his disappointment informed the room that refreshments would be brought in during the break. A quick glance at the agenda as he took his seat told him that several breaks had been scheduled including sandwiches and a fruit plate at lunchtime. Coupland's stomach started to rumble.

Felicity Thompson regarded the expectant faces staring in her direction and smiled. 'So, item one on the agenda: To establish the methods by which the joint investigation should proceed.' Coupland sank low in his chair and sighed. It was going to be a long day.

*

By the close of play it was agreed that staff on duty the night Savannah went missing, and their manager, would be interviewed at Sandilands at a mutually convenient time. There was no requirement for the local authority solicitor to be present. It had taken the best part of three hours to come to that conclusion. It occurred to Coupland, going by the demeanour of the people around him, that he was the only one there who didn't think that was time well spent.

'I just want to add,' said Stephen Bryant, his tone congenial when he looked in Coupland's direction. 'How gratifying it is to see that we all want the same thing. To determine how Savannah's disappearance was dealt with in its early stages, and the lessons we can learn from this.'

Coupland stifled a yawn.

'But what we mustn't do is feel the need to point a finger, find a scapegoat where there isn't one.'

Especially if that finger points at you, Coupland found himself thinking.

*

Nexus House

Across the city Superintendent Curtis listened as a high-ranking officer from the Sexual Exploitation National Enquiry Team, or SENET for short, highlighted the response being put in place at UK level to target gangs abducting children for the purpose of sexual exploitation. Similar incidents were being reported not just across the country but globally, resulting in a cross-boundary police response. Around the table were representatives from Europol – the EU law enforcement agency, Interpol, the National Crime Agency, Chief Superintendents from GMP's Child Sexual Exploitation and Public Protection units, along with the Chief Constable. Curtis's equal number at City Road station was also present. Chief Superintendent Alexander Slowe, from the Public Protection Unit, opened the meeting. He had a broad forehead which sloped down to a narrow chin, giving him the appearance of an inverted triangle. Curtis had gone through police training college with him, more years ago than he cared to remember. Partial to a drink and a flutter, Slowe had changed his middle name to Penguin after losing a bet. It was hard to see any resemblance between the devil may care rookie and the solemn faced officer addressing the room now.

'These predators have traditionally preyed on children living on the very edges of our society.' His voice was like the speaking clock. 'However, more recently, we are seeing reports of children from traditional, nuclear families falling prey to these monsters. In response, a global taskforce was initiated to track down these criminals. Our perpetrators fall into two camps: the gangs who produce these vile videos, by abducting, abusing and murdering the children online, and the people who pay to watch this material.'

Slowe explained for the uninitiated how the dark web worked, using a series of flow charts projected on screen and included in the handouts they'd been given. He described the router that accessed the sites on the web, how with a fake IP address they could make their location untraceable.

IP, wrote Curtis, on his handout.

'Internet protocol,' explained Slowe. 'Think of it like your computer's address. It's a string of numbers that tells another user your location.'

Curtis nodded his thanks, noticed he wasn't the only one writing this down.

Slowe continued: 'We've all seen the data published by The National Crime Agency showing that organised crime harms more people than terrorism. Forget drugs, the taking and sharing of indecent images of children is one of the fastest rising crimes of this millennium. Technology has enabled whole new illicit industries. Online child sex abuse draws a British audience of 80,000 people. That's equal to the UK's entire prison population. Members of these sites are like sick stamp collectors, posting thumbnails of the films they have downloaded and sharing them or swapping them with others.'

He named sites they had successfully shut down: Child's Play. Pacifier. Ridiculous site names that suggested the very opposite of what they peddled.

'We've made significant inroads identifying members of these sites, because credit card companies have at long last started to cooperate with us. Our digital forensic labs can even trace suspects who pay using bitcoins.'

Curtis wrote the word bitcoin down on his pad. Some sort of cyber currency, but beyond that he knew very little.

'The big worry now is live streaming, where offenders can pay to watch children being abused in real time. One specific live streaming site has come to our attention. They call it Utopia. A name as sick and twisted as the perverted files they share.'

Curtis sat up. The victims his murder squad were investigating had turned up on this site.

'It's impossible to gauge the size of its network but we know at least a dozen countries are involved. We have reason to believe the network responsible for the content on that site targets specific areas – setting up their operation and running it from local hubs before moving somewhere else. It's how they keep below the radar.'

He turned to Curtis. 'Your officers' investigation of Carly King's murder quickly identified similarities with two other local cases. Your team is to be commended on making the connection.'

Slowe looked over at the Superintendent from City

Road station but said nothing.

Curtis puffed out his chest.

'We know there are high level subscribers to this network. Wealthy men with pockets deep enough to buy whatever they want, including starring in their very own snuff movie. We knew they weren't acting on their own. Someone had to provide the *Lights, Camera, Action…* even if all that entails is a camera on a tripod in a dingy bedsit. Someone had to source the victims and that's where The Dutchman comes in. We believe he is at the heart of this operation.'

There was no need for Curtis to write *that* name down.

Slowe described the ruthless gangster to the uninitiated: 'The rich paedophile's Mr Fixit… Rubs shoulders with the cream of society…'

Curtis's opposite number raised his hand. 'This reference to "high level" players I keep hearing. How high are we talking about?'

Slowe's face was solemn. 'Where the real power lies in this country, around the globe for that matter.'

Slowe paused for a moment, cleared his throat a couple of times. 'Surveillance officers have tracked him into the UK. Into Salford in fact…'

Curtis picked up his pen and began writing again. When he looked up Slowe was looking straight at him.

'Our tech guys were able to hack into his encrypted mobile phone for some time before he was on to them. This was huge. We were able to read text messages he'd been sending round his criminal network.'

Curtis spoke up: 'Did this lead to the identification of his local cohort?'

Slowe smiled as he shook his head. 'I only wish that

271

was the case. However, it did shed some light on his modus operandi. We know he refers to the operatives on his payroll as "Passmen," and that there is one in each city of the UK.'

It seemed like DS Coupland had discovered as much as they had, Curtis thought, writing down the word *Passmen* and underlining it several times. He felt duty bound to ask the next question. 'I take it I've been summoned here to be told we're to step down?'

'Not at all. The extent of this operation is unfathomable. It would take 400 officers more than 40 years to crack the passwords and encryptions that this network use to cover their tracks. We can't afford to be precious. Closing the network is a priority for us, just as finding the men guilty of killing these girls is for you. If they turn out to be one and the same then even better. But no, we don't have the resources to do any more than we are already doing.'

'Can you shed any light on the passmen? We seem to have come to a halt.'

Slowe nodded. 'They remain dormant for most of the time, similar to terrorist sleepers. Then on The Dutchman's command they abduct the next victim for whichever rich client is in town, disposing of them afterwards.'

'Do you know which prison they're being recruited from?' Curtis asked.

'Prison?' Slowe's eyes creased in confusion.

'We thought they were recruited from jail,' Curtis explained.

'Ah, quite the opposite, in fact,' Slowe answered, his face clearing. He went on to explain what he meant by this, pausing while Curtis wrote it down.

WEDNESDAY/DAY 11

CHAPTER SIXTEEN

As was often the case when he'd spent the previous day chained to a desk, Coupland felt the urgency to make up for lost time. Unable to sleep, he'd showered quickly, throwing his clothes on in the bathroom so as not to disturb Lynn. He paused on the landing, resisting the urge to look in on Tonto. He listened for the toddler's heavy breathing which signified sleep, breathing out in relief when it came. He was becoming a handful, moods swinging between fury and joy, nothing in between. One of the toddler groups Amy had started taking him to had asked her not to bring him back. No need for that, in Coupland's view. Yes, he had a strong grip, and the other child's hair must have become entangled in it somehow, but no real harm done. He wondered whether there was a moment in time when parents of offenders reflected on their childhood for something they could point to years later and say, 'He was a handful at school…', 'He never slept as a baby…' looking for an indication of the trouble to come. Too early, in Coupland's view, to lose sleep over.

He crept downstairs like a seasoned cat burglar, grabbing his keys from the hall table. The drive to the station took half as long; the only traffic on the road were cabs doing the airport run, though not so many of those now. *Don't travel unless it's for essential purposes.* Coupland's mouth formed a grim line. In his line of work the public justified anything they took a mind to. There was scarcely a man in Strangeways who didn't think stealing was wrong unless it was to put food on the table. Only it was rarely food that was bought with the proceeds of crime. Mainly drugs and fuck off TVs.

A billboard beside a homeless shelter boasted '*Luxury apartments only 500 yards on the left.*' Might as well be a lifetime away, for some. Parts of Salford were being gentrified as though being working class was something to be ashamed of. Residential blocks boasted basement gyms and cinemas. Beside them bars that sold specialist beers and a selection of tapas. All exposed brickwork and Wi-Fi.

Coupland pulled into the station car park on automatic pilot. Found a space as close to the entrance as possible while finishing the cigarette he'd started at the lights on Belvedere Road. Eleven days since they'd found Carly King's body. In that time two more victims had come to light. The thing that had been worrying Coupland, that had kept him awake the best part of the night until he'd given up on sleep and headed in to work, pushed itself once more to the front of his brain where he could no longer ignore it. If it hadn't been for Carly the other victims wouldn't have come to his attention, yet she was the third victim, not the first. Coupland stubbed out his cigarette and sighed. What if she wasn't the last?

The CID room was empty except for the night shift DS, tucking into a KFC bucket. He held the bucket out to Coupland by way of greeting.

'Cholesterol levels say no,' said Coupland, as good a reason as any. The KFC round the corner closed at 10pm. If the contents of the bucket were still warm it was only because they'd been nuked in the office microwave God knows how many times, and no one reheating food waited for it to be properly cooked through.

The DS accepted Coupland's reason with a shrug, picked at a piece of gristle that had stuck between his teeth. 'Took a call earlier this evening,' he said. 'A woman claiming to have seen Carly climb into a blue car the night she went missing.'

Coupland had almost reached his desk. He swung round. '*Climb* into the car, did you say?' There'd been several sightings of Carly in the passenger seat of a blue car, but nothing more than that. The witnesses unaware at the time how important each detail would be. 'She claims she got in his car willingly?'

A nod.

'Why's it taken her so long to come forward?'

'Been on her holidays, apparently. Remembered seeing Carly on her way to the airport, saw her photo on the bus shelter when she got back.'

Coupland looked at his watch. It was half five in the morning; he wouldn't be able to phone this witness back for another hour and a half at least. Unless *she* worked shifts as well. 'Have you got her contact number?' he asked.

'I can do better than that,' said KFC, 'I sent one of my DCs round there double quick to take her statement while it was fresh in her mind. It's typed up and waiting for you on your desk.' There was a hint of smugness but he was entitled. Some working the night shift ducked their responsibilities by asking callers to phone back or leaving messages for the day shift to act on. KFC deserved to eat the remainder of his dinner in peace.

Coupland lifted the statement left on top of his

keyboard and skimmed through its contents. Elaine Tomlinson, 34, had been on her way to the airport to catch a flight to her timeshare in Lanzarote. She'd been driving behind a blue car which pulled up beside a bus stop without indicating. When she looked in her rear view mirror she saw a girl matching Carly's description open the passenger door and climb in.

'Don't bother trying to get a description,' KFC called over. 'All she can remember is the driver was white.'

Coupland didn't care. 'Carly knew him,' he muttered, working out the implications of this. He made himself a coffee while he waited for a decent time to call Ashcroft, poking around inside the communal fridge for something to stave off his hunger. Yoghurt. Hummus. Ready-made muesli. Nothing edible.

At 6am he hit 'dial.' Ashcroft answered after the third ring, his breathing heavy. 'Wakey, wakey,' chirped Coupland, 'Morning has broken and all that crap.'

'I couldn't sleep,' Ashcroft told him, 'been out for a run.'

'What happened to Maurice Kennedy?'

'I escorted him to Manchester Piccadilly and bought him a ticket back to Sutton Coldfield. Waved him off from the platform.'

'His mother came up trumps then?'

'Yeah. Seems he's a dab hand at DIY. Every time he goes to visit she has a list of jobs for him, everything from replacing loo seats to sanding down windowsills and touching up the paintwork. Tons of receipts from B&Q to verify the times he was there.'

'Cross-checked with the store's CCTV?'

'I checked them personally. Grainy images of him and

278

his mum wandering the aisles or sitting in the café. His alibi's rock solid. How was your meeting?'

Coupland grimaced. 'Arduous. It hurts your face trying to look that interested for so long. The good news is we can interview the staff whenever we want.'

'Shall we go over there this morning?'

Half an hour ago Coupland would have liked nothing more. Something about the manager of the children's home rankled with him, but there was nothing odd in that. It was his job to look for the worst in people. A skill that suited his personality down to a tee. But were the manager's flaws relevant to this investigation? Stay focussed, he reminded himself.

'You go. I need to speak to DCI Mallender. There's been a development.' He told Ashcroft about the witness that had come forward stating Carly had got into the blue car voluntarily.

'What are you thinking, relative, teacher?' Ashcroft suggested. 'We checked them all…'

'Turns out we couldn't have done,' Coupland reasoned, realising they were back to square one.

Coupland's next call was to the King family's FLO. The officer's voice sounded thick, as though the call had woken him, but Coupland ploughed on regardless. He told him about the witness sighting, asked him to check with Carly's parents whether there was a male friend or relative they'd forgotten to mention. He wanted names, no matter how obscure. This could not be another day where they drew another blank.

Krispy pushed the CID room door open with the side of his body, his hands circling two paper takeaway cups. He placed one on his own desk before carrying the other one over to Coupland. It was only when Coupland took it that he realised he hadn't touched the one he'd made earlier.

'It's only from the canteen,' Krispy said when Coupland removed the plastic lid to blow across the top of it. 'But I reckoned you'd be ready for one.'

'How did you know I was here?' Coupland looked at his watch; it was best part of an hour before Krispy's shift started.

'You always come in early after court days and external meetings,' Krispy answered. The only reason he knew that was because he came in early too. He shrugged off his rucksack and unzipped its central compartment. Pulled out a box of his favourite doughnuts and offered one to him.

Coupland gave a thumbs up, selecting one with icing the colour of ear wax, alternating bites of the doughnut with mouthfuls of coffee.

'Bit early for sugar,' observed KFC though he took one when Krispy offered it, rattling the remnants of his bucket at the junior DC like it was a fair swap.

Coupland updated Krispy on the sighting at the bus stop, asked him to put a call through to Carly's school when it opened, find out if there were any members of staff that could have come into contact with her that they hadn't checked out.

'*DS Coupland.*'

Startled, Coupland turned in the direction of the Super's voice. It was as if he was operating in some sort of twilight zone. He couldn't remember the last time Superintendent Curtis ventured down to the coal face when he didn't have to. Coupland licked icing from his thumb as he got to his feet.

'My office please,' instructed Curtis. 'I've asked DCI Mallender to join us.

'Bring your coffee with you,' he added as an afterthought and Coupland knew then it couldn't be a bollocking. Drinking coffee in the Super's office was a privilege denied to most, even if on this occasion it was one he would be bringing along himself.

It was closer to seven when Mallender joined them. Prior to his arrival their conversation had been stilted, each wary of the other without the comfort of their go-between. Curtis was pleased to hear that Ashcroft was stepping up to his promotion. 'He's a credit,' he observed, without specifying to whom.

Once Mallender was in situ Curtis briefed them on yesterday's meeting. 'First of all, we're not off the case,' he said to Coupland. 'I thought you'd want to hear that before I said anything else, put your mind at rest.' For some reason it didn't. Instead, the words *hot* and *potato* came to mind.

'What do they know that we don't?' Coupland joked, his voice petering out when he saw the look on Curtis's face.

'The Albanian trafficking gang you put away the year before last, there'd been talk back then of a lynch pin who went by the name of "The Dutchman".'

The smile froze on Coupland's lips. Even hearing that name put him on alert. An elusive criminal, he'd earned the nickname after serving time in a Dutch jail. He'd catered for the perversions of the elite by supplying them with underage migrant girls.

'When we shut down his trafficking network we didn't stop his operation. He's the one behind this network preying on our doorstep.'

'Last I heard he was living in Spain,' Coupland said. 'Costa Brava. In a town where estate agents offer bulletproof glass as a special feature, along with swimming pool and barbecue area. Who says crime doesn't pay,' he observed, his mouth forming a grim line.

'It seems Interpol have had him under surveillance,' Curtis told them.

'No surprise there.' Coupland shrugged, his mind going into overdrive as he tried to work out where this was going.

'The latest intelligence is that he's currently in the UK,' Curtis paused, 'Salford.'

A vein in Coupland's temple started to pulse. He had a way of putting his head to one side when he was trying to get to the bottom of something. Whether a toe rag's lie or an email from HR. Right now his neck was leaning at a precarious angle. 'Hang on a minute,' he began, eyes forming narrow slits. 'A man that we know trades in child exploitation has landed on our doorstep and nobody thought to warn us?'

'There's more, Kevin.'

Coupland stole a glance at Mallender. It had to be bad if the Super was calling him by his first name. The look Mallender gave him said he'd clocked it too.

'Interpol had access to his texts for a while. Their tech team has developed encryption software which meant they could read messages he sent and received.'

Coupland nodded, giving Curtis his full attention.

'He's had operatives working in Greater Manchester for a while. In his texts he refers to these operatives as Passmen.'

Coupland kept his emotions in check. He looked to Mallender for corroboration but he could see it was news to him too.

'Their title doesn't mean what we thought it did. They're not convicted criminals who were lackeys on the inside. They're men with clean records. As far as the law is concerned, guilty of nothing, not even a parking ticket. They're called Passmen *because* they can pass all the criminal checks,' he clarified. 'For all intents and purposes, they're as clean as a whistle.'

Curtis filled in some of the background. 'It's taken a while for their intelligence gatherers to work out what he was up to. When our victims were found on the Utopia site, DS Boydell's superior flagged it up to a colleague seconded onto SENET. Utopia is one of several sites on their watch list owned and operated by The Dutchman. His Passmen are gofers, similar to the role Austin Smith played.'

'Except Reedsy didn't abduct the girls,' Mallender reminded him, 'they were taken from the migrant houses – admittedly where they were being kept against their will,' he conceded.

'Carly wasn't abducted,' Coupland added, telling them about what the witness who'd come forward had seen.

'So there's a chance the other girls may have willingly got into this "Passman's" car?'

Coupland nodded. 'We have to consider that possibility. I know the Fentanyl was used to make them compliant during their abuse, but I also assumed it was to make it easier to get them into the car.'

'We all did,' said Mallender.

Coupland wasn't in the mood for someone to make him

feel better. He'd called it wrong. By thinking the Passman was a convicted criminal he'd sent the investigation down a futile path, wasting countless hours. By the sound of it though, he wasn't the only one who'd called it wrong.

'Did they know these girls were in danger?' His voice was low.

'Sorry?'

'Did the officers intercepting The Dutchman's texts know that he was orchestrating the abduction and murder of the girls on our patch?'

A flash of alarm crossed the Super's face. As though Coupland had strapped himself into a suicide vest and was about to pull the cord. He slowed the pace of his words, his tone saying, *easy now*. 'They didn't know where and how the passmen were going to strike, Kevin. They just knew they existed.'

Coupland wasn't having it. 'On our patch though! They knew that much! They should have warned us.'

Curtis threw his arms wide. 'And said what? How would we have traced them? Remember, this operative, passman, whatever you want to call him, doesn't have a criminal past. We can't go dragging members of the public in for no reason.'

Coupland wasn't so sure. 'Why hasn't The Dutchman been arrested? There's more than enough evidence to bring *him* down.'

'Think about it for a minute. Yes, they could lock him up but he's just the tip of the iceberg. He represents the gateway to politicians, judges, lords… people with status and enough powerful friends to make scandal disappear. This is where the real money is in the exploitation industry.'

And the real threat, thought Coupland. 'So he's free to carry on rubbing shoulders with people who fund rapes and murder and dress it up as entertainment that accountants jerk off to in their lunch break. Have I got that right or am I missing something?' Coupland struggled to contain his temper, to keep the incredulity out of his voice.

'The police service is fractured, Kevin. All these professional gangs need to do to outwit us is cross a border.'

Organised crime was rarely as visible or disturbing as the disorganised variety: public drunkenness or noisy neighbours. Even when police were asked to address it, they were tasked with tackling the symptoms – knife attacks, a drug squat – not the cause.

'What the public wants is local attention, and that's all we're equipped to give them.'

What he really meant was leave it to the big boys.

'We just can't afford to open up another can of worms. The manpower required by these cases is unfathomable.'

The child abuse case in Rotherham employed 144 officers. In February 2018, a 29 year old Birmingham University professor was sentenced to 32 years in prison for blackmailing hundreds of women and girls into torturing and sexually abusing themselves. It took the combined efforts of the NCA, the FBI, US Dept. of Homeland Security, Australian Police and Europol to catch him. This was a man operating on his own; what chance did they have against a well-connected crime gang?

'Don't think of it as letting him run free, more a case of letting those better equipped to deal with him take up the mantle. There's every chance it will result in a two-way handshake.'

Jesus wept, the Super had been on a leadership course again. Last year he was quoting *collaborative efforts*, the year before that *mutually satisfactory outcomes*. Now it was two way handshakes. HR needed to drastically update their lingo, given social distancing and all.

Curtis tried another tack. 'It's better to strike at the top. If we only go after those at the bottom of the pile we don't eradicate the problem, but a global police approach to take away the top tier, where the serious bankrolling comes from, could cripple the supply chain completely.'

Coupland had never experienced that level of optimism, that utter belief that if you wanted something badly enough, it would happen. He wasn't sure he could make that leap of faith. He let out a long breath. He felt exhausted. The energy he'd felt on his way into work had long since ebbed away, leaving something unpleasant in its wake. 'So, what's the deal? We go after the bottom tier but keep our hands off The Dutchman?'

The Super struggled to keep his face expressionless. 'I imagine it would've been something like that, if they hadn't lost him.'

Coupland threw his head back but the laugh he was aiming for came out strained. 'Jesus Christ-all-bloody-mighty. You couldn't make it up.' He looked around wild eyed, waiting for Mallender, if not Curtis, to speak out in agreement but it seemed those pips on the shoulder made you toe the party line. There were far too many chiefs in the force these days. Too many gazing at the wider picture when what was really needed was boots on the ground. Someone single minded enough to get the job done.

So, the powers that be were letting him go after the

'bottom tier' because they had their hands full searching for The Dutchman. Coupland hoped to Christ they had more gumption than the detectives on the trail of Lord Lucan. Or Shergar, for that matter. He massaged his temple with the fleshy part of his thumbs. He got to his feet. 'I'd better get back, Sir. I need to re-direct the team following the significant developments in the investigation.'

He managed to close the Super's door before muttering what he really thought. That a crack squad of international law enforcement agencies losing The Dutchman in Salford would have been hilarious.

If the consequences weren't so fucking tragic.

*

Sandilands Children's home
The staff at the children's home were a lot more amenable now they'd been given the OK to speak to the police by their boss. Ashcroft, having commandeered the communal lounge for the morning as an interview room, used the wooden arms of the wing back armchair he was sitting on as a makeshift table, his notebook and file on one arm, a plastic bottle of water on the other.

'No hard feelings,' said a heavy chested woman as she took a seat on the corduroy sofa, balancing a chipped mug of hot chocolate on her knee.

'As long as I leave here with an accurate picture of what happened in the lead up to Savannah going missing then we'll get along just fine,' he agreed.

The woman's name was Jackie Fields, 'But everyone here calls me Eggsie, because I'm always clucking around after them, like a mother hen.'

Mid-forties, she'd worked on and off at the home for two years. 'Well, it's not like I always wanted to do this for a living, know what I mean? It was always a stop gap, only I keep coming back.'

'Too fond of the kids to leave them?'

'What?'

'Doesn't matter,' Ashcroft replied, keen to get the show on the road. 'You were on duty the weekend Savannah went missing?'

'You already know that.'

'There were two of you on duty.'

'Yeah. That's normal. Two staff per shift. Not enough if the kids are troublesome but what can you do? A job's a job.'

'Is it usual for you and,' he glanced at his notes, 'Paul Woodhead, to do the weekend shift?'

'You mean Woody?' A shrug. 'Depends on the rota. If you mean do we always end up working together then no, but I'm pleased when I see that we're on the same shift because he pulls his weight. I never feel like I've been landed with all the domestic stuff when he's around.'

Not quite the response he expected from a mother hen, making him wonder if the kids called her Eggsie for an entirely different reason, or enjoyed the irony of it.

'Are either of you ever alone with the children here?'

'You mean like on a one to one? Of course, you have to give them the opportunity to open up to you.'

'And did Savannah open up to you? Specifically during the weekend in question?'

'Not especially. There'd been problems a few weeks before with men coming and going. Waiting outside in their cars for when she went out. Places like this are a magnet for them.'

'Did you report it?'

Eggsie looked away. 'I can't remember. Though I did mention it when you lot came round when we reported her missing. That's the same thing, isn't it?'

'Did she tell you where she was going on the night she went missing?'

'No.'

'Did you ask?'

A sigh. 'It doesn't work like that. If you push too hard for an answer they just tell you what they think you want to hear.'

No different to his line of work, Ashcroft thought. He took a sip of water. 'Can you tell me what happened when Savannah didn't return that night?'

Eggsie tightened the grip on her cup. 'We followed the procedures laid out in the local authority guidelines.'

Ashcroft stifled a smile. 'I suppose if I download a copy from your website it'll give me a step by step account of what you did that night?'

A nod.

'Your boss wasn't on site but he was on-call. How long did you wait before you called him?'

'Within reason.'

'Reason?' Ashcroft repeated.

'We rang a couple of her friends, well, people we assumed were friends, more just phone numbers of people who'd phoned here in the past and we'd taken down messages for her.'

'Do you have those numbers still?'

'I suppose I could have a look, see if we kept them

anywhere.'

'Did you pass these numbers onto the MISPER team that came round?'

'It never came up in conversation.'

'Was it at this point, after you'd rung round these "friends," that you decided it was reasonable to call your boss?'

'Ye-es.'

He glanced up sharply. 'You sure?'

Another nod. Ashcroft had made several notes while she'd been talking. He stopped now, replacing the lid on his pen to signify the interview was over. He looked across at her and smiled.

'That it, then?' she asked, groaning as she pushed herself off the sofa. She'd barely touched her hot chocolate.

Woody was 28 and looked it. Too young, in Ashcroft's opinion, to be in loco parentis of vulnerable children. This could be the reason he was rota'd with Jackie Fields more often than not, he supposed. Her maturity making up for the experience he lacked.

Short and wiry, he perched on the edge of the sofa gripping onto a can of own brand cola. His early answers matched his colleague's, though his delivery was hesitant. Pauses where Ashcroft wouldn't expect there to be, then words would gush out of him as though he couldn't hold them back – or simply trotting out a script he'd consigned to memory. Occasionally he'd take a sip from his can, his gaze never straying from the top of it.

Ashcroft leaned forward on the armchair, staring at the top of Woody's head until he made eye contact. 'I want to hear in your own words, what happened when Savannah failed to return on time. Take as long as you like.'

Woody's answer, when it came, was stilted. 'I didn't think much about it at first. I had my hands full with the other kids. One of them was running a temperature, another had wet the bed and the others were taking the mickey. By the time I'd finished the laundry and cleared away the plates from dinner I realised Savannah wasn't back yet.'

'What did your colleague have to say about that?'

'Eggsie reckoned we should sit tight. That Savannah was probably making a point – she'd been threatened with losing some of her privileges if she continued pushing boundaries. Eggsie was going to remove her TV. She used to do it with her own kids, said it worked a treat with them. So, it made sense not to flap.'

'When did that change? When did you start to feel that flapping was the right thing to do?'

'I found a couple of numbers in the office. School friends I think. I figured it was worth a try giving them a ring.'

'You figured, or your colleague?'

'Eggsie might have suggested I go and have a look.'

'And then what?'

'None of them had seen her. That's when I started to really worry.'

'Yet going from the statement I took from your boss earlier, you didn't call him until Sunday lunchtime. If you called Savannah's contacts late on Saturday evening, what did you do during the time in between?'

Woody blinked twice in succession. A nervous tic in the making, if he wasn't careful.

'Checked in on the kid with a temperature?' Ashcroft

prompted, trying to help.

A nod.

'Reassured the bed-wetter?'

Another nod.

Satisfied, Ashcroft, leaned back in the armchair, took several gulps of his water. 'Eggsie wasn't here, was she?'

*

CID room, Salford Precinct station
Coupland read through Ashcroft's typed up statements taken at the children's home, whilst listening to his summary: 'Turns out she had a part time job in a bar. When her weekend shifts at the home clashed she made sure she was paired with Paul Woodhead, a junior member of staff too gullible to refuse when she asked him to cover while she went AWOL. When Savannah didn't come home he called her three times during her shift for advice. She kept fobbing him off – at no time did she offer to return. She persuaded him to wait before calling their manager – she knew he'd want to speak to her to get her take on the situation; she was the more senior member of staff, after all. Even then she went home and showered before rocking up at 11.30am the next morning. When I asked her about it she told me her husband had been made redundant. She had no choice but to hold down two jobs to make ends meet.'

Coupland levelled his gaze on Ashcroft. 'Except she wasn't. She was doing one job instead of the other while claiming pay for both.'

Ashcroft had said as much to Fields herself, before telling her she'd be as well to look for other employment anyway, given her boss would need to be informed.

'It means the information she gave to the MISPER team who investigated at the outset was a lie. She didn't have a clue what Savannah had been doing as she was nowhere near the place, and this Woody had his hands full covering the work of two people.'

'So there you have it. The investigation was thwarted before it even got started,' said DI Little.

Ashcroft silenced him with a finger. 'Don't,' he warned, 'for one minute think this vindicates you. Half an hour with the staff and I worked out they were holding information back from us. You'd have worked out the same if you'd bothered to make the effort. Who knows, if you'd investigated it properly you might have caught whoever is doing this before two other girls had to die.'

Coupland held his arms wide, palms up as though holding back a tide. 'Let's focus on the here and now,' he urged, finding himself in the unfamiliar role of peacekeeper. What Ashcroft said was true, and if he followed that thought to its logical conclusion then Keri and Carly would still be alive. There were other factors that would have needed to be in place for that to have happened, though. Not least the requirement that Little and Clarke ditched their bigotry and engaged their miniscule brains.

Coupland had been waiting for Ashcroft to return before sharing what he'd been privy to in Curtis's office with the rest of the team. He brought them up to speed. 'It means we can eliminate anyone with convictions from the investigation, and as this 'passman' was known to Carly, it's possible the other victims had known him too.'

Krispy spoke up: 'I checked with the school like you

asked, Sarge. Carly's head teacher was adamant she hadn't come into contact with anyone that he hadn't already informed us about. The girls went to different schools, in addition Keri spent some time attending a pupil referral unit, but I've checked the staff rolls for all of them to see if a member of staff had worked in each one, but every search I put in drew a blank.' Pretty much the response Coupland got from the FLO when he called him back after asking Carly's parents about extended family members.

Coupland remembered something Keri's mother had told him. He crossed the room to his desk. Picked up Keri's case file, rummaged through until he found the phone number he was looking for. He pulled his mobile from his pocket and hit dial.

'Who is it?' There was music in the background, other voices; the one speaking to him was slurred.

Coupland's question was brief. Her answer, when it came, sent an electrical charge through him. He looked over at the others, the look on his face silencing their conversation.

'Keri was placed in temporary care when her mum relapsed. I asked her for the name of the children's home she was sent to the last time it happened.'

'Sandilands?'

'The very same.'

'Stephen Bryant is a person of interest, then?' asked Ashcroft.

'Not if you can't link him with Carly,' said Little.

Coupland could be a dark cloud at times, but Little denigrated everything. Or was it just everything that came out of Ashcroft's mouth?

Coupland reminded himself that Turnbull had been at City Road station yesterday with a production order for Keri's evidence files, was right this moment secreted in the EMU downstairs working his way through the boxes with the finest of fine tooth combs. It was bound to sting, Coupland reasoned, acknowledging the pleasure that he got from that thought.

'Both members of staff that Ashcroft interviewed referred to a list of acquaintances of Savannah's that they called on the evening she went missing. People who'd telephoned the home at some time or other asking for her.' Coupland held the statements out towards DI Little. 'Can you remember whether you checked out the phone records at the time?'

A sigh. 'Not really.'

'But you'll have notes, somewhere,' Coupland challenged, 'because no one wants the arse-ache of asking folk a year on what the reason was for their call.'

Little snatched the statements from Coupland. 'I'll see what I can do,' he said, his voice upbeat but fooling no one.

'Let's see if we *can* build a case against Stephen Bryant,' Coupland said, nodding at Ashcroft. 'Starting with what type of car he drives. His alibi for the nights Carly and Keri went missing.'

He walked over to the incident board, wrote Bryant's name on it, underlining it several times. 'Can you check out his career history, see if there's been any similar incidents where he's worked previously.'

Ashcroft nodded. 'You going over there now?'

'No time like the present,' Coupland said, patting his pocket for his keys.

CHAPTER SEVENTEEN

Coupland hadn't bothered ringing ahead. You could learn a lot from someone's reaction to an unexpected visit from the police. Whether they were biddable, defensive, or somewhere in between, it spoke volumes. Though lacking warmth, Stephen Bryant's greeting was polite. He didn't keep Coupland waiting when he asked the member of staff who answered the door if he could speak to the manager again, nor did he scowl when informed more questions were about to come his way.

'I rather thought your colleague had covered all the bases this morning,' he said good-naturedly, 'but no matter. If I can be of further assistance then fire away.'

Coupland thanked him, taking the seat beside his desk. He noticed that Bryant left his office door open this time, whether signalling to the staff he could be approached if they needed him or reluctant to be alone with Coupland without a third party present, he couldn't be sure.

Coupland nodded at the offer of coffee, recognising it as a delaying tactic, a chance for Bryant to prepare answers for the questions he saw coming. 'I hear Jackie Fields didn't cover herself in any glory,' he commented, referring to Ashcroft's discovery.

'You mean moonlighting when she should have been here?' Bryant shook his head. 'I was shocked, though I was more disappointed in Woody, to tell you the truth. I expected better of him.'

'How?'

'Isn't his the generation with high moral standards? Quick to tell us how we've ruined everything for those that follow?'

'Every generation has to rail against something,' Coupland reasoned.

'What was it for you, then?'

'Same as it's always been,' Coupland shrugged, 'I hate people taking something that isn't theirs. Especially a life.'

Bryant had filled mugs with coffee from a machine on a small table beside his desk. The milk was long life but you couldn't have everything.

Coupland clicked a sweetener into the mug and took a sip. Tepid, as he suspected. He took several gulps, leaving a centimetre of tarry residue in the cup's base before setting it back on the manager's desk, pleasantries concluded.

The entry phone in the hallway buzzed.

'Got it!' called out an adult female voice, before saying *hello* as she buzzed the door open. Coupland heard another set of footsteps as a familiar-looking man passed the open door carrying several flat boxes. Coupland could only see him from the side, but the buttoned-up way he carried himself, his awkwardness as he waited for the woman to issue instructions to a small child before taking the boxes from him.

'Enjoy!' he called out as he pocketed his tip, his gaze darting into the office as he turned, the smile freezing on his lips as he met with Coupland's scowl.

'It's one of the children's birthday,' Bryant explained, 'we let them pick what they have for tea, to celebrate.' He got to his feet. 'Excuse me while I go and wish them a Happy Birthday.' He headed in the direction of the kitchen and several excited voices.

Coupland used this time to compose a text to Ashcroft. He stepped into the hallway, took a photo of the pizza restaurant's delivery menu, which had been left on a small table. He sent the photo alongside his text, telling Ashcroft to get over there and speak to Darren Yates. His phone beeped with Ashcroft's reply: **Will do. By the way, checked out Stephen Bryant's history. He's clean**.

Which was more than could be said for Bryant's chin, slick with grease, when he returned to his office, apologising for taking longer than promised.

Under normal circumstances, an unblemished record would go a considerable way towards eliminating a suspect from an enquiry, but, to coin the most overused phrase this year, these were unprecedented times. Coupland got down to business.

'The names of the other victims in my investigation are Keri Swain and Carly King. Do either of those names mean anything to you?'

Bryant screwed up his eyes as though trying to conjure something up from the back of his mind. He dragged his computer keyboard towards him on the desk and started tapping. His hands moved deftly across his computer keyboard, operating whatever software he used with confidence. He surveyed the information displayed on screen once he'd hit the search button, waited for the results to come up on screen before turning it for Coupland to see.

'Keri was with us over Easter this year. Her mother is an intermittent drug user. It's a more realistic description, I think, than saying she is in recovery. If I'm honest I don't think she really wants to recover.'

Not anymore, Coupland found himself thinking.

Bryant pinched the bridge of his nose with his finger and thumb. 'I'm sorry,' he said, when he saw Coupland studying him, 'I'm just trying to get my head around this. Why didn't you tell me sooner?'

'I could ask the same of you,' barked Coupland.

'I had no idea it was the same girl! I hadn't given the other victims much thought. Even if I had, you've got to understand, I have so little day to day contact with the children I wouldn't necessarily have made the connection.'

'You did just now.'

'Only because your question suggested the names should mean something. I'm afraid I don't remember her particularly well.'

'Not even her potential?' Coupland asked.

'Sorry?'

'Forget it.' Coupland walked over to the window which looked out on to the main road. He jerked his thumb in the direction of the parking bay. 'Which one's yours?' he asked, clutching at straws.

Bryant looked up, followed Coupland's gaze to the row of parked cars. 'I don't drive, detective sergeant. Besides, walking is good for you. Half an hour each way and I've knocked the NHS exercise recommendations out of the park.'

'Walking, eh?' Coupland only exercised when he was chasing thugs. He wasn't sure what the NHS would think about *that*. 'What about when it rains?'

'My wife Amanda gives me a lift in.'

'What does she drive?'

'A VW Passat.'

'And the colour?' The problem with clinging onto straws was it was hard to let go.

'Metallic red.' He studied Coupland's reaction. 'You look disappointed.'

Coupland huffed out a sigh.

It was unlikely that Stephen Bryant was the *passman*, but he wouldn't be doing his job properly if he didn't ask what he was doing on the nights Keri and Carly were abducted. Ashcroft had already corroborated his alibi for the night Savannah was taken. A fiftieth birthday dinner party for friends, that he and his wife had hosted.

'I was here, DS Coupland, the staff will verify it. Both nights in question I was up to my eyes in paperwork. There's so much form filling in the job these days. No real time to get it done in the day. People are always surprised to hear how much red tape there is. I suppose it's the same for you. The public have no idea, do they?'

'Probably better they don't,' Coupland answered, readying himself to leave. No point everyone having sleepless nights.

*

Ashcroft saw the flash of apprehension on Darren Yates's face as he stepped out of his car opposite the pizza parlour on Bolton Road. Yates had been leaning against the wall, smoking a cigarette, chatting to another smoker wearing an apron and thunderbird style hat bearing the restaurant's name.

Yates stepped away abruptly, hurrying towards Ashcroft as though trying to head him off. 'You're not going to arrest me are you?' he asked, glancing beyond Ashcroft to the junction at the end of the road, as though expecting a police van to turn in with a convoy of squad cars as back up.

'Do I need to?' Ashcroft asked.

Yates was shaken. 'I've just seen the other detective who interviewed me with you last week. The mental one.'

'That's not very nice.'

'He's got issues if you ask me.'

'Just as well I'm not.'

'What is it then, only you'll have to be quick. If a punter won't pay up because their pizza's cold the restaurant docks my pay.'

'Seems a bit harsh.'

'You think?' Yates said, throwing him a look. 'I could tell you something that's harsh, though chances are you won't believe me.'

Ashcroft thrust his hands into his pockets. 'Why don't you give me a try? You never know, I might surprise you.'

He listened, his face impassive, as Yates said what he had to say, his mind filing the information away for another time. 'I still need to ask you some questions,' he said when Yates had finished.

Yates shrugged in resignation, as though this was all he'd come to expect from the police. 'Fire away,' he sighed.

'Did you know Savannah Glover?'

Yates frowned. 'Never heard of her, why?'

'She used to live in that children's home you just delivered pizza to. Only she's dead now. Same thing as happened to Keri and Carly.'

'No way,' Yates muttered. He looked up at Ashcroft sharply. 'You think I had something to do with that?'

Ashcroft regarded him. He was Keri's 'sort of'

boyfriend. He could have met Savannah at the home while visiting Keri, or whilst delivering pizza. It could also have been how he met Carly, and this restaurant was certainly within range of her family home for deliveries. A quick check with her parents and he'd know whether they'd ordered food from there or not.

'Where's your van tonight?' he asked, looking around for the white Ford Transit. Couldn't see it parked on either side of the road.

'The restaurant boss doesn't like me doing deliveries in it. Prefers me to use his car instead.'

'What colour is it?' Ashcroft asked.

'Blue.'

THURSDAY/DAY 12

CHAPTER EIGHTEEN

D CI Mallender didn't need to ask for quiet. The CID room fell silent the moment he and Superintendent Curtis walked in.

'As you all know by now, Darren Yates was arrested at 7pm yesterday evening. He's spent the night in custody so hopefully he'll be more talkative this morning than he was yesterday.'

'He's still "no commenting" then?' asked Coupland.

Mallender nodded. DCI Mallender had conducted Yates's initial interview alongside Ashcroft. It was Ashcroft's collar, it was only right he got to carry it over the line.

Still, he wasn't as happy as Coupland would have expected. 'I don't get it,' Ashcroft had said to him earlier, 'he had plenty to say when I slapped the cuffs on him. Then he clammed up the moment his brief arrived.'

The first two hours after Yates was arrested Coupland's time had been taken up conducting a search of his flat while Krispy and DC Robinson took statements from his landlady and the staff at the restaurant where he worked as delivery driver. 'SOCO is still giving his flat the once over, searching for anything that can link him to any of the victims.'

Other enquiries were proving to be more time consuming. 'The restaurant manager's car has finally been collected for forensic testing. He was threatened with arrest at one point when he locked himself inside the vehicle and refused to get out, but he saw sense eventually.'

Ashcroft had been in touch with Carly's parents, they confirmed using the pizza restaurant from time to time as it was Carly's favourite meal.

'Are we forgetting the fact that Yates's DNA isn't a match for the samples found on the victims' bodies?' asked Little. 'No,' said Mallender, 'We know he isn't the killer – the girls were murdered on screen by one of The Dutchman's rich clients. We can't be certain that the person who picks these girls up goes on to rape them either. We have to explore all possibilities.'

'You reckon he dumps the bodies though?'

A shrug. 'If he knows what he's doing he can minimise any evidence that links him to the crime – remember Keri and Carly's bodies were both covered in plastic – but I'm hoping he's been sloppy with this vehicle given it isn't his, and that forensics will find something that means we can charge him.'

'And the killer?'

'If it is Yates transporting these girls from A to B then he'll know locations, faces, all we need to do is pile the pressure on.'

'He's going to be a target when news gets out about his arrest – look what happened to Reedsy.'

'We can apply for a pace extension, put a gag on the press, Christ, we can put him in a safe house if necessary. Whatever it takes to get to the sick bastard who killed those girls.' Coupland looked at Mallender but his nod was slower than he would have liked. Had he already written off the idea of aiming that high? Accepted the killers were beyond their reach?

One step at a time, Coupland reminded himself, his hand seeking the lucky talisman he kept in the breast pocket of his jacket. The Lone Ranger badge Tonto had given him for his birthday. They'd got a suspect in custody who would likely lead them to the men responsible for killing the girls. He could feel it. A bit of positive thinking, that's all he needed.

Savannah Glover's name had been added to the list of victims on the incident board, but apart from a photo downloaded from Facebook which had been placed beside it there was no crime scene or PM photos as her body had yet to be found. Coupland sighed. 'Let's not rely on dog walkers to do our job for us. Get your thinking caps on and tell me what those bastards have done with her body.' He looked around the assembled detectives, his hand knocking on the desk beside him when there was no response. 'Hello? Anybody in? Why were Keri and Carly found but not Savannah?'

'Her body's better hidden,' volunteered Ashcroft. 'They panicked with the latest victims. If you think of the way they were found, they were dumped rather than buried.'

'Fair enough,' Coupland nodded. 'Let's work with that for a minute. So the first victim's burial site hasn't been disturbed yet. Why's that?'

'Lockdown happened. People weren't allowed out.'

'People still walked their dogs.'

'And more besides…' said a DC from the back of the room.

'Yes, but they were discouraged from travelling far to exercise, so the usual places you'd associate with bodies being buried were off limits.'

'Like the woods,' said Krispy.

'The countryside,' said another DC.

'They're all being accessed now, though, so why hasn't her body turned up?'

'A body'll stay hidden in the canal if it's weighed down or snagged on something,' Ashcroft replied.

'Maybe she was buried close to where she was killed, wherever that is,' said Robinson.

Which took them right back to square one.

Ashcroft tried to ignore it, but the self-satisfied smirk on Little's face was starting to rankle. When he announced to the room he was going to the canteen Ashcroft scraped back his chair. 'Think I'll join you,' he said, enjoying the irritation on the other man's face.

In the corridor Little was less amenable. 'I don't do small talk so get to the point,' he sniped.

Ashcroft refused to be intimidated. 'I just wanted you to know that I've worked it out,' he smiled.

'What?'

'Why you lost that interview tape. You know, that first account interview with Darren Yates. The one I asked you for but you couldn't find.'

They were facing each other but their voices weren't raised. To anyone passing they looked like two detectives discussing a case. *Nothing to see here.*

'Before I arrested him he told me something. Something that Keri had confided in *him*. She'd made a complaint to the police about the men who hung around outside the children's home she'd been sent to, propositioning the girls. She spoke to this inspector who didn't seem to give a toss. He didn't bother following up her complaint either. Ring any bells?'

'Christ, man, get a grip, if I had a pound for every allegation these Lolitas make—'

'—It's your duty as a police officer to record allegations of crime whether you believe them or not. If allegations weren't being recorded then neither were the names of the alleged perpetrators. How can you spot a pattern forming if you don't record crimes properly?'

'Have you heard yourself?'

'Yeah, except it gets better than that. Yates recognised your name. He went on to mention Keri's complaint during his interview but you still shut it down. And then those very same interview tapes disappear. Weird that, don't you think?'

'If you're that bothered why don't you report me to your boss?'

Ashcroft sighed. 'Because that's not how I do things. I'm no grass, but I couldn't let it go unsaid, either. I don't believe it's instrumental to the investigation anymore. I just wanted you to know that I'm on to you. That from now on in you do your job properly or I will turn you in.'

'I'd be careful if I were you. You go around issuing threats like that and you'll need to watch your back.'

Ashcroft's shoulders dipped. 'So, what's new?'

'I mean it,' hissed Little, 'one of these days you might call for assistance, only to find it takes longer than expected to arrive. Know what I'm saying?'

When both men returned to the CID room empty handed Coupland noticed that Ashcroft looked distracted. Maybe waiting around for SOCO to report back was getting to him, too. Little, on the other hand, looked like a schoolboy preparing for a fight in the playground.

Coupland's phone rang. He recognised the number, nodding to the team as he lifted it to his ear. The SOCO Manager: 'Darren Yates's flat is clean. No Fentanyl bottles stashed away, no rolls of plastic, nothing, in fact, to tie him to the girls. Forensics will take a bit longer, but I wouldn't get your hopes up.'

'Bollocks,' said Coupland, when the call ended, telling the rest of the room all they needed to know.

'Forensics can still come up trumps Sarge,' Krispy said, the way only someone young and unjaded could still see as a possibility.

'We don't have to let him go yet,' said Mallender. 'We've got till close of play.' He looked to the space where Curtis had been spurring them on from the side-lines. It was empty.

SATURDAY/DAY 21

CHAPTER NINETEEN

She thought at first he'd kicked his ball out into the street. He did it on purpose sometimes so he could 'accidentally' bump into his pal Ethan three doors down who was allowed to play out. They'd go no further than the end of the road; kick the ball against the gable wall of the house on the end. It would drive her mad but the couple who lived there didn't seem to mind. Either that or they were hard of hearing. When his moaning about being indoors got to her she'd let him accompany Ethan to the park, watching through the window while they crossed the road to the playing fields opposite. It was why they'd chosen the house. Its proximity to the school, and the playing fields beside it, made up for the fact their garden was the size of a postage stamp. He was small for his age and they mollycoddled him more than they should. She knew that, but knowing it didn't make her want to stop. He was forever telling them what his friends were allowed to do that he wasn't, and playing outside was one of them. She didn't mind if Ethan was with him, safety in numbers and all that. And he knew not to run after the ball if it went into the road. She should loosen up a bit really. Andy had been telling her that for ages now, *'You're too soft on the lad, let him spread his wings a bit.'* Though he never overruled her, after all she was the one who was with Toby the most.

She'd been glad of the peace if the truth be told. She'd

cleared the ironing and was about to make a start on the beds when she realised he hadn't come in for his lunch. There was soup left over from the night before. She lit the gas ring under the pan and stepped onto the front doorstep to call him in. She stood in the front garden, looking up and down the street. Tutting, she hurried inside to turn off the soup, making a beeline for Ethan's house.

*

Coupland pulled the collar of his coat up as he stepped out of the unmarked police car. The temperature had dropped a couple of degrees, fuelling the weathermen's hopes of a picture book Christmas. Likely that was going to be the only thing this year that would be traditional, the way things were shaping up. He slammed the car door shut, pausing to look up and down the row of red brick terraced houses overlooking the park. Traffic calming bumps were interspersed along the road to make it safer for pedestrians. Sleeping policemen, wasn't that what they were called? Their name lingered in the air like an accusation. A week had passed since Darren Yates had been released from custody. A week since Coupland had applied for – and been granted – a few days' leave. Fifteen-hour shifts take their toll after a while, especially when you're not making headway.

The press were growing tired. Even Carly, who'd been photogenic enough for her murder to make several newspaper front covers, had been relegated to the inside pages, the focus less on the shock and the horror of the event itself than on the inability of the police to make headway on the investigation. Coupland loved that. The ability of the police to go from hero to zero depending which way the wind was blowing. When he'd stepped in front of a bullet intended for a college pupil the previous year the Evening News couldn't get enough of him. *This too shall pass.*

Technically he wasn't due back until Monday, but, when the call came in from control he'd been the first person that Mallender had informed.

'You ready for this?' The DCI asked as he stepped round the car to join Coupland on the pavement.

'Like we have any choice?' Coupland answered as the front door opened before they'd even reached it, ready to swallow them whole.

The boy's mother was standing by the window. She turned as the WPC who'd let them in made the introductions, her gaze taking them both in. 'My husband's gone out looking for him! Said he couldn't hang around here answering the same questions over and over!'

They'd been given the briefest of details over the radio. Toby Roberts, 7, missing since lunchtime. Mother's name Lianne Roberts, 29, father's name Andy Roberts, 33.

Coupland wasn't much taken with the WPC assigned to sit with her. There was only one FLO on shift. He was still assigned to Carly's family, and had his work cut out for him keeping her father in tow. The WPC made Lianne a cup of tea when she first arrived but hadn't used the time since then to ask about Toby's school friends or the places he liked going to. 'I didn't realise that was part of the job,' she hissed when Coupland followed her into the kitchen to point out her short comings. 'I've haven't been on the training yet.'

'What, the Common Sense course?' he sniped, 'Yeah,

I can tell.'

He returned to the living room. 'Lianne, did you see anyone pass by earlier? A car, maybe, someone on foot…'

'Someone's already asked me that,' she sighed. The WPC made a point of jerking her head in agreement.

She'd been glad of the peace. The guilt she felt now for thinking that, for revelling in silence that seldom came her way. She'd as good as wished it on him, whatever 'it' was. Torment formed a stone in her throat, she made a choking sound. The WPC passed her a tissue.

'You told the first officer that arrived that you'd checked Toby wasn't with his friend.'

'I spoke to Ethan's mum. He's staying with his grandparents for a couple of days.'

'What about Ethan's grandparents?'

'They live miles away.' Her face was pale, drained. She had chin length hair which she kept tucking behind her ears. Not everyone had rushed back to the hairdressers after lockdown had ended. Some were still wary; for others whose hours had been cut it was an expense low on their list of priorities. 'The second lot of officers that came started looking round the house, as though I hadn't done that already! It's why my husband went out. He said it was pointless waiting around when we've looked in all the obvious places.'

Just then a car pulled up outside and her husband ran in, his eyes wild as he took in the detectives standing in his living room. 'Any news?' he demanded, trying to control the anxiety in his voice. 'I've spoken to all his friends' parents, nobody has seen him.'

'What is Toby wearing?' Coupland asked.

'His football strip.'

'City? United?'

'No, he joined the local boys' team. They've got their own kit.' She removed a photo on the sideboard from its mount. Two dozen boys grinned for the camera. Dark red jerseys with 'Noble' emblazoned across the chest on a green band. 'They'd just been presented with their kit from the sponsor. Toby was pleased as punch.'

'Can I take this?' Coupland asked, waiting for her to nod before placing the photo in an evidence bag. He wanted to tell her that there was no reason to be unduly worried. That kids went missing all the time. He could see the fear settling on her shoulders like a second skin. All those years of waking up each morning, expecting the worst, only for it to come true.

'He's not the sort to go off with a stranger,' she said. She moved to the living room window, as if staring long enough would make him appear.

*

CID room, Salford Precinct station

A new incident board had been set up with Toby's name along the top of it. A head and shoulders photo of him in his school uniform had been placed underneath.

'First thing's first,' Coupland said, handing the team photo of Toby in his football kit to Krispy. 'Get this blown up and circulated.' Coupland was agitated. There was to be a briefing in ten minutes but he wanted to be out there, looking, searching. Much as Toby's father had done before they'd arrived. The mood in the room had darkened. Two hours since Toby had gone missing and not a single sighting.

'Do you think it's the Passman, Sarge?' Krispy asked, saying the name that had remained so far unspoken. What was it with the young and their disregard for tempting fate?

Superintendent Curtis didn't need to clear his throat. All eyes were on him, waiting. The low hum that had preceded his entrance ceased as the assembled personnel waited to hear their instructions. 'I don't need to tell you the severity of this situation. The urgency with which we need to find Toby. Bring him home to his family.' The air was electric with anticipation. 'We must assume that the person who has taken him is the same person who abducted Savannah, Keri and Carly, and, together with persons unknown, inflicted upon them the worst possible harm. To not assume this would be a great disservice to Toby right now.'

Briefly, Curtis introduced Alexander Slowe, Chief Superintendent based at SENET, ten of whose officers would be responsible for assimilating intelligence and guiding the search. Two civilian computer operators had also been brought over from Nexus House.

The Chief Superintendent spoke quietly, setting out the parameters for an early search. Thirty uniformed officers were already combing the immediate vicinity around Toby's home. More were to be drafted in from surrounding stations.

DCI Mallender spoke next: 'We know there is a period of time between when the Passman abducts his victim and their murder. What happens in that intervening time I am thankful to say, for some of us still, is unimaginable. Somewhere out there this boy is being held, and abused, and that abuse is being filmed. Yes, we need to act fast, but fastidious is better. No loose cannons careering all over the place. You get a hunch, you call it in. Remember: channels of communication. Let's use the intelligence we have available.'

'One more thing,' said Curtis. 'The press office is mobilising local radio and national television. DS Coupland, I want you with me on that one. It'll be good to have someone who's been involved in this investigation right from the beginning.'

Not quite, Coupland thought, throwing a look at DI Little. What were the chances, Coupland reckoned. If Savannah's disappearance, if Keri's murder even, had been given the attention they deserved, would they be standing here today, scrabbling around for a little boy?

Phones in the incident room and at Crimestoppers had rung non-stop since Toby's photograph was shown on the teatime news bulletin. He'd been spotted in various locations around the north west of England. Each call had to be investigated. All Coupland wanted was for one fucking thing to go right.

'DS Coupland, have you got a minute?' The civilian call handler hit the 'hold' button before bringing Coupland up to speed. 'A passer-by close to where Toby lives saw a boy run out into the road, causing a motorist to hit the brakes. The boy was unhurt but shaken. Seemed happy to get into the man's car.' She handed the phone to Coupland.

'*Looked to me like he knew him,*' the eyewitness told Coupland, picking up from where she left off.

'Can you describe the motorist?' Coupland asked, holding his breath. Silence. Coupland looked up at the ceiling. 'Was he young? Middle aged? Old?' Coupland prompted. *Come on, come on, give me something I can work with.*

'*Late thirties, I'd say. Forty at a pinch.*'

'Facial hair?'

'*A beard. Yes, that's right. He had a beard.*'

How the fuck could you not remember that? Coupland thought. He kept his tone light. 'You're doing really well,' he coaxed. 'What colour was his hair?'

'*Dark.*'

Coupland thanked the caller, handing the phone back to the civilian with an instruction to send officers round to take an e-fit. 'Hang on,' he muttered, snatching the phone back. 'I don't suppose you can give me a description of the car, can you?'

'*Oh yes! A blue Nissan Juke.*'

Coupland stuck his index finger in his other ear. Had she really just given him the make and model of the passman's car? 'You sure about this, love?'

'*Of course I am,*' she said irritably, '*I've got one just like it.*'

Coupland's smile was cautious. There for a moment and then gone. After all, Toby was still missing.

A team of officers were assigned the task of tracking down registered owners of blue Nissan Jukes within the city. This would be cross checked against ANPR cameras together with CCTV near Toby's home in the run up to his abduction. Officers conducting house to house enquiries along the road where Toby ran in front of the car were instructed to check private CCTV footage for any sighting of the incident. A public appeal was also put out for dashcam material from any drivers or cyclists who were in the area at the time. Painstaking work that took time they hadn't got. Four hours in and it was starting to get dark.

The search team worked outward from the house.

Soon, the lines of officers inching their way along every field and ginnel would be replaced by dog handlers shining torches on every hedge while the dogs sniffed beneath them, the scent of Toby's pyjamas on their snouts. The same tasks repeated, over and over until a new line of enquiry emerged, giving them another place to search.

The chances of finding Toby alive were slim, but a chance all the same.

*

DC Turnbull had spent the best part of the previous ten days playing tug of war with the desk sergeant of City Road station's Evidence Management Unit. Initially he'd requisitioned a copy of the chain of evidence log from the scene of crimes manager who'd worked the scene where Keri's body had been found. He'd spent the next day trying to decipher their writing. Satisfied that he had an accurate inventory he'd arrived at City Road station at precisely the time he'd told them he was coming, stating, his tone polite but firm, that if an item couldn't be found, he'd be more than willing to look for it himself. Once the correct number of items were identified he brought them back to Salford Precinct, ensconcing himself in the basement as he worked his way through them.

He regarded Coupland now with a face like a lost dog that had been found. 'Happy as a pig in the proverbial,' he'd answered when Coupland asked him how he'd got on whilst working on someone else's turf. There wasn't a threatening bone in Turnbull's body. No reason why silverbacks like Little and Clarke would give him a hard time. 'I asked about the interview tape, Sarge, in case it had turned up, the way these things sometimes do.'

Coupland loved the fact that Turnbull had no side to him. From any other officer it would have sounded like a dig, especially as DI Little and his mini me were no more than a couple of desks down, but Turnbull prattled on oblivious. Sometimes a lack of self-awareness was a good thing.

'I think it's safe to say we can wave goodbye to any hope of it turning up,' Ashcroft commented, his glance at Little slow and deliberate, 'but good effort.'

Turnbull's face glowed. 'I found out something interesting though Sarge,' beaming when both Coupland and Ashcroft gave him their full attention. 'Keri's mobile phone records show she had been in contact with an unidentified phone number several times in her phone history in the three months leading up to her abduction. The calls last no more than a couple of minutes.' Turnbull paused. 'I spoke to her mum to see if she recognised the number. She said no one had asked her about this before.'

'For God's sake you know what these kids are like,' Little sounded riled, 'if we followed up every bloody call we'd get bugger all done.'

'Even an unknown number?' asked Ashcroft.

'It was likely some random hook up,' persisted Little.

Coupland was already shaking his head. 'Kids don't use their phones to ring each other,' he said. 'My guess would be that whoever was making these calls was older than her.'

Coupland turned his attention back to Turnbull. 'Did Keri's mum have any idea who it could be?'

The look Turnbull gave him dashed Coupland's hopes of it being a bearded Nissan driver. 'But then she mentioned something, made reference to Keri's *old phone*. I had to ask her to slow down a minute so I could make sense of what she was saying. Turns out Keri had persuaded her mum to get her a fancy phone on contract, in her mum's name since she was under-age. They'd had a bit of a rough year and she managed to guilt trip her into it. The handset in the evidence box – I showed her a photo of it – was her old pay as you go phone.'

'It was removed from her room along with other items of her belongings,' Little spluttered, 'standard procedure.'

'Did you not wonder why she didn't have it with her?' Coupland asked. Amy would need to be surgically removed from her phone. Truth be told, so would he.

Coupland saw where this was going. 'No one had put a trace on the new handset because they didn't know it existed.' He felt something inside him quicken. 'Tell me you rectified that,' he said, leaning forward, listening, giving Turnbull his full attention.

'Goes without saying that I'd put a request in to the network provider, Sarge, and here's the response. Took the best part of a week to come through but have a look at this: it's the last known place that Keri's new phone was used.' Turnbull held up a map of the triangulated area, the location of Keri's phone marked with a cross. Was this the miracle they'd been waiting for?

'Come here, you little beauty,' Coupland said, grabbing Turnbull by the ears and planting a kiss on the top of his head.

'Steady on Sarge, we're not from the same household.'

'Right now, Turnbull, I'd bloody well move Lynn out and you in.'

He turned to Ashcroft. 'Let's go and knock down some doors.'

CHAPTER TWENTY

Coupland had asked for half a dozen vans with as many uniformed officers that could be spared from the search for Toby to help find Keri's phone. The answer had been no. They couldn't do anything that would bring attention to themselves and put Toby in danger if he was being held nearby.

Coupland understood the hard place Superintendent Curtis was in. Balancing priorities was tough. Experts had been drafted into the search; going against their advice would be counter-intuitive. A compromise was found in the form of Coupland, Ashcroft and an unmarked police car. Better than nothing.

The map showed an area of five miles, covering a patch of Salford that had undergone prolonged regeneration over the last two years, leaving uncomfortable bedfellows. A derelict council estate dwarfed by an executive development. Residents had already started to occupy the prestigious Pennant Tower. Apartments here were opportunities for foreign investors, rather than homes. An income generator for pension companies. The people likely to stay in them would have flown into the city for a specific event. Or have money they needed to launder.

Coupland drummed his fingers on the steering wheel when the lights turned to red, his attention caught by a couple as they stepped away from the apartment block's entrance. The man was dressed casually, a cable knit jumper over designer jeans; his wife had on the kind of clothes that Lynn tutted at in magazines. Impractical outfits straight off the catwalk. She'd point to plunging cat suits and platform boots that were no stranger to a Slade stage set. 'Who the hell would wear that get up, Kev?' she'd laugh. Coupland now had the answer. *This* woman. It was like being at the zoo, watching some exotic species go about its habitat. The way they moved screamed money and plenty of it.

Half a mile along the road and it was a different story. A boarded up homeless mission beside a derelict yard where blow jobs could be purchased for £4.99, according to the handwritten sign pasted onto the fence that separated them.

'Christ,' muttered Coupland as they turned into Birchwood. The residents of this estate had been cleared out some time ago yet demolition hadn't started. It was like a ghost town. Row upon row of uninhabited houses. It only seemed like yesterday that youths rode up and down the rat run that bisected the estate doing wheelies on motor bikes. Scarves obscuring faces long before the government made it mandatory.

Coupland slowed in front of a row of houses. 'Where the hell do we start?'

'Keri's network provider has given us what should be an accurate location,' Ashcroft said, peering through the passenger window. The doors and windows on every house had plywood nailed across them. Abandoned toys littered the postage stamp fronts of several houses, as though the occupants had moved out in a hurry. 'It's in one of these,' he added, his finger pointing to the map then jabbing it at the window, 'It's got to be.'

He turned to Coupland. 'How come Keri's mum kept her contract going?'

'She told Turnbull she liked to phone her number every once in a while, listen to her voicemail message.'

Coupland parked the car at the end of the road so they could work their way along it systematically. He'd counted eight houses on this particular row. 'The estate was cleared out before Keri was abducted so let's focus on anything where the points of entry have been tampered with.'

The third house they came to a board had been prised off the window leading into the kitchen. Ashcroft peered through the gap. 'Probably a squatter,' he said, launching himself through it before Coupland had time to object.

When the back door opened Ashcroft held a finger to his lips. 'Shhh,' he said, 'unless you want to disturb sleeping beauty.'

The place was a midden but they'd seen worse. At its centre a man lay wrapped in a sleeping bag, his breathing even. A woollen hat with The North Face logo on the front was pulled down over one ear. A black parka hood poked out of the top of the sleeping bag, brown fur around its trim. The sleeping bag stank of cheap lager and piss. Drug-taking paraphernalia cluttered the floor beside him along with an iPad, several wallets and a pink mobile phone. Coupland pulled his smartphone from his pocket, tapping on the screen until he located Keri's number. He hit dial. Seconds later the shiny pink handset shrieked into life with a song Coupland had never heard of.

'*Whatthefuck*...' Sleeping Beauty sat bolt upright, his fists rubbing into his eye sockets.

'Rise and Shine,' Coupland told him. 'You're nicked.'

*

Interview room 1, Salford Precinct station
Coupland glanced up at the camera in the corner of the interview room, then across at the two-way mirror through which he knew that a small group of senior officers would be watching. The PACE clock was ticking. Already two hours had elapsed between arrest and a duty doctor carrying out a mental health assessment to confirm the suspect was fit for interview.

'He's sweating like a sumo wrestler's backside,' the custody sergeant had said when Coupland checked him in at the desk.

'He'll be coming down off something, that's all,' Coupland reasoned.

'All the more reason to get him signed off as compos mentis,' came the reply.

The duty solicitor, when he finally showed, was inexperienced, but Coupland had no intention of taking advantage. There was too much at stake. He'd play every inch of this by the book and if he needed to apply for a custody extension, he was confident he'd get it.

DCI Mallender had already called Coupland out of the interview room once. 'SOCO are at the squat now. A second search team is preparing to be deployed there depending on what they find.'

'We've found the phone, what more do they want?' Coupland already knew the answer. They needed evidence to show that Keri and Carly had been there. Without that, there was no reason to comb the area.

'What's your gut with this?' Mallender asked, nodding at the interview room door. The man waiting behind it wasn't capable of fetching and carrying victims around the city.

'I don't think he's a danger to anyone but himself,' Coupland answered. 'But he came by that phone somehow. And that's what I aim to find out.'

Back in the interview room Coupland regarded the man who'd given his name at the desk as 'Chad.' Matted dark hair worn long around his face. Dark circles under his eyes. An Amish style beard grew along his jawline. He'd been given a regulation grey sweatshirt and jogging bottoms to change into. His clothing had been bagged for testing.

Coupland pressed a red button on the recording device on the table and began to speak.

*

An hour later and Coupland found himself pacing the interview room. They'd made no progress other than ascertain Chad was a kleptomaniac. He claimed he'd found the phone, along with all the others in his collection, but he was buggered if he knew where.

'Why do you take them, though?' Ashcroft had asked.

'I thought the owners would want them back,' Chad replied. 'You know, they'd get a mate to ring their phone and I'd answer and they'd be so chuffed they'd offer me a reward.'

'Which you'd accept, of course.'

'Obviously.'

'How did that work out?'

'I met up with this guy who instead of being grateful gave me a kicking and robbed the bag I kept them in. Put me off after that. I mean, you've got to be lower than a snake's belly to steal off someone who's homeless.'

'You still "collect" them though, when you see them lying around?'

'Yeah, more through habit though than anything else. If it inconveniences owners like him, that's a bonus.'

'No one's rung this one then, to see if someone answers it?' Coupland inclined his head towards the sealed evidence bag containing Keri's phone.

A shrug. 'It rang a couple of times mebbe but I wasn't going down *that* road again.'

'You weren't worried that the phone could be traced?'

'Not after all this time. Why would anyone care?'

'How long have you been squatting on the Birchwood estate?'

'Not sure. A few months, maybe.'

'Where were you before that?'

'Overnight shelters, B&Bs, a couple of nights in the mission every once in a while. I'm not welcome in most of the shelters around here.'

'Why's that?'

'Because I take things that don't belong to me, of course.'

'Where do you go during the day?'

'Sometimes I hang about the gates of those new developments along Salford Central, you know, on the off chance someone's got spare change, but the guys on security move me on.'

Coupland sighed. His look signalling to Ashcroft to wrap it up.

Back in the CID room Ashcroft worked through the statement they'd taken to put together a timeline of the accommodation Chad had stayed in to identify where he'd been living when Keri had been abducted. 'He either found the phone close to where he was staying or where he used to hang out during the day, but without knowing how accurate his memory is it feels a bit like pin the tail on the donkey.' Ashcroft's tone suggested he'd resigned himself to it being a pointless exercise. In the absence of anything else at least it was constructive, Coupland reasoned, as opposed to standing by the window doing bugger all, as he himself was now doing.

Coupland looked out at the blackening sky. The city of Salford stretched out before him. Lights from the tower block windows of Tattersall emphasised pockets of darkness where only the brave or foolhardy would tread. He'd texted Lynn, told her he couldn't leave until the boy was found. Even if there were no leads to act upon, he'd be no use at home. Bitching his way through banal TV, pacing the floor as he waited for news. He was better off here, in the centre of things, coiled, ready for action. The rumble of a helicopter could be heard overhead. On the ground shed doors were being yanked open, while officers with shovels stomped over freshly dug vegetable patches. Crowds had gathered to gossip and hinder.

More sniffer dogs.

More house to house enquiries.

More officers on foot. In cars.

A long night loomed ahead of him, chivvying the team, combing through reports as they landed on his desk. Sifting, searching for information that would lead them to Toby. A night of coffee and cigarettes to keep him alert into the small hours of the morning. So much for the healthy lifestyle his GP banged on about. He kept a pack of Lisinopril in his drawer for times like this.

'You need to manage the stress in your life,' his GP had told him, having given up on getting him to pack in the cigarettes. Coupland had nodded like his comment made perfect sense, that it was in his power to stop murders from happening. *If only.*

SUNDAY/DAY 22

CHAPTER TWENTY-ONE

'Hurry up, knobhead.'
'I'm going as fast as I can! I can't see a fuckin' thing.'

'That's the general idea, isn't it? If we can't see anything then no one can see us.'

'No one can see us from the road anyway.'

'But they'll see your fuckin' truck, won't they, and that'll give the game away.'

'I thought you turned the lights off?'

'I did. But unless you want someone driving into the back of it or Five O giving it the once over we need to move, sharpish.'

A pause. 'You have done this before, haven't you?'

'Yeah…years ago though. With my ex's brother in law.'

'The one who's inside?'

'Yeah. But not for this.'

He stopped. Turned back to look at the way they'd come. Calling out: 'Don't think we can go any further, Dean! Remember we've got to lug the bastard things back.'

Dean stopped, muttered something out of earshot before turning round.

'What did you say?'

'I said, Shit-for-brains, that I'm trying to remember why I asked you to come.'

'Er, maybe because it's my truck we're using. And

my tools, come to think of it,' he said, the bag over his shoulder getting heavier by the minute.

'SHIT!'

'What is it?'

'I just tripped over something, dropped the fuckin' torch.'

'Maybe if you'd had the torch on you wouldn't have tripped over.'

'Everyone's a wise guy after the event. Come on, get over here and help me look for it. Aw… Jesus!'

'What is it?'

'I've just touched a fuckin' hand.'

*

Toby Roberts lay on a sheet of polythene which had been folded double. Naked to the waist, the milky white skin of his chest contrasted with the blackening bruise along his neck. There were mud and grass stains on his knees from his football kick about. One of his trainers was missing.

'Half of GMP out searching for him and he was found by two scallies out nicking Christmas trees in Kearsley. They've pretty much trashed the crime scene.'

Coupland heard Ashcroft's voice but continued to stare.

The boy, so small and broken.

*

Coupland's steps as he and Ashcroft approached Toby's front door turned to lead. Behind them, a car slowed before coming to a stop at the kerb. They heard a whirring sound as the window on the passenger side lowered. Coupland turned to see two heads turn in their direction.

The passenger already had his phone out, was pointing it towards them. Journalists.

Coupland ground his teeth. 'Move them,' he ordered without looking at Ashcroft, the set of his jaw making it clear he would stand all day staring at the closed front door if he had to. No way were those leeches going to get a glimpse of Toby's parents before he broke the news. Three strides and Ashcroft was by the car's open window. His movement was liquid, graceful, more suited to a running track than wasted navigating a garden hedge. He shoved his head inside the car, nice and close. Coupland couldn't hear him but he didn't need to, the vehicle sped off the moment Ashcroft straightened himself. He doubted it would be returning any time soon, though once word got out there'd be more journos, more photographers to contend with.

Coupland sucked in a breath. What he had to tell the couple inside this house was impossible to hear. He took a breath and knocked on the front door.

*

Viewing Gallery, Mortuary, Salford Royal Hospital
'Generally speaking there are few signs of defence wounds with children, as minors have no idea what is happening and are incapable of resisting…'

The bulk of Harry Benson's words washed over Coupland during the post mortem, however some managed to work their way into his brain: Torn. Ripped. Loose. Coupland had to force himself to stay. To *look*. But now he'd seen enough. Something hot and sour rose up inside him. He moved his hand to the top of his stomach, pressed down with the heel of his hand until the discomfort abated.

'Everything OK, DS Coupland?' Benson asked, though for once there was no hint of sarcasm.

Coupland nodded. He tried to shut Tonto out of his mind but it was impossible to look at the body of this damaged boy and not think of him. There were no words. He took a step back, throwing a look in Ashcroft's direction. He tapped his finger on his watch.

'We've got to go,' Ashcroft said to the pathologist instinctively, following Coupland out of the room.

*

CID room, Salford Precinct station

There were now four whiteboards along the CID room wall, each with a photo of the passman's victims staring down at them. A map on the wall gave the location of where each body had been found – apart from Savannah Glover's, which had yet to be located. Coupland's gaze glided over each photo, refusing to settle. He held up the interim PM report that Benson had fast tracked through. 'Do I really need to read it out? What those bastards did, after they filled Toby Roberts with Fentanyl? Is that what I have to do to get results?' Rage distorted his features. He realised too late that his voice was raised. 'I asked you when Carly's body was discovered, how it made you feel knowing the people who did this to her were going about the place like nothing had happened. How do you feel now? While it's still happening?'

He turned to Ashcroft. 'Am I the only one not sleepwalking through my shift?' Coupland picked up a chair, held it waist high, his hands gripping onto its arms as he thought about hurling it across the room.

'Kevin,' warned Mallender. Never had so much been conveyed in a word. *Rein it in. They need you to show them how to behave.*

Coupland placed the chair back where it had been.

Mallender took a step forward. 'Take a look around you, the team's on its knees.' He moved until he was standing in front of Coupland, lowered his voice, 'They're serving no purpose here. Their heads are shot. Why don't you call it a night and send them home?' Coupland stared at him. *Because there's a small boy in a mortuary who won't be going home,* he wanted to say.

Because there were sickos out there who didn't have a problem with that.

CHAPTER TWENTY-TWO

Superintendent Curtis's office

Curtis lifted a clothes brush from a cupboard and swept it along the sleeves of his tunic. Slumped in a chair, Coupland regarded him through tired eyes. There were far too many politicians in the force; he'd made his view clear on that to anyone who'd listen over the years. Too much posturing for his liking. More talk and bugger all in terms of action. But times like this, when something happened that went way beyond anyone's comprehension, Curtis seemed to spring into life. The public needed reassurance that the officers dealing with this were fresh faced and diligent. The last thing they wanted was some jaded detective dragging his knuckles behind him as he stepped up to the podium, speaking deliberately slowly to make sure his comments weren't peppered with obscenities.

Curtis straightened an imaginary kink in his belt with hands that had never wiped spit from his face, never been caked in someone else's blood. Coupland's hands were like meat hooks. Fat fists that would never move with dexterity over the keys of a piano but had blocked punches and pulled folk to safety. He slid a sidelong glance at Mallender who always looked as though he'd stepped out of a store window, an upmarket one at that. Coupland looked down at his own suit. Mallender had suggested he might want to go home and change ahead of the press conference, put something on that gave the impression he was on top of his game. Coupland had considered the DCI's suggestion for all of ten seconds, long enough to decide that several Marlborough Lights smoked back to back would be just as effective and a damn sight more satisfying.

It felt inhuman to put Toby's parents under the spotlight but the Super had stood firm. The public needed to be shocked into being vigilant. To keep their children safe. Which was a damn sight more than *they'd* managed, Coupland thought.

The family GP had given Toby's parents Diazepam. Their movements were slow, trance-like. They'd had to be steered into the press room and led to their seats. They were joined by Keri's mother on one side and Carly's parents on the other. An uncle who'd kept in touch with Savannah after she'd gone into care sat beside them. After giving out the briefest of details relating to Toby's murder, and reminding the public of the other victims, Curtis fielded questions from the press before drawing the briefing to an end. 'We have highly skilled officers hunting the people responsible for this and will provide updates as and when we are able to do so,' he concluded, 'but in the meantime we urge anyone with information to contact us.'

A reporter with thick brows and a large Adam's apple thrust his phone in front of Coupland as he left the briefing room. 'Have you got anything to say to the public at this time?'

Coupland narrowed his eyes, as though it were possible to look down the lens into the faces of the men who had done this. 'No, but I've got plenty to say to the scum

responsible, which I intend to tell them in person.' He
pushed forward to the exit, aware that if asked to expand
on it his reply might not be palatable for teatime viewers.

*

CID room, Salford Precinct station
Despite Coupland doing as Mallender asked and telling
the team to take time out, no one had taken him up on
it. He swallowed down guilt as he looked around. A few
desks away DS Ashcroft was in the middle of a phone
conversation, while other DCs tapped away on keyboards.
On the wrong side of a double shift, they moved heavy
footed. Tempers were fraught, conversations were
punctuated by swear words. Doors and filing cabinet
drawers were slammed. Nobody met Coupland's gaze
when he looked their way. Maybe he was the one who
was bent out of shape, he wondered. Maybe they'd make
more inroads into the investigation if he wasn't there.
He straightened his suit jacket, ran a hand through his
hair. He turned back the way he'd come, closing the door
behind him as quietly as possible. He managed a full ten
paces down the corridor before he smashed his fist into
the wall. His hand felt like it had exploded. Pain shot up
into his arm and shoulder but it still couldn't reach the
fury brewing inside him.

*

Leaning against the patio door Coupland stubbed out
the smouldering end of the cigarette he'd lit earlier and
forgotten. He fished out another from the packet. Unable
to find his lighter, he slipped back into the kitchen,

bending his head to light it from the stove. 'It's not how it looks,' he said as Lynn walked in and eyeballed him.

'I think it is,' she said pointedly, staring at the offending item in his hand until he returned to his position on the patio. He drew in smoke. Held it down inside.

Lynn opened the patio door, wrapping her arms around her to keep out the chill. 'You don't have to punish yourself, you know.'

'What for?'

'For what happened to that boy. I heard it on the news.'

'You heard the palatable version.'

Coupland followed her line of vision to the outer edges of the garden as she tried to seek out the latest addition to it: a Buddha sitting cross legged on a plinth of stones. 'It symbolises tranquillity,' she'd said, when he'd come home to find her lugging it out of the car boot. He'd had his eye on that spot for a goal post for Tonto, but he'd left it unsaid, not being a complete idiot. Cloaked in darkness it was impossible to make out anything beyond a threatening shape. She'd asked him to put lights up, the task added to the list of jobs he'd get round to when he had the time. She didn't ask much of him, yet he still failed to deliver.

He turned to see Lynn studying him. 'You smoke more when you're in the middle of an investigation.'

'Do I?'

She nodded. 'I can never decide if it helps you think straight or keeps you calm.'

'Is that what he's in aid of?' he asked, pointing in Buddha's direction.

'Well, it certainly looks like the fags have stopped working,' she observed, reaching for his grazed hand.

'You know I've got to go back to work, don't you? I can't stay here and do nothing.'

'I know. But there's someone who'll want to see you before you go.'

Tonto lay upside down in his cot, his head pushed against the wooden bars. His eyelids flew open as Coupland approached, as though he'd been lying in wait. Using the bars to pull himself into a standing position he chunnered until Coupland reached down to spring him from his cell.

'How's your day been?' he asked, hoisting the boy into the air and holding him at arm's length listening to his grunts and gargles, hiccups and farts. Tonto grabbed his hair and pulled at his ears, only stopping when Coupland blew raspberries into his chubby neck.

He wasn't sure how long they stayed like that. Holding his grandson while images of Toby's shattered body gnawed away at the corners of his mind.

CHAPTER TWENTY-THREE

The advantage of no longer being part of a murder investigation team was that weekends were her own, Alex reminded herself as she spooned second helpings of roast potatoes onto her plate, deciding the rest of the beef could be made into sandwiches for supper. She speared the last remaining Yorkshire pudding, ignoring Ben's shout of 'Oi, Mum!' whilst making a mental note not to have any more wine to compensate. She had cooked dinner, so it was Carl's turn to load the dishwasher while she mopped up the leftovers. The TV was on low, the boys' chatter drowning it out but when the news came on she excused them from the table.

'There's Kevin,' Carl pointed out, pausing what he was doing to hand her the remote control, knowing she'd want to listen. 'Did you know he was going to be on?'

'I'd heard a little boy had gone missing,' she said, pressing the 'increase volume' button. 'This doesn't bode well.'

While Superintendent Curtis described the latest young victim of this 'sadistic network' Coupland stood behind a row of what Alex assumed to be the victims' parents.

'Has he lost weight?' Carl asked.

'Shhh!'

Next minute a journalist was asking Coupland a question, although his answer had been edited out. A number for Crimestoppers, together with a message reiterating Superintendent Curtis's plea for information, appeared on screen beneath a photo gallery of each victim.

Savannah Glover. Scraped back hair and hooped earrings.

Keri Swain. A nose stud and bare midriff.

Carly King. The birthday girl beside a cupcake stand.

Toby Roberts. Grinning in his football strip.

Alex stared hard at the little boy's photo. It took a few seconds for her to realise what she was seeing. By the time the thought formed in her head she was on her feet. 'Are you OK to mind the kids while I go into work?' she asked, thinking that this was no time for a fashion parade; the jeans and sweater she had on would have to do.

'Like I've got any choice,' Carl grumbled, but by then the front door had already slammed shut.

*

Salford Precinct station

Alex was used to being called Ma'am at Nexus House. It felt right. Hearing officers in her old station addressing her this way felt weird, but she didn't discourage them. She'd worked hard for the title and the rank meant she didn't have to explain herself so much, so she could live with it. The team had never got round to giving her a leaving do. Lockdown caught everyone with their trousers down and although for most of them it had been carry on as normal there was no way GMP officers could be seen socialising, given the flack they'd got for dishing out fines to the public for breaching the rules.

'Well, as I live and breathe,' muttered Coupland as she entered the CID room. He was huddled with a group of officers she didn't recognise, reminding her that time moved on for everyone.

'Have you got a minute, Kevin?'

Coupland had clocked her civilian clothes; she wouldn't turn up out of the blue if it wasn't important.

She moved towards his desk, remained standing while he perched on the edge of it. 'I saw the press briefing,' she said. 'I don't know how relevant this is but I had to mention it.'

Carl was right, he had lost weight, but the stress of the job could do that. Staring at crime scene photos all day hardly whetted your appetite.

'I'm all ears.' Coupland's full beam stare locked onto her in a way most people found unsettling.

'There's a low life that's come to my attention. I think he's grooming a young girl on my safeguarding programme though I've no evidence to support this, and the girl won't tell me anything.'

'And?'

'I saw him drop her off at her home one morning. I did a PNC check on his car. He's clean, but I called round to his home.'

'Go on.'

'He wasn't in, but his wife gave me his business card.' She reached into her bag and pulled a rectangular card from a zipped pocket. The card read: Aiden Nichol, director of Noble Holdings Property Development Ltd. The logo above it was a wide green band with 'Noble Holdings' emblazoned across it. She handed it to Coupland. 'That's his company,' she said, letting it sink in. 'I called his mobile a couple of times, it just went to voicemail. Given the girl I saw him with made it clear she didn't want to talk about him there wasn't much else I could do.'

Coupland moved over to the bank of whiteboards, pulled down the enlarged photo of Toby Roberts' football team. 'Noble Holdings' on the same green background was emblazoned across their tops.

He brought it back to where Alex waited, waving it in front of her. 'Is one of these men the guy you saw giving your girl a lift home?' he said, indicating a row of men standing behind the boys; a combination of parent helpers and coaches.

Alex pointed to one of them.

'Toby's mum said he coached the football team, that that's how they got the sponsorship,' Coupland said, circling the man's head and shoulders with a biro pen.

'Maybe he got to be coach thanks to the sponsorship,' said Ashcroft moving from his desk to join them. Alex's presence had piqued the curiosity of several members of the murder squad, although some, still smarting from Coupland's hissy fit knew better than to poke their nose in where it wasn't wanted.

Ashcroft took the football team photo from Coupland, studying the man who, if Alex's suspicions were correct, had evaded them for the best part of a month. 'He looks no different from the men standing either side of him.'

'What did you expect?' asked Coupland. 'Horns?'

Alex exchanged a look with Ashcroft that seemed to say: *He needs careful handling but he's got your back.* There was no one she trusted more.

'The witness description of the bearded man seen

helping Toby into his car was spot on,' observed Ashcroft. 'What car does he drive?'

'A black Mercedes GLA Sport.'

Coupland's face fell. 'Our witness saw Toby getting into a blue Nissan Juke.'

'That's his wife's car. It was on the drive when I called round to his house. Here's his address.' Alex handed him the post-it note she'd jotted down his details on when she'd carried out the PNC check.

Coupland stared down at the street name and number. It was the house next door to Sandilands children's home. 'Christ, we couldn't have been any closer,' he muttered, showing it to Ashcroft. 'Easy enough for him to come into contact with Savannah and Keri. Gaining their trust over time by playing the part of friendly neighbour.'

'Keri wasn't there long enough surely? She only stayed there while her mum was in recovery.'

'He'll have found a way in, that's what they do.'

'But what about Carly? How will he have got to her?'

Coupland looked at Alex. 'How did he get to your girl?'

Alex considered this, conjuring up an image of the row of houses where Bez lived. 'There's a housing development being built across the road from her,' she said. 'What if that's one of his? He'd see her whenever he visited the site. A bit of chat here and there, innocent enough to anyone looking.'

It still didn't explain how Nichol would have got to Carly. As far as Coupland could recall there weren't any developments being built close to Carly's home, but then a thought occurred to him. He asked Krispy to check if Noble Holdings owned any developments close to Carly's school.

A quick search on the computer and Krispy could barely contain himself: 'Sarge! The company won the contract to build a new science lab at the school last year.'

Coupland had heard enough. He felt the familiar tingle when an investigation that had been stalling suddenly changed up a gear. 'We need to let the boss know.'

He and Ashcroft were at the CID room door when Coupland turned. 'You coming?'

Alex shook her head. 'I don't work here, remember?'

Coupland threw her a look. 'Our investigations are linked now. Everyone bar the international space agency is working on this – there's a chain of command you wouldn't believe, but Christ knows, this is the lead we've been searching for and you brought it to us.'

Alex followed them, thinking she should have made more effort on the sartorial front after all.

*

Within an hour, units had been mobilised and dispatched to Aiden Nichol's office premises and several sites around the city.

At his home, his wife's eyes darted from one officer to another as they removed his desktop PC and iPad. 'Where's his laptop?' Coupland asked.

'He always takes it with him…'

He saw her squirm at how foolish she sounded. Her mind racing as she followed a WPC into a squad car, arms circling her son. Questioning their life. Had any of it been real? Coupland had seen it before. The bewilderment of partners looking out on a once-familiar landscape to find it strewn with wreckage and for what? More money. More sex. *Different* sex.

They were taking her to a friend's house. How long that friendship would remain was impossible to say. She'd slept with a man who had sex with children before clearing away their bodies. His crime had left a stain on her, purely by proximity. She'd need to move away, start a new life. A life where she didn't put her faith in anyone ever again.

The blue Nissan on the driveway would be collected for forensic testing. Aiden Nichol's black Mercedes was nowhere to be seen. There'd been no sighting of him since he'd gone out for a newspaper two hours before.

'He's probably scarpered,' said Ashcroft. 'DCI Mallender's put an all ports warning in operation and airport police have been alerted. We've added his car to the ANPR hotlist. He's not going anywhere.'

Yet that wasn't what Coupland was worried about at all. When Nichol had left the family home earlier, no one was on to him. What if, for all intents and purposes he hadn't absconded – but was carrying on as before?

*

Chief Superintendent Stowe approved Coupland's request to circulate Aiden Nichol's photo online as 'Wanted, but dangerous.'

Krispy had been tasked with sourcing suitable photos from the company website. 'I was thinking of using this one, Sarge,' he said to Coupland, pointing to a full length photo of Nichol standing in front of a row of houses, handing a set of keys to a young couple. The caption beneath read: *All smiles for first residents in Lowry Rise development. Sharon and Simon Gregg were thrilled to learn they'd be the first people to move into the new home they'd bought off plan 12 months earlier.*

'Make the photo bigger,' said Coupland, studying the image as Krispy dragged the curser along the 'zoom image' bar.

'Are you happy for me to send this photo to the press office?'

Something niggled away at Coupland as he studied the photo. 'No, he's wearing a hard hat; we need people to be able to see his face. Find another photo but email this one to me.'

It took Coupland ten minutes to find the address on Google, another twenty minutes to drive there. Lowry Rise consisted of a compact row of town houses, the type that springs up when a row of shops has been demolished. The house Coupland parked outside was identical to the one in the photo Krispy had emailed him. 'Bingo,' he said, grabbing his car keys and stomping to the door.

Mr and Mrs Gregg were perplexed with the detective that arrived on their doorstep. Even more so when all he seemed interested in was asking them questions about their home.

'Have you seen the news this evening?' Coupland asked.

'Stopped watching ages ago, all that pandemic stuff was doing my head in.'

Not as much as learning that they'd bought their home from a sadistic bastard, Coupland reckoned, keeping his cards close to his chest for the time being. 'You were lucky then,' he prompted, 'that your move wasn't caught up in the lockdown.'

'I know, the whole plot was completed right on time, which is more than can be said for some builders you hear about.'

Coupland nodded, as though familiar with the issues buying a new build could bring. In truth he didn't have a Scooby. Lynn had made the arrangements relating to the purchase of their own home. Twenty years on it needed money spending on it that might be better spent on something new. 'Got yourselves a decent enough spot,' he observed. There were safer areas but they'd put the effort in bridging the gap. The house was alarmed and they'd installed CCTV at the back. Security lights lit the front of the property up like a beacon when anyone walked by. As long as they didn't get into a dispute with their neighbours they'd be fine.

'We did have a wobble about moving here at one point,' Simon admitted, 'but Aiden threw in a few extra features, a built-in microwave and spotlights in the kitchen, can't say fairer than that.'

'He even threw in a car parking space that on the plan had been a grass verge,' added Sharon, beaming.

'Now that I'd *love* to see,' said Coupland, already reaching for his phone.

*

'Oh, it's you,' said Jackie Swain. 'Wasn't expecting to see you so soon. I won't ask if you've made any progress,' she said, a half-smile playing on her lips. She must have tidied the flat before his previous visit, Coupland realised, because today it looked as though a bunch of marauding vandals had run through it doing their worst.

'I didn't mean to disturb you,' he said, though from

what he wasn't sure.

'Seems no point keeping on top of the place when there's only me to please,' she confessed, surveying the room through his eyes. 'Anyway, you're not here to check whether I fold the end of my toilet roll into a point, are you?'

'We've identified a suspect,' Coupland told her. 'If you check out Facebook or Twitter or the news later on, you'll see the photo we've put out. I wanted to give you the heads up.' Ashcroft had offered to update the victims' parents but Coupland had insisted on seeing Keri's mum in person. There was something he wanted to check.

Her hand had moved to her chest while he was speaking. Her movements were slow, as though motor co-ordination was something she'd yet to master.

'Something's been bugging me, though. You've always been insistent that Keri wouldn't go off with some bloke for the sake of it, and yet on the night she went missing that's what happened.'

'Not really, she was picking up a takeaway with her fella.'

'What if this fella wasn't her boyfriend? We've interviewed Darren Yates at length and he's adamant that he didn't see her that night. Besides, forensics have ruled him out now.'

'So?'

'The man we think abducted Keri is a property developer. We think he's involved in the rebuilding of this area once this block has been demolished, and that's how Keri met him. Their paths crossed while he was here, surveying the site. What I still can't work out is why she'd choose to get in his car.'

It didn't matter in the great scheme of things, Coupland knew that. But still. Call it some perverse form of nosiness, details like this mattered. To him at any rate. He'd been replaying in his mind what Darren Yates had said during his initial interview: *'She was always worried about something. Money or a place to stay.'*

As Coupland studied Jackie's clouded face he found the answer. 'Keri wasn't happy here, was she?' he probed.

Jackie hung her head. 'I'd started using again. She told me she couldn't hack it anymore. She didn't want to go back into care though. Reckoned she knew someone who'd sort her out with a place.'

'Didn't you ask who?'

'I'd lost the right to ask anything.'

'So, Keri went off with this man because he had a string of properties to his name. Would likely let her stay in one, for something in return.' It wasn't the first time the promise of a new beginning had brought about an untimely end. Probably wouldn't be the last, Coupland countered.

'You will get him for this, won't you?' Jackie asked.

'We'll get him,' said Coupland. Even to his own ears it sounded like wishful thinking.

CHAPTER TWENTY-FOUR

It was a trip to the shops. Nothing special. A packet of fags and a slow walk back while she smoked them. The busybodies who traipsed over their door kept saying she should pack it in, it wasn't good for Kayleigh to be breathing in all that smoke, not with her asthma. There was always someone poking their nose into their business – neighbours, nursery, probation, it was nice to be outdoors, anonymous, even if it was just for half an hour. Fifteen-minute walk there, fifteen minutes back, a quick ride in the daft car outside the supermarket so she didn't feel guilty about not taking her to the park. Not that Kayleigh ever complained. She was no bother really, loved the telly and never made a peep. She smiled as her daughter climbed into the car eagerly, her little legs tired from the walk. Her face lit up as she pushed the coin she'd given her into the slot.

The queue at the customer service counter was longer than normal. Lottery tickets and picking up online orders. The woman in front of her bought a book of stamps. She could have hand delivered the letter she was holding in person, the time it had taken to be served. Now it was her turn. A pack of 10 Mayfairs and a lighter. No, she didn't want the receipt. She saw too late the chocolate bar Kayleigh liked on the confectionary stand. She wouldn't mind, she reminded herself. She never did. She picked up the free magazine containing that week's offers. She'd give that to her, make out that it was a proper comic. 'Here, don't say I never get you anything...' she said when she stepped outside, only Kayleigh wasn't there.

*

Alex didn't hear her phone the first time it rang. Had been too busy hammering her fist against Bez's front door. Finally it swung open.

'What the hell?' Bez said when she saw Alex on her doorstep. 'What have I done wrong now?'

'Nothing,' Alex replied, easing her way in. A quick look up and down the street before closing the door behind her. 'I was just checking to see if you were OK?'

'Why wouldn't I be?'

'Where have you been? I tried calling you.'

'My phone had run out of battery. I was charging it up. Why, what's it to you?'

'The man that I saw dropping you off here...'

'Not that again! What about him?'

'He's wanted in connection with the abduction and rape of four young people. We have reason to believe he also disposes of their bodies after they've been murdered.'

Bez started to laugh. 'This is a prank, right? Some kind of sick joke to stop me from seeing him.'

'This is no laughing matter, Bez, I can assure you.' She explained how Aiden Nichol selected his victims, how he groomed them over time to gain their trust. 'Look, I'm going to have to take you down to the station dealing with this investigation. My colleagues need to ask you some questions.'

'Why?'

'There's a chance he may be hiding out somewhere he

used to take you.'

'He took me to a fancy apartment once. The night I stayed over and you saw him bring me back.'

'Did anything happen?'

'No! Though to be honest I thought it might.'

Maybe he could only get aroused when his victims were tied down, Alex wondered. 'Where did he take you?'

'I don't remember.'

'You're not trying to protect him, are you?'

'Why would I?'

'People like him are clever at making you feel special, that's all. They don't mean any of it.' Alex's ring tone could be heard trilling from the bottom of her bag. She lifted the flap to retrieve it, and saw there had been three missed calls from Coupland. She hit the call back button, looking at Bez as if to say she hadn't finished yet.

Coupland was brief. A little girl had been taken from outside a supermarket. '*The mother was reluctant to report it. Didn't want social work getting wind of it and pointing the finger at her. It was her dad who called us in the end, when he saw the item about Nichol on the news. We need your girl in, Alex. Now. Christ knows we need to get this child back alive.*'

Alex held onto her phone after the call had ended. Waited for the ping sound of an email coming in. She hit the 'open' button and gasped.

'What is it? What's happened?' Bez demanded, inching closer to see what was on Alex's screen.

Alex told her about the little girl that was missing. 'Her name's Kayleigh Lomax. She was abducted earlier this evening.' She swept a hand over her eyes. 'I saw her at the station once, such a sweet little thing.'

'Let me see.'

Alex turned her phone so that Bez could see Kayleigh's photo.

Bez swallowed. 'Her mum brings her into the café where I work. Has Aiden been grooming her as well?'

'Didn't need to,' said Alex, picturing the little girl in the station canteen, drinking fizzy pop. 'Stands to reason she'd walk off with a stranger. It's what she's been taught to do since she was a baby.' *Hold the nice man's hand…*

She caught the look that flashed across Bez's face. 'If you want to help her, come to the station with me and give my colleagues a statement.'

'Fine!' Bez agreed, 'let me get changed first.'

Alex moved around the downstairs rooms while she waited. The place had a lived-in feel that smacked of a teenager who barely left their room and an over-worked parent with no down-time to spare. Unwashed dishes littered the worktops in the kitchen. A washing up bowl with water in it left to go cold. A pile of used tea bags on the draining board sitting in an orange puddle.

'Bez!' Alex called out after checking her watch. An uneasy feeling settled on her shoulders. By the time she heard a thud coming from the bedroom above she was already on the stairs.

*

Superintendent Curtis's office
Specially trained public protection officers had searched Aiden Nichol's computer for illegal content. DCI Mallender read out their report: 'He had more than 500 images of children suffering abuse on his computer. Many of those clips culminated in strangulation – presumably

by the men he'd been paid to deliver our victims to. We've pieced together a timeline of his online activity – He's a regular visitor to the "Utopia" site. The frequency of these visits increased in the weeks before each victim was abducted and murdered.'

Coupland had applied for a warrant to excavate the parking bay at Lowry Rise. When the call came in that Kayleigh Lomax was missing he passed the task of managing the excavation onto DCs Turnbull and Robinson. He warned them that Mr and Mrs Gregg were no longer happy little bunnies now diggers were about to roll onto their land, and had instructed a lawyer regarding compensation.

Coupland joined the group gathered around the Super's meeting room table, putting together a search strategy for Kayleigh. Representatives of the CSE unit, Public Protection and the NCA were present but not in the same numbers as for Toby. Failure had a way of making folk melt away. Resources weren't being withdrawn as such; just no one wanted the responsibility of saying how they should be used. Bethany Davies, known as Bez, the one person who could have provided intelligence relating to where Nichol used to take her had gone AWOL. Alex, convinced that Bez would make contact with Nichol, was in the process of getting a trace put on her phone. The faces around Coupland were drawn, anxious. Cases like this defined where'd you'd be in five years – on route to commander or flushed down the pan.

'What's your view, DS Coupland?' a DI from the protection unit asked.

'That it must be squeaky bum time if someone gives

a toss what I think,' he answered, 'but this is what my gut is telling me: If Savannah Glover is lying under the mono blocking on the Gregg's drive, then she was dumped there because the location was convenient. Picture the scenario – Nichol tells a couple of labourers to dig up the grass verge in preparation; they turn up for work the next day to find someone's made a head start filling it back in. Half the hole's been filled in with rubble – it's not their job to question why, just to finish the job as they've been told. She *must* have been held close by.'

'We can't confirm any of this at the moment, it's all conjecture.'

Coupland eyeballed him. 'Conjecture which'll be verified in the morning, I'm sure of it. The point I'm getting at is that is that for the sake of convenience he picked somewhere close to where the murder took place. Close enough for him to be able to dump the body and cover it without anyone raising an eyebrow at him being there. I reckon if lockdown hadn't reared its head he'd have disposed of more of his victims this way. As it was, limited access to each site and the equipment on it meant he had to look for other locations to dump their bodies.'

The Super jabbed a finger at an enlarged map of the city which had been spread out across the table. Each Noble Holdings development had been circled, a site plan placed beside it. 'He's been involved in eight projects across the city. Tower blocks, converted mills, housing estates, you name it. The murders may have been filmed in one or more of these locations, but how the hell do we narrow it down?'

'If it were down to me I'd start at Lowry Rise,' said Coupland, moving his finger to the house where the excavation work was due to start as soon as Turnbull got the green light, 'and work my way outwards.' He traced his finger along the map in a straight line. 'Until I found the closest development. That's where I'd start looking for Kayleigh.' He stopped at Pennant Tower, jabbing his finger up and down on the spot.

CHAPTER TWENTY-FIVE

She'd been standing on the pavement for no more than five minutes when his car pulled up at the kerb. Not long enough for her to consider the truth of what she'd been told. Long enough to understand the consequences if she'd called it wrong. She'd already flicked the finger at one guy who'd propositioned her. Offered her £30 for 'the works,' whatever that involved. The girls standing on the other side of the road kept looking over, not entirely unfriendly, certainly a lot more amenable than their pimp would be when he showed up. She wanted to explain that she wasn't on the game but they didn't speak English. Eastern European, most of them, Roma gypsies groomed by men who promised them a better life. What did it matter, she thought. In the end all promises get broken.

She hadn't expected him to reply to her text. Much less a request that they meet. But then life was a transaction, and he'd made it clear she had something he wanted. He stared in her direction until she made eye contact, beckoning her over with his hand. The passenger window lowered as she moved towards his car. Tentatively she crouched so that she was eye level with him. His gaze wandering over her like a butcher eyeing a side of meat. She waited, desperate for him to tell her that none of what she'd heard was true, when her gaze settled on something lying on the back seat. Something that made the muscles in her stomach contract.

Without uttering a word she opened the car door and climbed in.

Unable to look at him she stared out of the passenger window. 'Where is she?'

'Who?' He sounded amused, as though they were

playing some sort of guessing game.

She turned to glare at him. 'A little girl has gone missing and that's her doll on the back seat. I should know because I gave it to her.' Even then she hoped he had a plausible reason.

He didn't speak. Instead he lifted a small bottle out of his coat pocket and sprayed it under her nose. There was an odd smell. Then all she wanted to do was sleep.

When Bez came to she was sitting in an armchair. She had no memory of how she'd got there, nothing beyond the point where she'd climbed into his car. She knew from the headache that was starting to form that he'd drugged her. She recognised the cotton wool feeling in her head, her hands were clammy and though she was scared the thud in her chest was slow. Opposite her, the little girl was asleep on the sofa. Bez eased herself out of her chair. She moved towards her; dropping to her knees she placed a hand on her arm to wake her but she didn't stir.

The sound of movement behind her made her turn her head. 'You were spark out,' he said, as though she'd woken from a nap rather than drug induced oblivion.

'What have you given her?' Bez demanded.

'Just something to make her sleep, same as you. You should have heard the fuss she was making.'

Bez remembered the doll lying on the back seat of the car.

'Here,' he said as though reading her thoughts. 'Give it to her when she wakes if you think it'll stop her making a racket.'

'Why did you take her?' She remembered what Alex had told her he did to his victims but she still couldn't believe it.

'You'll work it out.' His tone was harsh and he'd stopped smiling. Maybe there was another side to him, after all. She forced her brain to concentrate. Didn't those documentaries on TV tell you to keep your abductor talking? Because that's what he was now. No longer a guy in a smart car who liked to chat her up. She wondered what the advice on Crimewatch would be. She played the scene through in her head when they ran the reconstruction of her capture. *'Thanks to the quick wittedness of the victim, she kept her assailant talking while the police continued their frantic search…..'*

Only who would miss her, the trouble she'd caused over the years? Alex would have discovered she'd slipped out by now. Though she could hardly blame her, if she'd given up on her, too. She could send her a text, explain why she'd run out on her and give her their location. Her face brightened at the prospect. In the meantime she'd bide her time, let him think he had the upper hand. She looked away shiftily, fearful he'd read her mind.

*

Coupland sped along Chapel Street, blues and twos at full pelt, towards Pennant Tower. Sat on his heels was a convoy of police vans. An ambulance was on standby.

Coupland flashed the car in front until it pulled into the side of the road. 'Arsehole,' he muttered, overtaking two cars hard before returning to the correct side of the road. He tried not to think that this entire operation was based on nothing more than his hunch, greenlighted by top brass since the so-called crack teams had failed to come up with anything better.

Coupland eased his foot on the brakes as he indicated,

swung right into the tower block's private car park. He drove up onto the kerb, leaving ample space for the vehicles behind him. The letting agent had emailed a list of the apartment block's occupants through to him. She lived nearby, had agreed to meet him there with keys. One look at her face when she saw the convoy swing into the car park told him she hadn't grasped the gravity of the situation. That if she hadn't brought keys they were going in anyway. The rear doors of each van sprang open spewing out a sea of black as officers wearing baseball caps and body armour took up position.

Coupland took the keys from the letting agent before telling her to wait in her car. Signalling to an officer holding a battering ram that it wasn't needed, he inserted the key into the lock. There was a sound of static as several radios warbled into life followed by a command: '*STAND DOWN! REPEAT STAND DOWN!*'

Coupland blinked. He stared at the officers waiting for his signal and pulled out his Airwave radio. He hit the reply button. 'Please repeat. Over.' He waited.

The Super's voice this time. Firm. Insistent. '*I SAY AGAIN, STAND DOWN! Over.*'

Coupland dropped his head into his hands. 'Message received. Out,' he grunted, spreading his arms wide in a 'what the fuck gesture' before stumbling back to his car.

His mobile sprang to life. An incoming call from DCI Mallender. '*Save it, Kevin and listen!*' Mallender instructed. '*The call data analyst came back with a location for Bethany Davies's phone.*' The girl who had gone AWOL before Alex had a chance to bring her in. '*There's a signal coming from a homeless shelter… Ashcroft's on his way there with two units.*'

'I'm on my way,' said Coupland.

'Why have you brought us here?' Bez asked.

'There's someone I want you to meet.'

Nichol stepped back then, to give her a better view of the man moving towards them. The man was fat and bald. The jacket of his navy pinstripe suit hung open, revealing a belt that was already undone. Bez was more scared than she'd ever been in her life. More scared than when her dad crept into her room at night, his finger pressed against her lips to silence her. She'd taken herself to a different place then. Conjured up destinations she'd never been to, to block out the pain. These men were well-dressed and had money to burn but everything else about them was sleazy. The way they looked at the little girl, their eyes flickering with an interest that made her flesh crawl.

The little girl opened her eyes and began to whimper. The last meal she'd eaten had been a chocolate bar several hours ago, making her cranky. She kept pushing Bez's arms away when she tried to keep her close; even so a sixth sense kept her from approaching the men.

Bez held the doll up until it was in her line of vision. A nod indicated an agreement had been reached. The girl's whimpering stopped as Bez tucked Brown Dolly into her arms. 'What's your name?' Bez asked.

'Kayleee…'

'You remember me, right?'

Another nod.

The fat man smiled at them slack-faced, off his face on something that made him good humoured.

'She needs something to eat or she'll be no good to anyone. You can do me first,' Bez added, sensing a shift in his mood, 'while you're waiting.'

With a grunt Nichol took the little girl through to the kitchen, leaving Bez alone with the slack-faced man. His gaze travelled up and down her with renewed interest. He reminded her of her father. The special attention he'd show her when her mum went to work. She'd not been much older than this little one. 'Our little secret,' he'd said over the years, giving her pocket money to keep her quiet. Money that, as she got older, she spent on snap bags of weed sold from a van beside her school. It dulled the pain. And when that stopped working she tried something stronger. No one could fathom the change in her.

She turned as Kayleigh waddled back in the room clutching a sandwich. 'I can't do it in front of the kid,' she said, the dryness in her throat making her voice catch. She ran her tongue round the inside of her mouth. 'Besides,' she said, attempting to sound more confident that she felt, 'I'd like to see your room.'

The man grunted as he grabbed her arm and led the way. Her nostrils filled with his odour, making her feel sick. Fear formed knots in the pit of her stomach. What was he going to do with her? *To her*, for she knew damn well she'd have no say in it. She stared at him and wanted to gag. Beneath those fine clothes he resembled a slimy weasel. Vermin. Something mean and repugnant. She turned her head on the grubby pillow, smelling sweat that wasn't hers. A tripod with a camera pointed in their direction, its red eye recording her ordeal. She felt spaced out. Her mind's way of making her escape something her body could not.

So as not to frighten the child, her scream when it came, was blown out on a sigh

*

Outside the homeless mission

The windows of the homeless mission had been boarded up. A banner across the front of the building said 'Under refurbishment.' With all the redevelopment going on around the city no-one would give it a second look. Ashcroft waited for the officers to get into position. Checked in with control before giving the signal to storm the building.

*

Bez's hands shook a little as she put on her clothes. She wiped her mouth with her sleeve, desperate to be rid of the taste of him. He'd gone through to the living room once he'd finished, telling her he'd be back later, a glint in his eye that made her tremble in fear.

Kayleigh was in the living room watching TV. Reluctant to leave her alone with both of them Bez finished dressing quickly. The sound of arguing drew her attention. The men's voices were raised. She moved closer to the door so she could hear what was being said.

'Your face is all over the TV, yet you didn't think to mention it?'

'I didn't know! I had a few missed calls from my wife but then they stopped so I thought everything was OK.'

She'd never heard Aiden sound like that before. So *whiney*… He knew the police were after him though, she'd told him in her text. Lies came naturally to some people.

The fat man wasn't having any of it. 'Are you for real? You've got half of Greater Manchester Police after you yet you contact me like nothing's wrong.'

'I told you, I didn't know! Besides, I was just following orders. He's not the type of man that likes being let down.'

'And I am?'

The sound of cupboards being opened and items being removed.

'You know what? We're done here.' The fat man hurried into the hallway before adding, 'You do realise you're finished? The best thing you can do is get rid of those two and split.'

Bez shrank back into the room. He'd as good as told Aiden to kill them. She looked around the bedroom wildly as she tried to think what to do, before her gaze settled on the camera.

*

Bez stepped into the living room. Made her way over to the sofa where Kayleigh sat glued to the screen. She wasn't really watching TV; it was a programme about Brexit. She was doing what children do when they're scared. Making herself as small and as invisible as she could.

Bez reached across and gave her hand a squeeze. 'It'll be OK you know, just do as I tell you.' She picked up Kayleigh's doll, smoothing down its grubby clothes. New stains made the original one harder to distinguish but Bez could still see it, running along the hem like a watermark. Perhaps that was her problem. The dark streak inside her would always show through.

'What are you doing?' he asked, stepping up behind her.

'Looking for my phone,' she answered, winking at the little girl as she pushed the doll towards her. 'I wanted to see if anyone was looking for us.' In truth she couldn't think when she'd last seen her phone. Even if she found it there wasn't time to text Alex Moreton. He was growing impatient.

He smiled then, as though remembering a funny anecdote. 'I left it somewhere, while you were out cold. By the time the police track it down I'll be long gone.'

'Why don't you go now?' she asked, realising too late how eager she sounded. 'We can stay here. We won't try and escape, I promise.'

He took a step closer, began stroking her hair. 'All that effort I put into being nice to you. Can't go until I've had my reward,' he said.

Bez knew how to stand up for herself. She was no soft touch. She could bite, gouge, kick him in the balls. Easy to do when there was just yourself to think about. Harder with the little one. He pulled that damned bottle from his pocket again and sprayed something under her nose that made the room start to spin.

'As far as getting shit faced goes I've had better,' she said stubbornly, but her words came out slurred.

*

She opened her eyes as he climbed off her. She had no idea what time it was. She felt sleepy, or maybe hunger was making her lethargic. When he returned to the bed he was carrying something in his hand. A syringe. She willed herself to lie still. Submit. She was conscious of something tightening around her arm. The sharp scratch of the needle.

Her breathing became heavy. She told herself that even if no-one was looking for her, they'd be desperately trying to find the little girl.

A determination awoke in her that they *would* be

rescued. She pushed herself off the bed, dragging herself to the bedroom door. He was playing with Kayleigh. Tickling her but she wouldn't laugh. He was getting angry. Quietly, Bez moved towards the kitchen, her eyes scanning the room for a weapon. She lifted an empty bottle of wine from the kitchen counter, felt the weight of it in her hand. Moving soundlessly into the living room, she held her finger to her lips to silence the child while she smashed it over his skull. It stunned him long enough to let go of the girl. For Bez to grab her and yell at her to run into the bathroom. In her peripheral vision she saw him get to his feet, rubbing the back of his head as he lurched down the hall after them.

CHAPTER TWENTY-SIX

Ashcroft sounded as hacked off as Coupland felt. *'They're not here,'* he said when Coupland answered his call en route. *'Just her phone, lying in the middle of the floor like some elaborate hoax. What do you reckon we should do now?'*

Coupland had called just about every part of this investigation wrong. He wasn't sure he trusted himself to come up with another plan. Then again what choice did he have? Not like anyone else was queueing up with suggestions.

A beep on his phone told him another call was waiting. He hit the 'Hold' button and switched to the other call. 'This better not be fucking PPI,' he snarled into the handset.

'You told me to call you, Mr Coupland, if I had any information.'

'Who is this?' Coupland tried to place the voice, which sounded familiar, although he was buggered if he could put a face to it.

'Laughing Boy, remember? You spoke to me a couple of weeks back, asked me about Fentanyl.'

'This better be good, son,' Coupland answered. It had been a bastard of a night and he was in no mood to be jerked around.

'That's just it. I know you'll want to hear this.'

'Go on.'

'Ever since our meeting I've been looking at my customers sideways, well, not my customers obviously, since I promised that

373

inspector friend of yours that I'd given up dealing.'

'Yeah, yeah, I hear you. You don't do it normally but on this one occasion…'

Exactly. On this one occasion I happen to sell some random guy a couple of wraps of smack. He was lucky. I don't normally stock it but my dad's been leaning on me to shift some.'

'And?'

'And two hours later his face is plastered all over the evening news, Facebook, Twitter, Instagram. You name it, he's on there. Do not approach but don't let him pass "Go" either. So here I am, letting you know.'

Coupland swallowed. 'Stop talking,' he ordered. 'Just tell me where you were when you sold it.'

*

The banging had stopped. At first, when Bez'd pushed Kayleigh into the bathroom and locked the door behind them he'd kicked at the lock. Unable to break it he banged his fists on the door but after a while that had stopped too. Kayleigh lay nestled in her arms, her head buried into her ribcage. 'It's just a game of Hide and Seek,' she told her, 'Someone'll find us soon.' She moved her lips over the top of the little girl's head. Felt her arms tighten around her. 'It doesn't matter,' she said, when the girl whimpered as she emptied her bladder, too frightened to move even a few steps to use the toilet. Every part of her was tired. Had he intended to give her an overdose? Or was it another of life's cruel ironies, that she'd be killed by something she'd given up long ago. She was so tired. More tired than she'd ever been in her life. She smiled as Kayleigh's grip relaxed, her breathing deep and even. Bez closed her eyes. In her dream she could hear sirens.

Distant, but getting louder.

*

Coupland radioed the location Laughing Boy gave him to control before pressing his foot down on the accelerator, the convoy of vans speeding to keep up with him. It made sense the locations would change as each development was completed and Noble Holdings moved onto the next project. It explained why there'd been no match on the fibres found on each victim. It wouldn't surprise Coupland if one of the murders had taken place in the homeless mission. In Pennant Tower too, for that matter. Just not today.

After a couple of minutes a signpost announced Trinity Mills was coming up on the right. He'd asked for paramedics to meet him at the location. The use of Heroin, combined with Fentanyl, was a game changer for a recovering addict.

Coupland kept his eyes on the road. The needle nudged eighty. Slamming his foot on the brakes he swung into the car park of the former mill currently being converted into upmarket lofts. Cloister walls had been built across most of the building, with the apartments being formed behind them to create a big 'reveal'.

Coupland swung the car round in front of the building's entrance, waited for the officers arriving behind him to form a line. At the front of the line an officer holding a battering ram pulled his helmet's visor over his face.

Coupland gave his signal. The door caved in on impact. 'POLICE RAID! STAY WHERE YOU ARE!'

An explosion of noise erupted from the building as they surged inside: the sound of heavy boots on stairs as every floor was searched. A light was on in an apartment at the end of the hall. Coupland headed towards it, kicking open the main door before searching each room. A tripod had been knocked over beside an unmade bed in one room. An empty bottle of wine lay on the living room floor. Coupland's shoulders dipped. Had he missed them? He looked through the living room window. Aiden Nichol's Mercedes was parked in a courtyard at the rear of the building.

Coupland moved into the hallway, towards the officers that had followed him in. One stood in front of the bathroom door. He turned the handle, signalling to Coupland it was locked. A sharp kick and the door swung open.

The little girl lay half across Bez, her thin arms wrapped about her shoulders, her cheek pressed against Bez's cheek.

'Get the paramedics in!' Coupland yelled. He rushed forward willing them to be alive. He crouched down to pinch the skin on the back of Kayleigh's hand, blowing out a breath as the little girl sat up and rubbed her eyes. He sucked it back in when he saw that the arms holding onto her were blue.

*

'HE'S ON FOOT!' Coupland shouted to Ashcroft, his voice rising to compensate for the sound of the helicopter circling overhead. Officers and sniffer dogs were searching the field behind the mill. More units drove around the neighbouring industrial unit while foot patrols combed through footpaths leading into Grove Lane. Control had put out a request for emergency assistance,

376

Ashcroft, being in the vicinity, was one of the first to respond.

A team of SOCOs were currently swarming over the place. DCI Mallender was on his way over, accompanied by DI Moreton. Kayleigh had been taken to hospital for tests, but appeared to be unharmed. Bez wouldn't be moved until the pathologist had taken a look at her.

'How do you want to play it?' Ashcroft asked. They were standing in the yard at the rear of the building, Coupland half way down the third cigarette he'd smoked since prising Kayleigh from a dead girl's arms.

'Seems to me this bastard's going nowhere. If he's made a run for it our guys will pick him up soon. It's just a matter of time.' Coupland took another drag while Ashcroft considered what he'd said.

'You said "If".'

'I did, didn't I?' Coupland said, forcing his lips into a smile.

It was hard to put himself in the mindset of a ruthless criminal on the run, but if Coupland forced himself, he could see only one possible course of action for Nichol to take: lay low and wait them out. The layout of the mill was perfect. Five storeys high with a rabbit run of internal stairs and chutes which Nichol knew like the back of his hand. Although the apartments on the ground floor had been completed the remaining floors resembled a building site. A poster on the billboard Coupland had turned in at boasted a rooftop terrace and underground parking. They'd tossed for it. Which was why Coupland found himself on the top of the building while Ashcroft had headed down to the basement. Coupland kept his distance from the low wall around the perimeter of the roof. Tonto's father had fallen over a similar wall to his death; Coupland was in no hurry to join him. He lifted the tarpaulin covering a pile of building materials – nothing but scaffolding poles and planks beneath it.

His phone rang. Turnbull: '*A body's been found under the parking space at Lowry Rise, Sarge. Be several more hours before she can be removed but we've got a positive ID on her clothing. It's definitely our girl.*'

At least Coupland had called something right. He moved towards the edge, peered down at officers about to go into extra time on their shift. He saw one of them flash a torch into a skip. He made a mental note for SOCOs to check its contents in the morning, thinking Carly's phone and Toby's missing trainer could be among them.

He noticed something else too. Something that he struggled to fathom. DI Little and DS Clarke hurrying from the entrance to the underground car park looking shifty as hell. Without thinking why, Coupland whipped out his phone and began to video them looking left and right as they headed for the bank of police cars. A sense of unease formed in the pit of his stomach as his radio crackled into life. Ashcroft's voice shouted 'KNIFE!' across the airwave followed by him hitting his ten zero 'emergency' button.

'BASEMENT!' Coupland yelled into the radio, hurtling towards the stairs.

CHAPTER TWENTY-SEVEN

'Chris Ashcroft was a bloody good DC,' Coupland said to the detectives assembled in the CID room several hours later. They'd gathered quietly. With all that had happened it didn't seem appropriate to go to the pub to raise a glass. Instead they'd settled for several cases of lager from the Tesco superstore. Each detective held a bottle aloft ready for the toast.

'And I'm pleased to say he has all the hallmarks of a kick-ass DS,' Coupland beamed.

'I'll second that,' said Mallender. Lifting his bottle to his lips while Ashcroft took a half-hearted bow.

'I've only passed my exams,' he said modestly, 'Not captured the bloody Dutchman.'

Superintendent Curtis had been informed by Gold Command that The Dutchman had been staying in Pennant Tower, the apartment block Coupland had been about to raid. If Curtis hadn't told him to stand down who knows what might have happened?

Coupland had taken it remarkably well, considering. 'Look, we all have to make judgement calls as we see fit,' he said, eyeballing Little before moving on. 'We had no way of identifying him. Bastards like him operate below the radar – I could have passed him on the stairs and not known it.'

As it was, armed police had been despatched to bring him in but the apartment had been cleaned out. The lease paid by bank transfer from an untraceable account. The monster was on a lucky streak, that was all. And good luck, just like any other kind, comes to an end eventually. He'd come back to Salford, Coupland was sure of it. Only this time Coupland would be ready. 'At least the Super had the balls to tell me himself.'

'Anyway,' he added, his attention returning to Ashcroft, 'you captured the Passman. That'll do for me.'

A dozen officers had responded to Ashcroft's emergency call. It had taken six of them to overpower Nichol and remove the kitchen knife he'd cornered Ashcroft with. He was in custody now, awaiting an interview with senior officers from the Public Protection Unit. It was time to call it a night. Or rather 'day', since their actual shift had ended several hours ago. Coupland watched the detectives file out, taking longer than necessary to clear away his paperwork. There was something he'd asked Krispy to do for him, something that required the young DC's technical wizardry.

Ashcroft had changed into his running gear. Beers were all very well but it was the blast of cold air against skin as he ran the five miles to his home that would deal with the adrenaline coursing through him. His heart started pounding every time he recalled Nichol lumbering towards him with that knife. The sight of DI Little and his mini-me walking in on them, before turning on their heels to leave him to it, made him shudder.

He finished tying the laces on his trainers when a slow hand clap started behind him. He turned, pulling himself up to his full height. 'Well, well, well, if it isn't our very own Usain Bolt. Aren't you the flavour of the week?' Little asked. 'As long as it's banana.'

'I saw you,' said Ashcroft, 'running like cowards while I was cornered.'

'Nothing cowardly about it. I told you it didn't pay to get on the wrong side of me. Not my fault you didn't listen. Consider it a warning.'

'A warning against what?' Coupland asked, leaning in the doorway. 'How to avoid becoming a sad sack no longer fit for purpose?'

Little jerked a thumb towards Coupland. 'If he's the organ grinder,' he said, pushing his face up against Ashcroft's, 'what the fuck does that make you?'

Ashcroft's response was lightning fast but Coupland's was quicker. He grabbed at him, gripping his arms so he couldn't lash out.

Ashcroft swivelled his head in Coupland's direction. Shock registering in his eyes. 'What the fuck are you doing?'

'Assaulting a senior officer? Don't give 'em what they want. Trust me,' Coupland hissed.

Krispy walked in then, a smile on his face telling Coupland all was going to plan. 'You got all that?' he asked, patting the phone in his pocket.

'I have indeed, Sarge. Live streaming around GMP's intranet as we speak, along with your video of these scumbags leaving an officer in urgent need of assistance.'

'You bastards!' yelled Little.

'Still streaming as we speak,' smiled Krispy.

'Let's hope someone doesn't leak it to the press,' remarked Coupland, 'You know how the Chief Constable hates a scandal.'

'Don't chew my bollocks off for wading in,' Coupland warned Ashcroft. 'I wasn't doing this for you, I was doing it for me. I'm embarrassed, to think that when the public look at me they see THEM, some throwback to the days when it was OK to abuse Christ knows who because they were the wrong colour or religion or wrong fucking sex.' It never ceased to amaze him. Even when you'd set your expectations pretty low it was still possible to be disappointed.

Coupland turned to Little and Clarke. 'Cops like you,' he spat out. 'You make me ashamed to carry a warrant card. You're the reason why so many folk don't trust us. The public look to us to set an example, yet what do they see? That things haven't changed in thirty, forty years? What would have happened if other officers hadn't got to him on time? You'd be happy to have his blood on your hands?' Coupland wasn't a policy maker. He wasn't a bloody crusader either. But it galled him to think that attitudes which no longer had a place in modern policing were alive and kicking.

Fairness. Tolerance and inclusivity.

Were they really a thing of the past?

*

One week later

Coupland hadn't spoken to Alex in the aftermath of finding Bez and Kayleigh. He knew that Alex had stayed with Bez until her body had been removed from the mill and taken to the mortuary. When her name flashed up on his mobile he answered immediately.

'How's that greasy pole?'

'Getting slippier by the minute,' she answered, sounding weary. 'Do I charge Laughing Boy for supplying

382

the drugs that caused Bez's death?'

Coupland pinched the bridge of his nose. 'He was willing to incriminate himself to help us find a serial paedophile. In doing so he likely saved Kayleigh from significant trauma. He had no idea what Nichol's intention was when he sold it to him.' Navigating the law was never easy.

He tried a different tack. 'Will a prison term cure him?'

They both knew the answer to that. 'I met Shola Dube recently,' she said, as though avoiding the issue. 'That's how I came into contact with Bez.'

'Oh yeah?'

'I can't help wondering if she'd still be alive if Shola had been her social worker. You know, been in a position where she could influence change.'

'Do I detect a long-awaited note of realism, Inspector Moreton? In which case I'm sure you'll make the right decision regarding your dealer.'

Alex made a noise that sounded like agreement. 'I suppose he could be the subject of the case study I promised my boss. How, despite his offending background he helped police apprehend a vicious criminal.'

'There you go, then.'

'By the way. I thought you should know, the mayor's office is instigating a review into child protection in children's homes. The mayor has personally cited the outcome of your investigation as its starting point. How it's possible for girls to be abused by men who freely come and go without ever being challenged.' This lax attitude enabled men like Aiden Nichol to escalate their reach and commit serious sexual crimes. 'Both the council and GMP are being held to account, specifically the mishandling of the original MISPER enquiry and the culture of outdated attitudes towards young people in looked-after care. There's also going to be an enquiry into a missing interview tape. Does that mean anything to you?'

'Might ring a bell or two,' said Coupland.

'No regrets then?' he asked. 'With your move…'

A pause. 'The scope of Operation Naseby is bigger than I thought. My superintendent's on about setting up Project Blue Jacket as a response to the number of days schooling children of crime families miss out on, and Project Panther, where young people who want to report a crime are supported through the process.'

'Project Blue Jacket, Project Panther. Jesus wept, you're involved in more projects than a New York housing manager.'

'I thought you'd say something like that. The problem is that kids like these are at risk for a whole manner of reasons. Just as you fathom how to solve one set of problems another set arises.'

'You'll work it out.'

As Coupland ended the call, his desk phone rang. 'A visitor in reception for you,' the desk sergeant told him. When he gave the person's name Coupland raised his eyebrows, wondering if this meant good news or bad.

'We could go out for a coffee rather than have the slop in here,' Coupland said to Pauline Boydell as he greeted her in reception. She looked different somehow, though he couldn't place why. There was still a stoop to her shoulders, but the glasses were gone and if he wasn't mistaken, the merest hint of a smile.

'I don't care about coffee, I'm on my way to the

airport,' she laughed, swatting his offer away. 'I've a couple of weeks leave due and I'm going to spend it with my sister in Greece, and no, before you ask, I don't give a stuff about quarantine. If it means I have to take a month off the job then so be it, I've bloody earned it.'

He'd never heard her speak so freely, with such feeling, about anything other than the most heinous of crimes. It was easy to make the mistake of thinking of work colleagues one dimensionally, as though they operated in a vacuum, with no life of their own beyond the job. The thought of her getting shitfaced on ouzo warmed the cockles of his heart.

'I just wanted you to know there have been developments.' Her face grew serious for a moment. 'When specialist officers from the CSE team interviewed Kayleigh Lomax, she showed them where Bethany had hidden a memory card inside a split in the hem of her doll's dress. Amongst other things it contained images of Bethany's abuse, not just by Nichol but by another man too.' This account matched the teenager's post mortem, which had been virtually identical to the other victims, apart from the heroin overdose as cause of death. Coupland wondered if Nichol, used to The Dutchman's 'clients' killing each victim he sourced for them, had baulked at strangling her. Maybe, in some perverse way he thought giving her an overdose was kinder. Less like 'actual' killing. A way of minimising his crime.

'SOCOs never found the camera,' said Coupland. 'Maybe Nichol destroyed it thinking he'd destroyed the evidence.'

'Well, trust me, he didn't. The film contains unedited images of several men who are part of this network.

Their identities are being traced as we speak. One has already claimed diplomatic immunity,' she added, curling a painted red lip. 'They'll try running circles round the CPS, of course. Use contacts in the press to claim the investigation is a witch hunt. The evidence is solid though, you can be certain of that. She played a blinder, that girl.'

EPILOGUE

Coupland leaned against the kitchen counter, beer in hand. Beside him Lynn savoured a glass of wine. He angled his head to see her studying him. 'You have remembered it's your turn to cook, right?' she said, turning to face him head on. 'Can't bask on a good result forever.'

'Oh ye have little faith,' he said, moving towards the fridge and pulling open the door to reveal the ingredients required to make a chicken curry. It was a recipe Ashcroft had given him. He'd picked up everything he needed in the Tesco round the corner from the station, chucked in a bottle of her favourite red for extra brownie points.

'I take it all back,' she smiled, clinking her glass against his can.

She'd had a piece of good news. 'The mother whose baby had been removed at birth called me. Social services are going to review her case. With appropriate support in place there's a chance her baby will be returned to her.'

It never ceased to amaze Coupland, the difference between them. Lynn saw a happy ending when all he saw was the beginning of something else entirely. He kept this thought to himself though. At the end of the day he was happy when she was. No point in stoking trouble for the sake of it.

It had been backbreaking work putting together the CPS file for Aiden Nichol. The case against him was watertight. His DNA had been found on all of the victims, the memory stick Bez had hidden provided irrefutable evidence of the part he played in their abuse. He wouldn't be released while Coupland was still on the force, Krispy too, if the CPS played their part.

He'd left work earlier to find Jackie Swain waiting for him on the station steps.

'Thank you, Mr Coupland.'

'What for?'

'For getting Keri's name up there with the others. For getting all their names up. You know, the forgotten kids, because that's where they'd been relegated. Ironic really, that the only attention Keri ever got in her life was during the investigation into her murder.' She'd bowed her head. 'What kind of a mother was I, Mr Coupland?' she'd asked, looking up to reveal eyes that were glassy like she'd taken something. 'Don't worry. You don't need to answer that. I know I was the worst kind.'

Coupland wasn't so sure. He'd certainly seen worse. Though he knew damn well a response like that wouldn't help her. Nothing could. He'd never been a churchgoer. Had seen far too many horrors to think prayer could make a difference. But a line from a verse churned out at Amy's school assemblies came to mind: 'Let he who is without sin cast the first stone,' he said, his hand resting on her arm.

'No time to be maudlin though, eh, Mr Coupland? You promised you'd look under every stone and you did.'

Her smile when it came, was uncertain. 'It's Keri's birthday today. I've got mates bringing some voddy round later to celebrate. You'd be very welcome.'

'There's a chance I can get home at a decent time

tonight,' he said, shaking his head. 'But I'll raise a glass to her, how about that?'

Coupland drained his can now and threw it in the bin before helping himself to another.

Lynn sighed as she fished it out and placed it on the recycling pile.

'Better get this show on the road,' he said, switching on the TV while unloading the fridge of its contents.

Lynn refilled her glass and headed into the living room, at least two episodes of her favourite American drama ahead of her, if his previous attempts at following a recipe were anything to go by. The national news came on. In Newcastle, a man had been arrested on charges of indecently assaulting a girl of ten, and of gross indecency with another, younger child. These had not been isolated incidents: police and social services were working on the assumption that other adults and as many as a dozen other children were involved; the youngest of the children was the same age as Toby. The same news bulletin gave details of a telephone hotline that had been set up following the discovery of a child sex ring, offering refuge and advice to abuse victims. So far one hundred and fifty victims had been interviewed. So far.

More children. More Men. More cities. Was it possible that The Dutchman's reach was so wide?

Surveillance around The Dutchman and those he was paid to protect was getting tighter. The people he worked for were high ranking members of the establishment. It would take time to amass the evidence needed to bring them down. This was ground-breaking stuff, being monitored by organisations way beyond Coupland's scope of understanding. What he wouldn't give though, to be on the team that put that bastard behind bars.

After the briefest of internal investigations DS Clarke had been demoted and transferred to West Midlands Police. He went quietly enough. DI Little had put in for and been granted early retirement. The thought of it incensed Coupland no end, given his suspicion that the senior cop wasn't as inept and obtuse as he liked folk to think. Which meant he'd stalled the investigation into Keri's murder for more sinister reasons. After all, the Dutchman and his cronies didn't operate in a void. Someone needed to be working inside the system, smoothing their way.

He'd been about to take another swig from his can when he remembered something. Moving to the wall unit where the booze was stored since Tonto started walking, he lifted down a single malt. Poured himself a generous measure. He wasn't a whisky drinker by any means but he felt the occasion merited it. He raised his glass, recited their names one by one:

Savannah. Keri. Carly. Toby. Bez.

He moved to the patio doors. Looked out onto a garden shrouded in darkness. He'd finally got round to putting up Lynn's string lights. 'Not just for Christmas, we'll keep them until the lighter nights come back,' she'd said when she'd seen them. At least he'd got that right.

Coupland eyed his grandson as he toddled into the kitchen; cheeks glowing like he'd had a tipple himself.

'You ready?' Amy asked as she stepped in her son's footsteps.

'Hang on a sec,' said Coupland, knocking the contents of his glass back. He finished his drink as Lynn came in to join them.

'Hurry up,' she said, 'I've put my show on pause.'

Coupland lifted Tonto and pointed to the wall-mounted switch Amy had promised he could press when Grandpa got home. Tonto, quick to catch on, jabbed at it with a chubby finger. His eyes, wide like saucers, took in the multi-coloured lights criss-crossing the garden. Every corner lit up by shimmering beams. No darkness here. Tonto gasped and wriggled and clapped his hands together. If Coupland could bottle that sound he would.

THE END

Enjoyed *When Darkness Falls*? Read on for the first chapter of *Made to be Broken*, the next book in the DS Coupland series.

MADE TO BE BROKEN

CHAPTER ONE

A tent had already been erected around the body and the front of the truck. The police vans parked along the edge of the pedestrian square had attracted the attention of workers from neighbouring office blocks. An army of fluorescent jackets held back the crowd that had gathered. A reporter with scuffed heels and hair extensions watched two male detectives climb out of an unmarked car and made a beeline for them, shoving her phone under the nearest man's chin. 'Anything you can tell us about the victim?' She made it sound like an accusation.

'Quick off the blocks, aren't you?' DS Kevin Coupland paused as his gaze locked onto the familiar face. 'No motorway pile ups to get your false nails into?' he growled, aware that DCI Mallender was already at the cordon shouting his name as he beckoned him over. 'Saved by the yell,' Coupland added, dismissing her.

The Scene of Crime officer nodded as Coupland approached the cordon. 'Nice to see your media training in action,' she smirked.

Coupland had worked crime scenes with her before. She wasn't as thorough as Turnbull but she got the job done.

'You took your time,' she added, 'been here an hour already.'

Coupland jerked his thumb in the direction of the vehicle he'd driven over in. 'In case you haven't noticed, it's a car not a tardis.' It came out sharper than he intended. He'd never been one to take criticism well, especially when it wasn't deserved. 'For your information we've only just got the call, detective constable,' he added, reminding her of the pecking order.

The SOCO raised her hands and grimaced. 'Sorry Sarge, bad choice of words. Blame it on low blood sugar.'

It had been traffic's shout at first. The original report that came in had stated a collision between a truck and a pedestrian. When the first officers on the scene took the driver's account he claimed the victim had thrown himself in front of the truck. It was only when the truck's dashcam footage was checked that it was obvious he'd been pushed. The shout was assigned to Salford Precinct murder squad as they were nearest to the locus. The road – a major route into Salford's financial district – had been closed for the best part of two hours.

'Like what you've done to the place,' Coupland observed. Yellow evidence markers had been placed either side of a triangular sandwich carton and a mobile phone with a shattered screen. A leather wallet lay beside it. Further along, a black brogue lay midway across the road.

Coupland huffed out a sigh, his gaze travelling to the tent that had been erected around the front of the truck to conceal what was left of the body.

The SOCO followed his gaze. 'A lot of his personal effects were chewed up under the truck's front wheels, he must have let go of his phone trying to save himself. I'll get it to you once it's been logged. There were several business cards inside the wallet which I've passed to your boss.'

'And the driver?'

The SOCO pointed in the direction of a squad car with two occupants in it parked beside several police vans.

Coupland's nod was slow.

'Look on the bright side,' she said, 'at least you've got time of death.'

'As pep talks go, I've heard better,' Coupland muttered before heading into the tent.

DCI Mallender stepped back to let him get a closer look but there wasn't much to see. An arm was visible jutting out at an angle between the body of the truck's cab and the kerb. A heavy chrome diving watch on the wrist was intact.

'You hope to Christ when something like this happens that it's instant,' Coupland muttered, turning back to the DCI. 'That the poor bugger didn't have a Scooby what was literally about to hit him.'

Mallender handed him a business card taken from a folded evidence bag.

'Adam Sinclair, a financial advisor from Bridgewater Asset Management,' Coupland read aloud. 'We certain it's him?'

'The cards have all got the same name on them so I'm guessing they're his,' replied Mallender. 'I've taken a photo of what you can see underneath the truck's rig,' he added, handing Coupland his phone.

Coupland squinted at the screen, tapping it before widening the image with his forefinger and thumb. 'Jesus H Christ,' he muttered, blowing out his cheeks before handing the phone back as though it was contaminated.

'It'll be a closed casket,' he grunted, turning back to where Adam was pinned between two wheels. Only part of his face was intact. They'd be able to make an ID of sorts. The rest of him lay at awkward angles. Some body parts were beyond recognition. It was unlikely he'd be lifted into a body bag in one go.

'Fire and Rescue are on standby to move the truck once we give them the signal.'

Coupland glanced at the waiting crew with something akin to sympathy. His job was to work out who had caused this, but it was their job to get him off the tarmac.

Having no desire to see for himself what Mallender had already shown him on his phone he stepped away from the carnage. 'Want me to do the honours with this?' he asked, holding up the business card. 'I'll get his employer to confirm his whereabouts and send me a recent photo.' He waited for Mallender to nod his approval before stepping outside the tent, hauling in a breath as he studied his surroundings.

It was the part of the city where the old met the new. Concrete seventies-style office blocks dwarfed by glass and chrome towers. The commercial district was walking distance from Salford Central station. The streets were populated by sales reps searching for parking spaces and office workers nipping out for lunch. A construction site occupied the next block, tradesmen in high-viz jackets and hard hats moving about the site like worker ants on a hill. It was a public place to die. Broad daylight too.

Coupland eyed the CCTV camera on the office building behind him, his gaze sweeping the remainder of the block for another. They needed to move swiftly, get access to them before the footage was erased. An appeal would go out for dashcam footage from vehicles that had travelled along the same stretch of road. Passers-by would need to be traced, interviewed and eliminated. There'd been an incident a couple of years back, a male jogger in London had pushed a woman in front of an oncoming bus. Only the swift action of the driver saved her. The CCTV footage released at the time went viral, yet failed to catch the would-be killer.

The crowd that had gathered beyond the cordon were mainly workers and delivery drivers who for the time being would be unable to gain access to the retail units and business premises only steps away from where the victim fell. Beyond the crowd, a pedestrianised square where several wine bars with pavement seating advertised mid-week specials. Small groups of onlookers made their way towards them. No harm in a swift drink while they waited for the cordon to be lifted. A coffee shop nestled between a Slug and Lettuce and Toni Macaroni. Through the large glass window, sofas and high-backed chairs clustered around small tables. A man wearing earplugs sat in an armchair tapping into his phone.

Coupland stepped inside, ordered three lattes and a cellophane-wrapped chocolate brownie that he pocketed along with a handful of sugar sachets from the self-service counter on the way out. He headed towards the squad car parked in the blocked-off area of road, nodding at the officer sat in the driver's seat. A decent enough cop, though his lack of height caused a stir when he'd first joined the force, earning him the name Laptop because he was a small PC.

Coupland peered through the window into the rear of the car. A man in his forties sat with a foil blanket over his shoulders, the type given to marathon runners at the end of a race. He'd been driving the truck that had ploughed into the victim. He looked shell-shocked. The weather was clear and visibility was good, but nothing could have prepared him for what happened.

Coupland opened the door and climbed in, pausing before handing out the coffee. 'Preliminaries been taken care of?' he asked.

Laptop nodded, causing the truck driver to sigh.

'Let's get one thing straight. I wasn't on the phone, I wasn't texting. I had both hands on the wheel and was looking straight ahead, and I absolutely haven't been drinking.'

'Breathalysed at the scene, Sarge. Negative,' Laptop added when Coupland turned to him for corroboration.

Satisfied, Coupland held the cardboard coffee tray out so they could help themselves, fishing in his pocket for the sachets of sugar which he tossed onto the tray.

'Cheers Sarge,' Laptop said in a tone which suggested he was normally an afterthought when it came to detectives putting their hand in their pocket.

The truck driver's hands shook as he tore open a sachet. 'Supposed to be good for shock, right?' he said, tipping the contents into his paper cup.

'Ever had anything like this happen before?' Coupland asked, his question met with a vigorous shake of the head.

'Are you kidding me? I'd been warned about pavement suicides when I started in the job, but no one ever mentioned someone literally being thrown under the bus.'

The truck's dashcam footage had downgraded him from suspect to witness but he was a victim in this too. He'd never drive along this stretch of road again without bracing for impact. Recalling images that should never be seen. Skin welded to the front of his truck. Human smears on the tarmac.

Coupland glanced at Laptop. 'You taken his statement?'

'Yes, Sarge,' he replied in a tone that implied he wasn't a fuckwit.

Coupland took a gulp of his coffee, studying the driver over the plastic lid of his cup. He looked as though he'd been muscular once, before fast food and sitting still for hours on end took its toll. The forearm gripping his coffee was tattooed. A woman's face. Wife. Mother. Ex. Coupland couldn't be sure. 'Do you recall seeing anyone else on the pavement apart from the victim?'

The driver shook his head. 'Like I already said to the officer here, I was more interested in what was going on in front of me, on the road. The whole thing only took about three, four seconds, there was nothing I could do. I saw him jump out in the corner of my eye and I tried to swerve to the other lane to get out of his way. Then I heard a "bang" and knew it was too late.'

Coupland looked at Laptop pointedly. 'You've got this down as well?'

Another 'Sarge,' though this time through gritted teeth.

The truck driver gulped down the remainder of his coffee. 'I've still got deliveries to make. When can I get back to work?'

'The only place that truck's going when Fire and Rescue have done with it is the police compound for further tests. This road's going to be shut for the rest of the day,' Coupland responded, turning to open the car door.

The truck driver regarded him sharply. 'What about me? What do I do in the meantime?'

It was vital in these situations that a support network was in place for when the shock began to dissipate. Loved ones. Work mates. A manager who gave a toss about your welfare. Even so, the patience of those around you came with its own time limit. It was easy to look inwards. To absorb blame. To question whether you could have done more.

Coupland stepped out of the car, lowering his head to eyeball the truck driver once more. 'If you get offered counselling, I suggest you take it.'

*

The SOCO leaned into the back of an estate car, crosschecking sealed evidence bags against the Scene of Crime Log on her clipboard. 'I see you've acquainted yourself with the driver,' she said to Coupland, inclining her head in the direction of the squad car he'd climbed out of. 'Poor bugger. He wasn't bargaining on this when he started his shift today.'

'I'm sure the victim wasn't either,' Coupland observed, his eyes skimming the contents of each evidence bag. The black brogue with a hand-stitched leather sole. The designer watch. A torn triangular carton containing a sandwich the victim had expected to eat.

Coupland patted his pockets for the brownie he'd bought earlier. 'I nearly forgot,' he said, handing it over. 'Got something for that blood sugar of yours.'

'Blimey, I take it all back,' she gasped, in much the same tone Laptop had earlier.

'What is it with everyone? I can do nice, you know,'

Coupland said, his arms raised in frustration.

'You've got to admit, Sarge, you hide it well.'

Tossing his empty coffee cup into the nearest bin, Coupland followed a tree-lined walkway into a landscaped open square. The street sign attached to an adjacent building stated New Bailey Plaza, the address on Adam Sinclair's business card. The square consisted of a newly built development of smart office blocks and upmarket eateries. The open area was landscaped with shrubs and benches. Communal seating areas were dotted here and there. A place for people to linger, rather than rush from A to B.

Uniformed officers would soon begin making enquiries in neighbouring offices. It was feasible the culprit worked locally. Committed murder in their lunchbreak while nipping out for a vegan burrito. Coupland walked around the perimeter, his eyes scanning the offices and retail outlets. He couldn't think of the last time he'd been in this part of the city. He'd never had call to require any of its services: Private Banking. Financial planning. Accountancy. Law. The commercial kind, not criminal justice and conveyancing.

People moved with purpose between towering office blocks. Things were starting to return to normal for many, now lockdown had eased. In a few hours workers would swarm out of their offices into the square and avenues to either start their commute home or flop into one of the many restaurants for a bite to eat. The people that worked here dressed up to go to work. Tailored clothing from high-end stores, money to socialise with colleagues, not just friends. Even so, how many could afford a watch like the victim's?

Coupland pulled his phone and Sinclair's business card from his pocket. Keyed in the head office number for Bridgewater Asset Management before hitting the call button.

*

Afternoon briefing. CID room, Salford Precinct station.
'When I rang head office, the receptionist put me through to the company's MD, a Dominic Neilson. He confirmed that Adam Sinclair worked for them and was able to email me a photo of him taken a few weeks ago when he'd trounced his quarterly sales target.' Coupland held up the photo of Sinclair as he beamed into the camera, a champagne flute in one hand and a cheque in the other. Thick white hair and lived-in features gave him the look of an elder statesman, albeit one on the take. Coupland placed it on the newly erected incident board beside the photo taken at the locus. The likeness was uncanny, if you ignored the fact that in the crime scene photo half the victim's face was missing.

'Ashcroft is delivering the death message now.'

DC Turnbull peered at the close-up photo of Sinclair's watch that had also been pinned to the board. Beneath it the make and value. An Omega Speedmaster Moonwatch, just shy of five thousand pounds. 'Don't see many of them that aren't knock-off. Must be loaded,' he observed.

'Thanks for your sparkling insight, Turnbull,' Coupland said. 'Anything else you'd care to add, or shall I crack on?'

Turnbull was right though, this wasn't their typical shout, where a murder involved a drug deal gone wrong or a pissed-up brawl. Coupland pushed on.

'So, why would someone shove a pinstripe-suited businessman into the path of a truck in broad daylight?'

'What does the firm do?' asked DC Robinson.

Coupland studied Sinclair's business card. 'Wealth Management. Whatever that means.'

'Financial advice for those who no longer need it,' observed Mallender, who'd been happy to let Coupland run the briefing. 'They invest clients' money, take a percentage of profits made, and charge a management fee on top, even if the investments make no money at all.'

The assembled detectives considered this. Mallender, out of any of them, was the one most likely to know about such things.

'Imagine having so much money you didn't know what to do with it,' said Turnbull.

'Nope,' said Coupland, after a beat. 'I've a wife and daughter, remember.' Not to mention a grandson none of them bargained for.

Coupland inclined his head in the direction of a tall athletic black man who had entered the room. Newly promoted DS Ashcroft had been with the team for three years. Following a brief spell with the Met where a bright future as a poster boy beckoned, he'd returned to GMP to earn his stripes under his own steam.

Ashcroft inclined his head in return.

'How did his wife take it?' asked Coupland.

Ashcroft hooked a finger into the knot of his tie to loosen it. He shrugged off his jacket, placing it over the back of his chair. 'She's in shock. Wasn't able to say much. Said I'd go back later. FLO's with her now.'

Krispy had been studying his computer screen. 'Sarge!' he piped up, his tone causing Coupland to glance at him sharply. 'Adam Sinclair was released from HMP Manchester five months ago after serving a four-year sentence for death by dangerous driving.'

'Was he now…' observed Coupland. Then, to the rest of the room: 'I think we might have just found the reason.'

'Any information on the hit and run victim?' asked DCI Mallender.

Krispy shook his head. He was the most junior member of the team, his fresh face evidence his faith in people hadn't been crushed by the job yet. His fondness for icing-covered doughnuts, hence his nickname, resulted in his suits fitting him more snugly than they used to. 'Nothing as yet, Sir. I've put in a request for the crime report.'

Mallender nodded his approval. 'Check with local bail hostels and mental health units while you're at it. See if anyone's gone walkabout. Can't rule anything out at this stage, especially in light of this information.'

'Get onto the jail and find out who he associated with while he was there,' instructed Coupland, nodding towards DCs Turnbull and Robinson. 'Whether he was friendly with any known faces…'

Mallender regarded the incident board, studying the photo Sinclair's boss had emailed over before studying the crime scene photo. 'Our chap gets more interesting by the minute. Looks like he belonged to a private members' club too. The Clifton Club,' he added, pointing out the red and gold crest on Sinclair's blue tie. Coupland had thought it was smeared blood and tissue.

'You're the only person in the room who'd have picked *that* up, boss,' intoned Coupland. 'You know it?'

'Not personally.'

'Not got your name down, then?'

'I don't even think the Super would have the right credentials,' Mallender responded, keeping his voice low, glancing at the CID room door in case Superintendent Curtis had chosen to grace them with his presence.

Despite being involved more in operational matters, Krispy was still the go-to geek when online research was required. At the mention of The Clifton Club his fingers flew across his iPad with the dexterity of a concert pianist. 'According to the website its members include a lord and MPs from across the political spectrum.'

'And that's a reason to join?' Coupland's tone was incredulous. He added the name and address of the club to his daybook. 'Since Sinclair was wearing that tie there's a chance he'd been over there or was on his way. Possibly meeting a client.'

'Or his killer,' Mallender added. Coupland wasn't the only one keeping an open mind.

'Think I'll pay them a visit after I've spoken to his boss. Find out what they've got to say about our victim.'

'I'll go with you,' said Mallender, clocking the questioning look on Coupland's face. 'You know, in case an interpreter's needed.'

'Sir.' Krispy had angled his body towards DCI Mallender, though his eyes remained trained on his desktop monitor. Coupland marvelled at the number of devices he could operate at once and the ease with which he did so. Too many gadgets required programming these days. That or a password to access them. A central heating system at home he couldn't operate. Meter readings he could no longer submit to his energy supplier. A security alarm he couldn't set. Technology had locked him out of most of his personal life. As least he was still good for putting out the bins.

The DCI nodded at the junior DC. 'Got the background info I asked for?'

'Yes, Sir.' Krispy's brows creased as though he couldn't believe what he was seeing. 'Sinclair was jailed for a hit and run that killed a mother and baby nearly forty years ago.'

Several pairs of eyes swivelled in his direction, causing his ears to go a deep shade of pink.

'Did you say forty years?' asked Coupland.

'Sarge,' Krispy nodded. 'The mother's name was Marie Simpson. Her daughter, Sophie. Both killed on impact.'

An uneasy feeling formed in Coupland's stomach.

'Why's he only just served a jail term?' The question from a DC at the back of the room made Coupland push the feeling away. He tipped his head at Krispy to prompt him for an answer.

'Details are sparse. Looks like he walked into Swinton police station five years ago in a flash of conscience and handed himself in. He served four years of an eight-year sentence.'

'Got any details on the next of kin?'

Krispy shook his head as he read from the information on screen. 'Nothing on here, Sarge.'

'It'll be on the original crime report. Give Swinton a call and tell 'em you're on your way over to pick it up. Phone me when you've got the details.'

Picking up his car keys Coupland turned to Turnbull. 'Check we've got all the CCTV footage in from the cameras on both sides of the road and those looking onto the square where Sinclair worked. If not, bring them in. One of them must have picked up our guy, possibly his killer.' He turned to Ashcroft. 'Did his wife mention his time in prison?'

Ashcroft shook his head. 'No, though that could have been down to shock.'

'Only one way to find out, isn't there?'

Book Eight, Made to be Broken, is available now.

AUTHOR'S NOTE

First COVID disclaimer: I felt it wasn't realistic to write this novel and not make reference to the pandemic. I wondered, when I started it back in March, if too much commentary on it would make it feel dated. Little did I know that as we approach the end of the year we're still having the same conversation…

Second COVID disclaimer: Some fluidity is required regarding the COVID regulations I mention. The pandemic was part of the backdrop, not centre stage, so I have been deliberately vague regarding the start of lockdown and subsequent easing, to suit the story. Plus, the current set up baffles me – so when in doubt I've made it up.

I continue to be moved by the staggering facts I uncover during my research for each book. In particular, these figures left me open-mouthed:

'Every year 100,000 children and young people under the age of 16 go missing or run away from home or care.' – The Children's Society

At the time of writing, 250 children were linked to those deemed at being at risk of serious harm in Salford. 300 adults had 'Safeguarding' contracts.

GMP has lost 200 officers since 2010 as millions of pounds have been taken off its budget.

The Home Office fact sheet on Child Sexual Exploitation states:

'Law enforcement agencies in the UK are currently arresting around 450 individuals and safeguarding over 600 children each month through their efforts to combat online CSE.

Statistics from the National Crime Agency (NCA) show that last year 2.88 million accounts were registered globally across the most harmful child sexual abuse dark web sites, with at least 5% believed to be registered in the UK.'

For the purposes of authenticity, I try to be as accurate as I can; any errors are mine. Oh, and although passmen tend to run the pantry in jail, for the purpose of this story they needed to be cleaners – work with me on this.

ABOUT THE AUTHOR

Emma writes full time from her home in East Lothian. When she isn't writing she can be found walking her rescue dog Star along the beach or bulk buying hand sanitiser from a well-known online store.

Find out more about the author and her other books at: **https://www.emmasalisbury.com**

Printed in Great Britain
by Amazon